Advance Praise for *C*

"A very funny window into the culture of tech."
-**Kevin Roose,** *New York Times* bestselling author of *Young Money*

"Company of Foos is a really funny book. It nails the culture, mentality and zeitgeist of big tech like no other book ever has."
-**Bradley Tusk**, Author of *The Fixer* and *Obvious in Hindsight*

"Davidson packs more pop-culture references into the fun and compelling Company of Foos than an entire season of Family Guy."
-**Keith Wisniewski**, Author of *Too Small to Fail*

"Funny and timely."
-**Wayne Gladstone**, Author of *Notes from the Internet Apocalypse*

"Davidson has given us a needed morality tale for the New World Order."
-**Dustin Kidd**, Author of *Pop Culture Freaks*

"Paul Davidson's hilarious book makes me glad that I never had the smarts to work in tech."
-**Sarah Walker**, *McSweeney's Internet Tendency*

Company of Foos

PAUL DAVIDSON

FOO PUBLISHING
Los Angeles New York Milan Buttonwillow

Company of Foos is a work of fiction. Names, characters, places, and incidents are the products of the author's imagination or are used fictitiously. Any resemblance to actual events, locales, or persons, living or dead, is entirely coincidental.

Copyright © 2023 by Paul Davidson

Published in the United States by Foo Publishing

Paperback ISBN 9798891450431
Ebook ISBN 9798891210585

Printed in the United States of America on acid-free paper

pauldavidson.net

1 2 3 4 5 6 7 8 9 0

First Edition

Cover design by Paul Davidson
Chapter illustrations by Peter Thompson

"Now is the winter of our discontent
Made glorious summer by this sun of York;
And all the clouds that lour'd upon our house
In the deep bosom of the ocean buried."
-WILLIAM SHAKESPEARE, Richard III

"It has become appallingly obvious that our technology
has exceeded our humanity."
-ALBERT EINSTEIN

"Two men enter, one man leaves!"
-BARTERTOWN CROWD, *Mad Max Beyond Thunderdome*

Company of
of
Foos

Prologue

"**A**n intergalactic dictator would never lose his powers just by passing through the Earth's atmosphere," Derrik James announced to the room, which included myself, my Manager and a furiously scribbling, underpaid (but overly enthusiastic) Assistant. The sheer confidence with which Derrik announced his latest "developmental gem" partially had me convinced that somewhere, under a stack of comic books and unreleased manuscripts was a highly confidential, government-financed research paper entitled "Atmospheric Conditions and Their Impact on Foreign Biological Entities."

These industry types, sitting pretty in their Restoration Hardware-enhanced wood and metal, exposed-ceiling office spaces, always rubbed elbows with big wigs in other industries intent on ensnaring their own fifteen minutes of fame with an insignificant article or an anecdotal tidbit. "The mobsters and the savants already won their Oscars," a D-girl once told me. Now, astrophysicists, archeologists and anesthesiologists were making their way past the front gates of the studio lots with wild stories and even wilder financial asks.

I had made it past the front gates after years of trying. There were many turns as an underpaid (and not so enthusiastic) Assistant, working at movie studios and on the sets of TV shows while furiously writing screenplay after screenplay. There were many. Many were bad. Some were inspired. There was the one about the two college dropouts who accidentally stumble upon the Lost City of Atlantis and save its inhabitants from an archeologist's evil plan of destruction.

"It's charming," said my mother.

There was the one about the NASA cafeteria worker who accidentally gets trapped in a spaceship while delivering provisions on board and must save the day when it crash lands on the inhabitable red planet of Mars.

"It's a clever spin on those space movies I love," gushed my mother.

There was the one about the English barrister by day, who moonlights as crime fighter *Fancy Pants* by night in order to rid evil and injustice from the London streets.

"I went to London *once*," said Mom, over punctuating the fact that it was a place she would never return to by choice. "If only the way *you* portrayed London in your story was the true reality. Maybe then I'd plan another trip back." Glowing words, indeed.

The industry, on the other hand, found my scripts "unrealistic," "cloyed" and "self-indulgent." Despite it all, the writing got better and I eventually secured the triad of perceived success: the doting passive-aggressive manager, the aloof and busy agent and the almost non-existent lawyer (with an almost non-existent 5% commission). They did their best to give constructive feedback and rallied my internal creative troops to soldier on. And soldier on I did.

The previous year had been the most successful year in my entire life. I had sold a groundbreaking TV pilot about a jury to a major network who ended up not making it because it was "too focused on a courtroom," and a sci-fi comedy about an Intergalactic dictator who crash lands in Middle America. You know, the one where the Intergalactic dictator loses his powers when he crashes through the Earth's atmosphere? Needless to say, almost a year after the checks had cleared, I still found myself mired down in illogical debates like this one where my perspective and creative opinion meant nothing. Still, throughout it all, one thing kept me calm. One thing allowed me to breathe through the ludicrous nature of the developmental debates as I fought for what I felt was good and right. It was *fuck you* money.

No, not *my* fuck you money. My wife's.

"How do you know he wouldn't lose his powers?" I shot back to Derrik, while wondering how many other name-revision options he had contemplated before removing the "c" in order to create the 2020's version of a 1980's name. I came up with five that were all better creative choices than his, including one where all the Z's were silent:

Derreq

Derrawk

Darraq

Derec

ZDerezk

Derrik had the answer: "First, our atmosphere is primarily made up of benign gases like oxygen, carbon dioxide and helium. Second, any foreign entity tooling around outer space has already been exposed to high amounts of space radiation. If they've still got their powers after facing the stark reality of the Universe's infinite nature, and *then* they pass through our own atmosphere…?"

Carl Sagan, as I would later refer to Derrik when I was making fun of him to my friends, looked at my Manager, who nodded vehemently.

I glared at my Manager. "You're agreeing."

"I'm nodding," he shot back, defensively. "It's a biological response to hearing words. Still, he makes a compelling point."

"He loses his powers by passing through the Earth's atmosphere," I said, standing my ground. "If you had irrefutable data that proved otherwise, I would be open to changing it. But you don't." The pure eloquence with which I made my point was both depressing and soul-crushing all at the same time.

"This is disappointing," Derrik said somberly. "Very disappointing," he directed at my Manager. "Supremely disappointing," he directed at *me*.

My Manager made a kind of sad, droopy face – the kind that a *Kumon* tutor makes at your kid when he's obviously not comprehending the concept of the Pythagorean Theorem after four weeks of explaining to him just what *a squared plus b squared* equals. In my case, it wasn't that I wasn't "getting it" – it was the contrary. I got it and I refused to go along with it. We all stared at each other, quietly, for some time. We were breaking up. But…it was okay. Because, remember?

…*Fuck you* money.

Or so I thought.

Jess sat on the couch next to me, hysterical, half snot-sniffling and trying to catch her breath at the same time. Half a box of aloe-enhanced tissues lay everywhere as she blew her nose, threw one down, and went back to the box for seconds. And thirds. And fourths. Having had almost seven years of marriage under my belt with her, I knew not to even try and caress her arm. Or rub her knee. Or try and get in her face and wonder aloud if there was "anything I could do." No. I had been married seven years, so I knew that when Jess was this upset, you had to ensure there were at least three leg lengths between her and I (if a knee touched hers, the situation could get worse) and wait for the words to come out. Which were coming. Right at that moment.

"I'm such an idiot," she wheezed.

"You're not an idiot, Jess."

"Yes. I'm an idiot."

"Maybe it feels that way, but…"

Her face got serious, and I could have sworn she reversed the flow of gravity and sucked the remaining moisture back into her tear ducts. She had been known to do other amazing things, like book aging soap opera stars on *The Late Late Show*, so reversing gravity and negating tears didn't seem so altogether crazy.

"Can we just agree to disagree?" she sniffled.

Her idiot*ness*, mind you, had nothing to do with my own idiot*ness* previously practiced on a studio lot in Burbank. No, her idiot*ness* directly put the *fuck you* savings and checking accounts in extreme danger. See – just as I was sabotaging my own career, hers was being taken away from her in a coup reminiscent of *Lord of the Flies*.

"How dare they," she steamed. "After *fourteen* years at the studio. Bill said it wasn't anything personal, they just weren't going to pick up the option in my contract for another year. Nothing personal, my ass. When you don't pick up the contract of your Head of Publicity, it's totally personal."

In my head, I asked how many more months of salary the studio owed her.

"Bill isn't innocent in this whole thing," she continued. "If only he had a backbone, he would have protected me. And to think, after all the times I protected him."

In my head, I asked Jess when she thought she'd start looking for a new job. After all, finding a high-level Executive job in Hollywood didn't just happen overnight.

"I am so over the politics," she continued. "I need a break."

Sure, but what would you do with a break, I asked her again *in my head.* Our four-year-old daughter, Kate, didn't need a stay-at-home mom. There was a nanny. Nannies existed so working mothers didn't have to feel guilty that a Tik-Tok obsessed sixteen-year-old, wasn't actually watching their child.

"Cam?"

"Yes, babe?"

"You're not saying anything."

"I'm just letting you talk it through."

She leaned forward, across the three knee-length neutral zone, and wrapped her arms around me. Burying her head in the nape of my neck, she gave me a tender kiss and sniffled one last time. "Thank God for your rewrite money," she said, pulling back. "You are totally and completely my partner and I love you for it."

Yipee.

"One hundred thousand dollars," enunciated Jess. "That rewrite gig was worth one hundred thousand dollars." She stared at me, across the kitchen table, kind-of, *sort-of,* livid.

So, yes – I had filled her in on the day's events.

"Seventy-five thousand dollars," I corrected her. "Remember, commissions?"

"Yeah, okay. Seventy-five thousand dollars."

"And actually, the Writer's Guild takes another one and a half percent, so…"

"You couldn't have just made the changes? Would that have been such a big deal?"

"The atmosphere would clearly *strip* superpowers away from an alien life form," I proclaimed.

"Okay."

"Seriously. It would."

"But let's just say for a moment… Let's just imagine there are a million planets out there that can support life… Isn't it possible there's just *one* out there, where the atmosphere could possibly *not* strip away superpowers from alien life? Like a one hundredth of a percent chance? What's that called…*Beckham's Razor?*"

I gave her a look. It was *Occam's Razor*. Ah, the life of a publicist – where rag mag gossip about folks like David and Victoria Beckham superseded real documented science.

"Fine. Okay. But would it still have been such a big deal?"

"Yes!" I stood up, passionately, banging my palms on the table for added dramatic effect. "Sure, it sounds easy enough to just give in and not take away an Intergalactic dictator's super powers, but then what? Hmm? What's next, Jess?" I slammed my palms down again, turning away for a moment to gather my thoughts and come right back. "Before you know it, outer space becomes Las Vegas, the alien becomes a gambler and there's talking animals everywhere."

"So kind of like *Rain Man* meets *Dr. Doolittle?*" she grinned, shrugging.

Oh, how she drove me mad. I looked away, not wanting to smile. Somewhere behind me, she made a sound that had only one purpose – to make me laugh at the idiocy of it all. I turned back, unable to resist.

"I have no job," Jess said as she grabbed my hand. "And I'm asking you to help us… I need you to help our *family*… Cam, I need you to find a solution."

The "family" slash "male provider of the house" card. It had been so long since I had been the main provider of the house that it almost didn't work. Except, somewhere in the back bedroom, almost as if by cue, our four-year-old daughter stepped out into the living room, eyes still half closed. God dammit, she was the most adorable thing in my whole entire world. And that was before she even said a single word.

"Is evey-fing OK?" she lisped. Bingo. *Cue tears.*

Jess looked to me like most actors looked to other actors during that last moment right before the swelling dramatic music and the network commercial break. I had to say something. Something dramatic. Something dangerous. Something *stupid.*

"Yes," I replied, nodding in Kate's general direction. I squeezed Jess' hand, then nodded to Kate. "Everything's going to be okay." The calming effect was immediate.

At least for everyone but *me*.

The Loop

T hanks to The Company, I found myself wedged in between two glorious specimens of air travel companions. There was the non-deodorant using NFT geek (he wore a t-shirt with a digital piece of artwork he now owned), who spent copious time studying the digital edition of *Wired* magazine and a flannel-wearing grandmother on her way back to the Pacific Northwest after spending a "horrifically hot week" in the Los Angeles area visiting her offspring's offspring. Mind you, it had been a Winter time average of sixty-eight degrees for the last two weeks, so the chasm between "horrifically hot" and the reality of it all was more than I could comprehend.

Nor could I comprehend the strange in-flight magazine that *Alaska Airlines* had generously provided to me. I flipped through it, spending little time concentrating on the articles or the glossy outdoor pictures, but rather imagining the edge-of-your-seat brainstorming sessions the magazine's staff must have participated in on a monthly basis with their "keep it light but absolutely electric" story advice-giving Editor in Chief at the helm.

"Fish canneries. At night."

"The elusive Alaskan ice caves. On location."

"Bellevue, Washington – the new Fashion capital of the World!"

The room erupted in a wave of clapping because beating Paris at anything was always a reason to get excited.

I flipped back to the front cover, half expecting the masthead to be attributed to *The Onion*, but alas it was not. It was the *Dianetics* of the Pacific Northwest – while not completely all encompassing of what the experience entailed, it was a cult*ish* view at what the people of this strange, lush green environment found to be the most important aspects of their existence. It was the outdoors, exercise, healthy food, family life and…*bad freaking weather*.

Through the window, the moonlight shone across a sea of thick clouds, as the airplane continued its decent through the sheet of grey. The wings began to extend, angling downward, in preparation of landing. The cabin vibrated, the lights came on, and the plastic-gloved flight attendants made their last garbage run of the night. We were going to pass through the lower atmosphere, so to speak, and I hoped to God I wasn't going to lose any of *my* special powers. I would need them for tomorrow, when The Company put me through the paces.

Ah, yes – The Company. One search of their name on the Internet delivered bajillions of articles about them, their financials, their products, their problems, their flawed leadership, their meandering stock price, their past and their future. But that was the thing – they were a Goliath of sorts, with hundreds of thousands of employees worldwide, an annual profit in the hundreds of billions, and a new consumer using their product literally as often as a child was born somewhere in the World. All public opinion in the technology sector was that they were on the cusp of changing the industry again, with groundbreaking technological advances, pushes into the new media space, and a digital entertainment strategy that would revolutionize and disrupt the current space as we knew it. All I knew was that they paid well, awarded stock options, and despite a particularly infamous incident where employees rioted after warm towels were removed from employee bathrooms (it was the bicycle commuters, by the way) – The Company had pretty damn good benefits. Take that, *Cobra*!

Look, it was time for something new. In the wake of the *Atmospheric Incident of Burbank*, I found myself completely unmotivated to re-engage with the creative sector. Did I really want to spend the next twenty years of my life debating silly little details in silly little stories with silly little people? Could I even stomach it? It had taken me a decade to deliver one year of true success and it had not come easily. With a young daughter and an out-of-work wife, I would quickly become an angry, heart-attack worthy human punching bag. I had to seek out another alternative, if not for my own sanity for the sanity of those who I loved.

"You could write children's books," my Manager suggested one day over a plate of mozzarella cheese sticks and matzo ball soup at our favorite local deli. "Kids books really don't have to be based on any real logic whatsoever. I mean, look at that *Goodnight Moon* crap – they put a senile old lady character in there and she does nothing but *hush* every five pages about oatmeal. She's worse than the mother in *Psycho*. You probably wouldn't get much pushback on ideas that had no basis in real world logic."

"How many children's books have you published?" I asked, already knowing the answer.

After Jess's contract got paid out, and we paid off the credit cards (mostly sushi, furniture and frozen coffee drinks), the six-month financial outlook was less rosy than we expected. And with little to no experience working in a corporate environment, any other LA-based opportunity was a long shot. I networked across every social web portal I could, checking with friends and colleagues for potential opportunities. But none materialized. I was minutes away from suggesting Jess go back to work when my sister's best-friend called with a unique opportunity. The Company *wanted* creative folks from Hollywood to help market and sell their new, groundbreaking, innovative suite of media software products. *Innovation*. Wow, I loved innovation. I practiced saying it over and over again into the mirror until I could say it with a British, Indian and South African accent. *Inn-noooooo-vay-shun.*

I was being given the opportunity to fight for a job. If I could get them to offer it to me, I would return to Los Angeles the savior of the Murphy family fortune. I mean it wasn't like I really had a choice anyway. Jess had floated the family's finances for the last ten years while I had sporadically filled in the monetary sinkholes. If I were to regain my manhood and reclaim the colonial pastime of providing for ones' family, I would have to suck it up and do my best when the AM came calling.

I looked at my watch. Hell, it was only six o'clock. I had so much time to plan for the AM. I quickly pulled out my iPhone and pulled up the Notes section (yes, the Airplane mode was turned *on*). I tapped at the keyboard, putting my master plan in motion:

6:30pm: Plane lands, roughly.

6:35pm: Exit plane, stop by cockpit to find out if I *almost* died. Thank pilots.

6:35-7pm: Get bags, rental car, bottle of water. Stay hydrated!

7:00-8pm: Drive to hotel, check-in, hang up clothes so there's no ironing in the morning.

8:00-9pm: Study notes on The Company, be amazing.

9:00-10pm: Television show. Hotel room occupant's choice.

10:00pm: Fall asleep.

The timing would work out well, I thought to myself – intent and focused on having a good night's sleep and none of that rushed feeling that gave me (what the old folks called) agita. I would get eight hours of shut-eye, plus an hour to gear up in the morning before having to drive to the offices at seven thirty for an eight o'clock orientation with the recruiter. The plan was perfect. And far superior to what Danny Ocean put into motion in that horrific pile of steaming cow dung called *Oceans 12*.

Flannel Grandmother and NFT Geek both looked over at me at the same time, as I counted on my fingers like a certified loon. Hey, baby – genius wasn't pretty.

I felt extremely, overwhelmingly *powerful*.

I felt extremely, overwhelmingly *fatigued*.

There was something off about this seemingly innocent look-ing hotel room that The Company had booked me into. Something *evil*. Something that had prevented me from falling asleep since I had *turned off the damn lights* at ten o'clock. With every hour that passed came an-other hour of no sleep. The anxiety of never waking up because I had never fallen asleep was a mental M.C. Escher painting that I could not negotiate my head out of.

"What do you mean you can't sleep," Jess groaned through my cell phone. "It's two o'clock in the morning."

"It's this hotel room."

"What? What's wrong with the hotel room?" she sighed. "Does it smell?" Jess was one of those *olfactory* investigators – she'd walk into any room and tell you she smelled either rotten food, a dead skunk hidden under the floorboards or human feces. *Every single time.* Before long you'd smell it, too. There was that show about people who eat couch cushions and toilet paper so it was only a matter of time until TLC based an entire unscripted television show on people just like her.

"No. It doesn't smell. I *feel* something."

"You *feel* something. Like bugs?" She wasn't helping.

"No. I feel…like…the souls of a thousand desperate professionals who never made it past their interview because they *couldn't…fall… asleep.*" My hand touched the fuzzy wallpaper from underneath my pillow, revealing a turned-up corner and a stained yellow piece of drywall. "It's like *The Shining* up in here."

"Cam."

"What."

"You're a thirty-four-year-old man. Suck it up."

"I'm not technically thirty-four until I've lived the *entire* thirty-fourth year, you know."

"You'll do great, tomorrow," she shot back.

"Says the corporate professional to the guy who spent the last three years making up stories in the guest house."

"You're smart, your head is in the right place, and I love you," she said.

It was all I needed to hear. "Goodnight, Jess."

"Goodnight. Text me tomorrow. I want details."

"You know it."

I hung up the phone, readjusted my position, and maneuvered the cold side of the pillow against my face. And then, I lay there. Eyes open. Until seven in the morning.

No bullshit – I was nervous. I sat in The Company's main lobby being bombarded by shiny HDTV monitors on every wall, showing off the latest first-person shooter, hi-tech tablet and life-affirming software releases which were all accompanied by pumping electronica that no, wasn't headache inducing in the least. Around me, a slew of name tagged hopefuls were all waiting for their escorts to meetings, conferences or interviews. I took stock of the potential competition, making specific note of the suits in attendance.

"You sure you don't want to take your suit?" Jess had asked twenty-four hours earlier, as I stood over my empty suitcase, wondering how I had ever handled such seemingly complicated endeavors like folding clothing before I had someone in my life showing me how to do it.

"Suit?"

"This isn't happy hour drinks. This is a job interview. Best foot forward, right?"

"As long as my best foot forward isn't in a pair of dress shoes, that were specifically purchased to go with a *suit*."

"Your funeral, buddy."

"If it was my funeral, I'd be wearing a suit."

And in an ironic twist of ludicrous fate, I was the only fool in the lobby *not* wearing a suit. Damn. A wave of anxiety literally washed over me, causing tiny symmetrical beads of sweat to populate my back, neck, forehead and under arm areas. "We honestly would have hired him if he had dressed the part," someone with some modicum of hiring authority said repeatedly in my head. "All he had to do was wear a suit and his entire future would have been set." Somewhere in my head George Zimmerman of *The Men's Wearhouse* gave me the middle finger.

I did what I always did when I needed to give myself a calming pep talk and there was no one there [read: Jess] to do it. I pulled out my iPhone, opened the Notes app and started typing away. "*You're smart*," I typed. It didn't look right. I retyped, "*You're smart!*" It seemed so much more enthusiastic and got me feeling really good about just how smart the people behind my pep talk thought I was. "*Your head is in the right place!*" I typed on the next line, continuing the enthusiastic trend. Except it was *too* enthusiastic and made me feel like I was rooting my fellow contestant on during a particularly tough question on *The Family Feud*. I retyped, "*You've got great values.*" It had a different meaning, but I admired the new turn of phrase. Referring to someone's head-placement sounded more Dr. Frankenstein than corporate pep talk. But "*you've got great values*" was a universal sentiment everyone aspired to embody. Then I finished it up with "*She loves you.*" It was perfect. I was my own personal Stuart Smalley for the digital age.

Next to me, another interviewee in a suit leaned over. "You probably don't want anyone seeing your iPhone around here," he advised, pointing up to the numerous cameras on the ceiling. "Just sayin."

I cursed Stuart Smalley. The self-help guru probably wouldn't have ever gotten past the interview process here at The Company, either.

"There's four names on this list," C.J. the recruiter told me as he slid the paper across the uncomfortable wooden table. "If those discussions go well, there may be more people added to that list throughout the day."

"You mean, if the *interviews* go well."

"We don't call them interviews." C.J. half-smiled back, reminding me of a college girlfriend's ex-boyfriend who I kicked in the groin after a particularly tense debate over whether or not I had drunkenly tried to light his hair on fire at a house party. "Actually," continued C.J. "we just call this whole exercise…*the loop.*"

The Loop. Cue tense, heart-palpitating music *here.*

"So, if this first part of the loop goes well… Then who else will I be having casual, non-work focused conversations with?"

"Their names are secret. For now." The Company was starting to sound a lot like The Government. "Just don't worry about it," he continued. "Focus on being *you.* That shouldn't be so hard. If you're a right fit for The Company, then we'll make you an offer." C.J. pushed the list further towards me across the table, like he was trying to get out of paying the check. I took it, eyeing the paper. There were four names. Four interviews. Four chances at failure. Or maybe even more! The possibilities for total and complete disaster were well within my control.

"The Shuttle is outside," C.J. pointed, and reached out to shake my hand. "Great to meet you…and good luck."

I hoped the Shuttle had air conditioning.

Seven hours later, I found myself waiting in a hi-tech conference room for my seventh hour-long interview of the day. I had made it past the first four previously announced interviews, and been graced with a fifth and sixth "special surprise guest." I sat quietly, refilling my energy meter as quickly as I could, while waiting for the final headliner of today's festivities. I eyed the note card that had been given to me just before the last interviewer had deposited me here and left for greener pastures. It read, "You will be meeting with: Shane McCullough, GM Entertainment Software & Services."

I pulled out my iPhone, being sure that none of the devices hanging from the ceiling were cameras (they were WiFi antennas), and pulled up my text messages to Jess. The day had been long, but it had also been productive, which was illustrated by my brief yet extremely eloquent ability to communicate vast amounts of information with less than 250 characters. I scrolled to the top and read from the beginning:

"First one done," the 10:02am text read. "Potential new boss. Wore leather pants, used to live in L.A.. Sold me hard on The Company."

"This place needs people like you," I recalled her saying. "Someone with a varied background, a creative bent. We need out-of-the-box thinkers to get us executing on a much higher level. The products, the technical side of it – you'll learn that."

"I love to learn," I smiled back in an *aw shucks* Jimmy Olsen kind of way.

"Second one done," my 11:35am text read. "Uptight biz dev guy. We didn't agree on anything. It was kind of awesome."

"Great product, but priced above our competitors," he served across the desk at me. "What do you do?"

"Lower the price."

"Then we lose money."

"Better than losing customers." Bam! He picked up another ball.

"Your business development partners, namely me, come to tell you we have reached an impasse on a key deal you need to bring value to your product. We recommend not doing it. What do you do?" he served again.

"Is the deal *that* important to me?" I lobbed back.

"You tell me," he returned across the net.

"Well. If I asked you to get it for me in the first place, it's important. I'm not going to jerk you guys around. Get it done, buddy." He looked up from his notes, surprised.

"Third one, done," said the 1:05pm text. "Needy Engineer."

"Without engineers, the entire technology industry would never ship a product," he announced matter-of-fact, protected on his side of the table by a wall of unopened *Mountain Dew* cans.

"Engineers are the future. Train them well and let them…"

"Lead the way," he finished, smiling. "Righteous." He slid a can of soda over to my side. "Here. Have one."

There was the interview with the P.R. Manager, who asked if I had identified any areas for improvement with respect to the P.R. I had seen thus far for The Company (2:35pm). There was the Product Manager, who wanted to know how I dealt with ambiguity (4:05pm). And there was the Brand Manager, who challenged me to provide examples of when I had led a varied team of people with conflicting opinions to a mutually-beneficial solution (5:34pm).

I spun. And spun and spun and spun. Having perfected the art of pitching to a room of "creatives" where any ludicrous question demanded an answer that made logical sense, I had re-wired my brain to spin under such pressures. For some, forcing a square into a hole shaped like a triangle was paralyzing. For me it came naturally. Replace a talking dog with a pygmy marmoset? Easy. Turn a serial killer Priest character into a serial killer Bowling prodigy? Cake. That is, if I was motivated to do so. Here at The Company, on the day in question, there was no lack of motivation to make everything fit.

"Publicity isn't just a press release or a news story on a tech blog," I told the P.R. Manager. "If you want the normal world to embrace your products, you have to reach them where they play. Their social threads, their streaming shows, their *Instagram* friends' profile pages." The Company had been too focused on pitching the same old folks. The same old folks who knew how to reformat their hard drive and burn DVD images from their *FlixFix* discs. Normal, everyday consumers? They had no awareness about The Company's new products until someone they cared about raved about it. And yet these were the people who had the money. The Company needed to find a way to get them to spend it.

"Ambiguity only represents a chance for greatness," I told the Product Manager. "With no clear path, there lies an opportunity to forge one." I secretly wrote it down for the day when my Fortune Cookie business kicked into high gear. But it was true. Not knowing the future, as I was living at this very moment, represented a sea of potential opportunities. It was the same reason no one wanted to know about what would happen to them ten years in the future. Except if the future involved the eventual creation of *Skynet*.

"Had I led a ragtag team of disagreeing misfits to a final agreed upon solution?" I wondered aloud to the Brand Manager? It was my chance to be critical of myself, which my Dad the corporate management consultant, always said showed that you were humble and open to those "teachable moments" people who hated you, loved to give you. I hadn't. I had been a one-man army, focused on one man's solution. But it was "a muscle I was looking to build," that was for sure. Bring on the misfits and I would welcome them with open arms.

I scrolled to the bottom of my last text message and swiped the screen upwards to refresh the results. With a satisfying *bloop* came the expected response from Jess, "Keep up the good work, xoxo J & K." I smiled, starting to type my response on the phone when the door flung open to reveal none other than Shane McCullough.

"Do my eyes deceive me, or are you truly fingering away at that iPhone?" he questioned in the kind of sexy British accent you'd expect to hear on *Bridgerton* that made me even *more* conflicted. I stopped texting, frozen in my spot, unsure of exactly how fast I could swallow the phone without him noticing. People on late night talk shows had swallowed far larger (and sharper items), that was for sure. Instead, he reached into his pocket and slapped his own iPhone on the table, shielded from human stupidity and clumsiness by a see-through, yellow fluorescent plastic case. "Relax, mate. This thing is light years better than any piece of crap we've got here at The Company. Until we make something superior and more innovative, I'll be rocking mine as well." Shane's British accented performance of the word "innovative" put mine to shame. I quietly mouthed "innovative" to myself in a South African accent to remind myself I still had *something* that set me apart from everyone else.

I gave Shane McCullough a once over. He was obviously a fitness fanatic having come to our meeting in what appeared to be the result of a collision between *Under Armour* and *Nike*.

Besides his awesome looking iPhone, he carried a half-consumed green spirulina concoction and a plastic Tupperware container with the freshest looking salmon I had seen in months. His hair, short and styled to a T, defied gravity in much the way I had always hoped my hair could aspire to, but never had the wherewithal to do so. And by dissing The Company's products in his first thirty seconds, he definitely had my attention. When McCullough died, I was sure his obituary would be a really great read. Probably in *The New York Times*.

He kicked his feet up on the table (*look at those awesome shoes*) and took a swig of his green machine. "So, you made it all the way to me. Which means nobody had an allergic reaction to you."

"If you say so." I imagined the Engineer shaking my hand and then going into anaphylactic shock, only which could be cured by dumping seven cans of *Mountain Dew* over the affected areas. The bubbles would mean it was working.

"The real question is…" he paused, taking a bite of his salmon. "…why do *you* want this job?"

It was a valid question. It had two answers. There was the honest answer and then there was the answer that I knew gave me the best chance at getting the job. There was the financially-motivated, desperate need for a steady paycheck, completely over the day-to-day micromanaged creativity of my previous career answer. Or there was the passionate, technology-obsessed, tech savvy, I want to make a difference and revolutionize your product answer. I knew I could only pick one.

"Because I'm passionate, tech-savvy, and would be excited to leverage my unique set of experiences to revolutionize your product."

"Bollocks," said Shane.

"I kind of need a job," I backpedaled.

"So, you're hungry."

"You could say that."

"Let me make you hungrier," Shane said, as he popped out of his chair and grabbed a remote control from the white board behind him. His energy was infectious. Hell, just watching him tap away at the remote and cause a huge HDTV to rise out of the floor was like watching a Vegas performance. The screen powered up and soon revealed what looked like a digital Dolphin swimming around in a digital ocean. Doing tricks, flipping and diving. Having a grand old time. Shane eyed the Dolphin with a child-like glee, then turned to me with a wide smile on his face.

"You see the Dolphin?"

"Yes. Pretty Dolphin." Seriously? Did I just say *pretty* Dolphin? It was obvious that the McCullough factor, as some had called it, was already affecting me. *Smooth talker + pretty Dolphin = idiotic responses.*

"You see what the Dolphin is doing?"

"Uh, swimming? Doing tricks?" I went back to my safe place, "Pretty Dolphin."

Shane shook his head and pressed a few more buttons. The screen split. Now there was the pretty Dolphin doing tricks on one side, and a bouncing multi-colored ball on the other side.

"Now what do you see?"

"A bouncing ball."

"And?"

"A pr- ...a Dolphin." Now the Dolphin turned as if it was noticing the ball on the other side of the screen. As the ball moved, the Dolphin's attention moved with it.

Shane slammed the remote down on the table. "Everyone's got the technology to concurrently run multiple programs at the same time. *Multi-tasking,* right? But those software programs are running without any awareness or ability to interact with the others. What you are seeing here, my friend, are two completely different routines that are aware of, and interacting *with* each other. *This* represents the cornerstone of MediaMesh. A product that lets the consumer listen to their music and tailor a movie *to that music* at the same time. A software suite that allows you to play a game and video chat with friends who booted up the same game. When we ship this latest update to our software, it will mean more attention, more consumer adoption, and more need for people like you to market it, sell it and make it a success." Shane grabbed his iPhone, holding it up. "With this next iteration of MediaMesh, this thing becomes a worthless brick."

I eyed Shane like he was the second coming. I almost didn't care what was coming out of his mouth because the sounds were so damn *pretty.* I wanted to be here. I wanted to work here. I wanted the damn job already. Gimme.

"Any questions?" Shane asked me, circling back to his personal effects and picking up the protein drink.

"Any questions *for me*?" I was all for the song and dance, and don't get me wrong it was compelling, but how could this guy hire me if he didn't totally know me?

"I already know you, man," he smiled. "You want to make a difference. Make your mark. You're fed up being told what to do when you just want to do what you're passionate about. You're a galvanizing force and you just need that electric shock to get things going. I'm that electric shock, Cameron. Together we can create *lightning*."

He *knew* me. He *totally* knew me. He *knew* that he *knew* me. There was a lot of knowing me going on up in this here conference room. He'd sold me. Did that mean I had sold him?

"So does that mean I've got the job?" I asked.

"Great question," he said, reaching for the door. "Peace." And he was out. The door closed behind him, leaving me basking in the glow of the swimming Dolphin and the bouncing ball, regarding each other in a way no software program had ever done before.

January

It was *bad*. But not your every day run of the mill, "things were not so great" *bad*. It was two-hour long plane delay, turbulent flight, screaming child, "please don't kick my seat" airline passenger, nine bags of heavy luggage, twenty-three-degree weather, torrential downpour, missing children's jacket, no town car in sight *bad*. There we stood, on the curb outside the Seattle International Airport's baggage claim, drenched and fatigued in an afternoon darkness none of us had ever seen before. "It kind of feels like the End Times," I said under my breath, wondering just when the day had turned from overcast to *evil*.

"The End Times are supposed to be slightly sunnier," Jess shot back, smiling a smile that represented no happiness whatsoever. "And warmer."

Our adorable, innocent little Kate looked up, quizzically, putting a finer point on the discussion at hand. "Do they not have the sun here?" Aw, the innocence of youth. Never standing on ceremony, a child could assess a situation and without any malice whatsoever make the adults around them come to terms with the fact that they were the idiots who were responsible for the currently flawed situation. Kate had a virtual Hit List of awesomely insightful questions that made her parents feel like complete and utter nincompoops.

[Stuck at the border of the United States and Canada, *Age 3*] "How come you and Mom have Passport things but I don't?"

[Standing under me, while putting in a Princess light fixture, *Age 2*] "Those wires are making smelly, smoky sounds."

[At the local Playground, *Various ages*] "What is a mother-tucker?"

And since they were kids…no retribution. A parent's answer always had to be just as sweet on the flipside. "The sun is just hiding, sweetie," I said, tussling her mop of curly brown hair. "Someday, when he's good and ready, he'll come out to play."

"Oh good," said Kate. "Because this place feels like it's filled with monsters." Which was ironic, because just at that moment our tardy Russian town car-driving hulk of a man, Vladimir, jumped out of his car and made himself known. He could have introduced himself as the classic 80's Bond villain, *Jaws*, and I wouldn't have asked to see his gleaming dental grill.

"Murphys?" he grunted, realizing off our stunned open-mouthed looks that we were indeed the family he was looking for. "I take you home, no?"

"Good God, no," I replied lightning-fast, purely out of instinct and as a result of watching a thousand movies that started with that *exact* same question and ended up with people like Liam Neeson killing a whole bunch of really bad men.

"No, no? Or no, yes?" asked Vladimir.

"Yes, please," Jess jumped in. "Just get us out of this…*hell*." Vlad nodded, throwing the bags in the trunk of the Lincoln Continental and ushering us into the back of the comfortable (and dry) back seat. We piled in, strapping in Kate to a booster, and got ourselves settled. It was mere minutes before Vlad jumped in the front and we were on our way.

Canyon Park Estates sat nestled in the lush hills of the East Side of Seattle, in a suburban area just twenty minutes south of The Company and another thirty from downtown Seattle. The winding streets were the home to a myriad of other fantastical sounding neighborhoods, all with oversized homes and overdone gold-encrusted crests for places called Mountain View, Clearwater and The Estates at Altair. The entire East Side continued to be one of the most sought-after places for young families, with great schools, beautiful parks and consistently-rising real estate prices. Finding the house had been Jess' mission since December, and she managed it like we were competing in a kill or be-killed competition where the couples without a house after three weeks would be eliminated in a groundbreaking live television event hosted by Jeff Probst.

"Do you like two stories or one story? Colonial or traditional? Bright and airy or dark and cozy? Hardwood floors or carpet? Eat-in kitchen or formal dining room? Heated bathroom floors or warm towel racks? Bonus room or office? Solar panels or electric water heater? Furnished basement or three car garage?"

Jess handled it all, and in three weeks flat. We would be moving into a gorgeous two-story Colonial that was bright and airy with a mix of hardwood and carpet. In the months to come, every time I drove up to it or looked out from the second story bathroom window, I would audibly ask myself whose house this really was because I had never imagined it could have been mine. There was a wonderful eat-in kitchen, three car garage and yes, you guessed it, it came with *two* garage door openers. I was already mentally resetting the switches inside the garage door openers and bending their wireless radio technologies to my will when Jess snapped me back into reality – we had arrived at our new neighborhood.

"Canyon Park Estah-tes," Vlad announced as he swung around the corner and up the steep entryway to our new digs. But other than the flickering street lights that struggled to shine through the downpour, there wasn't a soul to be seen anywhere. No cars in driveways, no families lit up by crackling fires as they played charades in their living room, not a single sign of life existed anywhere. The welcoming committee had obviously packed up the streamers and the potato, chicken and couscous salads when they had realized our plane had been delayed. Somewhere in one of these houses was a virtual cornucopia of mayonnaise-drenched protein with our names on it.

"Sub-par lighting on that entryway," Jess pointed out, mentally taking note of everything that was wrong with her new stomping grounds. "And who is allowed to paint their house the color of a chocolate *Ding Dong*?" I imagined there had also probably been some kind of brownies or molten chocolate cake dessert as a part of our *Welcome to Canyon Park* festivities, as well. At least I wanted to imagine there had been some kind of welcoming committee put together by the friendly and organized residents of Canyon Park, but as someone would later inform me, this was just another example of the *Seattle Freeze* – if you were new and from out of town, people pretended you didn't exist. Not out of spite, mind you. It was just that it was cold and dark and the last thing anyone thought to do was cart a tray of Snickerdoodles over to your front door and risk slipping and falling on the ice-covered stairs. They would say hello. Someday. It could just take six months.

Mere minutes later, the three of us stood in the foyer of our new home, bags strewn throughout the entryway. The house was easily double the size of our digs in Los Angeles, yet had cost us slightly less. Every thirty seconds, Kate sped past us, running circles around the entire cavernous downstairs. With no furniture yet, our voices echoed throughout.

"Well, babe," I said, giving Jess' shoulders a squeeze. "Welcome home."

The word *home* echoed throughout the entire house, over and over and over again. We looked at each other, each forcing a smile. "The furniture can't come soon enough," Jess said.

I always found it amusing that in the most horrible of living situations some people tried to divert everyone's attention by coloring the moment as "it's just like Camping!" I contemplated if I were to be one of those "people" in our current situation, while my wife and daughter lay on a pair of wheezing blow-up beds in the middle of our empty living room. *It's just like camping!* I tried it out in my head, but it didn't sound right. I needed to build up to it. *Hey, girls! You remember when you said that you had always wanted to do something challenging that built character?* That wouldn't work, either. Knowing Kate, the next question on her Hit List would be something about the S'mores and when they would be ready since *all* camping excursions came standard with S'mores and insect repellant. No, I wouldn't go there. I would just quietly wait for the moving vans, which wouldn't be here until at least tomorrow.

Next to me, Jess could hear that I was thinking, which was always accompanied by a few body shifts and a periodic *sigh*. "Go ahead, start talking," Jess leaned over, whispering so that she didn't wake up Kate who was a few feet away on her own Princess-inspired blow-up sleeping bag. "Are you nervous about tomorrow?"

"Why? Should I be?" I hadn't been nervous. I had been excited. But had I overlooked something? Was I walking into a completely nerve-wracking scenario?

"It's great that you're not nervous. You're going to be awesome."

"Okay, sure. But, like -- what would you be nervous about?"

"I wouldn't. I love that shit."

"What *shit*?"

"Corporate shit. Politics. *Not* curing cancer, but solving problems. Sorry I said anything. It's your first day. People get nervous for their *firsts*. It's human." But she just said she wouldn't be nervous. What did that make her? "I'm human too," she continued, "so stop staring out the window and wondering if I'm an alien."

But I had momentarily moved on from her comment – there was a light or some kind of movement outside the house. I jumped up quickly, almost eating it on the wood floor as I made my way to the front window. Somewhere across the street I could have sworn I saw a garage door finish closing. Then, nothing. I half expected to see a frostbitten tumbleweed saunter across the street in an attempt to mock us, the latest Patsies to buy land in this frozen wasteland.

"A garage door," I turned back to Jess.

"A garage door."

"I swear to God I just saw a garage door close. Which means a car probably pulled into a garage. Which means…" I took a step toward Jess and widened my eyes using every under-utilized dramatic skill I had *never* learned. "People," I said. "There are people living in this neighborhood." Jess widened her eyes, sarcastically.

"I'll believe it when I see it," she said, motioning for me to get back into our luxurious air mattress. I got back under the covers, eyeing the still sleeping Kate, then flipped over to get close to Jess. I started shaking. Jess put her arm around me, rubbing my back.

"I'm not nervous. I'm friggin' cold. What is it, like fifteen degrees in here?" Jess picked up her pillow, which I swear to God was half frozen, and clocked me in the face.

"Welcome to NEO," the tour guide at the front of The Company shuttle proclaimed through the loudspeaker, drawing an overabundance of applause that was infectious enough to get me going as well. When was the last time I *actually* clapped for something? I had grown jaded in movies, scoffing at people who clapped during the credits. I refused to clap for street performers because then I would feel obliged to pay for entertainment I had obviously secretly enjoyed but refused to admit was good. I *had* clapped when waiters dropped full trays of dinner entrees now and again – no illusions why the Greeks made it a part of their celebrations since it was absolutely invigorating. But *really* clapping out of joy or excitement? There was something wrong with me. L.A. had sucked up my soul and turned me into a modern-day Scrooge. Well, no more, I announced to myself. I looked around, still clapping, and admired all the happy folks. I was just like them. I patted a guy next to me on the back and he did it right back. Ah, yes. The New Employee Orientation had just begun.

"My name is Tad, and I'm an evangelist for The Company," our self-appointed Captain of Fun continued. "It's my job to make sure you know how *great* it is to work here, the *awesome* benefits you have at your fingertips, and to provide you a Day One experience that prepares you to become a significant contributor to The Company's success. You will quickly find that The Company employs some of the smartest, most ambitious people in the World. The question is *how soon* will it be before you are just…like…them?"

Next to me, the concept of "how soon" was already being realized as one Indian dude wondered how another Indian dude had already gotten access to his e-mail for a job he had yet to begin.

"I've already responded to twenty-three e-mails and scheduled seven one-on-ones over the next two weeks," the first Indian dude whispered under his breath.

"But how could that even be remotely possible?" worried the second Indian dude, sounding like he had actually been asking about some horrific social or ecological situation that had befallen all the other humans on planet Earth. "We don't get our aliases and passwords until we meet with our managers on Tuesday."

"I met my manager at five-thirty this morning," responded the first Indian dude. "Then, since the Help Desk wasn't open yet I configured my new laptop myself, set up which domain to pair my alias with… I was working by six in the morning."

The second Indian dude's eyes lit up like he had just been given the secret to *The Secret*. He nodded, most likely working out in his head how he would abandon the tour and access his own domain so he could, too, be working before the rest of us. Meanwhile, Tad the Wonder Guide began the herculean task of familiarizing the entire population of the shuttle with The Company's elaborate and well-manicured campus.

The Company and The Walt Disney Company truly had much more in common than the words "The" and "Company" – they both had had the foresight to buy hundreds of acres of real estate in most-ly-remote locations for what would someday become the home of their Corporate Headquarters (or Amusement Park). Having done so in the mid-seventies, The Company's early success had allowed it to start building their campus in and around the East Side of Seattle, and they had never looked back. Now, there were hundreds of buildings everywhere, each with their own cafes, sport courts, futuristic "focus rooms" for individual or cooperative brainstorming and the kind of video-enabled conference rooms that made you *have to care* about how you looked. Over time, the campus had infested so much of the surrounding areas and grew to be so spread out that The Company decided to build one amazing hub of activity at the center of it all. They called it the "Studios" and it rivaled a place that some folks called *The Happiest Place on Earth*.

"Now we're entering the Studios Complex," said Mr. Personality, a.k.a. Tad. "The Studios were built in 2008 and are made up of four major compounds that house our most lucrative entertainment properties across the software, hardware and media departments." There were many *oohs* and *aahs* but the enthusiasm paled in comparison to what was to come. "And at the center of the complex," he continued, "is the Commons. This is a more than your mother's food court. These structures contain over forty different restaurants, a bank, a post office, a bicycle shop, a hair salon, five different mobile phone retail stores, a game room, an ice cream parlor, three coffee shops, an art gallery, the official Company store and a pair of full-size regulation soccer and basketball courts." *In my head*, I envisioned the entire crowd lifting Tad up on their shoulders, carrying him into the center of the soccer field and tossing him into a bed of roses. Instead, they just cheered wildly. The excitement was palpable and the questions were many.

Someone asked if the rumor was true – did the Seattle Sounders actually practice on The Company's regulation field? *Indeed.* Someone wondered if employees got discounts on high priced electronics and software? *Yes, as long as they didn't charge it to their Corporate AMEX.* A third person wanted to know if it was true that on one Friday every quarter The Company actually transported ponies, bouncy houses and a ludicrous amount of face painting professionals to the Commons for employees and their families to enjoy. True, true and *true.*

The tour continued. Past employee parks, athletic centers and even legal service facilities. Apparently, while on your lunch break, you could establish that living will, divorce your significant other (as long as she wasn't a current, in-good standing employee of The Company), and sue an off-campus hair salon for that Caesar cut they subjected you to. In the Shuttle, everyone stared slack jawed and wide-eyed at the possibilities that lay out before them. This wasn't an office park with three vending machines built next to a freeway on-ramp. This wasn't even *T-Mobile* – which *was* incidentally built next to a used-car dealership *and* a freeway on-ramp just miles down the road. No, this was high class. It made you want to work here. It made you *proud* to work at The Company. I found myself nodding along with my fellow employees. We were all drinking the Kool-Aid and it tasted *mighty good.*

An hour later I exited the Shuttle and into The Company's outdoor registration tent which surrounded the massive flagship convention center. It was adorned with the flags of every country and a digital billboard that cycled between two messages: "Welcome New Company Employees!" and "Your Future Begins Here!" All around me the machine was working to full effect. I stood, marveling at the choreography of the Shuttles – each pulling up, dropping off a group of thirty or so individuals, and continuing the dance out of the parking lot as another perfectly-timed Shuttle arrived. The in-house camera crews were also there, filming new employees exhibiting Spring Break-level enthusiasm for the Company's Intranet-focused news and television channel. I couldn't imagine the employees at The Company were spending their work hours perusing the in-house website, but the creation of a brand-new Excel template sometimes was a galvanizing watershed moment. At the far end of the tent in front of the entryway were tables, organized alphabetically, where volunteers affixed each new employee with their plastic-encased Blue Badge.

"Cameron Murphy," I announced to my own personal volunteer, who fished out a Blue Badge with a picture of my face already adorning the card.

"Always keep it with you," she explained. "And no tailgating."

"Tailgating?" I asked, confused.

"Okay, so when you swipe your way into a building, don't let anyone piggyback on your security badge."

"Piggyback?" Were we talking illegalities of the vehicular kind or something that my daughter stole from me every time I leaned down to pick up an errant sock?

"Everyone's blue badge is authorized for *only* the buildings they're supposed to have access to. Which means, don't let anyone else *in* when *you* open the door." She was done explaining, pointing towards the double-doors behind her. "Orientation is on the second floor. Take the elevator up, down the hall."

I made my way to the front doors, swiping my Blue Badge twelve times before the melodic *click* authorized my entry to the building. You better believe I made sure that the "questionables" behind me didn't try any of that *tailbacking* or *piggygating*. Everyone was paranoid. You didn't want to be the guy who was responsible for letting some investigative reporter into the inner-sanctum of The Company, only to leak confidential information all over the Internet. At least not on the first day. There'd be months and years in the future to get involved in that sort of thing, I thought, as the doors to the elevator closed and the closest person to the panel hit the button for the second floor.

"*Doors closing!*" reverberated through the elevator, in a pleasant almost-endearing female British accent. Everyone looked up, in unison, at the ceiling from where the voice emanated. There was an almost musical *sigh* throughout the entire elevator from its passengers as Daphne (the name I gave her the minute she spoke) let us know what was next. "*Second floor, doors opening,*" she pleasantly informed her group of admirers. Most of us aimlessly walked out, as if under her spell, and found our way in the main hallway that led to the auditorium. Behind me, I watched as the doors to the elevator closed – a few smitten individuals had decided to go back for a second ride. I headed down the hall, past various groups of gathered individuals. What, at first, appeared to be groups of friends mingling before the official start of the orientation sessions, were in fact groups of individuals hovering over a variety of amazing Company perks.

One group stood catatonic, staring at an entire wall of glass-doored refrigerator units. The sum of its total parts included every single possible carbonated drink, juice, milk and soy product you could ever imagine ingesting. "Coconut water!" someone cried to another, setting off a looting spree of epic proportions where pockets and bags suddenly became cold and rigid. These people were making salaries well over the poverty line, but free tropical liquids seemed to marshal them in a way social justice and political rallies never could.

Another group moved quickly and with purpose, cycling in and out of a hallway a few hundred feet down the line. As I approached, I bumped into an individual by accident, then watched as thousands of paperclips exploded into midair. As I took a few more steps forward I realized the hallway was not one at all, but rather an office supply repository. Pens, pencils, paper, datebooks, envelopes, paperclips, markers and more. People carted off boxes of brand-new dry erase markers and the accompanying eraser itself. Others lifted reams of paper and placed them in their bags. "Free paper!" someone cried to another, which seemingly had less of an effect than the free coconut water rallying cry, and which was communicated by a general malaise despite a few shifty-eyed looking newbies running off with stacks of white.

I passed by a final group as I approached the double doors to the auditorium, who marauded around a table stocked high with pre-wrapped protein bars and drinks. It was like an aisle in a supermarket, filled to the brim with every possible brand available. I grabbed one, tearing it open and taking a bite as I looked back from where I'd come, leaving Daphne to bond with the others. I smiled to myself. *Fuck L.A.*, I thought. *I'm never going back. This place is sweet.*

With The Company starting thousands of new employees every single week, they had NEO down to a science. They'd begin with a pre-record-ed message from Ben Packer, the charismatic fifty-something CEO, who had been a relatively recent hire after selling a billion-dollar Internet business solely focused on selling billion-dollar Internet businesses. "We welcome you and your families," he finished his message with, "be-cause without your families supporting your work at The Company, we would never be able to accomplish the unthinkable. I challenge you to go do amazing things starting right here on Day One." For the first time, my mind floated back to Jess and Kate. I picked up my phone, cycling through some saved pictures until I landed on one of them. I smiled. This was about them, too. I couldn't wait to walk through the door at the end of the day and tell them all about the great things I had seen. They would be so excited. So pumped. I visualized the three of us dancing in silly joy.

There were other speeches and videos, too. Most amazing was the fact that at The Company, health benefits were gold class. "Get as sick as you want," the Director of Human Resources told us. "Cough up a lung. Have a baby. Get diagnosed with schizophrenia!" The health benefits would cover it all. Plus, doctor visits *at your house*, prescriptions filled and delivered *to your door*, and if you actually ever went to the gym to work out? The Company would contribute to the monthly membership fee. There were folders and hand-outs for employees to better understand how they would be evaluated for promotions, bonuses and stock rewards. There was a brief teaser for a class focused on how to handle your e-mail in-box (I thought how silly that was since I had been handling my e-mail for years). For those who were afraid of driving or didn't have a license, there were free, WiFi-enabled autonomous shuttles delivering employees to the hundreds of Company locations throughout the Seattle area. And with each speech or presentation came yet another perk: *schwag*. Drink cozies, t-shirts, stickers, binders, water bottles, headbands, phone cases and more. It was like presenting at *The Oscars* and getting a gift bag of goodies for doing almost absolutely nothing. You can imagine how hungry it made us all.

Outside the auditorium, the lunch spread was already in place. Multiple food stations and chefs were standing at attention, carving Kobe beef, crafting sushi platters, tossing salads and serving up bread pudding in ten varieties. There were hot and cold sandwich bars, gelato sundaes, chicken wraps, vegan platters and more. I had to admit, after the morning I had experienced, it was kind of to be expected. But there was still room for some surprises, as a gleam of polished metal caught my gaze from across the room. I immediately made a bee-line for it, staring in awe at what was before me.

It was a portable, self-serving, completely intelligent *Starbucks* coffee machine – plucked right out of some futuristic space saga and dropped here, in the middle of this convention center. There were buttons for everything, in a well laid out simple to use interface. Choose your size of cup, choose the style of coffee you desired, land on the temperature you felt was appropriate and click *begin*. I repeated the steps to myself in sing-songy way ("Pick the cup and fill it up") as I banked four different combinations of hot drinks including Dark Hazelnut Hot Chocolate, and lined them up on the table before me. In the time it took me to arrange the *Starbucks*/Company co-branded cups in my usual OCD fashion, I had already determined how to lay off half of *Starbucks'* International workforce by simply showing them this device. That was it. The rest would take care of itself. The sobbing and general hysterics would be short-lived as they would all find more personally satisfying jobs elsewhere, I would tell myself.

"Cameron Murphy, you *bastard*." The words hit me like a ton of bricks, startling me into knocking over all my coffee as I spun around to see who had spoken them. It was a surprise I never could have called. Standing there, in a tight knit sweater and a pair of painted on jeans was none other than Romy Wallace. Back in Los Angeles, she was known as "the" new media agent, repping video game creators, new media visionaries and a slew of *YouTube* stars who were best known for their "snark." She had developed an entire cottage industry around the snark of today's youth, including pioneering the *Snark Food Review*, *Snark Music Video Goof* and discovering talents such as RJ Zimmer and his *Undead Snark*, who had racked up thirty-million views by dressing up like a zombie, packing himself in FedEx boxes and shipping himself to the doorsteps of faint-of-heart senior citizens expecting their Social Security checks. Those who liked her called her the Digital Diva, among other nicknames. Those who hated her called her a *bitch*. I had met with her years ago when I had been developing a video game based on a script I had written, inspired by a greeting card that had made me cry. My mother had loved it. The rest of the town, not so much. But despite that, Romy had been open to giving me advice and had treated me with the utmost of respect. Sometimes, in certain situations…*I liked her*.

"Romy Wallace!?" I reached out and gave her the hug she was obviously half-pregnant with. "What are you doing here? Do you have a client here at The Company?"

She rolled her eyes, then flipped her blonde locks behind her shoulder, leaning in more closely. "I'm working *here*," she announced, noticing the surprise on my face. "Those bastards at Legendary Artists were bleeding me dry. Sucking the life out of me. Challenging me to re-define the entire industry all at once and then at the same time they were stealing every idea I had and passing it off on their own withoutgiving-meanycreditwhatsoeverandIwassooverit." She took a breath. It was one thing I forgot to mention about Romy Wallace. She was passionate, that was for sure. And when she was passionate about something, she talked *incessantly*. Had you told me she had ADHD I would have told you that she was obviously not taking any medication for it.

Behind us, throngs of coffee worshipers had realized what I had discovered and were now waiting for their turn to use my new life's ob-session. "How about some lunch?" Romy asked, waving her open palms at the food stations like a regular old Vanna White. "On me." I laughed, starting to walk with her towards a table. "And don't forget your coffee," she turned back to point out. All four of the cups were spilled, half-filled, and totally *killed*.

"Oh, I don't drink coffee," I admitted. "I just *love* technology."

Over sparkling apple cider and Chicken Cordon Bleu, Romy and I caught up on how our lives had landed us here. It was ironic, in a *two-thousand spoons when all you need is a knife* kind of way. She represented the side of the Industry I never understood – people who defined their success by the success of others. I represented the side of the Industry she loathed having to deal with – talent who always believed their success was sole-ly due to one person...*themselves*. Yet both our actions...both our own self-inflicted ultimatums had driven us out of Hollywood and were moti-vated by the same exact aspiration.

"Dude, I wanted to make a difference," she continued. "I didn't want to have to take orders from those Barneys at Legendary. They didn't believe in the coming digital revolution. They wanted me to focus on talent who were known for shooting *Mentos* out their butts. I was sitting in my office, staring out the window one day and wondered to myself where the next truly disruptive opportunity would come from. It wasn't in that suffocating little asbestos factory, that was for sure. I picked up the phone and called my friends at The Company. Within a week I was here, interviewing. They made me an offer the next day."

"An offer to do *what*?"

"I'm starting in Business Development for a new media product," she explained, making a sick-face. "I'm told that if I kick butt and get a few quick wins under my belt, I can be the GM of my own product within the year." My eyes slightly glazed over as I let it all sink in. Getting promoted to a General Manager was like being "made" at The Company. It seemed Romy's years of Hollywood caché had put her in the catbird seat. "We should stick together," she continued. "Homies forever, *riiii-ight*?" An alliance. The two of us. I imagined just how powerful the two of us could become…

In my imagination, the scene changed to something out of the *Game of Thrones*, with me in my chain mail, unsheathing a gleaming behemoth sword and gazing bravely at the horizon. A horizon which, at that very moment, seemed to move and vibrate under the glare of the setting sun. But it was no trick being played on my eyes. No, the shadows of a thousand marauding warriors and their clanging armor, approached rapidly. Their hunger for death was no rumor – their actions proved that. I turned, startled and then relieved to find Romy standing beside me, in her own medieval battle-gear, a small dagger in one hand and a broadsword in another. The scene widened, and yet our metal-encased backs touched as we evaluated the situation. "They are almost upon us," Romy said without releasing her gaze from the incoming deluge. "We must stay together or everything we hold dear will fall to their swords." I said something back. Something courageous. Then I squinted my eyes in an extra-brave look that obviously signified my brazen *braveness*. Somewhere deep down I released a frightening rallying cry.

In the real world, I choked on a piece of chicken, coughing it up into a napkin. "Oh, Jesus are you okay?" Romy asked, handing me a stack of twenty more.

"I was just trying to agree," I said, wiping my mouth dry. "Homies, for- *forever*."

She reached out and grabbed my hand in an awkward handshake that easily pointed out how *un-Street* I was. Still, it was the thought that mattered. "You get my back, I get yours," she winked, as we both dug back into our luxurious meals of privilege. "Hollywood in the house."

My energy was infectious as I drove through the early evening's darkness, following the directions of my newfound GPS friend at the helm. Ben Folds' *Song for the Dumped* blasted on the stereo system, being piped through my brand-new smartphone, which sat next to my new game console, laptop computer, and state-of-the-art retina-enabled flat-screen tablet. They had all been given to us in glorious *Oprah*-fashion, with a "there's just one more thing we'd like to share" zinger from the day's NEO facilitator. "We want you to be evangelists of our own products," she announced excitedly. Which I'm not sure anyone actually heard because they were all screaming so loudly when they noticed the wrapped boxes underneath their chairs. My voice was hoarse, too. What can I say? Peer pressure.

I turned past the front entrance of our neighborhood, pivoting my head from side to side as I ascended to the top of the development, craning my neck to find any sign of life. Still nothing. Where were all the people? It was six-thirty at night. I made a turn onto our street, then a quick right into our driveway, pausing to reach up for the garage door opener. Behind me, a streak of light passed by, accompanied by the growl of a luxury automobile. I quickly abandoned the garage door opener, bursting out of the car and onto the sidewalk. At the end of the cul-de-sac, I could have sworn I saw another garage door close. But I couldn't be sure. Was I seeing things? My curiosity gave way to pure disbelief as snow flurries began wafting down and around me. *Well, now today really feels like Christmas*, I thought to myself, getting back into the car.

In the garage I stacked my new electronics on the hood, retrieving the rest of my schwag from the trunk. I couldn't even carry it all in one trip, despite trying and failing a minimum of three times (while attempting to play my own personal real-life version of *Electronics Jenga*). But then the most amazing, MacGuyver-*esqe* idea materialized, and I proceeded to *wear my schwag*. I put on the "The Company Can!" t-shirt, shoved one hand in the drink cozy, pulled on the fuzzy winter hat and shoved pens and office supplies in my pockets. I was a one trip kind of guy. If it took two trips, I'd leave what I didn't care about behind. It was a good thing I only had one child.

I slowly and cautiously made my way up the garage stairwell to the door. Inside I could hear Jess and Kate having a conversation. I grabbed the doorknob quietly, turned it slowly, and *burst* out into the house. Like a completely giddy fool I landed on both feet, let out an un-intelligible high-pitched sound and cheered, "Look at all this amazing stuff I got!" At least, I got to the "*look at all this amazing st-*" part before I noticed Jess and Kate sitting in the center of the kitchen, surrounded by boxes and candles. They were eating…

"Cold beans!" Kate announced excitedly. She used a plastic fork, cautiously fishing for sustenance through the jagged metal top.

"Yay. Cold beans." Jess regurgitated in a monotone voice. "Because the electricity and gas won't be turned on until tomorrow. And how was your day entertaining the crowds at the hockey game, darling? How many t-shirts did you shoot into the stands?"

I stripped my winnings and sat down between my girls, giving them both the kisses they deserved for (a) dealing with me, (b) moving to a brand-new city *for* me and (c) managing what had been a tiresome day of directing movers and boxes throughout all the rooms of our new house. Kate took another scoop of the cold beans, offering me another bite. "No thank you. I'm not hungry," I smiled.

"Aside from taking really good care of you and showering you with expensive gifts, did they feed you well today?" asked Jess.

"Yes, I ate fine," I replied, feeling somewhat guilty. Jess had been with me for years, she knew my "guilt tell." All she had to do is cock her head and roll her eyes at me to get the answer. It had worked seamlessly during the *I Rear Ended Some Other Guy With Your Mercedes of '05*, the *Yes, The Bachelor Party Did Have Strippers At It of '07*, and the *Okay, So I Ate Both Drumsticks Off That Costco Chicken Without Even Thinking of Saving One For You, Situation of Last Week*. "Chicken Cordon Bleu," I volunteered. "But it wasn't *that* good."

"Chicken Cordon Bleu?!" She punched me in the arm.

Jess and I stood in the doorway of Kate's new room, arms around each other, gazing at stacks of more boxes. It was like someone with a sense of humor had setup a mini-New York City skyline in the five hundred square foot space. From somewhere deep inside the cardboard Manhattan, a voice whispered "Mommy, Daddy? Good night…"

"Goodnight, Kate," we spoke back in unison.

"Wherever you are," I followed up. There was nothing but a quiet *tee hee* and then we flipped off the light and closed the door.

Back in our bedroom, Jess filled me in on a harrowing day, filled with moving men, cable guys, toddler temper tantrums and a neighborhood shrouded in cloud. She had already culled together a slew of recommendations for local Pre-Schools, determined to have Kate enrolled and attending before the week was up. Thursday was our first school tour, at *Mountain Ridge Academy*. It housed classes from Pre-K all the way to Fifth Grade and was known for their unique extracurricular activities like chess, horseback riding, French, piano and beat poetry.

Jess flipped back onto the bed, obviously fatigued, then turned to me. "What am I going to do once she's in school? I'm going to be sitting here, all by myself…all day long. It's going to be like *Groundhog Day*."

"She doesn't *have to* go to Pre-School."

"Oh yes she does," she responded without a thought, "or else I will suffocate her with a pillow." I leaned down, looked Jess in the eyes. She looked back up at me. "Seriously. What am I going to do while she's in school and you're at work getting foot massages and eating sashimi?"

"What do you *want* to do?" I asked her. "You can do anything. I mean, who gets that opportunity? You're free of the political studio bullshit. You get to do whatever you want on your own terms."

"I just don't know what my own terms even means," she frowned. "I mean, if I'm not the Head of Publicity, then who the hell am I?"

"You're my wife. And Kate's mother."

"Don't get me wrong," she said as she held my face, "but if I'm going to survive up here in this darkness, I'm going to need a little more than that." She kissed me, then flipped over to her side of the bed, turning off the light.

It was twenty-nine degrees and pouring. Normally, it would have made for a quick drive in Los Angeles, where people had death wishes and heavy feet. But in Seattle, despite being drenched in rain more than six months out of the whole year, the drivers *could not handle it to save their life*. People braked when the rain picked up, they swerved around puddles in their four-wheel drives and they generally freaked out if a rumbling of any kind seemed close, using the *Poltergeist* "how far is that Thunder" math (a mile per second until you hear the roar, FYI). A fifteen-minute back-up on this particular morning was due to two lanes of packed traffic waiting for a pair of ducks to cross the street. I loved animals and all, but *really*?

I followed a slew of cars piloted by fellow Company employees (every car had the same rear window parking tag which is how I knew) into the main structure for the office buildings across the street from the Studio complex. Despite the hard sell about the *Disneyland* experience across the way, the startup feel of MediaMesh had landed the team a sizeable structure across the freeway in Building 87.

Building 87 was a part of the old-school construction in The Company's history, and it reeked of office park instead of Apple store. It was made of bricks and mortar, instead of the Studio building's metal and glass. Inside, it was an open space warehouse with cubes instead of the glorious offices everyone got across the freeway. It reminded me of the sneaky trick Mom always used to play in an attempt to get out of actually having to pay for fast food. She'd make a homemade burger, slap it on a fancy bun and slather it with gourmet ketchup and tell you it was "just as good as the *Big Mac*." But alas, it never was. Needless to say, Building 87 was no *Big Mac* like the Studios were. It was an overcooked burger with a bun that had gotten slightly soggy, but it was a burger nonetheless.

Despite all that, no one was sitting dejected and depressed inside Building 87. There was a kind of frenetic energy and excitement that permeated the entire space. Cubicles were redesigned as pirate ships with elaborate wicker thatch roofs and virtual zoos with life-size stuffed gorillas and monkeys. Music played on an endless loop throughout the space, adding the soundtrack to everyone's daily routine. Employees handled the stress of their days in two very distinct (yet similar ways): some battled each other in violent, often acrobatic *Nerf* gun battles while others battled work crumpled over their computer screens. There were flashing beer signs, glowing lava lamps and Dolphin posters everywhere with the stenciled words "swim to where the puck is going to be." The old Gretsky adage was alive and well, repurposed illogically for the tech sector. Had he known his inspirational words were being paired with an underwater mammal, I suspect he would not have been pleased.

My new manager, Leah Norton, waved to me from across the sea of cubicles as she stood in front of one of the many glass-enclosed focus rooms. She oozed enthusiasm and a genuine passion that made me glad she would be my entre into this new society. She was a nurturer, that was for sure, further demonstrated by the motherly hug she gave me as I followed her into the room and she closed the door.

"Cameron. Look at you," she smiled, "you are *actually* here! Can I tell you how great it is to have you as a part of my team?"

"It's so great to be here," I replied. "Really, it's just been such an exciting experience so far." I held up my new laptop and new smartphone. "And with benefits like *these...*"

She laughed, then got extra comfortable as she pulled her legs up under her body and stretched her sweater up and over her legs. It felt like one of those nights in college, just shooting the shit with the girl next door. She cocked her head, as if giving me a once over, and then said "Are you ready to make a difference?" There was only one answer, and this time it was from my heart.

"Willing and ready. Just tell me what to do."

Leah sat back up, pulling out a crumpled piece of paper and flattening it on the table. "Let's get you logged into the network with your alias and password," she said as she turned around my laptop and started typing. *Why did she crumple up my alias and password*, I wondered to myself. I figured I'd leave it alone as she swung my laptop back towards me. "First step of any first day... Heck, of *any* day... Get your mail."

I laughed. "It's my first day. I don't think you'll find much in there *yet.*"

I turned to the screen just as Outlook, the Official E-mail Client of The Company, was booting up. Leah slid over next to me as the screen popped open and the in-box appeared before us. It was empty. I looked over to Leah. "Wait for it," she smiled.

I looked to her just as a pleasant "*ding*" reverberated from the computer and my inbox began filling with new e-mails. They came and they came. What was fifty, became one hundred. What was one hundred, became one fifty. The numbers kept climbing. And climbing. When the e-mail count had finally stopped, it read two hundred and thirty-seven e-mails. "Who are all these e-mails for?" I asked, wondering if she'd typed in the wrong alias and password. This wasn't e-mail for *me*, was it? How could it be? Today was my first day.

"They're for you," she stated, matter-of-fact.

"How is that possible?"

"Oh, the minute you accepted the offer, everyone started adding you to e-mail threads and meeting invites. But don't worry, not every single mail is something you've got to deal with." *Thank the Lord,* I thought. "Just the ones with *red bangs.*"

"Red bangs?" I repeated, not even wanting to try to predict what that meant.

"Red bangs," she repeated back. "Red *exclamation marks* next to the e-mail. It means that those mails are the most critically time-consuming issues that must be dealt with as soon as possible. We really encourage all our team members to refrain from using a red bang unless it really, truly represents an issue that will cause catastrophic results if not resolved ASAP."

I looked at the in-box. Scrolled from top to bottom. There were seven e-mails *without* red bangs! For those in the World who could still do math in their heads without the crutch of a digital calculator, that represented two hundred and thirty e-mails. That had to be handled *now.* By a guy who had been in his new job about, oh, *twelve minutes and thirty seconds.* I scanned over the subject lines. It was like reading complete and utter gibberish. A wave of terror flashed through my soul as I blankly stared at all that *damn red.* Couldn't they have made them *beige bangs*? Or *teal taps*? Why did they have to sound so damn life-threatening? Somewhere outside, a hail storm started raining down baseball-sized ice boulders, reverberating as they pelted the facility. I imagined one particularly large ice sphere punching a hole through the aluminum roof and careening head-on with our focus room, smashing square into my head and causing me to collapse violently onto the floor, limbs shaking uncontrollably.

"Are you okay!?" Leah would yell, panicked.

"I'm not sure," I mumbled back, half unconscious already. "But what I am sure about is that due to my current *very serious* medical situation, those e-mails are going to have to wait."

Back in the real world, Leah sensed the pure terror that was passing through all of my extremities. "Listen. You'll figure it all out. Like everyone who has come before you," she proclaimed, still smiling that genuine, peaceful, engaging...smug, pandering, spiteful smile. I wanted to slap it off her face.

"I will," I lied. "I totally will."

"Team meeting in twenty," she said, getting up and opening the sliding glass door. "See you then." She closed the door, leaving me to stare blankly at the list of mails. I shook it off. Everyone went through this. It was like a hazing ritual. Meant to challenge me on my first day and to see if I could handle the pressure. I'd show them I could.

Twenty minutes later, Leah introduced me to the rest of her team, comprised of the sales and marketing folks responsible for getting companies to buy MediaMesh and getting customers to use the product. With a major new standalone version being rolled out for the software suite in just over two months, there was lots of work to be done in ensuring that the new multi-media, multi-tasking mode (read: dolphins & bouncing balls) was communicated clearly, branded successfully and accompanied by a go-to-market plan that would get the word out in both the tech and entertainment sectors. I would be responsible for identifying the right partners to sell the product to and partner with my new wingman, Everett, to verbally pitch the companies on the opportunity. *Pitching companies*, I repeated in my head. At least that was something I knew how to do.

"Nice to finally have a partner in crime," spoke Everett, eyes closed. While he was well-dressed to the point of over-doing it and well-spoken to the point of sometimes being *too* eloquent, every single time he talked he *closed his eyes*. People around the room would follow his bobbing head as he spoke, wondering like in a game of Russian roulette when the end was finally going to come. "It will be absolutely fantastic to leverage each other's skills to pitch our potential clients." *Of course, it would*, I thought. *Because now there will be someone in the room who can actually look at the people*. I knew how to do that, too. I was great at opening my eyes.

Leah introduced the rest of the crew. There was Elise Jenner, the Marketing Lead for the product. She was passionate, personable and seemingly always tapped into the next horrible thing to impact the team, the product and The Company. "We've got some amazing things in the works with tech press and VIP enthusiasts," she excitedly announced. "But my boyfriend's best friend, who is *very* high up at Reuters says that he is hearing the entire Company is going to be shut down before the end of the year. It's *really* bad."

"That's not true, Elise," said Leah.

"I'm just telling you what I heard," said Elise. "That could impact our entire marketing plan." I nodded at Elise. It was a very astute statement in a *bizarro* world kind of way.

There was Eric Garcia, an amenable numbers cruncher who appeared to be happiest when he was deep in an Excel spreadsheet. Gil Potter, a Brit who was focused on a slew of ambiguous special projects that all seemed to be in various stages of development. And Gail Lockwood, a mousy wallflower with *bite* – she always seemed to answer a question about the work she was supposed to have completed with a statement throwing someone else entirely under the bus.

"Gail, how's the social media plan coming?" asked Leah.

"Ask Gil. Until he speaks with Reddit, I'm at a stand-still."

On the way out of the conference room, Elise pulled me aside. "I'm taking you to lunch later," she whispered. "If you're going to survive here, you're going to need all the download you can get. And I have got *a lot* of download."

"Lunch sounds nice," I said. "Where should I meet you?"

"At Studios," she said, raising her eyebrows. "Where the food is made to order. Never eat the crap around here. They use the leftovers from local homeless shelters and pass them off as fresh."

"That can't be true," I said, disbelieving.

"I'm just telling you what I heard," Elise shot back, giving me a forearm grab and shuffling off on her own way. Meanwhile, my smartphone vibrated and I looked down at the screen. I was due for a meeting somewhere in Building 88 in ten minutes. I bolted for the door.

The conference room chairs at The Company were some of the most amazing, ergonomically-correct chairs in the History of chairs. There were chairs that aspired to be ergonomically-correct, with cheap mesh backs and styro-foam lower back support. And there were chairs that delivered on a superior ergonomically-correct experience, with the materials obviously developed by none other than N.A.S.A.. The Company spared no expense when it came to their employees' spines. I sat back, reclining, and watched the room fill up with a variety of folks I had never met or seen before in my life. This being my first meeting with folks from across the Org, I was fascinated to see what it was all about. I checked my smartphone (I had still refrained from opening up my laptop to this point) to read the subject line of the meeting in question. "*Sync on Medi-aMesh Advertising Opportunities*" read the invitation. I sat up, interested. Seeing as though I was invited was a testament to the fact that my opinion and involvement was obviously necessary to move forward the initiative.

"Who's Cameron Murphy?" asked a grey-haired man near the front of the conference room.

"That's me," I responded, somewhat surprised that people were already taking notice.

"Floor is yours," he replied. "Do you have a deck to present?"

The *floor was mine*? *Did I have a deck to present*? What floor? What deck? I stared around the room – everyone eyed me to see what my next answer would be. A woman from across the table shoved a black computer dongle towards me, as if I had some idea of what to do with the snaking, black cord. I threw it back at her, across the table, panicked. She looked at me, confused.

"I don't have a deck to present, I'm afraid," I said. I looked for where the door was, estimating how long it would take me to bolt for the exit. What the hell was going on here? Didn't people know that this was my *first day*!?

"Fair enough," said the grey-haired instigator at the front of the conference room. "You can always just speak to it."

Speak to *what*? What was I supposed to be speaking about? I seriously looked around for Ashton Kutcher. This had to have been some kind of elaborate episode of a new spin-off of *Punk'd* meets *The Game* – where someone's life was completely ruined by hiring them for a new job, moving them to a faraway locale, then demanding they speak in a meeting where they knew absolutely *zero* about the subject. I waited for a moment, hoping for someone manning a boom mic to come crashing through the ceiling.

But no one came. No one started laughing. It was just me. I had two choices. I could get up in front of an entire group of strangers and fake my way through a presentation that I knew absolutely *nothing* about. Or I could be honest and tell them they would have to postpone today's meeting due to me knowing absolutely *nothing* about the subject matter at hand. Neither sounded good. Or productive. Only career limiting.

Instead, I stood up, cradling my stomach. I let out a *gurgling* sound that caused a few people to cringe and roll their chairs away from me. "Stomach bug," I wheezed, as I grabbed my laptop and fled for the door.

"Are you okay?" asked the grey-haired troublemaker at the front of the conference room.

"I will be," I coughed, bursting out the door.

As I fled down the hall, the meeting participants came out after me – following. "We'll reschedule for next week!" someone yelled. But who it was, I had no idea, since I was already too far away.

From the outside, The Commons was an architectural masterpiece. On the inside, it was a foodie's dream come true. This wasn't the house built on *Cheetos* and fried chicken, this was a gourmet, four-star culinary extravaganza. Elise walked me through the downstairs, past the bicycle shops and the post office, in and around the "stage" where a jazz band was playing, and towards a long string of food preparation areas where chefs sliced beef, prepared sushi, took hot bakery bread and rotisserie chicken out of the ovens…

"And the salad bar was voted *Best Salad Bar in the Pacific North-west* by The Seattle Times," she began. "It's partially because they developed a unique chilling feature that distributes the coldness throughout the metal pans versus just using a single fan refrigerator unit."

"Wow," I said, while really thinking *wow*.

"The clown town General Manager of the food service org was fired twelve months ago, *before* we got that Seattle Times mention," she continued. "A Corporate VP choked on a frozen piece of chicken back when they were using the refrigerator unit and it totally malfunctioned. He almost died. But the chicken has been super moist ever since."

I dove right into the salad bar while Elise hit the carving station. Award or no award, this was literally the best salad bar I had ever seen in my entire life. There were five kinds of salad. There were three kinds of chicken. Tofu. Lobster. Shrimp. Bacon. Garbanzo beans. Peppers. Seventeen kinds of dressing. Years ago, I remember waking up from a dream that for whatever reason focused on a fictitious Bacon Balsamic Ranch dressing. *My dreams are coming true*, I thought, as I poured a dressing with that exact name atop my heaping Devil's Tower of vegetative goodness.

Next to me, a strange older fellow with a wispy red Gandalf-like beard, mumbled to himself while he combined no less than three different dressings atop his *feng shui*-esqe salad. He measured and poured with such accuracy and eye-hand coordination, it was like he had practiced it on multiple, if not dozens of occasions. The plate itself was organized by colors. Reds blended into purples which blended into oranges and then greens. Peppers to eggplant to fruit slices and lettuce. It was anything but the type of chaos I carried on my plate. Later, when I thought about it in more detail, I would decide that there was something *mathematical* behind the way he had organized the meal.

"You just stood toe to toe with Simon Davis," Elise whispered when we sat down at the table, shoveling a slice of beef covered in double-baked potato into her mouth. "He's a legend."

"Simon Davis?" I replied. Sadly, for me, the kind of legends I knew about were responsible for things like *wookies* and caped crusaders, not technology. It would be something that would have to change.

"Murphy, you had better spin up quickly or you are going to drown," she said as she finished destroying the bite in her mouth. "Simon Davis was the twenty-fifth hire at The Company," she began. "He was a part of the team who developed the first user interface for the first piece of computer software. He *invented* the Start Button."

"He invented the Start Button. That can't be true."

"Before him, people had to use those crappy menus to choose a program. Remember those? You booted up, picked a number and it ran the program? Then came this genius and the start button. One button to rule them all. When everyone else had become jaded or unbelieving, Simon Davis was the guy who got shit done. He made things happen."

"So, what is he doing now, besides making salad?" I joked.

"Nobody knows. Not even me. He's got some lab somewhere in the bowels of the campus. One day he was developing what was supposed to be a product that would change the world, the next day his product and his whole org were getting shut down. He's got major anger issues. Kind of dangerous. But they keep him around because he's…"

I was picking it up. "…the guy who invented the Start Button." Elise nodded, then took another bite of her lunch.

"You'll get there," she said. "Everybody does."

Headmistress Julie, which we had been instructed to call her (and which sounded like the horrible combination of lawyer and stripper), spread professional high-gloss pamphlets across her uncomfortable mahogany desk. "Mountain Ridge Academy," she said in what appeared to be the same *faux*-British/American accent Madonna had previously acquired "is about providing children the opportunity to identify and follow through on their passions. At Katie's age she will find herself at a challenging crossroads, where the choices she makes will forever impact her life's trajectory."

Jess and I shared a look and smiled, as she dug her nails into my knee. Not only because Jess, who grew up tortured by those who called her *Jessie,* hated to hear her daughter's birth name being mauled by someone named Julie, but also because we both agreed on one very important child rearing detail... Kate didn't have any choices to make at age four. Her dictatorial parents were going to make every single decision for her. We had agreed. Seriously, we had.

"The curriculum looks very distinct," I said politely, eyeing framed pictures around her carpeted office of children in uniforms at the piano, playing chess and braiding the hair of drugged-out looking llamas. "Llamas, huh?" I asked rhetorically.

"Some children aspire to be veterinarians and so we give them the opportunity to interact with God's blessed creatures."

"How many children are in the school?" asked Jess. Headmaster Julie swallowed, then seemed to pull herself together before answering.

"One hundred and thirty-two, presently."

"And how many can the school support?" I asked back.

"Up to three hundred," she said. "But we aren't looking for numbers. It doesn't matter to us how many children attend, as long as the ones that do are growing and learning and excelling." She stood up, straightening her suit and motioning to the door behind us. "Why don't I give the two of you a little tour? You can see those little darlings in their natural habitat."

"The llama or the children?" I asked. Jess pinched me. *Hard.*

The tour was depressing. Not only did the facility feel empty and the framed children's art on the wall feel *eerie,* but the empty corners and maze-like walkways reminded me of the Winchester Mystery House – a San Jose tourist attraction supposedly haunted by the ghosts of the individuals who once were. At one point, Headmistress Julie took us into a Kindergarten classroom where children worked diligently at the kind of math problems even *Good Will Hunting* would have gotten a headache from.

"Children?" she said, clapping her hands. Without any additional instruction, they dropped their work like little brainwashed robots, stood in a line and began reciting a poem about being responsible.

"We must be responsible," they chanted in unison. "We must honor our fellow man. We must aspire to be the best human beings we can be. For when we are our best, the World is a better place. And when the World is a better place…"

The assimilation can begin, I thought in my head, imagining all those creepy kids in all those horror movies where the parents realize their adorable squirts are actually possessed by the Devil.

"…no man will be treated any less than another," they finished.

Headmistress Julie clapped enthusiastically while Jess and I did our best to fake it. As quickly as the children had stood up and recited their scripted performance, they were back down at work. There was no emotion, joy or fun to be felt anywhere.

We walked out into the hallway, away from the children, where Headmistress Julie pulled us aside. "So, are there any questions I can answer for the two of you before I provide you the application for Katie?"

"Do any of these kids eat paste? Like normal kids do?" asked Jess. Headmistress Julie swallowed, not quite sure how to answer the question.

February

*T*hree full weeks at The Company had passed, and with it had gone the total darkness and below thirty-degree weather of the Seattle wintertime. Still, overcast clouds and consistent rain storms kept us shut in our over-sized house atop the hill, often feeling like housebound criminals whose ankle bracelets refused to let them venture too much further past the mailbox. What had started as a sarcastic, jaded version of *Where's Waldo*, with the *where* referring to our neighborhood and the *Waldo* referring to our non-existent citizens, quickly turned into a real life CIA-like stake-out with the whole family involved. Kate was responsible for using her trademark crow call from upstairs if she saw movement out her window. Jess, having gone out and purchased a pair of binoculars from the local REI, could sit comfortably on the couch while watching *Real Housewives* and still get a great view out the front windows and across the street. I monitored the late-night shift in the case of an after-work drinks or late-night corporate meeting that resulted in one of our *fictitious* neighbors revealing themselves out in the open. So far, we had seen little more than a rapidly closing garage door. There had been no welcoming committee, baked goods or HOA fee requests.

We had found a pre-school for Kate called *Hillside Academy* that was, for all intents and purposes, a day care center filled with normal everyday children who ate paste and had never heard of a llama. With every story about an errant bodily function or an ingested toy or potential-poison, Jess and I became more and more satisfied that we had chosen wisely. Though, the morning routine was something new for Jess, who had moved on from rolling calls and managing celebrity appearances on the morning shows to battling ponytails, lunchboxes and conversations with the mothers at drop-off.

"I had a twenty-minute conversation this morning about where to get the most reasonably-priced leggings," Jess lamented one night, then faked like she was vomiting. "Then, when I picked up Kate, I miraculously found that I had a fairly strong opinion to share about pre-pubescent yeast infections." She flashed me a *what have I become* kind of face.

"It's all about the kids," I observed.

"Yeah," replied Jess, deep in thought. It wasn't her life goal, but when she committed to something, she went balls out a hundred and ten percent. The transformation from a working stiff to the stern matriarch of the Murphy family was slowly happening before my eyes. As a part of the complete and total cleansing of Hollywood out of her system, she had decided it was time to trade in her Mercedes S-Class for something much more utilitarian. With four-wheel drive. And snack trays in the back seat…for the kids. You know, because it was *all about them.*

"An SUV," she announced to me at breakfast one day, while she was tagging pages of recipes in a myriad of cooking magazines, then writing them down on note cards for inclusion in her latest extravagant meal plan.

"You want an SUV?" I asked, confused, concurrently responding to the twelve e-mails that had magically appeared on my smartphone while she had uttered the words "an" and "SUV."

"Since no one is subsidizing the car anymore," she began, frowning, "it doesn't make financial sense for us to have one. Plus, if you could see the way the rest of the SUV mommies at Hillside glare at me when the car growls up to the drop-off area, you would want to get rid of it too. I kind of think they're worried the Mercedes will steal their husbands."

In Hollywood, you were what you *drove.* More often than not, your car payment was equal to your mortgage. In Seattle, you drove a car that could get you up the hill in a freak snowstorm, that had enough room to carry camping equipment and hiking gear, and which could tow your boat to the lake. Even the hundreds of millionaires at The Company who had become richest beyond their wildest dreams when the stock had split, refrained from showing it off through what they drove. It just wasn't the Pacific Northwest way. For Jess, taking the Mercedes out of the girl was her way of taking the "Hollywood" out of her soul. It was like acknowledging her career as a publicist was over. Yet she played it bravely, only tearing up slightly when the car salesman at the Dodge dealership let her sit in the driver's seat of the new Durango we had been ready to pull the trigger on.

"I know, it must be overwhelming to be buying a brand-new car outright like this," he said, eyeing Kate and I in backseat as if to say "I got this one."

"That's not what's making me tear up," Jess replied. "It's just…" she worked up the nerve to say it. "I'm sitting in Pleather. I never thought I'd be sitting in Pleather ever again." Then she bawled. An ugly snot-sniffling cry I hadn't seen since she'd been fired. Perhaps she hadn't gotten it all out before. Perhaps it was all coming back. But it was the last time she'd say anything about the Pleather or the fact that the car had specially-designed dispensers for *Purell*. She knew, just like me, that some things would have to change.

Working at The Company was not too much different from the plot of the movie *Speed*. You were expected to move as quickly as possible, constantly being slowed down by other people and a variety of complications rapidly being thrown at you. Meanwhile, there was a cadre of "nemesai" (nemesis, *but plural*) who wanted to see you fail and tried to expedite your untimely demise under the cover of anonymity. If the speed at which you handled problems was kept at a constant and rapid pace, you could guarantee your continued survival for the week in question. But slow down? Trip up? Pause to use the lavatory? *Kaboom!*

All that being said, the constant activity and threat of perceived failure made the whole experience more exhilarating. *So this is what it feels like to be a bomb diffuser*, I would often think, as I answered a phone call, raced to a meeting, built PowerPoint slides and figured out how to sprint from one side of campus to the other with no meeting buffer whatsoever. It may not have been perfect and it probably wasn't what I had expected, but it gave me a rush that I had never felt before. It necessitated a new way of thinking and living. You had to multi-task *everything* or you would get lost in the shuffle. I had successfully perfected the "end of the night, standing up peeing, brushing my teeth, cleaning out my inbox and catching up on Jess' day" *multi-task* without incurring any injuries, errant leaking or marital counseling sessions.

At The Company, I had thankfully put an e-mail action plan into effect, reserving five minutes every thirty minutes to check and respond to red bang deliveries. If there had been no new e-mails in the last thirty minutes, my next check would occur fifteen minutes later – assuming that if no e-mails were coming through there was obviously some delay from the server. If a check at thirty minutes resulted in no new e-mails, and a second check fifteen minutes later also resulted in no new e-mails, a "Defcon 2 Plan" (checking mail every two minutes) went into immediate effect, superseding any meetings, calls or meals that may have been on the docket. In The Company, there were only three reasons for someone not getting e-mails *every few minutes*: a downed server, a mistyped password, or the end of the physical world as we knew it.

The *E-Mail Anticipation Action Plan* as I had dubbed it inside my head, also had after-hours contingencies as well. If I were to awaken anytime between the hours of Midnight and five AM, I was *not* permitted to check e-mail. If I did, not only would it reveal a list of e-mails and issues that I would then spend the rest of the night spinning over, but it would (as punishment) activate the original daylight plan into effect. I had written down such rules in my new smartphones' Notes application, as it represented a legally and binding agreement with my own psyche. I figured it was as airtight an argument as it could be, barring visiting the Commons' Legal Offices for further clarification.

With the e-mail situation somewhat under control, I was finally able to spend some time focusing on the *actual job* I had been hired for. According to Leah, there were three things she wanted me focused on over the next two months. First, getting to understand the full feature set of the product so I would be able to sing its praises with potential external clients. Second, I would need to ensure that any engineering or coding that would be done on the product would be delivering on features I felt were necessary to help with customer adoption and engagement. Third, I needed to make sure that I was partnering closely with Marketing and special projects (Elise, Gil and Gail) to ensure they were fully aligned with the first two requests.

"And what about sales?" I asked, curiously. "How many units of the product need to sell in order for us to make money?"

Leah looked back at me, with that adorable half-vacant cocked-head look. "You mean *profit*?" she asked.

"Yeah. Profit."

"Don't worry about profit," she replied. "Just worry about being a *great* teammate!"

Did I mention the job was ambiguous? Everyone's job seemed to overlap with another person's job. Often at meetings, three people were working on the same initiative, without being aware that others were, too. What *was* success, I wondered? In Hollywood, it had been very clear. Sell a movie. Make money. Repeat until rich. Here, the ambiguity of it all made my head hurt. Especially when my own idiotic words came back into my head. *"Ambiguity only represents a chance for greatness,"* I had said in my interview loop, clearly without any knowledge about the true inner workings of The Company or the lack of "greatness" I was currently feeling. The truth was this – ambiguity represented a chance for OARP meetings. Meetings where everyone, intent on *owning something* at The Company, would debate about exactly who owned what.

Leah wrote the word OARP in big black letters on the whiteboard, with the entire team present for the discussion. "Since it appears as if there's some confusion as to everyone's roles and responsibilities these days," she lectured, "I felt it would be helpful for us all to re-sync on the team's OARP."

"Urp?" I repeated, confused.

"OAR-p," said Gil, in a British accent that just made it all sound so official and serious.

"Here. Hold on." Leah erased the word OARP and rewrote it, leaving space between each of the letters so she could write them out. They were "Owner", "Approver", "Reviewer" and "Participant."

"Aah," I nodded, still without any clue whatsoever about what it all meant.

"Every project we work on here at The Company where multiple stakeholders are participating must adhere to the OARP model," began Leah. "The owner drives the program and the approvers get sign-off while the reviewers and participants represent the broader virtual team."

"I'm hearing that the OARP model is supposed to change," said Elise. Leah just glared at her, fatigued with fighting her on what was true and what *wasn't*. Elise wasn't deterred. She just continued on. "One of the Chiefs of Staff told me that the Owner category would change to Facilitator and that Participants would become the collective Team. That way the wider group has input."

"So...FART?" chimed in Eric uncharacteristically, since there were no numbers involved in his statement.

"People, please," shrieked Leah, tossing the black marker onto the table. "Can we just focus on what it *is today*? Are there any questions?" Leah, the usually calm, happy person that she was, seemed to be changing right before our eyes. I wondered what it was, but that was the least of my questions. This company-sanctioned OARP business was twisting my mind into knots. The feeling took me back to my debate about the intergalactic dictator in that the logic I was being presented with, made no sense whatsoever. But this was different. This was The Company. Where I was challenged to question authority, push on things I felt didn't make sense and share my opinions. I cleared my throat – now was *that* time.

"So, let's say I'm the Owner," I began, with everyone listening. "Do I get final approval since I own the project?"

"Yes," said Leah.

"Great. Ok. Then what do the Approvers do?"

"They approve the project as well."

"And if they don't approve it? Since I'm the owner, and have final approval, doesn't that kind of render the Approver's approval useless?"

Leah thought about it for a second. "No. The Approver still has the opportunity to review the project before you make the final approval."

"Then what are the Reviewers, reviewing?"

"The project."

"But they don't have approvals."

"No."

It was like Abbott & Costello's *Who's On First* routine. Except that routine was created to be funny. The OARP was created to streamline the business decision process and it was obviously not doing that at all. At least as far as I could tell.

"And what about the Participants?" I asked. "Do they get to review the project before it's final?"

"Ex…actly," replied Leah, now appearing unsure.

"So why not just call the Participants, reviewers? They're reviewing, just like the Reviewers, who also don't get to approve. And while you're at it, since the Approvers don't get *final* approval, shouldn't everyone just be a Reviewer with no approval power at all?"

There was a long stretch of silence and it was shattered by the sound of my smartphone vibrating on the conference room table. I saw that it was Jess – she never called me during the day. "Sorry, one second," I said as I cradled the phone to my ear. As I did so, everyone turned to Leah, who turned to look at the OARP on the whiteboard and started what appeared to be an internal monologue about the legitimacy of the hair-brained scheme.

"Hey, I'm in a meeting," I whispered into the phone.

"I got the most amazing marinade for the steak tonight," Jess shared excitedly. Usually, those middle of the day calls had been about a promotion or an argument with a high-powered agent. The mid-day marinade call was a new one. Still, Jess seemed extremely enthusiastic about the situation, so I was just as happy. For the first few weeks in January there had been a subtle, almost unperceivable sadness in her eyes, which I had associated with the cabin fever we were all feeling. If marinade excited her, well then…bring on the marinade.

"That's wonderful news," I whispered again. "Can we talk later?"

"Okay!" she replied, happily. "I'll keep you posted."

I hung up the phone, turning my attention back to the meeting. Leah erased the OARP from the board and let the dry eraser drop to the floor like she just didn't care. It was silent for some time, with each of us around the table sharing a WTF look with each other. Leah wasn't saying anything, and then without warning she filled up on oxygen and took a big breath.

"Perhaps we can find another way to identify ownership of a project," chimed in Everett, who closed his eyes the whole time, but at least squinted in the general direction of Leah.

"It doesn't matter," Leah sighed.

Elise perked up. "Because The Company *is* being shut down!?"

"No. Because at this afternoon's All-Hands meeting with Shane, he'll announce that as of tomorrow, I will no longer be your Manager." The room was suddenly deathly quiet.

My phone vibrated again, this time with a text. I covered it up, peeking at the screen. It was from Jess. It read, "Grilling onions, too! Mmmm."

Shane McCullough burst into the large conference room like someone running with the bulls in Barcelona, clad in yoga-wear from head to toe like he had just come from his morning workout (he did). He clapped, hooted and hollered as he worked the room of fifty or so MediaMesh team members into a huff, pounding his hands to the sky like he was raising the roof with T-Pain. Today's All-Hands had been on the books for weeks, and it would be Shane's opportunity to get everyone excited for the planned release date for the product update, the global marketing plan that The Company would be funding, and we hoped – an announcement that the product would be featured at December's Entertainment Technology Show in Vegas. It was there, every year, that CEO Ben Packer would put on a star-studded, hi-tech keynote speech that would kick off the conference and give lip service to the products that The Company was fully invested in. If your product got mentioned there, not only had the leadership of The Company taken notice of the leader behind the product (i.e. Shane), but it represented a bright future for the product itself and the money that would be invested into it over the next twelve months. There was always the reaction and opinion of the Press, which could submarine a product in forty-eight hours, but getting your work in front of the general consumer was the golden opportunity everyone wanted.

"Helllooooo Mesh Heads!" shrieked Shane, channeling a mix between a QVC host and a personal trainer. "How's everyone faring this fine, glorious, overcast day?" The team hooted and hollered, jostling people to all sides – including me. The McCullough Factor was still well-intact since I had last witnessed it, drawing me into his sphere of influence as I clapped excitedly.

"Good. Perfect," said Shane. "This is the enthusiasm I want to see.

That I absolutely adore seeing. Because if there was any lack of passion here today, I would simply have to ask the question, *have all of you been living in a cave!?* Have you somehow forgotten the path we are trailblazing?" Shane tipped his head to someone at the back and a brand-new slick logo for MediaMesh appeared on the front screen. Everyone went wild. And for good reason. In the same way a screenwriter would cream himself after seeing the movie poster or movie trailer for a product he had created in his head…that he had toiled over for years… This was the same thing for the room of hard-working employees. Someone, somewhere, did their best impression of a Dolphin screeching.

Shane made another head motion and the logo changed to video of someone using the product in a testing lab. "We've got our beta up and running in a test environment," he pointed out, "and as you can imagine we've had great success bringing the multi-task awareness feature to life. With three more sprints left to go this year, we've still got a long road of engineering and coding work to be done. But we are feeling good about delivering on our most basic promise of *your media, meshed*." The tagline needed some work and a bass-voiced announcer saying "*in a world…*," but we would get there, I was sure.

Different teams went through their status updates. Engineers presented what they called "roadmap slides" – detailed charts outlining when they would code what. Legal and business development teams outlined their progress on getting media companies to sign off on the usage rights we were asking for so that people like Tom Cruise couldn't sue The Company for allowing consumers to put the original artistic intent of *Mission Impossible 7: Death Sentence* at risk. The problem with creating new and unique ways for consumers to engage with their entertainment was that they technically didn't own their entertainment when it was digital. But that was a whole different problem altogether that no one was losing any sleep over. After Elise and Gail gave a quick overview of some of their Marketing and Social initiatives, Shane took the "stage" again with a more reserved look on his face.

"I wanted to take a moment to call out Leah Norton," he began. "Leah, can you stand up?" She did, uncomfortably, as the rest of her team shared knowing glances across the packed room. "Leah has decided to take an exciting new opportunity in another area of the company," he continued. "I wanted to thank her for all her hard work on our team, and wish her the best of luck in this groundbreaking new endeavor." The room clapped. Leah and Shane shared a look. It wasn't one that appeared warm in the least. "I'll be announcing Leah's replacement soon," Shane finished up, then challenged the group to go do "great things" for the rest of the day.

Exciting opportunity for who, I thought to myself. Leah had obviously not delivered for Shane in the way that he had hoped, and so she was sent packing. I reflected on my own performance over the last month – it too seemed all surface and no substance. Would next month's All Hands meeting involve *me* taking on a "groundbreaking new endeavor?" The problem was navigating what people called the "highly matrixed" Company, where dozens of product groups had thousands of people who all needed sign off from virtual teams of employees, and which made getting anything done seem completely overwhelming. The e-mail had just been the start of it all. Meetings with no focus or resolution continued the trend. And the vocabulary used within The Company was making it completely hard to follow what anyone was saying.

"Just download me on your sync with the virtual team from the roadmap meeting," a Director from the Advertising team asked me days prior, sending my mind into the kind of endless loop that caused people to spontaneously explode.

"What is it you want to know?" I asked, trying to use words that made some semblance of basic grammatical sense. Despite everyone telling you "there was no stupid question" there were *tons* of them and I was doing my part to keep filling the quota.

"I need to know if I still have to support *foo* or not," he shot back.

"…if you still have to support *you?*" I asked.

"Not *you*. *Foo*." Holy crap, it was maddening.

"What the heck is *foo?*" I asked, chalking up another stupid question. Mostly because I didn't know what the hell *foo* was, but also because I was a grown man using the phrase *foo* in a corporate conference room with people in button down shirts tapping away at laptop computers.

"*Foo* is the feature that the engineering team *will* build in time for the product's release, but which no one currently has actually thought up. But the advertising team originally committed to support and message that feature through ad buys and brand sponsorships," he answered. I was still completely lost.

"What does *foo* do?" I rhymed, sounding like Dr. Seuss, and proceeding to imagine how the master rhymer might have crafted a classic literary masterpiece based on this insane drivel. *What does foo do? Do you know who knew about the foo? Was the foo blue? Was it a new blue foo? Could you chew a foo? What about Lindy Loo, who was great with glue? Could she glue a new blue foo to a bubbling stew? Nobody knew.* The segue was awesome, especially in light of the statement to follow.

"Nobody knows. We suppose. That's why we call it *foo*." The logic was air-tight for a Children's book, which I'm sure my Manager could have sold to a publishing house. That aside, it drove me completely and utterly mad.

I asked myself the same question I had asked myself on that flight back from Seattle, after feeling excited about a brand-new life in a brand-new city in a brand-new job. Was I up to the task? Could I really do it? How could I shake this feeling that I was a total imposter, pretending to know what I was doing, in a world that seemed more foreign than every single world created by James Cameron. Yes. Even that *blue* one with the flying horse people.

It took me about five minutes before I realized I was standing like an idiot in the middle of the Commons, staring blankly at all the glorious food options. It was probably because I wasn't really thinking about what I was going to have for lunch. Instead, I was reflecting on what I had experienced so far at The Company. I had been warned by many – it wasn't an easy transition going from a creative environment to a corporate one. Ironically, all those rules I had been so fed up with in Hollywood couldn't hold a candle to the logic that was in place around a whole new set of Company guidelines. When I had signed my acceptance offer, I recall dismissing C.J.'s advice to give myself time. That it took many new employees four to six months to fully wrap their head around how things worked. So, sue me – I was an overachiever. One month and no progress made me want to slam my head against a wall made up of glass and metal.

As I filled up my salad plate, reviling in the glory that was *fresh Artisan lettuce leaves*, I thought about my new game plan. I couldn't keep going along the current path accepting the broken system. There had to be a better way.

As I drenched my salad plate in the taste sensation that was a *Bleu Cheese Avocado and Anchovy* balsamic dressing, I wondered whom I could turn to for advice. It would have to be someone with intimate knowledge of what was broken, and enough of a backbone to offer solutions to fix it.

As I turned to walk towards the cashier, to pay for the lunch that laughed in the face of all other lunches that came before it, I slammed right into none other than the legendary Simon Davis. He protected his masterpiece of vegetables, all arranged by shape this time (instead of color), and just glared at me as if to suggest my ability to control my own motor functions was in dire need of re-calibration.

"I'm sorry," I started to say, but his ZZ Top beard and lanky Steve Jobs' body had already moved on, swiping his Blue Badge to pay for lunch and heading out the door. I made a split-second decision that probably wasn't the right one, but was backed up by the kind of courage I hadn't exhibited in years. So, I tossed my salad in the garbage without paying for it and chased Simon Davis out the door.

Being stealth isn't as hard as the movies make it out to be. The normal, everyday corporate campus is filled with foliage, electrical generators, stairwells, benches and garbage pails. *Ergo*, an enormous collection of hiding options.

I ducked. I weaved. I checked readings on electrical generators. I ensured air conditioning units had adequate freon readings. I mimed throwing out garbage while hiding near the receptacles and sat admiring the skyline as I perched on benches, turned slightly, so no one could identify me in a lineup. Meanwhile, Simon Davis took me on a journey further away from the Commons, across multiple streets, and towards a building with such a small number that it was obvious it had been one of the very first to be built.

Building 12 was a squatty, brick-laden structure with a single window over the front door. There was no signage, no visitor parking spots and no home to any legitimate business group at the Company, which I would later confirm by a quick search on the intranet campus map. Simon Davis made his way towards the front door, salad in one hand, other hand protecting his Blue Badge, which was hanging from a contraption on his belt. I quickly scuttled across the lawn, did a somersault that planted me under the cover of a well-manicured hedge, and popped up *Fortnite*-style to ensure I wouldn't lose my mark. Simon Davis, mumbling to himself incoherently, reached the front door where he swiped his badge, waited for the *click* and proceeded to enter the building.

I had to move quickly. I sprung over the hedge and ran to the door as it started to close, sprinting faster than Harris Green, a fellow Elementary School colleague of mine who was known for his inability to run the 100-meter dash in less than three and a half minutes. By comparison, I was the next Usain Bolt in training. I eyed Simon Davis, who was already making his way down an indoor hall to an elevator, as I lunged for the door handle.

It *clicked* shut as I collapsed on the landing. But I was far from finished. I quickly whipped out my Blue Badge, swiping it across the security pad, proud of my split-second ingenuity. Except that feeling of ingenuity would be short lived – instead of a click, a painfully obvious *buzzer* rang out. I did not have authorization to enter this building. Still, I tried five more times. Five more *buzzers* rang out. In the building, I watched as Simon Davis entered an elevator and disappeared into the abyss.

Behind me, a young woman approached the door, swiping her badge on the pad. It *clicked* and she opened the door. But not before looking back at me, suspiciously.

"No tailgating," she demanded, eyeing me with disdain.

There's a gigantic over-sized raccoon stealing crap from our mailbox, I thought to myself as I rounded the corner of our street and spied a strange creature poised in front of the residents' outdoor mail kiosk. Perhaps my mind had gone there because I had a desperate need to *be* the hero in all of Kate's drawings. *Guy battles raccoon* had been my most grandiose paper battle to date, and perhaps it was my brain's way of saying, "Hey Cameron – there are battles you can win in life, so why not try this one?"

The reality of course, was that the raccoon was none other than a *real, bona fide* human neighbor. I rolled down my window and yelled "Hey!" in such a way that I must have startled him just enough to keep him from running away. He was an Indian man who wore khakis and a dark Member's Only jacket that covered a half-tucked in dress shirt. On his belt hung no less than three beepers. Yes, *beepers. Didn't they stop making those in 1994*, I wondered as I quickly parked the car and ran up to the man in question.

"You!" I said, out of breath. "You *exist!* My wife and I weren't sure that you were real, but now that I can see you…and feel you with my own hands," I said as I squeezed his forearm, "she will never believe I caught you out here." The words and the touching made him appear more uneasy, which was evidenced by him glancing longingly at his slightly-cracked open front door across the street. The warm lights stretched out into the street, beckoning him to come home. *Perhaps I can make a break for it*, I imagined him thinking to himself. *It may be my only chance for survival.*

I lunged for him as there were people to prove wrong in the Murphy household.

"We're home," I screamed from the foyer, closing the door behind me and my newfound neighborhood mail buddy. "You'll never believe what I found outside!"

Two pair of footsteps reverberated throughout the house as Jess and Kate rounded the corner from the kitchen and into the foyer. Kate instinctively went to attach herself to one of my lower extremities, but then noticed the strange man standing beside me. Meanwhile, Jess was covered in food, including things like flour, that I was totally sure had nothing to do with the dinner she had been texting me about *all…day… long.* Her hair, up in a pony-tail, had splashes of mustard and what appeared to be relish in it. Again, condiments that had *nothing to do* with dinner.

"Honey?" Jess stopped, taking stock of the situation before her. "You didn't tell me you were bringing home a…"

"A *human* neighbor. A real live human neighbor," I finished her sentence, excited. "I win, by the way. Go ahead, say it. Say 'Cameron, you discovered a human neighbor, you win the contest.'" Sudhir was relatively comfortable, despite the fact that this whole situation felt like the beginning of the latest new-and-improved *Saw* movie.

"I'm Sudhir Kurian," said the human neighbor that I had caught *outside our house*, resulting in me winning the contest that had been put into motion the month prior by yours truly. *Say I won*, I projected with my eyes towards Jess.

Jess smiled politely at the man. "Hello, Sudhir. It's nice to meet you. You live across the street?"

He smiled, nodding. "Yes. It appears as if your husband has taken quite fondly to me."

"*Say I won*," I whispered to Jess again.

"Daddy won!" said my beloved firstborn, who obviously knew when to stoke the egotistical fire that raged within my soul. I stuck out my left leg, as if to reward her – she latched on like a Koala bear hugging a tree.

"Are you hungry, Sudhir?" she said, ignoring the rest of her blood line. "Do you like steak?"

"I would be honored," Sudhir smiled genially; obviously confident that if he had not yet been chopped up and eaten by this strange family across the street by now, dinner was probably a pretty safe bet.

Jess watched all of us as we battled, knife in hand, to cut through the slightly (nay, completely) blackened steak before us on our plates. "Don't worry," she piped in, "people who eat food that's been charred are *not* more susceptible to getting cancer. Trust me, I asked Google."

Sudhir was a true soldier, politely cutting his filet into a hundred tiny pieces and ingesting each one with a swig of water, much like the strategy of a prisoner who is forced to eat shards of glass as a unique but torturous form of covert physical harassment. Kate added another classic question to her Hit List, asking "Should they all taste like black rocks?" Jess just smiled at her. What did I tell you? No retribution whatsoever.

Sudhir was an engineer. But not like the soda-swigging, t-shirt wearing ones I regularly crossed paths with at The Company. He was more reserved and more thoughtful in how he expressed himself, explaining to us that he had been with a start-up company for the last eighteen months and had viewed the experience as a once-in-a-lifetime opportunity to learn from some of the most influential and creative people he had ever met in his life. His family, on the other hand, including his wife Teha, had grown tired of the experiment, since he often left in the morning before they got up and came home after they'd gone to sleep.

"Not fans of your job?" asked Jess, concerned that at some point she might feel the same way about mine.

"On the contrary," Sudhir said, revealing his *beepers*, "it is *these* that they hate. They call them my *children*." He pointed each one of them out as he spoke. "This one goes off when the client has gone down, which requires me to get up and login to the server and reset the entire database. *This* one goes off when the CEO's testing account in India has locked up – I am then required to drive into the office to pair his I.P. with a new environment no matter the time of day. And when *this one* goes off, it signals a fatal hard drive failure."

"So, what do you do when *that* happens?" I wondered.

"Pray to God I still have a job to go to in the morning."

Dinner had been nice, if not simply based on the fact that there was someone *new* sitting with us around our kitchen table. More importantly, we learned that the neighborhood was filled with families whose working parents were all employed by one major technology company or another. Long hours, early mornings, late nights – when you coupled that with the fact that no one ventured outdoors until the fog had lifted, it made sense why we had not seen anyone during the last six weeks.

"March or April," Sudhir had hypothesized. "That's when people will start to show themselves." Until then, we could be on stakeout all we wanted, but we would rarely see more than a speeding car and a rapidly closing garage door.

"Hermits," Jess stated matter-of-fact. "We're living in a village of hermits."

Upstairs, I supervised Kate in her nighttime routine of complaining, detaining and shirt staining. How she couldn't keep toothpaste in her mouth made zero sense to me, but even less sense was why parents ever had to go through this tooth brushing charade. When she finished, I tucked her into bed, then lay beside her, staring up at the pink-colored ceiling. This was the point in the day when I would ask Kate what she did at school and she would tell me she didn't remember *anything*. Money well spent, I thought.

"But what did *you* do at work today?" she asked sweetly, curling her arm inside mine and resting her chin on my shoulder.

"I worked," I said, figuring she probably wouldn't understand all the hiding behind trash bins and hedges I'd been involved in.

"But what do you *mean*," she pushed. "Did you do art?"

"I would definitely have to say no."

"Did you have recess?"

"Not a lot of down time, honestly."

"Did you take a nap?"

"Not on purpose," I said.

"Then *what*?" she demanded. "What kind of things did you do with your friends?" Ah, it was so simple to a four-year-old mind, who could only comprehend a world where (a) people *had* friends and (b) those friends participated in some kind of creative, care-free activities. She poked me, prodding for an answer.

"I worked on lots of projects with my friends." I had to give her something.

"Did you bring any of them home for me to see?" she sat up, curious. "Like I do for you?"

"Well, I didn't really finish any of them."

"When *will* you finish them? I finish an art project every day," she challenged.

"I'm not sure," I shot back. And I wasn't. When the hell would any of the things I was working on actually get *finished*? Things at The Company didn't seem to ever get finished. They were worked on, debated, discussed, thought through, revised, presented…and so on. "There are so many, sweetie," I said, "it's hard to know."

Kate patted my head; with a maturity I hadn't seen come from her before. "Just do one thing, Daddy," she nodded. "Do one thing really great and *finish* it. Then bring that home so I can see."

Just do one thing really great.

Finish it.

Then bring that home.

It reverberated in my head. How simple it was. *One big win*, I thought to myself. Just one. Let all the noise completely melt away and just focus on one damn thing. It was so simple and so clear all the logic in the world couldn't deter me.

For a four-year-old kid, she was a pretty damn good career counselor.

I walked in through our bedroom door, making a bee-line for the bathroom. It was always my last stop before I collapsed next to Jess in the *TempurPedic* bed we were still financing on one of our credit cards. You financed a car. You financed a boat. But a bed?

"Four hundred-thirty dollars left to go," Jess would say later that night, premeditatedly heading off my annoying financial question at the pass.

Back in the bathroom, after doing my business and thanking my lucky stars that I could still urinate without any pain whatsoever, I noticed that the loose end of the toilet paper had been folded into some kind of origami flower. I ripped it off, taking it with me back into the bedroom. "What is *this*?" I said, shoving the origami toilet paper flower at Jess.

"Origami flower," she beamed.

"When did you have time to learn how to make an origami flower out of toilet paper?"

"After I learned how to marinade and barbecue steak," she replied. To which I decided to hold my breath and a dozen of responses that, while amusing to the general TV sitcom audience member, would have resulted in me sleeping in a bed that was completely, totally paid off.

I slid, then sunk into the bed, rolling over to present the origami flower to Jess. "You have more talents than I ever imagined," I lied.

"Screw you," she laughed, throwing it onto the floor. "You know, I have *a lot* of time on my hands when you and your daughter are off interacting with *real people*."

"Really crazy people," I replied.

"His eyes are still closed, aren't they?" She had heard the story multiple times before.

"Yes. But the big news? Leah quit. Or was fired. Or something."

"You already lost your manager?" she sat up, stunned. "That must be, like, a record or something. What are you going to do?"

Do one thing. Really well. And finish it. Kate's voice reverberated in my head.

"I'm not going to let it affect me," I said. "I'm going to use it as an opportunity to show everyone that Cameron Murphy can make a difference."

"You're talking in the third person, now?"

I continued, ignoring her. "Cameron Murphy can succeed, even in the face of ambiguity. Move my cheese, motherfuckers? I'll get it back!" God, I felt *powerful*.

"Actually, when they move your cheese, you're supposed to *not* chase it. That's the point. You don't want to *want* that old cheese. You've got to…" I just grabbed her and kissed her, shutting her up. It didn't always work, but this time it worked wonders.

Do one thing. Really well. And finish it. I leaned back in, and got to work.

"You look like *shit*," Romy Wallace said to me, as we sat opposite each other in a pair of oversized couch-chairs in the Studio D Atrium. The Atrium area was where all informal meet and greets took place in the Studio complex, and they spared no expense. A café monopolized one wall, glass staircases ascended the length of the building, and flashy tech-infused art hung all over. There was even a huge Elephant by the front doors, a remnant of last year's Entertainment Technology Show, that no one seemed to know what to do with. Now it was stop number two for all the kids who visited their parents at The Company. The free chocolate milk, well, that was number *one*. Romy chewed a piece of gum voraciously, always pivoting her glance in the event someone she knew came walking by.

"Maybe that's because I've been working my ass off, non-stop, for days."

"Special project?" she perked up, curious. "Tell me *now*."

"And we believe the educational applications for *MediaMesh* will grow exponentially with…" Everett closed his eyes again, while attempting to repeat the memorized talk track while pointing to the PowerPoint slide, while trying to be personable. I *clapped* my hands, snapping his eyes open. He looked fatigued. We had been doing this for hours. Thanks to B.F. Skinner and my college psychology course, the Skinner Box was in full effect. Every time he closed his eyes, I would clap again – and it was wreaking havoc on his nerves.

"Again," I said. "We've got to get this pitch down."

"Urgh," he mumbled. "How much longer?"

"How much longer are you going to speak to a conference room with your *eyes closed*?" I accused. "Why do you do it, have you ever really thought about it?"

"People are distracting," he explained.

"Well, until the zombie apocalypse, there's going to be a lot of people," I clapped. "Let's go again. We keep doing it until we do it *really well*."

Everett reset, opened his eyes, and started again.

"And what about you, *hot shot*," I threw back at Romy. "You said you were working on an entertainment product. What is it?"

She looked around the Atrium, making sure no one was in ear-shot. "It's vaporware," she shook her head. "Total bullshit hardware that will *never* ship… And which I am totally *kicking ass* on."

"Sounds like a horrible product."

"It is."

"So why do you sound so damn excited about it?" I asked.

"Oh, Murphy. Get your head out of your ass. Tell me you've figured it out already. It doesn't matter what crap you're working on. It doesn't even matter if it's good. It just matters that you're the one who's making things happen. Are you making things happen?"

"And we believe the educational applications for *MediaMesh* will grow exponentially with your students and the faculty," Everett presented to the room of suits from the Portland School Board Special Projects team, eyes so wide he looked extremely passionate. And strung out on drugs.

"He's very excited," an older woman leaned over to me and whispered.

"Let me demonstrate some of the ingenious ways a student in a Portland Public School's music class could compare two classical pieces as performed by different symphonies and their conductors," he continued, spinning up a demo on the screen. Each time he turned, I could tell he was stretching those eyes open to keep them from closing. Everyone else, not so much.

"I love his passion for this product," said the Finance exec sitting next to me.

People applauded. And it made Everett's eyes open and close like crazy because I had conditioned him to be afraid of "the clap." But it didn't matter. Not in the least.

"Look at you. You closed a deal. *Nice* job."

"Yeah, and about thirty minutes later, I had a meeting with Shane McCullough for next week drop onto my calendar," I bragged. At The Company, no one asked to setup a meeting – they just dropped it on your calendar. At times, you'd get invited to meetings with people you'd never even heard of. Actually, most of the time.

Romy nodded, giving me the once over. "Making inroads, I see," she seemed to reluctantly offer up. "Keep me posted on everything. And whatever you do, don't get all *weird* on him." Good God, if she'd only been there for the *pretty Dolphin* moment.

"I'm eccentric," I shot back.

"Yeah, dude. Whatever. Just don't waste the opportunity. *Carpe diem!*"

In my imagination, I found my iron-clad self standing side by side Romy again – with the warrior horde closer since I had last visited this fictitious place. She pointed to her eyes, then mine, signaling that we were two warriors in tune. Two warriors with similar goals. She screamed *Carpe Diem* again, racing head on towards our destiny. I raced after her, trying to keep up, but the armor seemed heavier than I had expected. I felt weighted down. Romy looked back at me, turning slightly, and gave me a look of critical disappointment.

Back in the real world, she was still talking.

"Don't do that insecure writer thing with him. Just be normal. Honest advice – trust me, I know how this place works."

I wouldn't act insecure. Or weird. Perhaps smitten. In a very male, heterosexual 'you inspire me' kind of way. *He's only the Dolphin whisperer*, I thought. *He's only the guy who made me want to move here and take this job*, I thought. *He's only the guy who fired my last boss.*

I sat outside Shane's office, while he wrapped up with another person, quickly tapping through my ever-burgeoning list of e-mails. I watched as twenty-three e-mails all popped up in one swift kick – clicking through them to only discover they were twenty-three e-mails from people saying "thanks", "thank you", "TY" or "totally agree." When people disagreed, they either sent flaming tirades or didn't respond at all. But everyone wanted to be sure you knew they agreed. I quickly "replied all" and made sure I had registered my own appreciative comments, as Shane started to open the door...

"You're a galvanizing force and you just need that electric shock to get things going," Shane uttered to the guy in a suit, who was so taken with him that it kind of made me feel like a complete and total idiot. Also: a jealous girlfriend. "I'm that electric shock, Justin," he continued, shaking his hand. "Together we can create..."

"*Lightning*," I mouthed to myself as Shane finished what was now apparent to me to be a wholly-unoriginal statement. I eyed Shane as he escorted the potential candidate towards his Admin. Justin was *me*. I was *Justin*. Except Justin wore a suit. *A fucking suit*, I thought. *What is it with all these people and their suits?*

But in reality, my anger towards well-tailored clothing was only taking the brunt of it because I had been an idiot simpleton and I was just now realizing the error of my ways. I had gone through the Loop and it was Shane's final words that had me convinced he knew exactly what I was looking for in a new opportunity. It had been a total snow job, which was now completely obvious to me. The singing-and-dancing magic-trick enabled Shane McCullough show seemed to fade off in the distance, as the lights came up and all the secrets were revealed.

"Join me," said Shane, motioning me into his office, barely even looking me in the eyes.

I hopped up, walked into his luxury box, and sunk into the only bean bag chair available to me. Conveniently, Shane had the only normal sized-person's chair in the whole space. Towering over me, he looked down as I cradled my knees together like a Kindergarten student being reprimanded for picking his nose and eating it. *Not that there's anything wrong with that.*

"I thought it would be a good opportunity for a sync," he continued, "seeing as though you have now been here almost two months."

"I closed a deal," I muttered, as it was the first thing that came to mind.

"*One* deal."

"Really well."

"Excuse me?" Shane asked, confused.

"I just meant, that I closed the deal really well." Kate would have been extremely proud of her Daddy. Shane didn't seem impressed. Perhaps I felt that way because he was picking food out of his teeth with the edge of his business card. It reminded me of two things: first, he got food stuck in his teeth *just…like…me*. Second – he was a General Manager at The Company. It mattered what he thought.

"I don't care if you close a deal horribly or you close a deal with clowns and noise makers. Closed is *closed*. That being said, I do care about *how many* you close."

"One," I reminded him.

"That's the problem, as I see it," he frowned. "I know you've been without a Manager, and I know spinning up at The Company can take time… But you're going to be out of time soon, Cameron. I need you to step up and be the guy I thought we hired."

The one with the lightning, I asked rhetorically in my head?

"If you can't be that person," Shane continued, "then perhaps we should re-evaluate our employment agreement."

A slew of images sped through my head. There was the one of Jess, Kate and me living in our SUV and eating nothing but cold hash browns from McDonald's. There was the one where Jess looked me straight in the face, disappointed, and said something to the effect of, "you were right – you're not a man." There was George Zimmerman, of *The Men's Wearhouse*, flipping me the bird. *Again.*

"I *am* that person," I replied, flop-sweat and all.

"Then let's get this thing going," he responded, getting up and motioning for the door. "Let's try closing more than *one thing* at a time." I nodded, and walked out as he shut the door behind me, thinking *never trust a four-year-old kid to give you career advice.*

March

"**I**'ve got *gossiiiiiiip*," Elise proclaimed in a sing-songy kind of way, closing the focus room door behind her and sitting opposite me. You had to give her credit – she was at least enthusiastic about all the confidence-crushing leaks she uncovered, despite the fact that her sources may not have been fully reputable. "Shane's hired a new Manager to replace Leah," she whispered. "Starts next week. Supposedly coming from the Mobile group."

"And how do you know that?" I asked, suspicious. Every time she brought up a new piece of gossip, it made me think back to that moment in *Ferris Bueller's Day Off*, when an equally-as-cheery blonde student proceeded to explain just how she had known Ferris had "passed out last night at 31 Flavors."

"My boyfriend's a UPS driver." It was true. She loved him to death. It was the perfect example of those *opposites attract* stories you always heard about, but were never quite sure they truly existed.

"Uh huh," I acknowledged. He literally was dropping off packages all day long.

"He was delivering a package to Mimi Gelner."

"Okay."

"Who is best friends with Frank Dulles."

"Go on."

"Frank works in the Mobile group."

"I'm with you so far." Her eyes were lit up like New York City on Christmas. I imagined her story as the physical representation of the *Formerly Dick Clark's Rockin' New Year's Eve* crystal-encased ball – with each detail of her story revealed, the ball moved closer and closer to the bottom. When it reached the bottom, that's when the party started.

"While he was at the door, and Frank's wife was signing for the package, he overheard Frank in the background on the phone, talking about how one of his Directors was leaving to go take a management role that just opened up in Shane's group. For MediaMesh. Managing Marketing and Sales." She let out a big breath, sinking back into the couch, as if she had just finished an extra tiring spinning class at the gym. I half expected her to pull a sports bottle out from underneath the table and *squirt* a stream of water all over her face.

"And what is this person's name?" I asked, curious.

Elise looked around, covering her lips so no one could read them through the glass. *Seriously.* "Gennifer Layton," she said. "Gennifer with a G. Supposed to be a total nightmare."

Gennifer with a G, I internalized, reminiscing about *Derrik without a C*, and hoping to God Elise's *U with a P and an S*-boyfriend had gotten it wrong. If he hadn't, then Elise and her secret network of *Wikileaks*-like intel was more valuable than I had ever imagined. People, and that included me, often perceived Elise and her streaming-consciousness of happenings as bullshit. As unimportant. But if she was truly connected and her insights were correct, she would end up being like the Nostra*dame*us of The Company. Having Nostra*dame*us in your back pocket wasn't a bad thing.

In the meantime, the *Bean Bag Incident* or what I was also referring to as the *Shane Smackdown of February* had not done me any good. I took back to the Notes section on my phone, writing myself inspirational pep talks to get me past the fact that the leader of my division had zero faith in me. *"I don't care if you use clowns and noisemakers to get a deal closed"* he had told me, coldly. *Nobody ever suggests their employees enlist the help of clowns to solve a problem unless they've already completely written them off*, I thought to myself. I was sure of it. My imagination fully convinced me I was onto something:

Police Captain to Hotshot Detective: *"Find this serial killer before he strikes again, Jenkins! I don't care if you have to use a clown to help you do it."* Confidence in Jenkins' ability to do good work? Not so much.

Symphony Director to Flawed-Yet-Genius-Composer: *"This concert will make or break the future of this institution. You've got to write something that will change the World. Get a clown to handle the string section part of it if you need to.* No, Symphony Director did not think that the Genius Composer was anything *close* to "genius."

Make-a-Wish-Foundation Founder to Professional Baseball Player: *"Little Timmy looks up to you as his idol. His final wish is to meet you in person. Bring a clown if you think it will make it more fun."* The last thing Make-A-Wish beneficiaries wanted was a clown in their midst. Nobody thought clowns were a good idea. Not even Shane.

So here I was, worried about performing, with Nostra*dameu*s stressing me out even further because of a potential, impending new Manager. I had not closed a single deal and Everett's new facial drama (a.k.a., *Surprise Eyes*, not to be confused with *Bette Davis Eyes*) was freaking people out even further. Every opportunity that came across my desk represented an opportunity that I had already lost. I lamented. I spun. I worried. Then, one evening in bed, I found myself in the middle of an Intervention.

"Cameron, we need to talk," said Jess, flipping over so we were staring at each other's faces.

"We're paying off the *TempurPedic* bed this month and you want to finance a pair
of new *TempurPedic* pillows?" I joked.

"No, and no." She cradled my face, so I couldn't be distracted by beeping or vibrating technology, which often turned me into the equivalent of a canine hearing the mail truck. The cradling meant that she was serious. She had previously cradled my face two years into our relationship when I had still *not* proposed. She had also cradled my face when I had developed a certain illogical fear of holding our newborn baby. And she had cradled my face when I had successfully grown, and decided to keep, a *goatee*. Now she was cradling my face again. I put the jokes away, *for now*. "You need to *do something*," she said. "You need to snap out of this funk you're in."

"The head of my division…the guy who hired me… He thinks I'm an idiot."

"Did he tell you that?"

"He suggested that I go close some deals by…" I began. But she had heard it all before.

"…using *clowns*," she interrupted me. "I know the clown story, Cameron. But the only clown here is *you*."

"That's low."

"You're low. Look at you. Stop worrying so much about what the guy thinks about you because all that's doing is turning you into a self-fulfilling prophecy. What do you need in order to get back out there and show them that you're the resourceful, kick-ass guy that I know you to be?"

"I did kick a guy in the nuts once," I reminded her. She just glared at me. I knew what the glare meant. She was right. So, what did I need? *What do you need?* I asked myself. I needed someone to direct me through the labyrinth that was The Company. I needed to understand what I could do and couldn't do. What were the rules? *Were there rules at all?* It had to be someone who obviously had seen it all. Who had done it all.

"I need to talk to Simon Davis," I said, convinced.

"So, talk to Simon Davis," she said matter-of-fact. "…Who is Simon Davis?"

"Twenty-fifth hire at The Company. Legend. Looks a bit like someone's unshowered homeless Uncle. But there's a reason he's still here. There's a reason The Company has kept him around."

"I'm going to focus on the *legend* part and not the *unshowered* part," she said, growing serious. "How do you get to him?"

"I know where his office is. I just need to figure out how to break into his building," I sat up, scheming.

"Wait," Jess sat up next to me. "Break into his *what?*"

I cradled her face, looking seriously into *her* eyes. "I've got an idea," I began, "so trust me." She tried to pull her head out of the face-cradle, but I was just too damn strong. "Just know that it will be far superior to anything that Danny Ocean put into motion in that horrific pile of steaming cow dung called *Oceans 12*."

"You and *Oceans 12*," she mumbled, her face half sealed shut by the immense power of my face-cradle move. "Focus, please."

And focused, I was. I could see it all in front of me, in a virtual plan that was hatching itself before my very eyes. I would use The Company's Intranet portal called *Who* – a relative who's who of employees, their teams, their locations and org structures to find those who worked in the elusive and mysterious Building 12. I would set meetings, dropping them automatically on all their calendars, for the same date and time. Much like pressing every call button of an apartment building resulted in at least one *buzz-in* from a clueless and oblivious resident, there would be at least one individual in Building 12 who would accept my meeting invite. It would allow for my Blue Badge to get authorization to enter the building. Once inside, I would travel to the elevator, take it down into the depths of the building, and locate the office space of one Simon Davis. I would enter his office, introduce myself humbly and with respect, and he would embrace me for my perseverance and pure ingenuity. Simon Davis would welcome me with open arms.

Ah yes. My focus would result in *success*.

You are a complete and total failure, I thought to myself, standing on the other side of a lab door in the depths of Building 12. A lab door, mind you, that had just been *slammed* in my face by none other than Simon Davis.

The plan had worked like a charm. In fact, it had worked better than I had expected. My meetings had been met with extreme curiosity, with over four individuals accepting my requests. From there it had been simple. An authorization to the building was added to my Blue Badge, I entered without any complication whatsoever, and descended in the elevator to the floor I was now standing on. It wasn't hard to find Simon's office at all, due to the fact that the *entire floor* was his. I hadn't quite determined that until he had opened the windowless office door, eating an eggroll, and wearing some kind of *Star Trek: The Next Generation* pair of Geordi LaForge glasses that obstructed most of his eyes. In the split second the door had been opened, I crooked my neck to look past him, realizing that the massive office space behind him was less office space and more *laboratory*. There were walls filled in with computers, individual stations with foreign looking technology, and a huge ceiling to floor refrigerator. A gleaming Harley sat parked in its own section of the room, surrounded by its own tools and repair station. Heck, he was the twenty-fifth employee at The Company, what did I expect?

"Mr. Davis," I began. "I'm Cameron Murphy. I bumped into you the other day at the Commons and I was hoping…"

"Don't know you," he said. And slammed the door.

That had been twelve minutes and thirty-two seconds ago. Since then, I had been going over the exchange in my head, wondering if I could have been stronger out of the gate.

Mr. Davis, your help will change my world.

Mr. Davis, I use the Start Button all the time.

Mr. Davis, have you ever tried the Bacon Balsamic Ranch dressing at the Commons?

All three were far catchier than my own egotistical introduction. I pulled out my phone, trying to text Jess, but there was no signal whatsoever. It was probably why I had also received no e-mail in what was now fourteen minutes and forty-eight seconds since the twenty-fifth hire of The Company had slammed a door in my face. As I stood there, debating whether or not I should round up to the nearest minute when telling my story of failure to my grandchildren someday, Simon proceeded to open the door again to see if I was still there.

"You still here?" he grumbled.

"Mr. Davis, have you ever tried the Bacon Balsamic Ranch dressing at the Commons?" I tried, desperate. It threw him off, slightly. He ran his greasy egg-roll hand through his wiry red beard, then pulled off his Future Man goggles so he could give me the once over. It took every ounce of effort in my body to not adjust my stance to one that I knew would have been "more pleasing to the naked eye." He pointed to my cell phone, which was the latest pre-release version from The Company.

"What's the firmware release on that phone?" he asked. I held it up, looking at it. I wasn't sure what exactly firmware was, or where I could find it. "It's not written on the outside, it's in the code," he said, snatching it out of my hand and turning around to go back inside his laboratory as he tapped away at the screen. I stood there, unsure of what was going on. "Well, don't leave the door open," he yelled back, without even turning around.

I ran after the twenty-fifth hire of The Company, and shut the door behind me.

An hour later I was still there, watching Simon Davis poke at my phone while it was concurrently hooked up to some contraption in one of his many workstations. Every once in awhile he'd murmur something about *firmware* or *proxy* or *packet* and get excited and then frustrated a moment later. He tapped away at a computer while a flat screen revealed thousands of lines of code being scrolled through rapidly. Simon Davis was looking for something, but what it had to do with my phone, I had no idea.

I peered around the room, venturing a few steps in multiple directions to get a closer look at what was going on in this space. At each workstation sat multiple computer screens, with boxes hooked up to a variety of The Company's technology. There were game consoles, phones, laptops, tablets, virtual reality and augmented reality headsets, and much more. Some hardware looked like nothing I had ever seen before.

"There it is!" he shouted, turning to me and pointing to a highlight line of code of the overhead flat screen. "You see it?"

"That highlighted portion, yes of course," I agreed. "Very nice." What was nice about it was anyone's guess. God knew my guess would probably have been wrong.

"*Not* nice!" Simon growled, shoving his roller chair across the room and slamming it into the wall. "It's potentially catastrophic!" He grabbed my phone, jacked out the cord, and pitched it high-speed across the lab and into a concrete retaining wall like a Major League pitcher on steroids. It smashed into a billion pieces, plastic and glass flew everywhere.

"What the f-!" I yelled. "That was *my* phone!"

"Your perception may elicit a feeling of ownership," he replied, "but everything you have been given as a gift, is in fact owned by The Company. Basically, they *own you*." He turned away, shook a thought out of his head and looked back at the code.

"Still," I complained like a whiny teenager whose parents had taken his car driving privileges away, "that phone had *my* e-mails on it." *What right did he have*, I thought, to destroy other people's property?

Who did he think he was?

"What's your level?" he challenged me, now facing me head on. I just stared at him, slightly nervous. Hell, *completely* nervous, who was I kidding?

"Sixty-three," I replied.

He pounded his chest (which sounded like a drum incidentally) like a gorilla in *some* mist, *somewhere*, needing to prove his superiority. "Seventy-five," he spat. For those at home – CVPs at The Company were in the low seventies. Ben Packer, the CEO, was rumored to have been recently upped to eighty. Simon Davis, a man who was living with his motorcycle and destroying other people's phones in the basement of a windowless building, was a seventy-five. "When a seventy-five destroys the phone of a sixty-three, you just say *thank you* and assume there was a *very good* reason for it."

"That phone had all my e-mails. My appointments. My personal messages, too. I've only been here two months. I was already drowning, how the hell am I supposed to function now?"

"Your *stuff*," he began, almost treating the word like a curse, "is safe. I downloaded it before it got corrupted. I'll upload it to a *better* phone before you go."

"Corrupted? Why?"

"Because of the code," he said, calming down, turning back to his screen. "Those geniuses up there took five-year-old code and thought they could pair it with brand-new hardware without making any adjustments to it whatsoever." He tapped at the code again. "They probably couldn't even understand *how* to refine it."

"How do you know it's five years old?" I asked.

Simon sat back down in his roller chair, locking his hands behind his head. "Because it's *my* code," he said, putting his futuristic glasses back on. "And *they* stole it."

Thirty minutes later I found myself walking, dazed, back towards Building 87. My data had been restored, uploaded into a new cell phone that Simon had given me. "This one has the *right code*," he had explained. Eventually, according to Simon, the code would find its way into the hands of the "geniuses upstairs" who would realize the error of their ways and re-release the beta version of the software to the general employee base. But not before everyone's personal data would have been "irrevoca-bly deleted", spinning everyone up into a frenzy that would drive down productivity and "drive up churn" – which basically meant that the vor-tex of drama would paralyze everyone and reduce the Company's ability to move more quickly and be more nimble.

"You just saved The Company from probably the biggest public-ity nightmare ever," I complimented him, while checking out the new phone – everything was there as it was before.

"*Biggest*," he mused, smirking. "This is nothing. What do you think I've been doing for the last thirty years?" He had looked back at his laboratory, eyes scanning all the technology from The Company. "The reason *I'm* still here? To make sure The Company *is*."

It had come across less like ego and more like *fact*. The initial mystery as to why Simon Davis was still at The Company had been made clear to me in that one moment. He was cleaning up after The Com-pany's mistakes from his hidden bunker underneath the campus. He determined the solutions, ensured they found their way to the powers-that-be, and continued to ensure the future of The Company remained unquestioned. Between the beard and the attitude, Simon Davis was like a modern-day Gandalf from *The Lord of the Rings*. Instead of preventing monsters from passing, he was preventing misguided products and mis-aligned code from passing into the hands of the consumer.

"Do you mind if I come back sometime?" I had built up the nerve to ask him, seconds before he had locked me out of his lab once again. "I could really use some advice from someone like you."

"Are you dogfooding any new software products?" he asked me, referring to the practice of employee guinea pigs testing (or, dogfood-ing) software before all the bugs had been worked out.

"Yes. MediaMesh," I replied.

"Oh, that piece of crap?" he said, grinning. "Bring your laptop next time so I can look at what they've screwed up there… And I'll give you five minutes." I nodded. It was a deal.

By the time I had crossed the freeway and found myself tromp-ing up towards the double doors of Building 87, I had replayed the entire Simon Davis experience back in my head. I had set out a plan of attack and it had mostly delivered on my expectations. Not only would I get to pick his brain on how to find success in year one at a company he had remained at for thirty, but perhaps he'd have a perspective on Media-Mesh that would help me as well. It was obvious to me that, somewhere, George Clooney was kicking himself in the ass.

The invitation to our Coming Out Party was Princess-themed, covered in glitter and a faint scent of bubblegum that was welcoming nonetheless. I had spent extra time that morning showering and shaving, choosing a particularly young-minded athletic outfit for the occasion. Jess had spent the morning plucking and primping, as our Coming Out Party would put us in close proximity with new and exciting people who could potentially become our new best friends.

"What kind of best friend do you think *you* want?" Jess had asked me the night before in bed, eyes wide with anticipation of our party the next day.

"He's got to be kick back," I began, thinking back to my college fraternity days, "with a great sense of humor and a real sarcastic wit. Not an excessive drinker or partier, and definitely not into baseball. I judge people who are *really* into baseball since it's such a soul-sucking boring game. What about you?"

"She doesn't take herself too seriously," reflected Jess. "She's got one daughter and works as a patent attorney but has enough flexibility to grab coffee with me in the middle of the day since she owns the practice. She took it over from her father when he passed away." I glared at Jess; this was getting morbid. "Old age," she punched me. "*Just* old age."

The two of us laughed hysterically, before we calmed down and our faces landed back on our pillows opposite each other.

"Maybe we *will* meet our new best friends tomorrow," I imagined.

"At our daughter's friend's fourth birthday party?" Jess questioned. "At an indoor facility filled with bouncy houses?" We shared a look. It was anyone's best guess. In this strange new land where people jogged in the rain and only ate food that hadn't been genetically-modified, meeting our new best friends at an indoor birthday party wasn't so blatantly out of bounds.

We made it to *Bounce Bazaar* later that afternoon. It was housed in a huge warehouse in an office park of warehouses, just North of our suburban haunt, and mixed Gen-Y sensibilities with an awkward Indian mosque-feel. It was next door to an indoor trampoline park, three ballet studios, a YMCA, a gymnastics club, a karate dojo and a massive indoor sky diving *slash* roller skating park. While this would be our first trip to an indoor birthday party populated by gigantic Godzilla-sized air-plumped slides and obstacle courses, it would not be our last. We had already RSVP'd to three more that would take place over the next four months. *All in the same location. All with the same style invitation.* I guessed it was better than *Chuck E. Cheese*, although I wasn't quite sold on that fact. Main reason? *No singing animatronic mice.*

Jess and I escorted Kate to the front desk of the Bazaar, signing away our lives in the event our child was maimed or killed, and entered into the massive facility where sweaty shoeless children were already wreaking havoc and risking concussions on the multi-colored monoliths of fun. Wrapped birthday presents populated a back table, decorated sitting areas were prepped and ready for the soon-to-be delivered *pizza d' resistance*, and parents stood quietly in a variety of spots staring blankly at their smartphones, looking up only periodically to be sure their child hadn't been sucked into an open-air vent.

"Hi there, I'm Sofia's dad Wayne," said Wayne. He was Sofia's dad. Beside him telling us, you knew he was because he wielded a huge digital camera with a lens so long you'd half expect he was going to be taking pictures of a one-of-a-kind stellar event or a triathlon of some kind later that night for Getty Images. It was the only explanation because there was *no reason in Hell* that he needed a telephoto lens to take pictures of his little Sofia crawling through a maze filled with multi-colored plastic balls. "Which one is yours?" he asked, because he had to.

"Kate," I replied, pointing over to a particularly scary-looking obstacle course that required children to scale an army-regulation wall, crawl through a tube reminiscent of getting an MRI, and then squeeze their bodies through two over-sized rolling pins in order to escape.

"Awesome," said Sofia's dad, and then he was off to the next parent to ask them which one was *theirs*. Somewhere in between his in-depth, undercover journalist-like questions, he took a few more long-range shots of Sofia eating a gummy worm. *If only he'd had a wind machine for that "eating a gummy worm in a tornado" look*, I thought, he could have locked up the Life cereal photo competition before half the entries had been submitted.

"Do you see your patent attorney friend anywhere?" I asked Jess, prodding her. She looked around the room – it was a sad group of morose-looking parents who appeared more like zombies than the heavily made-up ones you saw on TV. "What was her name, again?"

"Meg," she replied. "And no. Meg's obviously not here. What about Rick, your Commie-bastard baseball-hating homebody?"

"Not his scene. He's somewhere else, *kicking-back*."

Jess let her shoulders drop, then eyed the massive space. She didn't show it often, but I could tell when her quick wit took a backseat to real thoughts. "What is it?" I asked her.

"Your best friend Rick and I," she began, resting her arm around my shoulder, "we have a lot in common. This isn't *my* scene, either."

"I don't think this is *anyone's* scene, to be honest," I shot back.

"Not the party, darling. The daily grind. I'm living *Groundhog Day*. The same thing every day, over and over and over again. It ain't pretty." Meanwhile, Kate was now screaming out for Jess, hanging up-side down with one leg tied up in the ropes that she had been using to scale the blow-up wall. "One second," Jess said, as she ran to rescue her four-year-old.

I watched as Jess untied her, then gave her an extra boost to get up and over the massive wall – dumping her into the next challenge of the catacombs. Jess tromped back to my side, taking a breath. "Where was I?"

"*Groundhog Day*."

"Right. It's weird. I don't even have an end of the week to look forward to. At least you have a work week and on Friday you know you've got a weekend to enjoy. For me there is no weekend. Every day is…" Kate was screaming again for Jess – this time she was stuck in the MRI tube. Jess *sighed*. "One second…"

Jess couldn't get to Kate from the outside, or through the mesh wall – the inventors of this monstrosity had made damn well sure of that. She had to scale the wall herself, pulling herself over the top, then collapsing next to the entrance to the tube. At which point she used her foot to jam Kate through to the other side. Tears turned to smiles, and Jess found her way back to me.

"No weekends," I said, heading her off at the pass.

"Thanks. So, anyway, I keep getting this feeling of…" As soon as Jess had started, Kate began shrieking from the roller pins. She was neither here nor there, her little body stuck in place. Jess just rolled her eyes, giving me a hard pat on the chest, and heading back to save her firstborn. Unfortunately, this time, as Jess jammed her own adult body in between the two rollers and squeezed Kate loose, she ended up getting stuck herself. I watched her wriggle for at least a minute before she, too, screamed out for *my* help.

It was my chance to prove my manhood. I had waited for this moment ever since I had cried that horrific *ugly cry* when Kate was born. Even the hospital staff had laughed, remarking that mine had been the most heinous cry in the history of delivery room cries. I think someone even took a picture. Needless to say, I scaled that red nylon wall with ease, pushing myself through the MRI tube with skill and panache. Then I got to the roller pins, seeing nothing but a pair of legs sticking out. They were Jess' legs.

"I'm here to save you," I yelled over the Justin Bieber music that was assaulting the senses.

"My hero," Jess yelled back, fatigued. "Now just *pull* or something." I grabbed both her legs, bracing myself on the MRI tube behind me. I didn't have much leverage, but I pulled with all my might. She didn't budge an inch. "Great job," she yelled again, sarcastic.

"Hold...on..." I yelled back. I backed myself up against the MRI tube, jamming myself as far into the nylon as I could, creating a human slingshot effect. When I was good and ready, I propelled myself at the small space between the two blown-up rolling pins and I went *flying* through. When I opened my eyes, I was lodged in between the two roller pins, parallel with Jess. I struggled to move, but I couldn't. It seemed that two adult bodies had now made the prospect of escape even tougher. Physics *or something*.

"Hey, Cameron," Jess said, annoyed. "Thanks for *saving* me."

My arms were pinned at my side. I couldn't even squeeze them free. She just closed her eyes, looking away. When turned back and opened them to look at me, they were red with tears.

"I'm not cut out for this *crap*," she cried. "Look at me. I am not a birthday-party, stuck in an obstacle course, peanut butter and jelly-making stay at home mom. I went to work in a power suit. I solved real world problems. Not anymore. Now if I find a lost beret or get through folding all the laundry before the end of the night I guess I'm supposed to think of that as a huge accomplishment. But I *can't*." Then the cry turned to a bawl. "And it's *dark* outside, like all of the time."

"Babe, c'mon," I said, trying to console her by rubbing my trapped shoulder up against hers. It just made me look like a beached seal, so I stopped as quickly as I had started. "Maybe it's…" I started to say, with my mind already having finished the statement and my vocal chords not quite sure it was the right thing to say, "…that you haven't been taking enough Vitamin D? Doctor Samuelsen *did say* it could cause very serious side effects."

Jess glared at me. "Congratulations, you are now officially a *real man*. Give me a break."

"You say that like I just suggested you're being over-emotional because of your *period* or something." *Keep digging that hole*, an unfamiliar female voice in my head replied.

"So now I'm over-emotional. And it's my ovaries fault." Jess, painfully, turned her head the other direction in between the rollers. Now I was just staring at her head.

"Turn back around. I'm sorry. Please." It took a minute, and a lot of neck muscles, but she finally found her way back to the other side.

"I don't know who I am living for anymore," she said. "Everything I do is for someone else."

"That *someone else* is your *family*."

"I know. But I also need to find something to do for *me*."

"Then we'll find that *something*," I assured her. "Whatever you want. I swear."

"Do you?" she turned, still sniffling through the tears. "Because if you promise me and then renege on it, I'm going to hurt you."

"I promise," I said, just as Sofia's Dad started taking action shots of us with his telephoto lens from the other side of the mesh.

"Great moment, you two!" he shouted, excitedly, unaware that Jess would never want an eight by ten. He stared at us, realizing we were stuck beyond human comprehension. "You kids stuck? You need some help?"

Gandalf really should close his mouth when he eats salad, I thought to myself while watching Simon Davis devour his latest creation from the

Commons' award-winning salad bar. He had been halfway through when I had arrived, laptop in hand, to initiate our second meeting of the minds. He grunted for me to hand him the laptop as he chewed through a particularly leafy bite of lunch, took a sip out of a bottle of Mexican *Coke,* then motioned for me to sit opposite him while his systems downloaded the software off my device.

"Don't worry about your *e-mails,*" he teased me, as salad-dressing spittle peppered the table between us. "I'm just copying the disc image and you'll get it back just as it was."

I just sat there. Quietly. Not really knowing where to start. I wasn't sure of the procedure here, and the last thing I wanted to do was send Simon off into a tirade, rendering this opportunity useless. He finished his last mouth full, sliding the plate to his side like a warrior finishing a juicy leg of meat, then finished off the last swig of soda. "I don't have all day," he said, "so if you've got a question, you'd better start asking."

I nodded, taking a breath. "I've only been at The Company for three months," I began. "I don't get it. The Company is completely splintered, there's people everywhere doing the same jobs, my Manager got reassigned and so now I'm reporting to the CVP who doesn't think I'm selling enough of the product and yet the product itself isn't even fully fleshed out. I've got meetings to plan meetings, there's process that doesn't make sense, and I'm buried under a wall of e-mails that make getting anything else done almost impossible. I am making zero progress and I'm worried I'm also going to get let go at some point which will completely screw up everything since I moved my entire family here for an opportunity that now seems far different than I originally expected." I let out a breath.

Simon rubbed his chin, contemplating. "Noise," he said.

"Yes," I agreed. "The Company is…"

"Not the Company," he interrupted. "*You.*"

"Me?"

Simon got up, rummaging through the desk drawer behind him, and revealed a small plastic ball and a stopwatch. He put the ball next to the soda bottle on the table in front of me. "Get the ball into the bottle," he said. "You've got one minute." He *clicked* start on the stopwatch.

I was confused. "Uh, can I ask *why*?"

"Fifty-five seconds left," he shouted, eyeing the ball and the bottle. Great, now I'm on *Survivor*, I thought, as I grabbed the ball and started trying to jam it into the top of the bottle. It was barely making it in – I'd get it slightly in the top, then it would squeeze back out. "Thirty-seconds left," he shouted at me, this time even louder – which startled me into trying a completely different plan of attack. I shoved the ball in as far as I could, then started banging the top of the bottle against the metal table, hoping the force would bring success. *The twenty-fifth hire at The Company challenged me to jam a ball into a bottle*, I thought, likening it to Professor Stephen Hawking asking someone to chew three packets of Saltines in less than thirty seconds. Both situations were untenable, and no one would ever believe they had happened.

"Ten seconds left," he shouted at the top of his lungs, causing me to muster all the strength I had in slamming the bottle against the table. With about five seconds left, the bottle completely *shattered* – sending chunks of glass all over the floor. The ball bounced off into the distance.

I stared at Simon, who sat back, grinning ear to ear. *What a smug asshole*, I thought to myself. *What was he trying to prove*? He got up, retrieving a dust pan and mini-brush from the wall, and proceeded to sweep up the glass on the table and floor.

"Try and shove yourself into a mold you won't fit into," he continued, pointing to the shards of glass, "and you're going to crack up." He emptied the glass into the garbage, then sat down opposite me. "Like me," he said, reflecting. "Like *me*."

A light bulb in my head went off. Or lit up. He was totally right. If I kept trying to jam myself into some already-established mold of The Company, I would totally go completely mental and crack up. He had obviously gone through the same exact thing himself and yet he was still here. This guy was a *legend* who had burnt out and found a way to sidestep the pitfalls that were coming at me head on. *The ball and the bottle,* I repeated in my head. Holy crap, this guy was like the real-world equivalent of *Mr. Miyagi*.

"So, how do I avoid it?" I asked. "How did *you* avoid it?"

Simon pointed to the bouncy ball, still rolling and bouncing off in the distance. "You let yourself go," he said. "You ignore the noise. You ignore the process. You ignore what you think you're expected to do. You go where your instincts take you. Those early years at The Company, when innovation and inspiration drove everything? That was when the real magic happened." He disappeared into his head for a moment, visualizing something that caused him to flash a genuine smile I had not seen before. Then the smile turned to a frown. "When the day came that they tried to shove *me* into that bottle, I took myself out of the equation. Make no mistake – if you can't succeed based on who you are, then any sliver of success is on someone else's terms. I wasn't going to settle for someone else's terms. Someone else's terms are always *shit*."

"Easy for you to say," I stated, matter-of-fact. "I mean, look at who you are."

"Look at who *you* are. It's that easy. Just be you. Say what's on your mind. Don't accept bullshit or jump through idiotic hoops for no particular reason. Do that, and you will either own it or fail trying. And that kind of failure isn't failure at all."

I nodded, realizing the mistakes I had made since I started at The Company. I had come in, excited to be valued for my unique, out of the box thinking. I had taken the role with the promise of having a voice. But the minute I had started, I had muted that part of me in an attempt to fit into a mold that didn't embody any of those qualities. I had to be me. I had to make my voice heard. Whether or not it fit into what everyone else expected. Whether or not it was unpopular or criticized. I had to be the guy who believed that an intergalactic dictator *could* lose his powers passing through the Earth's atmosphere. I had been him before. I could be him *again*.

Shane McCullough and his *pretty Dolphin* had nothing on Simon Davis. That was for *damn* sure.

For the next three weeks, the *Me Being Me* one man show (note: working title) toured the halls of The Company with reckless abandon. Gone was my concern for operating outside the guardrails that had been set up especially for my arrival. Absent was my worry for what people would think if I spoke out of line. Obliterated was my patience for the inane inner-workings of how The Company chose to do things. I had decided to *Costanza* my life up – putting myself on the line and hoping that doing the complete *opposite* of what everyone expected me to do would reap huge benefits and save me from the literal and figurative *mold* that was solidifying around me.

Sale commitments for MediaMesh had gone through the roof,

now that I had chosen to jettison Everett's all-singing, all-dancing, *wide-eyed* Vaudevillian show. Multiple OEMs (the manufacturers of the hardware devices we were targeting to ship the product on) committed in the room to shipping their products with the new version of our installed software thanks to focusing less on the product (which always turned into a blinking, talk-tracked mess) and more on the relationship.

"We're not here to meet about MediaMesh," I would pronounce to the packed rooms of momentarily-confused potential buyers. "We're here to meet about our *future* together," I'd say. "Do you want to be in business with The Company or in business for a single product?" It was the same methodology I had heard my Agent and Manager repeat over the phone to potential studio or network partners in Hollywood as I eavesdropped in their offices. Did they want to be in the Cameron Murphy business where we would develop a true relationship that would span multiple projects and years? Or did they want to exert so much effort on a "one and done" opportunity? One was a partnership, while the other was a *transaction*. Sitting there in those ergonomically-correct conference room chairs, with warm cookies and chilled coconut water in front of them, the idea of partnering with The Company seemed worth the small price they'd have to pay for sidling up to MediaMesh.

"Will the guy with the scary wide-eyes be our account manager?" some would ask, referring to Everett in the back corner, looking like one of those creepy kids from *The Ring*.

"No. No he won't," I'd reply, and the expensive pens would come out of the suit pockets so we could put ink to paper for our future *relationship* together. Everett didn't mind in the least, especially since all he had to do was stare motionless at a pre-determined spot on the wall off to the side. We were a team, the two of us, knocking them down one by one.

"Heard you've made some headway...*without clowns*," sniped Shane one afternoon as he passed by my cube. I just nodded, hardly even giving him the time of day. Because I wasn't going to suck up just for the sake of sucking up. That wasn't *me*. Not anymore.

Somewhere in between all those sales, I had found myself at a kick-off meeting for the social media plan around MediaMesh. Remember, at The Company, "kick-off meeting" isn't like the kick-off of a soccer game, where the game *actually starts* after the kick-off. Here in the over-planned, over-scheduled Universe of The Company, kick-off meant something slightly different.

"The goal of today's kick-off meeting is to determine who the right stakeholders are for this project," a Senior Director from the Community Outreach Team explained.

"Then who are all of *these* people?" I asked, pointing to the eleven people in the room.

"The individuals, who I assume, believe they are the stakeholders for this project," he replied, wanting to just get to the part where he projected something inane on the screen.

"Are any of you folks a stakeholder for this project?" I asked rhetorically. A chorus of "no", "not me", "my boss is", and "will there be lunch served in this meeting?" bounced back and forth against the walls, reverberating. Mr. Senior Director, who I would later call Frank Torres because that was his name, wasn't happy.

"Great. What happens after you determine who the stakeholders are?" I asked. My new best friend, frustrated, put down the computer A/V cord to address me.

"Next steps would be to schedule a meeting with the stakeholders, establish roles and responsibilities, and then discuss action items based on those R&Rs. Once that's complete, we meet back up to check progress on those action items."

"How many meetings is that?" I asked.

"Three."

"We're going to spend *four hours* of our lives doing all of that?" I asked, completely stunned.

"Well, if you can wrap up all that work in *this meeting*, be my guest," he challenged.

The *Thunderdome* was on. I wasn't going to take that challenge lying down. The rest of the room eyed the two of us like a pair of gunfighters poised on opposite sides of a dusty town's Main Street. Who would be the quickest draw? As evidenced by my ability to get everyone's "official stakeholder" on the live video conference and resolve the roles and responsibilities question in ten minutes…*it was me.*

I looked at the clock. We still had forty-five minutes left in the meeting. "Let's quickly assign action items based on our areas of ownership," I said as I jumped up to the white board and began scribbling furiously. The rest of the room was energized, and in the time it took to play *five* rounds of Pictionary, we had established all the action items, resolved who would deliver on them, and agreed to a thirty minute follow-up meeting to wrap up in a week. The entire room let out a raucous *cheer* as we grabbed our things, hung up the conference line, and started filing out the door. There were handshakes and back-taps (the manly kind) and thanks all around. Except for one individual. Mr. Senior Director. Who was sitting quietly in the back of the conference room, head buried in his laptop.

I paused, at the door, looking back before I left. "Anything to say?" I asked. Embarrassed, he tapped away at his keyboard, refusing to make eye contact. I opened the door, took a step out, and looked back one last time.

Wherever I went, the feeling traveled with me. I smiled, exhilarated by the fact that as I continued to trust my instincts, I continued to find success. There was a noticeable change in the air and the whispers in the halls began to form a chorus of positivity that just made me work harder. The bottle had opened up to fit *me* and not the other way around.

"People are talking about you," Elise revealed later that day as we walked into Building 87 together.

"Yeah? What are they saying?"

"That you are a wild card. That people should steer clear of you. That you have a death wish."

"Like Charles Bronson," I replied, puffing up my chest.

"I once met Charles Bronson," bragged Elise. "His moustache had dandruff." I wanted to say that there was no way it was true, but I had learned from Leah's mistakes.

I always loved to ask crazy "what if" questions to my friends. *What if* you had to choose between losing your left leg and having a dead raccoon carcass in your stomach for the rest of your life? *What if* you had to choose between living life always crying grape juice or having to carry a dwarf around in a backpack twelve hours a day? *What if* the only way to be a "happy" stay at home mother was to affix a strange luminescent contraption around your neck?

It was a question I was seconds away from asking Jess, who wore a strange circular light around her neck and presented a table filled with awful looking protein bars and powders to me.

"It's a happy lamp," she proclaimed, adjusting it so the light would shine directly in her eyes, causing her to constantly blink since her body's *survival instincts* desperately wanted to stop her eyeballs from completely melting into nothingness. *Look away*, the motor functions that controlled her pupils screamed out.

"A happy lamp," I parroted back. "Are you happy?"

She picked up a protein bar from the kitchen table, ripping it open like she'd been trapped on a desert island for months, and took a huge bite, masticating it as she talked. "I really feel much happier," she mumbled through the chews. "Happy quotient, ninety-one percent."

"Oooo…kay," I accepted, turning my attention to the boxes of protein bars, vats of shake powder and a mint-in-box heart monitor that had very clearly cost *us* three-hundred dollars. "Talk to me about this cult you've just joined."

"*Not* a cult," she finished chewing, taking another bite. "Melinda says that the combination of this light, a surge of protein every four hours, and consistent exercise will not only reduce stress and depression, but completely improve my cholesterol and outlook on life."

"Melinda?"

"My *nutrainic*." It sounded like a sneeze. I handed her a tissue. She took it from me and threw it on the floor.

"What's a *new…*"

"*Nutrainic*," she repeated again. "Nutritionist. Trainer. Psychic. Although I didn't choose to opt in for the psychic counseling part." Jess could tell I was obviously not drinking the protein-shake along with her. She flipped off the happy lamp light switch and parted the seas of protein bars on the table so she could grab my hands.

"This is a *me* thing," she said, looking me right in the eyes. "Remember, you promised? Does it really matter how silly *you* think it is, if it makes me happy?" I must have searched my soul far too long, as Jess punched me in the arm. *Hard.* "You told me I could kick your butt if you didn't support me."

"Do you have to call it a happy lamp?" She let go of my hand, pulling a box from beneath the kitchen table. The brand of the lamp was none other than "The Happy Lamp."

"Yes, Cameron. I do. That's its name. Do I have to call you Cameron? Could I call you Stan instead?" I clearly treated it as a rhetorical (or *stupid*) question, ignoring it.

"Do you promise not to force me to do *any of this* with you?"

She put the box back under the table, flipping the light back on – illuminating her extra creepy/happy face. "If you don't want to be *this* happy, then that's *your* choice."

"Great," I said, standing up. "Should we hug now?"

"Sure," she said, approaching me, arms outstretched. Needless to say, it was completely awkward trying to hug her with that contraption around her neck. She had to swing the lamp one way, crook her neck the other way, half hug me with one arm while wrapping her leg around my waist. "This is going to change everything," Jess said, pulling back from the hug and turning the happy lamp to a higher, more "turn away from the light, Carole Anne," level of brightness.

"It already *has*," I smiled, meaning something completely different.

April

It was six o'clock on an especially gloomy afternoon; the clouds were about to open up with a torrential downpour the morning Weatherman had been referring to as "*The Potential End of Human Existence.*" I raced across campus to Simon's secret lair, fighting my way reluctantly through one of Jess' protein bars. They had mysteriously found their way into my laptop bag over the last few days, and when hunger got the best of me, I miraculously found a way to ingest them. *Fine,* I thought. *So, I'm eating her damn protein bars. But she'll never get me to wear that damn lamp collar.*

When I entered Simon's laboratory, he was off in the far corner, covered in oil and working on his motorcycle. Not only could the guy write code and re-build hardware, but he could keep a "classic" bike growling like a tiger no matter how ancient it was. I had done my research after spotting the bike on my last visit to the space – Simon had scored a 1936 EL V-twin, it was a Harley Davidson regarded by historians as the first truly modern motorcycle. Front and rear brakes, foot clutch, tank shift and suspension built into the seat. The antique was worth more than the price of a luxury house on Mercer Island, which was like the Beverly Hills of Seattle but without the 'tude. How did I know? There had been a fairly lengthy article back in the late 80's, when the founders of The Company saw their stock options split again and again. When the money started rolling in, they started spending like crazy. This had been Simon's ultimate prize. That, and a rare endangered African parrot he named *Hal*.

"Laptop's on the table over there," he pointed, head still buried in the shaft of the bike. I went over to it, picking it up – it appeared intact and scratch free, which was lucky for anyone or anything entering Simon's space.

"That it?" I asked, closing up my laptop bag. "We square?"

"We're square…for the moment," he said, continuing to work on the bike. I stopped in my tracks, looking over at him. *For the moment*?

"Thought that would get your attention," he said, cranking a wrench around a bolt.

"What is it? What did you find out?"

He put down the wrench and looked up at me. "Piece of advice. You'd better start looking for a new job at The Company," he said, lifting himself up off the ground.

"Don't screw with me," I stammered, as my heartbeat rapidly went into overdrive. Those sweat beads started to form again all over my extremities. What the hell was he talking about?

"I don't have time to screw with anyone," he said, wiping his oily hands on a pair of black denim overalls as he stepped towards his workstation. "In fact, you should thank me for being as generous with my little gems of advice. People used to pay me twenty-five thousand an hour for those things."

I just stared at him. *Blankly*.

"That software you're hocking over there at MediaMesh," he said, continuing, "it's living on borrowed time. It ain't ever gonna see the light of day."

I took it all in. And felt nauseous. *It's probably the protein bar*, I thought, wanting to blame Jess. Then the room started spinning and I saw the floor rushing up to meet my face. I landed with a *thump*, then opened my eyes to see Simon's meticulously clean boots a few inches away. I leveraged the remaining active brain cells in my skull long enough to wonder *what the hell* he was talking about.

Ask him when you regain consciousness, I reminded myself, as the world went completely *dark*.

Mitch DeForrest was a young, hotshot entrepreneur who had turned a million-dollar trust fund into a billion-dollar portfolio by the age of 23, then mysteriously disappeared from the public eye into the jungles of South America for an entire decade. When he emerged at the ripe old age of 33, he did what any billionaire entrepreneur ~~who had drawn a line through every item~~ on his *bucket list* could do – he accepted a job at The Company as a Corporate Vice President of the Emerging Media Division. Because when you've:
    ~~climbed Corcovado in Rio de Janeiro with your eyes blindfolded and your monkey guide screeching in your ear while rain showers pelt your shirtless body~~...
    and...
    ~~wrestled rabid Iguanas while making guacamole for a tour group from Israel~~...
    and...
    ~~hiked barefoot into Argentina then competed and won first place in a horse riding competition populated by *evil* gauchos~~...-
    Well, you could accomplish anything you set your mind to. Yes, even in a corporate environment. At least, that's what Mitch would tell you, if you ever sat in one of his *infamous* meetings where he came off as the secret love child of *Jackass'* Johnny Knoxville and the former CEO of Yahoo, Melissa Mayer.
    "I fell out of a hot air balloon at six-thousand feet this past week-end," Mitch announced to the room, which included Shane and the rest of the core MediaMesh team. Now was the opportunity for Shane to present the roadmap and future plans for the product to Mitch so he could sign off on the last batch of fiscal year funding so that the team, product and initiatives could all be completely bankrolled. "I hit three trees on my way down, slammed into a pile of jagged rocks, then floated down the river in *class five rapids*, before I was able to pull myself out using the tail of a bear that was fishing for lunch," he continued – the entire room hung on every word he spoke. It was ridiculous. *Who was this guy*, I wondered, and why was he here at The Company? From the look on Shane's face, plastered with a smile that was definitely not a ninety-one percent, I could tell he was just biding his time until he could get back to

the slides on screen.

Knowing this meeting was happening today, I had been spinning on it the whole evening prior, staring at the clock as it climbed from eleven o'clock to midnight to two in the morning. Jess' hearing was finely tuned to my "stress sigh" as she so adeptly put it, and she could troubleshoot the reasons for my insomnia while her eyes were still closed and while, I believed, she was actually still sound asleep.

"Whafff esss et?" she would mumble, still dead out.

"It's what Simon told me," I said, turning to her.

"Stoffp thinkennng," she would mumble back, experiencing REM sleep, eyes totally closed.

"If you knew that the people working on your product were unknowingly building something that wouldn't work on any of the new chipsets, spelling untimely doom for everyone on your team… Wouldn't you say something?"

"*Spider!*" she shouted out in terror, eyes still closed, apparently encountering something in her half-awake, half-asleep imagination.

"I'll take that as a yes?" I asked her, as she settled back down into her pillow.

"Yeffff," she mumbled back, now dreaming about making a protein shake, *allegedly*. "Goffa say somthenn."

With the remainder of the bear's tail story wrapped up, and Mitch D's sneakers planted firmly up on the conference room table, Shane set the stage for the asks he would be making. There was the additional heads he'd need Mitch to fund, so he could more quickly get additional engineering and coding done on the software in order to meet the delivery date. There were millions of dollars in marketing spend required to adequately promote the release of the product. Shane presented screenshots of the user interface, research studies that proved that media-savvy consumers *wanted* to their competing apps to talk to each other, and potential brand tie-in opportunities with movie, TV and music content providers.

All the while, all I kept hearing was Jess' rambling, mumbling voice saying, "*Goffa say somthenn.*" The voice started low in the back of my head, then continued to a grumbly high-pitched tenor. It half sounded like the creepy kid from *The Shining* repeating it over and over to me with his crooked little finger. "*Goffa say somthenn,*" came the words again. *"Goffa say somthenn, Mrs. Torrence."*

"This looks wicked," shouted Mitch D, jumping up out of his chair and walking over to the screen to get a better look at the video product demo. "Have we thought about burning the final version of the software onto tiny little USB drives and dropping them over low-income housing projects? Kind of like a philanthropic gesture but one that leverages the social graph?"

Shane looked to Gail. Social media was her thing. Dropping USB drives into housing projects where no one had laptop computers, tablets *or the money to buy them* seemed square in her roles and responsibility charter. "Have we thought about that?" he asked her.

"Yes," she lied nervously, scribbling down notes furiously. "I'm still waiting on a few calls back from the...*uh*...low income-housing... projects?"

"Great!" replied Mitch D. "I'd start with Detroit. Then New York. Then Los Angeles."

"Goffa say somthenn," the voice echoed again in my head.

"On the user interface," Mitch began, eyes rolling up into his head as he brainstormed the next disruptive idea, "is there any way for the entire experience to shut off when someone else in the room starts talking to the user?"

"That would require building a voice recognition component," Shane replied. "It would be a fairly extravagant additional engineering expense."

"What if we outsourced it to high school students?" Mitch D spitballed.

"Goffa say somthenn," slipped out of my mouth in an eerie whisper. Unfortunately, the whisper was whispery enough to get Mitch D's attention. He spun around, pointing to me.

"Dude, so say it, then!"

It was a regular cavalcade of voices in my head as time slowed down and Mitch D waited for my response. There was Simon Davis, reminding me to *"just be you"* and that *"failure wasn't failure at all."* My old Hollywood friend Derrik reminded me that *"if you don't inherently believe...the audience won't either."* My third-grade teacher, Mrs. Diamond, appeared to remind me *"don't forget to take the bathroom key when you go to the lavatory."* I suspected she meant something to the effect of, if you're going to take the time to go the distance (or go to the bathroom) you'd better be sure you fully commit (and bring the key). I had started urinating, *figuratively*. Every guy knew you couldn't stop once you started, *practically*. Spilling the beans was the only choice, *logically*. *Mrs. Diamond would have been proud*, I thought.

"Have we done our due diligence to ensure that the code we have been developing for the last ten months will actually work with the new chipsets on the touchscreen tablets we're pre-installing the product?" I asked. We hadn't. Simon had laid it out for me. The Company had closed a significant deal with a major hardware manufacturer to include MediaMesh on their millions of new touchscreen tablets. The hardware was late. The folks writing the code were doing so without test devices. They would soon realize that MediaMesh wouldn't work and the significant deal would disintegrate, taking with it any reason for the product division's existence and all the progress I had made. If we backpedaled now, there was some potential opportunity to salvage what had been done. Perhaps the product could be re-built from the ground up and jobs could be saved. But the clock was ticking and I would have to move fast.

See, when you knew a bomb was going to blow up, it was your duty to get as many people out of the blast radius as fast you could. There was no time to count the wires, clip the red ones and hope nothing exploded. I had to get everyone out *now*. *Just call me Mr. Bomb Diffuser Guy*, I told the crowd of people I had saved, from a pulpit, in my imaginary after-the-fact press conference. Someone, somewhere, threw a bouquet of roses at me. Which I caught with my left hand.

I was right-handed, FYI.

Shane didn't share my positive outlook on the situation. He let out an almost animal-like grunt from his throat and turned his head to glare at me like I was the Priest in *The Exorcist* throwing Holy Water on his face. It was a wicked look that I had never seen before. The others, around the table, had their mouths open in stunned silence.

"I thought you were going to say you knew some high school students," Mitch D replied. "But *this*. Well, this elevates the conversation, that's for sure." And then, he turned to Shane. "Is what he's saying…*true*? Have we done our *due diligence*?" Shane didn't know what to say. He was, for the first time *ever*, speechless. Mitch D waited for an answer.

"This *can't* be true," Shane spoke up. "And from where in the hell is *he* coming up with this? He's only been with the company for three months. He's in sales. He's not an engineer, for bloody sake!" Ah, how the *Bridgerton* accent disappeared in times of chaos and uncertainty.

"Where are you getting this information…" Mitch D looked to me, *snapping* his fingers at my face so I would tell him my name.

"Cameron. Cameron Murphy."

"Cameron Murphy," Mitch D repeated. "How did you get this intel?"

I couldn't give up the ghost. I *wouldn't* throw Simon under the bus. Not because I didn't think he could handle it – the guy was a badass. It was because this was *my moment*. It was my choice. Ever since I had taken Simon's advice and started approaching things at The Company on my own terms, everything had improved. I wasn't going to stop now. Hell, it was only a job. It was only one tiny moment in time. It was only The Company. I stared, *blankly*.

"Get me an answer on this *today*," Mitch D demanded, turning to Simon. "If this is bullshit, we *riff* him. Out on the street. …But if he's right?"

Everyone in the room, including me, filled in the blanks in our heads.

An hour later, while still waiting for the fallout of the morning meeting with Mitch D, another surprise landed in my lap. The surprise came in the form of a frumpy, shorts-wearing, bun-headed, rosy-cheeked replacement Manager doing business under the moniker-

"Gennifer Layton with a G" whispered Elise, sitting next to me in the conference room with the rest of the team while we watched her hook up her laptop so she could project on the screen at the front of the room.

"You were right," I nodded. Elise smiled, obviously quite proud that her underground network of random Seattle delivery men and food service workers had delivered on true, actionable data. I had to admit, I was impressed. If Elise was right about *this*, how many other things would she end up predicting?

My thoughts shifted as the room turned dark – Gennifer with a G tromped back to the front of the room and put her hands on her hips as she prepared to introduce herself. *Things can only get worse from here on out*, I whispered to myself, intrigued to see just what "worse" would actually mean.

"I…am…Gennifer," spoke Gennifer with a G, directing everyone's attention in the darkened conference room towards the elaborate PowerPoint presentation on screen. The letter "G" bounced onto the screen, then faded and blew up like a balloon (with accompanying balloon blowing *sounds*), only to be joined by the rest of her name – each letter faded in and accompanied the floating "G". "A little about me," she continued, as multiple photos twirled from off the screen and landed in a collage much like a vision board of sorts. There was a picture of her with her family and dog. A picture of her standing atop a mountain, after a particularly tough climb. One showed her digging up weeds in her garden, while another showed her scrapbooking with a particularly motley crew of crafting cohorts. Gennifer with a G gave the room tidbits about each of them, before advancing the presentation to the next slide with a particularly overdone origami animation that crumpled the last slide into a ball, refolded it into a crane, then transitioned to a new slide entitled, "My Greatest Hits."

I am not going to last five minutes with this insane woman as my Manager, I lamented, as I watched screenshots of previously animated PowerPoint decks float in and out of our eye line, accompanied by the Lionel Ritchie song "Dancin' on the Ceiling." I looked over to Elise who made the crazy sign with her twirling hand up by her head. If it wasn't for the music, we might have heard the crashing and yelling before it had reached just outside the conference room in question. But have no fear, the tornado was coming, and it was right outside the door.

The door burst open, slamming so hard against the inside wall that a Wi-Fi antenna on the ceiling came crashing down on the floor, landing at the feet of the breaker and enterer. It was Shane McCullough. Red like a beet, hair characteristically out of place, eyes blood-shot and swollen. He scanned the room like a Terminator, evaluating each body in the room to see which one would match his mark. His mark, of course, was none other than *me*. I imagined him grabbing the table with one of his superhuman arms and tossing it behind him, but he just walked menacingly around the table to get to me.

Ah, *Me Being Me*. My one-man show had now put me directly in the spotlight. *It's really warm being in the spotlight*, I thought, immediately crossing off "Tony Award Winning Actor" from my list of life's desired accomplishments.

"Mitch D wants to see you *now*," Shane growled. I could have sworn that Gennifer with a G uttered a "*oh no he dinn't*" at the same time.

"Did he say why?" I asked, cautiously getting up.

"NOW," he yelled, which was more than enough reason for me to get up quickly and head out the door, but not before I looked back at the room of my three-month old teammates. Everett blinked at me – it was his way of saying 'goodbye.' Gail, Gil, Eric and Elise all eyed me confused. Shane took a breath and shook his head at me before turning to look back at the rest of the team. What he had to say to them, I did not know – he slammed the door in my face. I stood there alone for a moment before getting up the nerve to take my first step towards the exit of Building 87.

"Of course, you still have a job," said Mitch D, tapping at a scorpion through the glass of its office-constricted habitat. "But it ain't that crap one you were doing before," he continued, vaulting over the back of a chair and hitting a perfect landing directly in the seat. It was obvious, in that very moment, that falling six-thousand feet into a ravine hadn't impacted his ability to do indoor office gymnastics. Good for him. I bet he was good on the horse vault, too.

"I'm not following you," I said, respectfully. "Are you asking me if I want to choose the new job in place of the one I currently *still* have?"

"Read my lips. *MediaMesh is gone.* Kaput. It was an incubation project and I just pulled the plug. Because you were *right*. Shane was building something that was never going to deliver on The Company's promises to our hardware partners. So. Congratulations."

"What about all those people? My co-workers?" I asked, concerned.

"Listen to *this* guy," Mitch D bellowed to some unseen Corporate lackey, "he drops the bomb on Hiroshima and then wants to know if everyone is OK. Snap out of it, Murphy, I'm telling you what your next job is. You don't have a *choice* in the matter. It just *is*."

It was the unique logic of The Company. In the real world, outside the hallowed halls of this decades-old institution, if someone thought you would be good for a new opportunity they would ask if you were interested. If you weren't, you kept doing what you were doing. At The Company, when a Manager or Senior Executive offered you a new opportunity or suggested adding double the workload to your already overwhelming job…you just accepted it with a smile on your face. Declining, rejecting, questioning, diverting or divulging any dissenting opinion would set your career trajectory on a path of utter and complete failure. You would forever be *that guy* who turned down that job and deserved to get *that scarlet letter* on your shirt. The one that denoted you were a lazy, ungrateful, disloyal little bastard.

"Relax!" Mitch D said, noticing my unease, "The job you lost is now being replaced with a *promotion*. This is like the fastest promotion I've ever given someone at The Company since I've been here. I'm not doing it to screw you. I'm doing it because you impressed me. Because I saw something in you… I saw a bit of *me* in *you*. And when I see *me*, I like to give *me* a leg up. So that's why I'm giving *me*…I mean *you*… the opportunity of a lifetime."

I hadn't ever climbed a naked monkey or made guacamole on a horse, or whatever it was he had done, so I wasn't quite sure how he was seeing any part of his egotistical self-absorbed personality inside of me… But the word "promotion" kept ringing in my head. It had a nice sound to it. It probably came with a bigger salary, too.

"For the *same* salary," he quickly finished his thought.

But the word *promotion* continued to ring in my head. Three months in, I wasn't expecting more money. I was just expecting to survive.

"Memphis," he said. "The product's code name is *Memphis*."

"Memphis," I repeated.

"We also call it R-thirty four," he stated.

"So, it's a product you call Memphis and R-thirty four."

"The R&D Department refers to it as *Operation Insight*."

"Uh huh," I was losing my enthusiasm in a sea of confusion.

"What do you say…*Perrier*?" he asked.

"I think three code names is enough," I said, watching Mitch D.

as he got up and made his way around the back of his desk.

"No," he said, revealing a bottle of *Perrier*. "I was asking if you wanted some *Perrier*?" I nodded yes, relieved the product only had three completely incongruous naming conventions. That meant that the secret details of whatever product this was, would only get leaked and posted on the Internet *three* times before The Company actually wanted anyone to know about it. There was some misguided logic to the madness, that was for sure.

I accepted a cold glass of fashion-water and took a sip as Mitch D. sat back down opposite me. "I want to promote you to Senior Director of Memphis," he said.

"And what does that mean, *exactly*?" I asked.

"You own the product. You direct the product teams who are already building the technology. You hire a team to ensure one thing and one thing only..." I waited, hanging on his every word. "That Ben Packer falls in love with this product. So much so that our beloved CEO highlights it in his keynote speech at December's Entertainment Technology Show."

I took a sip of the bubbly water. The bubbles tasted richer. Fuller. They had more body. Maybe it was the same damn carbonated water but I was evolving, right there, into a completely new person. The Mitch D. inside of me wanted to eat a jagged light bulb and then jump out of a helicopter on skis into an active volcano.

"This is where you define or destroy your future," he said, deadly serious. "If you deliver for me, which puts *me* on Packer's short list, then I make you a King here. You fail, and not only do I strip away the promotion, but I fire you and ensure that the only job you can ever get is as a vendor. Whose only job is to take massive Excel spreadsheets and highlight every other cell with a slightly different shade of grey. *All day long*."

"Why would anyone hire someone to do that?" I asked out of curiosity.

"To punish someone," he said, holding back a look of sick satisfaction. Then he *laughed* a riotous laugh. I laughed with him, but wasn't quite sure if either of us really thought it was funny. I felt a non-menopausal hot flash pass across the entire surface of my body.

"What do you say?" he asked, hand outstretched and primed for a shake.

"I thought I didn't have a choice."

"You don't."

"Then put 'er there," I said, shaking his hand. We both nodded, smiling, enjoying the collaborate hand shaking moment. *You give good handshake*, I thought, as I squeezed his hand even harder. He squeezed back. The back and forth, give and take handshake pulse meant it was a legal agreement. In Manila. *But still.*

Three months in and I had been promoted. I was the new Senior Director of Memphis. I would hire a team and turn my passion and creativity into corporate gold and a spot in our CEO's keynote speech at December's Entertainment Technology Show. God knows I had the talent. I had the moxie. I just had *no idea* what the hell the product was.

Foo, someone would tell me later.

The promotion news had traveled quickly among the Murphy inner circle. Three minutes and twelve seconds after I had texted Jess about the stupendous-yet-foggy details about my meteoric rise at The Company, the requests for familial interviews came fast and furious.

"Did the CEO come to congratulate you?" asked my Mother over the phone, convinced that anytime her firstborn son did something great, the highest ranking individual in the land was *obligated* to come kneel at his feet.

"No. He didn't. But I wouldn't expect it," I said speaking loudly through the Bluetooth speaker in my car. Less because of the placement of the technology and more because she was going *deaf*. "He's the CEO," I yelled. "He doesn't have that kind of time."

"If he wants to keep that CEO position, he'd better find time and realize how important all the little people are," she proclaimed. "I am *not* feeling good about this CEO now," she lamented, "and it's upsetting me. I have to go."

When I arrived home and walked into the house, the fact that all the lights were off initially startled me. But it was the whispering and giggling in the background that convinced me I truly had the best family in the entire world.

"I'm hoooooome," I yelled, pretending I didn't see the glowing candles making their way towards me at the front door.

"Surprise, Daddy!" Kate yelled out, just as she flipped on the lights. To be honest, I jumped back in horror. Less because of the lumpy, lopsided, homemade cake with the misspelled "Congradulayshens Daddy!" scrawled across the top; but because of Jess.

Not only was she wearing the happy lamp, and wearing workout spandex that had sweat stains from an earlier session, but there were large Band-Aid like strips all over her exposed skin. On her nose, cheeks, forearms and calves.

"Good God, Jess," I said, leaning forward to get a better look. "What happened?"

"Yay, Daddy!!" she exclaimed, sing-songy, jumping up and down in front of me while the cake continued to collapse on one side. "We're so proud of you!!!" Kate was amped up because of Jess, jumping at my feet. A chunk of loose cake landed on my shoe like a bird had just taken a crap on my head. It was chaos.

"Jess!" I grabbed her, stopping the bouncing. "What's wrong with you?" She stopped bouncing, out of breath, eyes still wide with joy and energy. "What's all over your body?" I said, referring to the adhesive strips.

"Oh, these things?" she smiled, trying desperately not to bounce. "Caffeine patches! Supposed to give you extra energy and…*oomph*!" She started to bounce again, speaking through her staccato breathing: "I…feel…so…happy!"

Then she collapsed into my arms, looking up like a wounded puppy. "I…am…so…tired."

Thirty minutes and twenty-two adhesive caffeine patches later, I sat cradling Jess' head in my lap on her side of the bed. I held a cold washcloth on her forehead as I worked to unlock the happy lamp from her neck. When I finally figured out the combination, her eyes started to flutter as she seemingly came back to the land of the living.

"I'm sorry I ruined your party," she said, looking up at me.

"It's okay," I began, "but what in the hell happened? What possessed you to-?"

"I was feeling great. Took my Vitamin D. Worked out, felt invigorated *and* happy. And Kate was home, so you know if I was feeling that way, it was all working according to plan. Then I remembered that my nutrainic sent me these energy strips to try. I thought it said to use eleven. It may have said one. The happy lamp kind of creates this blind spot…right around this area," she motioned to the *entire room*, meaning *everywhere.* "I must have misread."

"I'm going to go out on a limb and hypothesize that it said *one.*"

"Yeah," she said, turning on her side and cradling my leg, "you're probably right."

She snuggled up even closer, closing her eyes and getting comfortable, then grabbed my hand and placed it on her head. That meant she wanted me to rub her hair. Which I did. Over and over and over again as she *sighed* beside me. Inside, all I kept thinking was that I got screwed out of a celebration. Instead of congratulating me on the phone, my mother found a way to criticize the CEO of The Company. Instead of having a party for me at home, my wife had overdosed on adhesive caffeine patches. *A man's house is his castle,* I mouthed to myself. *If he comes back from a triumphant battle and the Queen and his loyal subjects can't even stay sober long enough to celebrate, then what kind of King was he?* Where was the respect? How could I be made a King at work if I wasn't seen that way in my own lands?

I got up and walked down the hall to Kate's room, peering inside. Part of me was looking for someone to talk to about my day, and despite periodically seeing a glimmer of maturity in Kate's eyes I had to remember that she was just a four-year-old little girl. I stepped up to the side of her bed, looking down on her sleeping peacefully, in and among her own pile of loyal (stuffed) subjects. Her life was simple. The big decisions focused on what snack to have, what toy to play with, what crayon to choose or what temper tantrum to select for a variety of unfair adult decisions. She wouldn't even get what I was talking about.

"I just got promoted today," I would tell her.

"What's a promotion?" she'd ask.

"It's like getting more responsibilities."

"Like getting to be Lunch Passer Outer?" which was obviously the equivalent of a CEO in her Pre-School world. No, she wasn't the right audience for my blathering emotional concerns.

I kissed Kate, exiting her room and staring out the front windows across the horizon. The moon hung high in the sky and shone brightly, lighting up the entire mountainous region surrounding the East Side of Seattle. The clouds still hung low, but there were changes coming. I could tell. Not only would the clouds dissipate soon, but so too would the restrictions previously placed on my ability to excel at The Company. But that was where it got scary.

What if I didn't deliver? Mitch D. had made it clear as day. Allow *him* to fulfill his destiny and get in with the CEO, and my future would be guaranteed. Fail him, and I would lose it all. It wasn't something I could tell Jess. She had her own issues and challenges. The last thing she needed was the added stress, knowing that if I didn't hit a home run that we would be right back at that uncomfortable table, having an even tougher decision to make.

"I think it's best that you just leave the country," I imagined Jess saying.

"Leave the United States?" I would ask her, confounded.

"I can't risk crossing paths with you ever again," she would say as her face tensed up, "because then I will have to repeatedly punch you in the ear for destroying our lives."

I felt alone. I recalled that someone, once, had said that if a job didn't scare you it wasn't worth taking. Based on my level of fear, this had to be one *helluva job*.

I felt less alone, but a little silly – standing in the darkness, drenched in the light from the moon, starting to feel empowered and enabled. In fact, in that split-second, the adrenaline rush coursing through my veins convinced me that I *could* become King. It was possible.

The King of Memphis, I whispered, feeling a chill roll over my back. It felt good. I wanted it. I would show everyone, especially my family, that it could be done.

"We call it R-thirty four because it is the thirty-fourth iteration of our next-generation entertainment recommendation engine," said Rafi Johansson, the half-Indian, half-Swedish leader of the *Island of Misfit Engineers*. Mind you, there were tiny factions of Engineers everywhere throughout The Company, all working on side-projects in startup atmospheres hoping that they would make enough progress to be given a green light to move forward. That meant more heads, more financial support, and a product leader to shepherd everything along. For all intents and purposes, my presence in front of them meant that things were following that trajectory.

I sat in a big oversized leather couch in a living-room like mosh-pit on the third floor of the Studio A building, surrounded by Rafi's soda-slurping team and their conceptual drawings, UI sketches and storyboards showing how the product would eventually work. Rafi and his team of ten had been working on the core underpinnings of the product for Mitch D., who had now handed off the entire project to me. I sat, taking notes on my phone, listing off the basic concepts of the product that I had gleaned thus far.

R-thirty four was, in a nutshell, a computerized algorithm that told you what movies and TV shows to watch, what music to listen to and what books you would love. Consumers would be able to download the app onto any device they owned, then sit back as the algorithm synced with their social networks and friends' lists to decide what it thought you'd like best. The only problem was that, *they already existed* in one form or another somewhere else.

"So, what makes it 'next generation?'" I asked. "Any service I use today has its own algorithm with recommendations. It has charts, top lists, and what my friends were previously engaging with."

"This recommendation engine," Rafi began, defending, "is *one* engine for *all* your entertainment. Our competitors' services have *multiple* engines for *multiple* kinds of entertainment."

"I don't get it," I said, doing my best Tom Hanks in *Big* impression.

"Our engine will be better. More innovative," Rafi said, quite pleased with his answer.

There was that word again. "Innovation," I repeated, in my trademark South African accent, which nobody picked up on or complimented. Having been at The Company for months now, it had taken me until this very moment to realize what people meant when they uttered the word "innovation." *Innovation* was "*foo*" decked out in a party dress, with make-up, and a whole lot of perfume. It was the second (of five) *Stages of Oblivion* in a world where people who had no clue what would set their product apart from all the others, kept upping the game by upgrading the terminology they used to "wow" those around them.

Stage 1: Foo. No one knows what the feature is, but "foo" will be amazing!

Stage 2: Innovation. That amazing feature, whatever it is, will innovate!

Stage 3: Differentiator. That innovation, whatever it may be, will be so different from others' products, that it will be a game changer.

Stage 4: Game Changer. Some amazing feature, that will be so different, the entire game as we know it will have to change to even be able to contemplate the weight of its impact.

Stage 5: Disruptor. Still not completely aware of what the innovative, differentiated, game changing product feature could be – it will disrupt everyone else's business and get them to bend to the will of The Company.

The bottom line was this: no one truly knew what success looked like, and so they threw out adjectives to keep the wolves at bay. But not me. The *King of Memphis* was howling at their front door.

I stared down at my notes on the phone, just as a text message popped onto the screen. "Sorry about last night," it said. "I'm so proud of you." It was from Jess – and in that split second of receiving the text, feeling the emotion, and then looking back up at Rafi and team, I had an epiphany that was nowhere near the world of *foo.*

"You want a next generation recommendation engine that *matters* to people?" I asked, standing up in front of them. They nodded, cautiously, unsure of where I was going. "People watch movies or listen to music because it is an emotional activity. They engage in these things because it makes them *feel.*" The group nodded intently, listening to my pitch. I was in the zone, much like when I was pitching an idea to a Producer, and the wheels inside my head were asking and answering questions more quickly than any new twice-as-fast Intel chip could. Everything in the real world was moving slowly, but inside my head it was going a mile a minute. I thought about writing. About how words and phrases elicited emotional responses. Jess' text reminded me of that in that one moment – "I am proud of you" was the phrase that popped onto my phone. It made me feel. It made me happy. It made me *love.* If I was going to watch something or listen to something, I was in the mood for something that made me feel *even more* of that emotion.

"I don't care what my friends are watching. I don't care what they're listening to. Instead of focusing all our attention on that, why not take the words and phrases in my e-mails? In my texts, status updates, even the tags attached to the pictures they take? Use *those* real time emotions and build it into an algorithm that returns recommendations that are significant for *me*."

Rafi was nodding. His team noticed. "So…we build a new algorithm from *scratch*?" he began, "that cares about *you*. We base it on your *words*, not your actions. That what you mean?"

"Exactly," I said, getting excited. It was right in my wheelhouse. "Words *are* emotion. Emotion *drives* action. Action drives-"

"Money," Rafi finished. We both shared a knowing look, and we were there right on the same page. It was as if we were doing the Vulcan mind meld in that very moment. We would build a recommendation engine that capitalized on people's emotions, right in the moment, giving them no other choice but to buy the entertainment they had no idea they were even looking for because it made them feel. We had to make them *feel*.

"That's *innovation*," I said. I was *damn* good. Holy crap…*it* was.

"We'll have to call it R-thirty five," another Engineer piped up, simply because it represented yet *another* time they'd be rebuilding the damn thing.

"We'll call it *Memphis*," I said, now completely attached to the ludicrosity of it all. The room was with me from that point forward. They had taken the journey with me, had seen it with their own eyes, and totally and completely knew it. *Had this been a movie pitch*, I contemplated, *I would have just gotten a three picture deal*.

"Yo, Murphy!" the voice echoed throughout the atrium of Studio A, as I was making my way down the glass stairwell towards the ground floor. There, looking up, was none other than Romy Wallace. She wore a three-quarter sleeve L.A. Raiders jersey that had obviously been the one she wore as a teenager, or it was yet another thinly veiled plot to get more male attention in the corporate world. She gave me a painful jab in the ribs as I reached her, causing me to drop my laptop onto the ground, generally making a spectacle of myself.

"What's this, UFC or something?" I whined, picking up my laptop and bracing myself on the edge of a chair behind me.

"Toughen up, dude," she smiled, patting me more gently on the shoulder. "What are you doing over here in belly of the Engineering beast?"

I perked up, realizing I hadn't seen Romy since everything had gone down. In our last conversation she had made me feel insecure, questioning my ability to even handle Shane McCullough. Of course, now, the tables had completely turned. It took me less than three point five seconds to let the brag out of the bag. "I was promoted," I said, watching for some kind of envious or surprised facial tick. "Mitch De-Forrest put me in charge of a pretty amazing new product. I'm running it to ground, hiring a team, the whole nine."

"Reeeaaaallly," she drew out, nodding and smiling the kind of smile that the Cheshire cat would have been jealous of. "Got your eye on the Entertainment Technology Show Keynote, I suppose?"

"Of course, I do…" I said, wishing I hadn't said it.

"That's very *very* interesting," she shot back, measured. *Why was that interesting*, I wondered. *Let it out. Spill, bitch.* "Especially since just about a week ago, I was promoted to GM of the product *I've* been working on."

My heart sunk. Just what I needed. I figured there were many product groups who had their eyes on the Keynote of the ETS, but they were not being led by Romy Wallace. She was a ballbuster who didn't believe there was anything she could do that was *questionable*. Let's face it – she scared me. Her brusque attitude and physicality had made her a great ally, but knowing she would now be a competitor made me dig deep and pull out an insult as best as I could.

"This is your 'total bullshit hardware that will never ship' that you mentioned?" I asked as sweetly as I could, concurrently trying to take my passive aggressive attitude and dump barrels of flammable liquid onto Romy's internal fire.

"That's right," she said, unaffected. "I'd bet on *my* bullshit before I ever bet on someone else's." The words came out cold, calculated…and *vague*.

In my imagination, I found my iron-clad self, back in the battle, finishing a desperate run across the dark landscape – having caught up with the sword-wielding Romy. The warrior horde was now closer to us than ever before, and the clanging of their swords and shields reverberated all around us. Things moved in slow motion as I reached out to grab Romy's shoulder to let her know I had finally reached her side. But when she turned, she was not the Romy I had expected. She morphed from an iron-clad warrior into something far more dangerous. Her hair grew long and dark, her iron dissolved to reveal a sweeping black robe. Her eyes sunk in more deeply, surrounded by black lines that caused her dark pupils to appear even more pronounced. Instead of a sword, she held a wooden staff with a glowing green orb at the top. Her metamorphosis was complete and she let out a cackling, ear-shattering laugh. Once a warrior, by my side, she had turned into an evil, magic-wielding *Sorceress-Bitch*.

Back in the real world, I smiled. Genially. As best I could on the heels of the verbal challenge that had been set out at my feet. "Well, I hope things continue to go well for you," I said, not remotely hoping that at all. "Good luck with that."

"Thanks, pal. But I won't need it." She pretended as if she was going to jab me in my *other* uninjured side, causing me to flinch. "Because I was bred for this *Hunger Games* shit." She pretended to pick up an imaginary bow and arrow and shoot one straight at the head of a passerby. Then she grinned, turned, and strutted out of the Atrium.

I watched her go, kicking myself that I hadn't seen her before as clearly as I was now. What did I expect? She was an agent. From Hollywood. With an almost inhuman desire to beat everyone else at the big game. Somewhere in my head, I heard the sound of an evil magic staff clash with the sound of a steel-plated sword.

Romy Wallace is my nemesis, I thought, as I got up from the couch and headed for the exit. *May I destroy her and scrape her defeated carcass from the Earth.*

"So, is this what you meant by me *owing you*?" I asked Simon blindly, my entire head encased in a modified fighter pilot's helmet, with a blacked-out visor completely keeping me from seeing anything.

"Something like that," he said, soldering wires to a circuit board, or something that sounded quite like it. God knows what he was doing out there, but as long as I could keep talking, it would keep me from guessing just what "harmless experiment" he was about to put into motion. Everyone had seen *The Fly*. I knew about the kinds of crazy things that happened in underground laboratories, hidden from prying eyes.

"We haven't talked about MediaMesh since I was last here," I said, hearing a strange buzzing sound come from outside my black Universe.

"That's because I already know what happened."

"How?"

"You seem to forget that I'm *me*," he said, hammering away at something with a metal hammer. "Shane McCullough got what he deserved," he said with labored breath, obviously exerting some level of physical energy on whatever he was working on outside my helmet.

"You know Shane?"

"Know *of* Shane."

"So why do you say he got what he deserved?"

Out there, Simon let out a *sigh*. "Because I know his *type*. People who believe they are Gods, above all others, eventually need to be shown that they are mortals down here, just like the rest of us."

"People call you a legend. How much different is that from a God?"

"Bullshit gossip," he said, sitting back in his chair and remaining quiet for a long while. "People call me a legend because they believe that I did everything by myself. Which I didn't. There were others. But people don't remember the others when you do something good… Or when you do something bad. They just remember *you*. I'm no Legend, or God or Saint. I'm just one man trying to make up for my mistakes. One man just trying to make a difference."

"What did you do?" I asked, thinking that now was my chance – the fact that Simon didn't have to look at my face was making it easier for him to talk to me.

"It's what I didn't do," he said. There was another long pause, followed by him clearing his throat. "Enough talk. Tell me if you feel this." Somewhere out there I heard a switch get flipped.

Suddenly, an electrical shock passed through my skull with such force that I could have sworn I'd just been hit by lightning. I *screamed out*, pawing at the helmet to try and take it off. "Getitoffgetitoff!" I screamed, as Simon quickly detached some wires and ripped it off my head. He was shaking his head, eyeing the smoking helmet, now sitting on his workstation.

"Are you trying to *kill* me!?" I yelled, patting down my static electricity-enhanced hair.

"The voltage limiter apparently isn't talking to the circuit board," he proclaimed, investigating the bottom of some electrical components. "It was supposed to be a slight, pleasant feeling accompanied by visual cues."

"Nothing in this laboratory falls under the category of *pleasant*," I spouted, still steaming (literally).

"Ah, yes. Mr. Senior Director speaks," Simon spat at me. I looked at him surprised – I hadn't told him about the promotion. "I'm *me*, remember? I am the eyes and ears of this institution."

I was still pissed. I got up, grabbing my bag, and started heading for the door. "Yeah, well I have *a lot* of work to do now that I've been promoted, so you'll forgive me if I don't stick around to get electrocuted a second time."

"Just remember one thing," he yelled after me, as I started to open the lab door.

"Yeah, what's that?" I said, turning around.

"The *people*. Remember the people."

"What people?"

"The MediaMesh people. Your old co-workers. Who are now looking for jobs because you had a hand in revealing what was *really* going on."

"I can't help every single one of them," I said, starting to turn back around. The gall Simon had. He gave me the MediaMesh intel. Now it was all on me?

"Don't be remembered for what you *didn't* do," he said, turning back around and returning to his fiddling. I let it sink in, closed the door behind me, and headed for the elevator at the end of the hall.

May

I was lying in bed next to Jess and Kate the morning that it happened. I had been tossing and turning the night before, clock-watching the whole way through to the AM. There had been a particularly noisy rainstorm accompanied by the kind of forceful howling wind that made you question how entrenched the roots of the twenty-story trees in the backyard really were. Kate had come in around three in the morning, unable to sleep and scared of the sounds. There was no work the next day, so we piled her in between us for a sleepover of sorts.

At first, when I saw it, I half expected it was a dream. I noticed it out the corner of my eye, creeping into the room slowly and meticulously, as if it knew we were all sleeping there. It entered at the window just next to my side of the bed, then made its way to the carpet and across the room towards the bookshelves and the TV. I lay there completely paralyzed at the sight of it, rubbing the sleep out of my eyes so I could be sure. After a few double-takes, I knew it wasn't a dream.

"Wake up," I nudged Kate and Jess quietly. "You have to see *this*." The two of them rubbed their faces in their pillows then turned toward my side of the room. Both of their eyes went wide.

"It can't be," said Jess, mouth agape like she was starring in one of those disaster movies where the White House was about to be destroyed by a space ship, tsunami, terrorist bomb, tornado, atomic hurricane, destructive superhero finale battle or CGI-animated monster of sorts. "Is it…?" she paused, not wanting to say the word as she sat up to get a better look.

"*Sunlight,*" I spoke the words calmly, and with measured caution. "It's May. And there is sun shining through our bedroom window." We all looked at each other and busted out of the bed, doing the happy dance all over the sunlight-covered floor. Jess pulled open the shades, Kate rushed into the bathroom to do the same. We went running, screaming through the house like a trio of ridiculously silly mental patients. I held my cell phone above my head, blasting The Beatles' "Here Comes the Sun." It was like winning the overcast lottery.

We got dressed, ate a quick breakfast and ran out the front door, throwing it open wide. Down the cul-de-sac and across the street there were people everywhere. Picking up the papers on their doorsteps, hosing off cars in their driveways, attaching boat rigs to the back of their SUVs. There were early morning joggers, gardeners trimming hedges, and a blue sky that I had forgotten even existed in this part of the world. There were high-fives, cats being rescued from trees, and children learning how to ride bicycles without training wheels for the first time. Somewhere, a baby was born naturally, with the help of a doting doula. I could have sworn I heard the gurgling cry. But perhaps I was just projecting.

In my imagination, everyone started singing and dancing like any typical opening number of your favorite neighborhood musical. They linked arms, hoofing it up in unison as the men swung the women into the air, and as brass horns and tubas filled out the lyrical harmonies of a hundred neighbors with a spring in their step and a song in their hearts:

> *Good morning, good day,*
> *It's a wonderful time to play,*
> *See the elk and the deer,*
> *Dear old neighbor, don't fear,*

The sun's out and it only took until May. It was a virtual *Oklahoma* in front of my rose-colored eyes, as neighbors started to notice us for the first time.

"Good morning!" chimed a sweet middle-aged neighbor, who saw us standing on our doorstep and came running up our front walkway. "I'm Loretta. Live right there down the street. Been meaning to come over and welcome you to the neighborhood."

"We moved in four and a half months ago," I smiled, shaking her hand.

"We know! We came over as soon as we could. Please let me and Jerry know if you need anything," she sang as she motioned to a fatigued old man who was mowing his lawn with one of those 1950's manual hand mowers. He waved, re-adjusting the wife-beater that was falling off his shoulders.

"That's really nice of you," smiled Jess, giving me a WTF look as Loretta made her way back down the stairs, passing Sudhir and a crew of other neighbors on their way up.

"What did I tell you?" he smiled, showing us off to The Kirkmans, The Mooreheads, The Chens and The Shaffers.

"Welcome to the Neighborhood," smiled Mrs. Kirkman, handing over a platter of cookies and cupcakes that *looked* four months old. Maybe they were.

"Here's a list of helpful numbers I thought you could use," said Mrs. Shaffer. "Local doctors, gardeners, coupons for setting up cable and phone service."

"You look just like your shadows," Mr. Chen said.

Handshakes and hugs abound, we made the acquaintances of all of the garage door closers we had witnessed over the last four months. For silhouettes and specters, they seemed like a pretty friendly bunch, and we wished them well as they left us alone with Sudhir.

"We thought you were lying," I joked with him, as a family of cute raccoon babies and their parents walked right past us across the stairwell gate. Kate eyed the animals with the kind of wonder a child experiences when a shiny silver dollar has shown up under her pillow, in exchange for a tooth.

"Where are we?" asked Kate, confused at how drastically her surroundings had changed overnight. "Did we move?"

Sudhir laughed, then felt his belt as one of his pagers went off. "I must go," he said, waving goodbye and heading down the stairs.

"No, Kate," I pulled her close, as a family of deer ran across the street and into the trees. "This is still our home. It's just...a *sunnier* version of it." She grabbed me tight as I looked over to Jess. There was a smile there, but it wasn't the one I was expecting. The sun was here! People were abound! No longer would we be prisoners trapped in a world of overcast solitary confinement.

"The sun, babe," I pointed to Jess, smiling wide.

"I see it," she nodded, giving the best smile back that she could. But it was obvious there was more on her mind than just the weather.

"If I don't get this job," the suit-laden young man sitting across the un-comfortable wooden table said matter-of-fact, "my wife and I may have to consider giving up our child for adoption." I looked at him, yet another one of the candidates on my very own "loop" who was vying for one of four positions on my mysterious Memphis product team, and was disgusted. His total and complete disregard for human life...all for a full time job at The Company?

The difference between looping as a potential employee and looping as a potential *employer* was worlds apart. The latter was riddled with uninformed, socially-inept, technologically-inferior stalker types.

There had been the older creepy dude who had obviously re-searched my entire life on the Internet, saying "I've always found the name Kate to be absolutely charming." He made sure to comment on the types of movies he loved, stressing "My favorite films are the ones that inject comedy into sci-fi, like for example any movie that involved an intergalactic dictator crash landing in middle America would be on the top of my list," having obviously read the press release about my most recent and most psychologically-scarring script sale to date.

There had been the mousy Emo girl, who insisted she knew ev-erything about today's strategic landscape of entertainment and tech-nology, only to read me an article from *Wikipedia* entitled "*Today's Entertainment and Technology.*"

There had been the *Magic Talker*, who never actually answered *any question* despite responding to each one for five minutes or more with impressive-sounding words. There had been a regular cavalcade of not-so potential employees that I would later dub *The Flat Top, The One*

With The Bermuda Shorts, Cuckoo Fran & Ollie, Mysterio, James and the Giant Peach, Chews with Pencils, The Onion, Vin Doozie, The Gambler, Equilibriu-Man, Sniffy, Ear Lobe, Clam-Hands and *Soul Patch Sister.* Not only was spending sixty minutes with each one a painful hour of my life that I would never get back, but trying to figure out how much to pay the people I'd actually hire (if I ever found them) was an exercise in pure, illogical nonsense.

By the time I had completed the *Process That Makes No Sense*, I had been lucky enough to find three individuals who didn't threaten the lives of unborn children, ramble on about playing the tambourine like Shirley Jones or just plain *suck.* But there was still one more golden ticket I had to give out. And I knew just who that person needed to be.

"That clown town is working on a *special project,*" Elise said, using finger quotes to describe just what Shane McCullough had been up to since that fateful day three weeks ago. "He had a total and complete *Jerry Maguire* meltdown," she demonstrated as she flailed her body in all directions, manically. "Then he gave everyone two months to find a new job."

We were walking and talking through the main campus, drenched in glorious sunlight, past throngs of employees eating lunch, playing soccer and participating in outdoor meetings much like the one I had called with Elise. After having been through what I now called *Loop Fatigue,* I had still only landed on three of the four roles I needed to fill. The one significant slot that I had not found someone for was the Marketing role. It was Simon's words that came back to me one night, reminding me to "remember the people." Elise was the kind of people I couldn't forget.

"I have a role I still need to fill on my team," I told her, watching her face light up with glee. "It's a Marketing role, overseeing the go to market plan around Memphis."

"Memphis," she repeated, stopping in her tracks. "The next generation entertainment recommendation engine?"

"It's *confidential,*" I said. "How do you know about Memphis?" She smiled.

"Don't underestimate my underground network of intel," she

grinned. "And yes. I'll take the job."

"But I didn't offer it to you."

"But you were going to. In about five minutes from now."

I didn't even need to ask her how she knew. She *just did*. And it just validated the exact reason I had reached out to Elise in the first place. She might have been full of drama. And she might have created stress and swirl on a team of even-keeled people. But if I were going to make it to Las Vegas in December, I would need every bit of help I could get. I needed a psychic. I needed a soothsayer. I needed the female Nos*tradame*us for the digital age.

Elise accepted the offer five minutes later.

#

At home, Jess had taken to calling me "the Coal Miner" in reference to the fact that I often left before my family awoke in the morning, and often returned by the time everyone was in bed asleep. My return was often met with saran wrap covered "reheatables" that ranged in menu item from "cold-yet-undistinguishable protein dish" and "yellow vegetable medley" to "fish-of-some-kind with kale." As was clearly evidenced by the healthy-yet-confounding meals, Jess had added "Mystery Chef" to a list of hobbies intent on eviscerating daily boredom.

The days got longer and the e-mails got longer still. Once terrified by the forever-filling e-mail box, I became yet another Company man returning the favor. The "red bang" e-mail became my calling card, depositing that red trademark accouterment with every message I sent. And I wasn't doing it out of some misplaced sense of revenge. Over time, whether it was the result of growing my purview or simply settling into the daily rhythm, I honestly believed that *every single e-mail* represented an extremely time sensitive issue that had to be handled *asap*. I *had* to give it a "red bang."

Each night at home, after choking down the Mystery Chef's latest concoction, I would wander my way through the family room and upstairs – past the open crayons, half-finished books, couch cushion forts and jewelry boxes, visualizing the events I had missed out on with Jess and Kate while I had been at work focused on my own success. *This is for them*, I'd remind myself, replaying the one-on-one meetings, team meetings, goal setting meetings, virtual stakeholder meetings and recently revised O.R. (*owner* and *reviewer*) meetings. *They understand why I'm so busy*, I'd say, trying to convince myself that my absence would make the heart grow fonder. My internal justification usually ended with me losing to Harry Chapin, whose lyrics to *"Cat's in the Cradle"* would ring out in my head – reminding me about the father who ignored his child, who then grew up to ignore him back. *"He'd grown up just like me... My boy was just like me..."* I never wanted to punch a folk singer more than Harry Chapin, which made me feel even more self-loathing. Although, *Harry Chapin was already dead*, I'd think. *...He already got his.*

What a bastard I was. I crept upstairs and into Kate's room, sneaking up towards her bed and caressing her hair as she lay innocently asleep. "I love you," I told her, whispering. I had convinced myself over the last few weeks that even if my daughter was fast asleep, any conversation I could have with her was obviously getting through to her subconscious psyche. Despite not seeing her as much lately, all those late-night whispers would prevent any later-in-life psychological issues and subsequent shrink bills.

She tossed, rubbed her eyes and added yet another question to her Hit List. Contrary to the general Hit List, this one landed on the *Parental Guilt Hit List*. The question was simple, and pierced a virtual dagger into my heart.

"Daddy," she whispered, "don't you sleep at work now?"

I was getting to be a pro at navigating our pitch-black bedroom without any light whatsoever, and changing, brushing teeth and setting my alarm without nary a sound. This had been going on for a few weeks now, and other than the weekends, I started to believe that I *could* be blind and get through life pretty well as long as I only had to live in my bedroom. Still, *braille*? Didn't need it. *I scoff at you braille*, I thought to myself, as a slid into bed and pulled the covers over my head.

"Aren't you going to kiss me?" a raspy voice whispered from across the equator of the still-not-paid-off bed.

I fumbled with my flashlight app, turning it on, and swinging it in the general vicinity of Jess. I was met head on with something that kind-of, sort-of sounded like my wife but didn't look anything like her at all. There was a nose strip, white hardened face cream, a single caffeine patch on her forehead and the battlefield whereto errant eyebrow hair once lived. As she leaned forward with an extra-mushy pucker, I saw the bags under her eyes. *Jesus Christ*, I thought to myself, what has happened to my Jess? This was not the Jess I had left Los Angeles with. This was…something *different*.

Instead of saying a thing, I flipped my smartphone around and pulled up the texting app. I typed, "Text and e-mail only, remember?" and tapped *send*. On the other side of Jess, her iPhone lit up with a *bloop* sound. She reached behind herself without looking, felt for the phone, and brought it back around. She read the text and let out a deep, fatigued *sigh*.

Right. What kind of crazy technology-obsessed loser was I? *I wasn't.* This was *work*. Just days prior, Rafi had presented me and my new team our own Memphis-enhanced smartphones. Each one had the recommendation kernel built into the hardware, tracking and logging all the e-mails, texts, social networking posts, Tweets, and so on. The mandate was simple. Use the smartphones for *everything*. Instead of conversations, text your loved ones. Instead of a phone call, send an e-mail. Instead of two-hundred and eighty character statements, Tweet them instead. After one week of logging conversations we would sit together and see if my genius idea of personalized, real-time recommendations tied to the consumers' emotional state happened to be genius at all.

"Are you going to kiss me?" the text *dinged* onto my screen. I quickly fumbled for the emoticon keyboard, planting a digital wet one by the cursor and hit send. *Bloop.* Jess' eyes scanned the screen, reading my text again. She sat up, turned on the light on her side table, and revealed further evidence of her complete and total disregard for her looks. The huge ice cream stain on my college fraternity sweatshirt didn't help her case.

"Are…you okay?" I typed and hit send. *Bloop.* Jess shook her head, so over this, although to my credit it had only been going on for three days. She started typing.

"I volunteered at Kate's pre-school math party today," she texted back. *Ding.*

"That's great, no?" I texted back. *Bloop.*

"I was looking forward to being social," she texted back. *Ding.*

"That's great." *Bloop.*

"Not if you're the Bingo dealer." *Ding.* She held up her hands, they looked worn like she had scrubbed them endlessly with a Brillo pad. I typed back a question mark. *Bloop.*

"You do not have any idea what it is like to have another children's snot juice leak onto your hand," she texted back. *Ding.* I winced, not loving the vision.

Jess grabbed my smartphone and sat on it, then put hers down. "Cameron," she said in her raspy, tired voice, "I need human interaction. With *adults*. With *you*. Otherwise, I am going to have a total and complete breakdown."

"Even with the happy lamp?" I asked, regretting my choice of words.

"Look at me," she said, doing that face cradle I hated so much. "Read my lips. Total breakdown. And P.S.? It will be *bad*."

A few days later, my new team and I found ourselves in a conference room with Rafi and team, who had previously sent us off on our own version of a technological Lent. We had been challenged to refrain from talking or communicating like typical homosapiens did in an attempt to fill the Memphis recommendation server with petabytes of real world, real human data that represented our relationships, conversations, strides and struggles. Today, Rafi would light up the algorithm server, which would process all of our electronic correspondences and return what we hoped would prove that this was truly the next generation recommendation engine we all hoped it could be. My team sat at the front of the conference room table as each of our devices were hooked up to the master hub, waiting as the servers were lit up for the first time.

I glanced over at *my team*. *My team*, I said to myself again. How in the hell did I have *a team*? Even as a kid I was banned from all organized sporting rituals that involved inclusion onto a team-like structure, primarily due to my inability to deliver anything but *sucky results*. Yet now, here I sat, lording over my own empire of employees. If only all those high school Varsity letter jocks who had turned into fat construction workers could see me now.

I took stock of the team in all their glory; there was Jane D'Allegro, a sweet, dark-haired nurturer, whose inability to stop war gaming every single decision she obsessed over showed in her nubby, jagged fingernails. She would be responsible for chasing new partnerships, business opportunities and making this a breakeven or better business.

Next to Jane, sat Dustin, slightly stocky and always wearing a black t-shirt with a reference to either pop culture or a type of computer language. The overabundance of Linux penguin appearances spoke to his independent spirit and unbridled geek passion. He would take that passion and turn it towards the social sphere, drumming up interest and VIP support in the ramp up to an actual release, which would build the buzz months online ahead of Las Vegas.

Then there was Bernard, the aged legal counsel for the team. Bernard was sixty-seven. Bernard looked like Santa Claus after a year on the Atkins diet. Bernard carried around Tupperware containers all the time, most of them filled with strips of chicken or garbanzo beans, both of which could stench up a room within five seconds of cracking the corner of the container. Bernard was a man of few words, but when he uttered them, it often contained the phrases *legal precedent, you shit-head* or *corporate guidelines*. Bernard would make sure we didn't do anything illegal, so you can imagine how quickly he took on the role of "angry patriarch" in the group.

"Can you lend me some money for beer and then can I borrow your car to go to a party?" Dustin asked him one day, screwing with him.

"Listen up, you shithead," he said, louder than you'd expect. "Corporate guidelines state that no employee may lend or authorize the use of their motor vehicle to be used to purchase illegal substances during working hours. There's *legal precedent*, by the way." Usually, everything that Bernard spouted was followed up by a growl reminiscent of the Hell dogs from *Ghostbusters*.

Bernard was a Hell dog himself, and came highly recommended. Even Elise knew his name, reminding me that she had heard he "almost had been hired by O.J. Simpson to defend him."

"That can't be true," I had said, falling into typical patterns of those who came before me and will remain nameless from this point forward.

The overhead projector *whirred* to life and we all watched as the screen powered up to reveal a grid that was labeled with each of our names. Rafi pulled his feet beneath him, sitting on the ergonomic chair like a kid restless to be done at the dinner table, balancing his laptop on his knees. On-screen, a progress bar quickly filled completely green, flashing the message "Uploading Complete."

"Thank you for helping us beta-test this early version of Memphis, version two," Rafi began. "Thanks to Cameron's ingenious suggestions and leadership, we rebuilt the backend and pivoted the algorithm's focus from what your social network cared about to what we think *you* care about based on your real-time interactions with those in your life. What you're about to see is the output from that new algorithm, accompanied by a new alert-driven interface that will verbalize the vocabulary and key phrases used to generate the resulting recommendations."

I didn't quite know what the hell he was talking about until a small speaker icon appeared on the bottom right of the screen and a pleasant British woman's voice came through the speakers. "Memphis ready," the woman spoke. From the sound of her voice, she was obviously attractive, well-toned, and probably would have never given me the time of day. In the real world, it was exactly the type of woman who could tell me what to do. Or what to watch. Or what to buy. It was *perfect*.

"Let's begin," said Rafi, hovering the mouse over the first box labeled "Jane." He clicked a button and a slew of text scrolled quickly by. If you squinted you could make out a portion of blurred texts and e-mail messages. Then the scrolling text gave way to a myriad of recommendations, which my new British lady friend began to reference.

"Stress… Blind date… So overwhelmed it's funny…" said Chloe, the British voice of Memphis, who I had named in that very moment due to her poise, intelligence and dry sarcastic sense of humor. Next to me, I witnessed Jane, squirming in her seat as the recommendations started to appear. "You might like *Bridget Jones' Diary*," Chloe said, "and *The Devil Wears Prada*," as the movie posters appeared in her grid. Chloe continued, announcing a slew of other movies and books where the protagonist and Jane seemingly had loads in common. It was the typical story of a woman feeling out of place, overwhelmed by the day-to-day, and looking for love in all the wrong places. A Barbra Streisand album showed up, too.

"But that's not-" Jane began to stammer, then slumped down in her seat as everyone turned to look at her, seemingly wanting her true opinion. "I *own* every single one of those movies," she said, re-lenting.

"One for five," one of Rafi's statistical henchmen said as he wrote the score up on the whiteboard behind us.

"Let's keep going," I said, noticing the rest of the team eyeing their connected devices with disdain. Elise subversively attempted to pull the cord out of her phone, but my look diffused *that* bomb as well. Rafi turned our attention back to the screen and hovered over Dustin's part of the grid. He clicked on the button to execute the next set of rec-ommendations.

"Hotties… Variant cover… Must have…" spoke Chloe. "You might like *Jay and Silent Bob Strike Back* and the *Kingdom Come* graph-ic novel," she said, populating his grid with geeky science fiction, com-ic books and the latest album from *The Lonely Island*. Dustin nodded, with a big smile on his face, less embarrassed and more embracing.

"Oh yeah, that's me," he said proudly, letting his geek flag fly.

Chloe continued her assault on the team, calling out the key phrases that repeated themselves over and over again in each of our electronic communications. Elise's recommended movies ranged from *Three Days of the Condor*, *The Manchurian Candidate* and *Charlie's An-gels* while Bernard's recommendations revealed more about the man than any of us could have imagined – surfacing up nothing but movies, comic books and television episodes focused on *My Little Pony*.

"I have granddaughters, you *shitheads*," he grumbled. "*They* use my phone to watch the damn shows. I don't text for shit's sake." His defensiveness was way more amusing than the perceived reality that Bernard was a *Brony*, which was obviously, completely not the case. We thought. Potentially. Maybe, maybe-not. It was anyone's guess. Or not. *Whatever.*

"A good edge case," said Rafi. "We have to ensure that the kernel suspends data collection when the main user signed in is *not* the owner of the device and we can use facial recognition to double-check that." Another one of Rafi's engineering henchmen (who I would later refer to as *Dr. Detail*) scribbled down every single piece of feedback that made it out of anyone's mouth.

Then it was my turn. I was so pumped watching the recommen-dations come to life with the glorious Chloe at the helm, that I didn't put much thought into what might come up on my part of the grid until the words actually started appearing.

"Kiss me… Cuddle me… Help me…" Chloe spoke eloquently, making me momentarily uncomfortable with the two affectionate phrases and the reality that punctuated them both. I smiled through them as they appeared, trying to separate my thoughts from the situation I was dealing with at home. It was obvious to me that Jess had become extremely dependent and needy over the last set of months and was hungry for something…or *someone* to help her. *Kiss Me… Cuddle Me… Help me…* While the rest of the folks in the room may not have gleaned the significance of the three phrases together, it weaved together a story that both made me feel uncomfortable and guilty all at the same time.

Chloe's silky-smooth voice chimed back in, suggesting the movies *Pretty Woman* and *Love Actually* along with *Sleeping with the Enemy*.

"Isn't that the movie where Julia Roberts fakes her death to escape an abusive husband only to run into the arms of a new love interest in a small town?" asked Dustin.

"Aren't you the guy who shouldn't, in any way, know the brief plot summary to *Sleeping With the Enemy*?" Elise joked.

"I'm not an abusive stalker husband nor is there any abuse in our life," I said defensively. "That particular suggestion feels *off*." Which it was. But the way Chloe and Memphis took the themes of my real-time life and turned them into suggestions was intriguing. And exciting.

I wanted to share the joy with the one person who I cared about the most. Still the middle of the day, Jess would be at home alone, and would never suspect that I would walk through the front door so early on a work day. I headed for the parking garage – I would drive home, surprise her and share the awesome news.

The parking garage elevator doors opened up and I stepped out into the underground, weaving through parked cars on my way to the far edge of the fourth floor. I passed by a particularly overcrowded motorcycle parking area, filled to the brim with dozens of extremely pricey "million-dollar motorcycles." The story behind the phrase had been relayed to me many times – how in the days of The Company's richest stock rewards, employees would often cash in stock one week to buy a motorcycle, only to wish they had waited. For when the following week would arrive and the stock would split again, what was worth twelve-thousand one week would be worth fifty times that the following week. And thus, the "million-dollar motorcycles" legend was born. I half wondered if *that* had been how Simon had purchased his.

I pulled out my keys as I approached my car, ready to wirelessly unlock it when I noticed a strangely *familiar* individual out of the corner of my eye. My immediate instincts, ingrained in me from the years of training I received while playing *The Last of Us* in my man cave, were to find cover immediately so I could get a clearer look. I dove down, slammed my head against a tire, and nursed my head wound as I crept up to look through the closest car window.

And there she was. Ten car lengths away, standing by the trunk of her car, talking animatedly to a man who had his back to me was… *Romy*. Somewhere in my head, a tribe of African women warriors let out a lyrical shriek – the kind they would make right before they ripped their enemies' hearts out. *What is she doing here on the 4th floor?* Just having her anywhere near my vicinity made the competitiveness rise within my blood, which also ironically felt a little like acid reflux. She waved her hands in that annoying way she normally did, probably bragging about some other ridiculous product she didn't care about but which she would usher into the history books. *She's got nothing on me and Memphis*, I thought. At least, that's what I thought until the man with his back to me turned around.

It was Shane McCullough. He blathered on about yet another "game changer" in his self-important British accent, waving his hands in enthusiastic accordance with Romy's hand motions. The two of them could have been supplying their voices to the next generation version of *Peanuts'* cartoon teachers – *wah wah wah wah wah waaaah* all the way home.

In my imagination, my iron-clad self, stood face to face with the evil, magic-wielding *Sorceress-Bitch*, her wooden staff with the glowing green orb lighting up the surroundings in an evil shroud so paralyzing, I could not move. "Your mortal powers stand no chance against my magic," she cackled, striking a pose that threw up her black robe in dramatic slow-motion, that was accompanied by a blinding flash of light. When my eyes could see again, not only was the *Sorceress-Bitch* standing there, but by her side was a black Knight wielding an on-yx-colored blade. He reached up to his helmet, flipping up the faceplate, revealing a pair of glowing eyes that accompanied a very familiar face. "Together, we are unstoppable," the visual representation of Shane bellowed. I stared at the two of them then over my shoulder at the Horde – they were also closing fast. The situation before me represented a challenge I currently had no solution for. Blocked on both sides, I was fresh out of ideas.

Back in the real world, I cursed to myself – watching Romy and Shane part ways and pull out of the parking lot in their respective cars. *A Mercedes and a Porsche*, I lamented, watching them speed away. *German cars,* I thought, shaking my head. *Figures.*

I got in my car, throwing my head back against the headrest. *Et tu Romy*, I said aloud. *Three* times. What project could they possibly be working on together? What shared motivations did they have? Romy had a reason to want to beat me, especially with Las Vegas at stake. And Shane? I had caused the complete dismantling of his pride and joy. If he didn't want revenge, he was not the egotistical person I knew him to be. The two of them together represented an alliance I had not expected. They were the *Master* and *Blaster* to my Mad Max. And everyone knew what happened when you put Cameron in the Thunderdome. We all would enter… And *they* would *leave.*

I flipped on my sunglasses. Put the car in gear. I backed up, *peeling out* as I swung ninety degrees. I caught a glimpse of myself in the rear view, giving myself a particularly confident sneer. *Handsome devil,* I thought someone else who saw me in the rearview mirror might have thought. I let my foot drop hard, punching the gas with reckless abandon.

The car jumped and stalled, coughing up a lung.

Back at home, somebody wasn't just coughing up a lung, they were coughing up their soul. The sounds were unbearably loud as I entered my house that afternoon, excited to surprise a good-natured Jess with the exciting developments about Memphis, unaware that I would be met with something far more heinous.

"*Read my lips. Total breakdown.*" Jess' words echoed in my head as I rounded the corner to find her collapsed on the family room carpet, wrapped up in Kate's *Little Mermaid* blanket, face swollen from crying, body heaving from uncontrollable fits of hyperventilation, eyes completed trained on a network soap opera that blasted loudly through the surround sound. She hadn't seen me yet, and I took the opportunity to duck below the pony wall, in an attempt to assess the situation before actually poking the bear with a stick.

"Just checking in – everything okay?" I texted. *Bloop.* On the other side of the wall, I could hear her pause in her total breakdown and reach for her cell phone. The clicking of the keyboard echoed over the TV, where a bare-chested Wall Street Mogul ravished an almost bare-chested blonde Nuclear Scientist *slash* Interior Decorator twin.

"It's not. I'm mad at you," she texted back. *Bzzzt,* vibrated my phone. With all the texting lately, I had minimally ensured any texts vibrated rather than the annoying alternative.

"Mad at *me*? Why me?" I texted back. *Bloop.*

"Because you are *never* here for me. You dragged me up to this god forsaken place and left me alone. Now I have nothing," she texted back. *Bzzzt.*

I slumped down further to the ground, getting a better two-handed grip on the phone, readying to type a mini-*War and Peace* explaining that this had been a mutual decision. That we were here because I had saved the family from destitution. But my elbow knocked the phone in such a way that it hit the hot key for Memphis. The recommendation engine spun up.

"You might like *Kramer vs. Kramer* or *War of the Roses*," Chloe's voice reverberated out the speaker of my phone. *Shit.* I quickly jammed my phone off, only to hear the shuffling of a children's blanket-encased livid wife turning towards the audio cue.

"Cameron?" she questioned, projecting her voice. *Shit shit shit.* I had to think of something clever and endearing. Something that would diffuse the situation. As far as Chloe was concerned, we were on the cusp of divorce or a violent mutual death, so I had to act quickly.

I slowly and cautiously rose. "Remember a few seconds ago when you said I was *never* here for you?" I said. Jess *screamed*, scared silly. It didn't have the impact I had hoped as the breakdown returned full force.

I ran over to her, kneeling at her on the floor, trying to put my arms around her. She pushed me back. Hard. I braced myself from falling backwards, face surprised at her blatant physicality. She saw how surprised I was, and did it again.

"Come *on*," I yelled, wrapping her tightly in Ariel's face. "Stop it."

She struggled to get out of her Disney*fied* trap, finally giving up out of pure fatigue. I let her slump down to the carpet, where she collapsed.

"I didn't sign up for this," she said.

"We agreed to come here, together."

"I guess I never expected it would *feel* this way. I guess I never expected *I* would feel this way."

"What way?" I asked, laying down next to her so our faces were closer together. I used my thumb to wipe the tears that continued to well up in her eyes.

"I'm lonely."

"What am I, *chopped liver*?"

"You are *never* here, Cam. Even when you are, you're still not here. You're *distracted* by work. I can't ever get your attention. It's like I'm doing all of this all by myself."

"That's not fair," I said, defensively, knowing that it actually *was*. I had been absent for the last few weeks. I had been so focused on Memphis that I had rarely saw Jess or Kate. I was never good at multi-tasking work and life, I thought, reflecting back on the moments in the past when I had disappeared for weeks on end to finish a screenplay. But back then had been different, since Jess had her own work to keep her busy. Here in Seattle she had *nothing*.

"What can I do?" I said.

"Be *nice*," she said. "Be *present*," she shoved me. "Be my partner. Not my roommate."

"I will try my best," I nodded, pulling her even closer.

"Not try," she crooked her head to look into my eyes. "*Do*." Had it been Derrik, I might have made a Yoda reference, but it just didn't seem like the right time or place.

Jess turned, gazing up at the soap opera still on the TV. "Was it a sad part?" I asked, giving her the benefit of the doubt despite the fact that a circus midget had kidnapped a pop star and was driving them off a cliff into the Panama Canal.

"I wasn't crying because of the show," she said, "although it kind of set me off because it reminded me of how I used to book the *people* on that show for appearances. I used to shadow them on press lines. I used to get the *New York Times* to write about them." I gave her a look of surprise. "*The New York Times* online," she clarified.

"What do you mean, it 'set you off'?"

"I miss having a *job* that doesn't involve carpooling and hair combing. I need an outlet. I need to solve problems," she said. "I need to resolve conflicts, come up with creative ideas, interact with real adults in real adult situations. And I need you to, once and for all, take me seriously and help me do that."

"Then I'll do it," I said, thinking for a beat. "What *exactly* do you need me to do?" She wiped her eyes, pulling the blanket off her, and revealing some burlap sack of an outfit that needed to be burned immediately.

She had a thought, evidenced by her wriggling out of my embrace and turning to face me with a mischievous grin. I was glad to see the emotional change, but leery of what was coming next. She had obviously ruminated on this one many times before this particular moment.

"Bring me to a meeting. Just *once*. Let me remind myself what it used to feel like. Maybe it sparks some ideas."

"You want *me* to bring *you* to a meeting at The Company?" I stared, slack jawed. "But you don't even officially work there."

"You're always saying how these meetings are bloated exercises in futility, no? Where half the time people don't even know everyone in the room? I'll observe. I'll sit in the back of the room. No one will know any better."

I paused a long pause. It was the kind of pause a person made when a relative in desperate need of a kidney asked you to donate your spare one. Nobody truly had a *spare* kidney, or else we wouldn't have been given two of them. And at The Company, no meeting was insignificant or disposable… *Shit.* I couldn't even think it in my head without the bullshit alarms going off. Half my day was filled with insignificant meetings that had no impact on *anything*.

"Do you want *Kramer versus Kramer* up in this here hizouse?" she asked, jokingly. But with a hint of dead pan seriousness.

June

In war, Generals often wouldn't wear uniforms or stripes on the battlefield for fear of being identified as such, increasing the risk of capture
or subsequent assassination. At The Company, employees often wouldn't
wear suits, ties, dresses or any other professional Wall Street-*esque* fash-
ions for fear of being identified as a "person of interest." Because if you
weren't rocking high tops, flip flops, logo t-shirts, tank tops, jeans or
Dockers, you were either interviewing for a new job or meeting with
CVPs in an attempt to build your empire and steal away employees from
another team. People were always leery of a button-down shirt or a casual
sports jacket, and the questions embodied the epitome of passive-aggressive misdirection.

"Nice threads. Going to a bar-mitzvah?"

"Lookin' sharp today, Pal. Interviewing for CEO?"

"I see the Madoff look is back in season."

Yet when Jess walked into an official conference room for an official meeting that I had *unofficially* told her about – the Wall Street-
hot power suit, high stiletto heels and hair blown out like the 90's were
back again *look* didn't raise any ridiculous questions or uncomfortable
thoughts. But was ZZ Top's "She's Got Legs" playing in my mind as she

casually found a seat at the back of the room, keeping to herself? Did half the room look at her, pondering via inner-monologue who she was and what level of hierarchy she had descended down from? Did she break out a yellow legal pad, fountain pen and start taking notes like she had a bajillion concerns and questions to address in today's brownbag meeting about Corporate Responsibility and Ethics? Yes, of course, and *definitely*.

I had chosen a meeting carefully for her coming out party. I had steered clear of meetings with my team or org stakeholders. Instead, I had invited her to one of The Company's many "brownbags." These were meetings designed to instruct and inform employees on a variety of topics that ranged from business overviews and product walkthroughs to International and Legal guidelines. They called them "brownbags" because I assumed, at some point, before all the free drinks and over-priced boutique restaurants that had cropped up at The Commons, people had actually, unbelievably, brought their own lunches to work in…yes you guessed it – brown *bags*.

Sitting across the room, I shared a quick glance with Jess, who put on a pair of sharp-looking glasses and tried not to show any emotion whatsoever. Inside, of course, I knew she was screaming with delight at the fluorescent lights, conference room chairs and a myriad of discarded office supplies on the table and floors. "Remember," she had told me that morning, "no matter what we do *not* know each other."

"What if they arrest you?" I posited, playfully.

"*Especially* if they arrest me," she replied, obviously dedicated to the ruse at hand. It would give me a chance to employ the help of a Bail Bondsman, which had always been a personal dream.

I looked up at the clock, as did others in the room. It was already four minutes past the start of the meeting and no one had arrived to get things moving. At The Company, the rule of thumb was that if no one showed in ten minutes, everyone was free to abandon the meeting in question. It wasn't a *rule* per se, as sanctioned by some governing body at a high level in the hive mind – but rather a crowd-sourced *opinion* that had wormed its way into the consciousness of the worker bees.

"We're ready if you are," someone said, leaning over to Jess. It wasn't nearly a surprise seeing as though she was the only person within a mile wearing a *suit*. A few others, including me, waited to see what this woman's response would be.

"Oh, no – I'm here to participate…just like you," she said, turning back to her yellow pad and trying to diffuse any awareness of her presence as the conference room door opened to reveal the actual person who owned the brownbag.

"Sorry folks, so sorry," said the Corporate Responsibility and Ethics Guru as he quickly hooked up his computer to the overhead projector and sat down at the last remaining open seat. "Today we're going to talk about ethics and how to ensure that your actions at The Company adhere to the high expectations the senior leaders have for all of us. As a part of ethics, we'll discuss how being honest, protecting internal secrets and confidential information from outsiders, and not taking advantage of The Company's generosity all represent significant areas of concern and focus in today's corporate climate."

The next forty minutes represented the most uncomfortable forty minutes of my entire life as every topic on the docket seemed to be perfectly tailored to the scenario where I had illegally invited Jess to the meeting in question. Snuck someone into The Company without true purpose or necessity? *Check.* Allowed a non-employee access to confidential areas of Company buildings while products or services were being developed out in the open? *You know it.* Provided or gifted supplies or items of a monetary value, like yellow legal pads, pens or post-its to family members or friends? *Yes sir!* I sunk lower in my seat as the session went on, ensuring my laptop bag was ready to go so I could sneak out before I had been caught. With fifteen minutes left, our Guru of gab opened up the floor for questions.

"These ethics guidelines have changed since last year," announced a silver-haired woman, obviously far more concerned with consistency than content. "Can you speak to the methodology and specific changes included in these revisions?"

Another employee across the table from her chimed in before the Guru could. "I think we should use the time that's left to focus on questions about ethics specifically and we can take an action item to follow-up on the changes to the policy later," the guy eating a yogurt parfait shot back.

You had to laugh. *Everybody* at The Company had to get a thought in edgewise. If you didn't speak, you didn't exist. As the silver-haired

Woman and the yogurt parfait Guy began debating more passionately how the remaining time in the brown bag meeting should be used, the one person who *wasn't supposed to exist* decided to make her thoughts known.

"People... *People!*" Jess got everyone's attention, placing her stack of office supplies on the table in front of her. *Damn her*, I thought, as I gave her the evil eye. Of course, she didn't see it because she was making a point to not look in my direction. "Are we *seriously* arguing about policy version control when we could be using the time to ask questions about real daily scenarios?" Then she stood up, and started pacing.

Good God.

"I know I would *much rather* spend my time discussing how to put these learnings into practice," she continued, stopping behind the Guru to give him a double-shoulder squeeze, "than debating operational issues." Jess made her way to the front of the room, passing in front of the screen as she made her way around the horn. Her eyes were lit up, she was feeling the buzz – and there was no stopping the train. "I mean, why waste time on worthless endeavors," she continued, pointing to her eyes then the eyes of everyone around the table, "that only reduces our ability to be productive and proactive? If that's your bag, then you might as well leave this building right now...and head home instead, where you can wipe snotty noses and carpool screaming children to swim lessons... Where you would be forced to listen to stay at home mothers drone on about loose teeth, scabs and food allergies. Where you might find yourself spreading prescription-strength hemorrhoid cream on a four-year old's *ass*. Is that really what all of you would rather do?"

The entire room shook their heads "no" – it chilled them all to the bone. Nobody truly knew what the hell was going on here, but I suspected some assumed it was some secret Ethics group good cop/bad cop routine that had been covertly arranged for today's session.

"Neither do I," said Jess, grabbing her office supplies and pausing by the door. "So, make it count, *people*. Before you don't have a choice."

She was out. The room was silent for at least ten seconds while the Guru regained his own composure – not quite sure what had just happened.

"She has a point," said the silver-haired Woman.

"Can four-year-old kids get hemorrhoids?" asked the yogurt parfait guy.

I got up and bolted for the door.

"Oh my God," Jess breathed, nodding. The two of us sat on an outside bench, in the glorious sunlight, just outside of the Studios buildings in the middle of the grassy quad. "Don't take this the wrong way, hon," she continued, "but that was orgasmic."

"I'd go with *panic-attack inducing*," I said, scratching my head. "What were you thinking in there?"

"That's just it," she said, eyeing the notes on her yellow pad. "I wasn't. It was all *instinct*."

"So, great," I said sarcastically, taking the office supplies back from her. "And what is your instinct telling you *now*?"

Jess paused, straightening herself up. "I'm a solver, darling," she said, wrapping her arm around my shoulder, gazing out at the horizon with a look of adventurous hope. "And what I realized in there just now is that Los Angeles hasn't cornered the market on problems. Doesn't matter where I am - there are people, organizations and *meetings* that need my help."

"It's a big world out there," I said, eyeing said fictitious adventurous hope at the horizon. Of course, Jess was already drinking her own Kool-Aid.

"So, I'll be busy," she grinned, giving me a kiss on the cheek. "There are worse things than that."

Oh yes, I thought. *Yes they are.*

Mitch DeForrest was never quiet. Nor was he ever stunned into silence. Yet there he was, sitting at the head of the conference room table, mere seconds after Rafi and my team had presented the Memphis recommendation engine tests to him, having trouble finding the words. Did he hate it? Did he love it? You desperately *wanted* him to love it, because if he did, then you'd have Mitch D on your side. He'd go to the ends of the Earth for you. He'd even save your life - as was evidenced by the fiberglass cast on his right arm; the result of our resident MacGyver rescuing a fellow mountain climber from a fatal fall the previous day. "The power of one single arm," he had claimed confidently on his way into the meeting that day, "beat God at his own game."

"Words *are* emotion," I said, tossing a packet of results down the table to him, where they stuck underneath his mammoth cast. "Emotion *drives* action. And action drives money. What we had previously was a copycat product. What we have now is market leading."

He nodded, biting his lower lip. "*Wicked* good," he said, repeating it five more times in a whisper as he gave the entire contingency at the table a confident glare. "Can I just tell you," he said, standing up and pacing the room, "that during this entire presentation I felt no pain in my arm despite having shattered my Humeral Lateral Epicondyle and Flexor Digitorum Sublimis?"

Everyone nodded, smiling. *Epicondyle-what* everybody in the room wondered, while I personally wondered how to spell it. Mitch D. must have sensed the confusion, so he clarified, "Memphis is so good, that it made me forget the pain. Sign of a killer product. *Escapism*, people!"

Then came the snapping. When Mitch D. was excited, he started snapping at people. He was a good snapper. I thought I was a good snapper, but I was more of a thin treble snapper to Mitch D's thick full-bodied bass snapper. Ben Packer, our CEO, was also a pretty stellar snapper. *Great timbre,* I remember thinking when he had snapped at the camera during his video at NEO. Apparently, snapping and your ability to do so successfully, had some indirect correlation with your position in The Company.

"Next steps?" he *snapped* in Rafi's direction.

"Lock down the algorithm. Eight-man weeks of coding before we take it to focus groups," Rafi spouted back.

"Product wise?" he *snapped* at me.

"Early sneaks with taste makers and digital bloggers. *Wired* magazine. Explore partnerships, build the marketing and social plan, build a business model around affiliate programs so when people buy a product based on our recommendations, we generate revenue." As I finished each of my statements, Mitch D. *snapped* along. It was like a low rent version of *Hamilton* except there were no singers or dancers – just a guy in an arm cast who thought he was God.

"Okay, now… I'm feeling it," Mitch D. bounced in place. "Ideas… They're coming." Everyone looked to me, scared for their life, because when Mitch D. had ideas you knew they were going to challenge logic, space and time all at once. We held onto our armrests, preparing for the worst. I pulled out my smartphone and started to take notes.

"Let's reach out to *FlixFix*," he excitedly announced, scrawling the name of the company on the whiteboard for extra dramatic effect. "They are the undisputed streaming movie service with over a hundred and fifty-million unique monthly subscribers. We find a way to partner our engine with their service."

It wasn't a question. It was matter-of-fact. Still, a reasonable request based on *FlixFix*'s global market penetration. "Jane, take an action item," I said, turning to her. She smiled, but it was that kind of smile you gave right before you blew chunks.

"*FlixFix* is notoriously against sharing data or generally partnering with anyone," she mustered the courage to get out, diverting her eyes the minute she had said it.

"Are you telling me," Mitch D. swung around, directing it to Jane, "that if we landed in front of *FlixFix*'s corporate headquarters on a flying elephant while holding a gigantic twenty-four karat gold check in the amount of a *billion dollars*, they would still be against partnering with us?"

"Do we have a flying elephant?" she asked, sidestepping the obvious question of finances because everyone knew The Company *did have* a billion dollars to blow.

"Beside the point," Mitch D. shot back. "Would they be open to partnering if we did?"

"A flying elephant *and* a billion dollars?" she questioned back.

"Yes."

"Well, I'm sure I can't say they *wouldn't* be open to partnering if that situation arose."

"Thank you," Mitch D. *snapped* back, leaving Jane to figure out how to find the elusive gravity-immune creature categorized *Elephantidae* of the order *Proboscidea* and learn how to ride it into the air space of the one-and-only Beverly Hills.

"Now, the one issue I foresee," he continued, "is that people won't want to install Memphis without knowing how great it is, and they won't know how great it is unless they install it. How do we feel about pre-installing it without requiring a consumer's authorization to do so?"

"How do you feel about five to ten years in a Federal prison?" asked Bernard, mouthing *"you shithead"* under his breath.

"If the NSA, a *Federal organization*, can do it – why can't we?"

"Because they're the *government* and we're not," Bernard shot back. You had to love Bernard, he was so close to death anyway he didn't care about ruffling feathers of higher ups.

"Double check for me," Mitch D. replied.

"Yeah, I'll be sure to do that," Bernard grumbled.

"OK. Finally," Mitch D. *clapped* his hands, then machine-gunned a selection of *Glengarry Glen Ross* salesman snaps around the room, "celebrity spokesperson. I'm thinking…Roger Ebert. The most trusted human movie recommendation engine in the History of mankind."

"Roger Ebert is dead," I spoke up, pantomiming the spilling of my virtual forty-ounce beer in memoriam, which no one noticed or understood. I pulled back my virtual forty embarrassed, much like I'd done when someone had left me hanging, waiting for a handshake.

"I don't care if he's dead. He's our guy. Get him." This was Mitch D. at his finest, I thought. Sure, perhaps we could have stitched wings onto an elephant especially in light of all the great work that had been done giving Dolphins replacement flippers, but barring digging up the world's most famous movie reviewer from the dirt – I wasn't quite sure how we'd swing it.

"You mean, like get his Estate to give Memphis a plug?" asked Dustin, smartly trying to think around the conundrum currently on the table before us.

"No. I want *him*," demanded Mitch D.. "Hell, they got Tupac to sponsor a vacuum or something after he died, why can't we get Ebert?"

"Actually, he did a concert," responded Dustin. "And it was his hologram."

"So, get his *hologram,* then. How do we get in touch with his hologram?"

"Everything having to do with Ebert has to go through Chaz," piped in Elise. "I once met Chaz at the Telluride Film Festival," she announced. "Biggest ballbuster I've ever shared a spicy shrimp tempura role with."

"Who the hell is Chaz?" asked Mitch D., now slightly fatigued by the line of questioning he had spun up.

"Chaz is…*was* his wife," Elise finished up. "I can try to get her number through some of my more reliable sources."

"Okay, so *action items*," I piped in, checking my own notes on my phone. "Rafi's on point for the software build." He nodded, totally on board, as I looked to my team. "Jane will research the *FlixFix* flying elephant partnership opportunity, Bernard will double check that we can't operate like the NSA does, and Elise will call Roger Ebert's widow to see if his hologram can be our celebrity spokesperson." I turned to Mitch D. "Does that sound about right?"

It sounded *insane*.

"*Golden*," Mitch D. said, standing up and going through a comical set of motions just to reach the door handle with his cast-encased right arm. "I'll get updates from Cameron in our one-on-one. Great work everyone! Keep it up!" As he excited the door, he started to say "I'm feeling greatness coming on…" but it was short lived due to some run-in with an aluminum hallway garbage pail. Rafi ran to the door to look out.

"He's okay!" Rafi shouted, arms up like a referee in the end zone.

I turned to look at the rest of the group. Their contorted, disgruntled faces said it all.

Simon Davis had a tricked-out metallic silver golf cart. It had been given to him on his twentieth anniversary at The Company, in lieu of the pounds of M&Ms and the heavy crystal paperweights employees at the five, ten and fifteen year marks were so lucky to have received. It had a polished silver name plate affixed just under the ignition with the words "Simon Davis. For Your 20 Years of Service. Thanks for 'Starting' us up." I hadn't known that Simon had the golf cart, nor had he ever mentioned to me in our short discussions that he owned one or drove one across campus at mind-numbing speeds. Truly, the only way I knew, was because on my way across campus to my new office in Studio D, he drove over both my feet.

"Get in," he said, concealed in a hoodie and sunglasses, and looking more like the Unibomber than even the Unibomber could have claimed.

I looked up from the sidewalk, holding onto both my feet because *they hurt*. "Are you crazy?"

"Kid. Get in this golf cart if you want to live," he said, poking his head out of the hoodie just enough to make it sound serious.

I got in. Mostly for the story, but also because with him there was always a slim chance his warnings might actually be real.

Simon hit the gas (if that's what you preferred to call it) and the golf cart sped forward, swerving quickly out of the center of the Commons and onto the back roads used by The Company's service vehicles. We quickly entered an area that was unfamiliar to me in all my travails on campus, behind structures, warehouses and the errant professional "four-square" court.

"What the *hell* is going on!?" I asked, out of breath, turning to the maniac at the wheel as tree branches *snapped* as we careened past. Apparently, I was the only one stressing out.

"Nothing really," he replied stoic, eyes focused on the road ahead. Um, ninety seconds ago it had been a life-or-death situation and now Simon was calmer than I had ever seen him before.

"Get in this golf cart if you want to *live?*" I repeated, questioning the validity of his statement now that there appeared to be no pressing issues or dangers.

"An *expression* of timeliness," he replied. "Like, *get your hands in the vehicle NOW*," he yelled – startling me to do just that as the golf cart took a sharp detour, down a tiny driveway, through overgrown trees and brush, under an overhang, and in through what appeared to be a metal-grated garage door that was open and ready for the vehicle's arrival. The golf cart slammed to a *stop* once inside and the grating behind us closed automatically. A machine *whirred* to life and the platform on which we were parked began to descend, brick walls rising above us on all sides.

There were pictures, magazine articles and old banners on all of the walls – they slowly rose around us as the lift descended further. Mostly, there were articles highlighting the heyday of The Company, with shots of the original founders and their dated hair styles and ancient computers. With each ten feet we descended, the further back we went in time. A significantly younger version of Simon Davis smiled out from a few pictures, seemingly just at the outset of what would become the longest beard growing experiment in the History of beard growing experiments. I felt like the Jules Verne of elevator photo and news clipping time travel.

"Where are we?" I asked, turning towards the wistful Simon, who gazed at the walls longingly.

"My *other* workstation," he nodded, turning his attention to the space in front of us as the lift came to a grinding halt and a new gate rose before us. "The one that's *off* the grid. That no one knows about." Simon got up and out of the golf cart, heading past the gate and down a concrete hall. Something mechanical started to make a *buzzing* sound in the background, startling me – so I quickly got up and gave chase as fast as I could.

Simon had called it a 'workstation' but no one would have argued had he called it a *home*. For all intents and purposes, it was, with a full kitchen, living room, bathroom and bedroom – all surrounded by glass and painted metal that made the underground loft feel like a *Tesla* dealership. On one side sat multiple metal lab tables, covered in wires and in-progress tech, on the other a wall of monitors that appeared to track the entire campus of The Company. Simon made his way to a double-wide refrigerator that looked like the front grill of an eighteen-wheeler and pulled out a pair of cold beers. I stood there, mouth agape, in the center of it all.

"You're like *Batman*," I said, half expecting an older butler to show up with tea and a crumbly dessert of my choosing.

"*You're like Batman*," came a high-pitched mimic, which turned out to be a Parrot who had just landed onto Simon's shoulder as he made his way back to me.

"Cameron, meet Hal," he said as he reached up and gave Hal a crumbly dessert of his choosing. "He's an African Grey. One of the most intelligent birds in the world."

Of course, he was. Would I have expected any less? If the twenty-fifth hire of The Company, who was also one of the most revered technological visionaries of the last three decades was going to have a pet... It had to be,

endangered

extremely smart, and

skilled in the art of mocking the less intelligent

I tilted the beer back, taking a swig, although I couldn't even tell you what kind of beer it was or how it tasted because I was so stunned by the virtual onion Simon kept peeling in front of my eyes. With each strip came another amazing revelation and a slew of burning questions.

"Do you live down here?" I asked, taking it all in. "And where, exactly, is *here*?"

"I said 'off the grid' when what I should have said was *under*," he nodded. "Directly under the campus power grid. And yeah, these are my digs. Have been for the last ten."

"Ten *years*?"

"*Ten years*," said Hal. I glared at him. Simon gave him another treat. *No wonder.*

Simon turned and walked away from me, resembling a pirate, with his shoulder-perched parrot buddy and his cold brew in hand. He jumped onto the leather couch, turning back and motioning for me to join him. I followed, sitting opposite him in a chair. Simon eyed me, quiet, until it started to get uncomfortable. I had to say something. I needed to understand-

"Why *me*?" I began. I'd already let him poke through my phone and my laptop and find new ways to save the Company. But that had come and gone. Now I was just another guy at The Company who was trying to aspire to even one percent of what he had accomplished. Why was Simon Davis so interested in me?

Simon took a long swig of his beer and placed it down on the glass table in between us. "I'm here to help you," he said. "Because there are people out there, and you may not know it yet, who want to do the opposite."

Of course, there were. The list was long enough to make me proud and nervous all at the same time. There was Leah, my old manager, who I'm sure could claim I had something to do with her firing. There were my fellow MediaMesh co-workers, whose jobs had disappeared after I had conveniently engineered a coup. There was Shane McCullough. There was Romy Wallace. Some could even question Mitch D's intentions.

"But why *me*?" I repeated.

"Because…you're *me*," he exhaled. "Before I allowed those backstabbers up top to shut down my projects, poison my creativity and cause me to sacrifice my ingenuity." The words stung Simon as he spoke them. He shook his head, reflecting on the words which had made his long road even more real in that one moment. "Maybe if I can help you,

I'll have done something worthy at the end of the day."

"Something *worthy*?" I repeated, unbelieving. "But what's all *this*," I said, trying to turn him back into the intimidating and scary-intelligent twenty-fifth hire who re-arranged salad enigmatically by color, "that you're *creating* down here? God knows I can't pretend to even understand what any of it does, but if it's yours its got to have potential."

"That garbage," he pointed over his shoulder at the tables, "is called a time waster. None of it will ever benefit a single soul."

"Like all the work I've seen you do hasn't impacted a single soul?" I challenged, thinking back to how Simon had saved The Company from shipping products with broken technology. For a guy who was responsible for so much, he had so little faith in himself.

"Fixing other people's mistakes is a world away from *creating* something that matters," he disregarded. "My time came and went. And it was a good run. But that's history. Now it's time for someone else to make a difference. That's why…*you*."

"But who the heck am I?" Honestly, who was I to Simon Davis?

"Do you really have to ask that question after what you've accomplished in the last six months? You're the guy who had *zero* experience in the tech sector and shit for prospects in Hollywood and landed a job at The Company…"

"I had *some* prospects," I said, defensively.

"You're the guy who faced down the bullshit hierarchy and inane company policies while trusting your instincts instead of surrendering to your fears. And it got you noticed. Noticed enough to land a promotion in a product group where your ideas have already shaken things up. You're the first person who ever put Shane McCullough in his place!" he said, taking a deep breath and letting it out with an air of satisfaction. "That's who you are."

"What do you mean…I'm the guy who put *Shane McCullough* in his place?"

"Exactly *that*," he said. "And he deserved it, the bastard." A million data points swam around in my head at that very moment, causing me to wonder just what the connection was here between Simon and Shane. It had been the second time he had mentioned him in front of me.

"And that matters to you…*why*?"

He paused. Then let it out. "Because if it weren't for that back-stabbing bastard, Shane McCullough, I wouldn't be where I am today."

I sat in my office, contemplating life, the Universe and *conversation*.

The Shane McCullough and Simon Davis connection had my insides twisted into a knot. For the first time in months, I was questioning my actions and wondering who exactly had been behind them. Simon had clearly given me information that, if shared, would have potentially caused the shutdown of MediaMesh and the appropriation of Shane McCullough's unique talents into another area of The Company with far less impact or influence. But he hadn't sought me out or forced my hand. I had illegally entered Building 12 with my superior breaking and entering Navy S.E.A.L.-like skills, and had waited persistently at his door until *he* had given in. I was the one who had made the decision, thanks to the eerie whispers and sleepless mutterings of my adorable wife, to speak up in a meeting where Mitch DeForrest could have fired me on the spot; but promoted me instead. Or had I? Had someone else been pulling my strings?

Had it been Simon?

I tried to snap myself back to reality. What I needed to focus on now were the things I *did* have some element of control over. That was *Memphis*. That was protecting the project that would solidify my place at The Company while keeping the wolves at bay. The wolves that Simon had so ominously claimed were already circling my bloody, pungent carcass. There was no turning back now. I was living in a real-life version of the Robert Frost poem "The Road Less Traveled" with only two roads and one palatable outcome. There was *Failure Avenue* (the left path), which involved allowing Memphis to fail, losing my job and destroying my family's faith in me. And there was *Success Way SE* (the right path, in more ways than one), which involved manning up, fighting back the wolves with everything and every*one* in my corner, and making my family proud. Truly, there was only one *right* answer in a double entendre kind of way. Anything else involved me returning to Los Angeles a complete and total failure.

Which could…not…happen.

As the dread grew, the door to my office burst open. Rafi stood there, out of breath, with a look of total panic on his face.

"What is it?" I asked, spinning around in my chair.

"Need you *now*," was all he said.

"Is something wrong?" I asked, getting up, grabbing my phone.

"That would be an understatement," he said, bolting out the door and sprinting down the hallway as he yelled back, "follow me!"

There was *moaning*. And there was *screaming*. I chased down Rafi into the conference room where his entire team of misfit engineers were running around like chickens with their heads cut off. They were completely beside themselves with a nervousness and fear so palpable that the room felt thick with it. Oh, and there were *breasts*, too. And other female parts accepting male parts into their darkened palaces of pleasure.

"Porn," Rafi spoke, disgusted, directing my attention to the recommendation test grid, which was now filled with a slew of movie posters with the kind of imagery no Employee Handbook had ever explained how to handle. The faces and expressions and gaudy colorful fonts clogged up the screen like a hairball jammed in a cat's throat. "Memphis has been compromised," he said, throwing his phone onto the table in disgust.

And to add insult to injury, Chloe – the lovely cultured British voice of the product, was rambling off movie titles that she was sure we would *all love*, that I was sure no one would want their co-workers or extended family hearing out loud *ever*. Not even in the privacy of their own home. Chloe was a very *bad* girl. I imagined the Union Jack going up in flames.

"How did this happen?" I demanded, needing to take the tone of the guy in charge. "Everything was working. We're weeks away from having to demo this in front of potential VIPs and tech bloggers. We can't show them *this*!" And any delay would push us off our plan, which would reduce our ability to deliver the kind of package that would be needed to convince Ben Packer that we were the rock stars Mitch DeForrest wanted us to so desperately become.

Rafi eyed his team. "We're into it. But this wasn't our doing. Someone hacked into the code and completely altered the filtering method for the algorithm. Instead of hiding *this kind of content*, it did the exact opposite. It opened the floodgates."

"And we're locked out of making any changes to the code," said another one of Rafi's team. "It's going to take us at least eighty-man hours to get back in and fix this."

"Eighty-man hours?" I looked to Rafi.

"We've already started," he said, nodding to the team. They scrambled, turning off the projector, grabbing their technology and exiting the room. Rafi was the last to go, pausing at the door as I shook my head in dismay. "We've got it, *jefe*," he said. "And we'll get it done."

About ten seconds after he left, my cell phone *buzzed* with a text. It was from an "anonymous number." All the text contained was a single emoticon. A yellow face, slapping its cheeks with a look of horror. On a sunnier, happier day I might have marveled at how the emoticon had captured the childlike mischievousness of one Kevin McCallister after trying his father's aftershave while stuck in his Chicago home...*all alone*. But it wasn't sunny. And it wasn't happy. And it was no coincidence.

Simon had been right. *Someone* was out to get me.

July

*J*ane was crying uncontrollably.

"An elephant with w-w-wings," she sobbed, wiping her dripping nose across her shirt. At first, the crying fits had been embarrassing for me, driving me to avert my gaze from the ten-car pileup happening before me. Eventually, I just found myself fascinated. Let's face it – ten car pileups *did have* a *CHiPS-like* romanticism about them. *In my head*, I began referring to her as "Ponch" whenever she'd approach.

"I think we can both agree that Mitch D. is not expecting you to find a flying elephant," I placated her. She started to say something and I knew what it was, heading her off at the pass, "And no – there is no twenty-four karat billion-dollar check *either*." Oh, how Jess' recent breakdowns had prepared me well for what I was dealing with at this very moment.

"I'm just… Then what does he want?"

"Results," I said. "Get us a conversation with *FlixFix* however you can." Truly, once you made it past Mitch D's extreme personality, you could see the forest from the trees. "It's not the journey that matters," I said, imagining one of Hollywood's talented (yet overpaid) movie trailer voice talents speaking, "it's where you end up." *Cue music. Billing block. Winking Tom Hanks.* Ponch… I mean, *Jane*, looked at me. Took it all in. And the post nasal drip started to dry out.

"You are an amazing b-b-boss," she said, enamored. "You've managed a team of people before, haven't you?" *No. No I hadn't.*

"I've *managed* people," I said, using a grammatical loophole to make her feel like she was in good hands. She blew her nose as loud as a lighthouse foghorn.

"Well, *mister*, you are *good*," she said. "Look at me. I feel better already. I'm going to write you a note giving you feedback on your management style," she committed. "I like to give feedback. People underestimate just how helpful feedback can be. Positive *or* negative."

Oh, that's right. In addition to the forms and the forums and the meetings and the evaluations and the career counsels – there was feedback. Everybody *loved* giving feedback. Feedback was the answer to everything. Feedback, feedback, feedback.

"I welcome your feedback," I said, using the tools provided to me by my HR counterparts, to ensure I was open, accepting and welcoming of any and all useless criticism.

Jane got up, sniffled in her lingering tears and errant liquids, and headed for the door. "*You*," she pointed, smiling. "Fantastic." I nodded, watching her as she made her way out the door, closing it behind her. She poked her head in front of the window, smiling and mouthing "thank you." I smiled back.

Seattle in July was a glorious time. Never hotter than eighty-five degrees, never sunny enough to cause the news to report on heatstroke, never overcast enough to require Vitamin D. And it never applied to me since I was always *holed up in my office* holding one-one-one's with everybody and their mother. At least I had a window. I'd often look outside and see parents frolicking with their visiting children during lunch breaks. Employees soliciting unique food trucks that sold curry-infused fruit salads. Hugs, friendships and laughter. Just not with Bernard, the grumpiest, most-amusing, legally-trained bastard I had ever met.

"Total *bullshit*," said Bernard, who wasn't laughing at all. I turned back from the window toward him where he had shuffled a stapled document towards me at the table. I looked down at them. They were Bernard's commitments.

Commitments were the Company's way of keeping employees honest, focused and productive. At the beginning of every year, each employee committed to everything they'd accomplish over the next twelve months *in writing*. Their Managers would approve the commitments, assuming they believed they represented an accurate view of what could be accomplished in the given time. If the end of the year came and they hadn't met those goals, their annual review would be bad. If they exceeded those goals by the end of the year, management would refer to them as sandbaggers. If they hit them *exactly*, they were an "average employee." Bernard was, in the very moment he handed over his commitments, what people liked to refer to as "uncooperative."

"You have *three things* listed on your commits," I said, referencing the almost empty form.

"And I'll do 'em all," he said, slapping his hand on the table for added effect.

"You kind of need to, generally, commit to more than this," I stammered through, genuinely nervous that Bernard was always about six seconds away from snapping completely. "It's important for you to find *stretch* projects," I said, referring to the practice of adding completely unrealistic but exciting projects to ones' commitments despite never thinking they were possible.

"Doc says I shouldn't stretch for *shit*," he said, grabbing back the commits and crumbling them in his hand. "Corporate guidelines state that 'commitments must represent an employee's expected performance output to the best of their knowledge'. *This* is what you can expect. And *this* is why you hired me. I'll get'er done, don't you worry about that, son."

Then Bernard straightened out the doc, flattened in front of me, added some extra spit to smooth it out, and walked out the door. He didn't stop to smile through the window or tell me how great of a Manager I was.

The Nostradameus Sessions, as I had labeled them in my head, occurred as often as thrice weekly, regularly took place in my office with the door closed and shades drawn, and always involved information delivery by Elise via "quatrain" and rolled out in *four* very distinct but linked categories:

I. "Oh My God" or Unbelievable Happenings

II. "The Sky is Falling" and other impending doom

III. Overheard with Unreliable Resources

IV. "I'm Tellin' You It's Gonna Happen" Forward-Looking Predictions

Elise stood up in front of my whiteboard, ensuring that she had closed the blinds to my office window, then rapidly scribbled an org chart across the entire white expanse. She would often sketch out various sections of the Company's org chart so she could make special-colored indications next to each individual while she rattled on about gossip that involved them, their teams or someone that was connected to them.

"Oh my God," she began, on this particular day in question. "You are not going to believe what I heard happened at Packer's leadership retreat last week." She took a red dry erase marker, making asterisks next to the box labeled "Ben Packer, CEO" then scribbled an avant-garde circle around the square.

"Shouldn't we talk about the marketing plan?" I asked, while she drew.

"Uh, no" she said, turning back to the board where she continued scribbling. Faced with the option to talk about work or *really talk* about work, Elise always deferred the boring stuff for a later date. And the minute she started rattling off her intel, I was back in the vortex of drama. It pulled me in every time. I couldn't escape the *sucking* due to Elise's pure unadulterated enthusiasm in the material. *If only she could bottle this and sell it*, I thought, as she turned back to me with the story at hand.

"So, Chiun Lu Kei, he's the clown town who has been building some ultra-secret new product they're calling *Boise* or *Banana*…I'm not sure… He's been working on this presentation for Packer for like months to get final funding to build the product. Packer authorized like fifty million dollars for the R&D. So, Lu Kei presents the deck to the room. And like three slides in Packer is like 'shut it down' and Lu Kei is like 'the PowerPoint deck?' And Packer is like 'no, the entire product' and Lu Kei is like 'I'm not sure I understand,' and Packer is like 'what is it about shutting down the entire product you don't get?' and Lu Kei is like 'you've already invested fifty million' and Packer is like 'and I'm not going to lose any more.'"

She took a breath. "Of course, I'm just paraphrasing," she finished.

"What was wrong with the product?" I wondered.

"Not the product. The *presentation*."

"What was wrong with the presentation?" I asked, confused.

"Pelicans," she said, eyes wide with a WTF look on her face. She nodded. Then smiled. Then nodded some more. She was like the Marcel Marceau of Corporate facial gossip.

"Pelicans?"

"*Animated* pelicans. Every single slide had an animated transition with pelicans. I guess Lu Kei went on and on about how pelicans have some religious significance or something… Packer's fine with religion, he supposedly once talked to God who told him to kick red meat to the curb. Anyway, it's the animated PowerPoint transitions that he *can't stand*."

"You're telling me that Ben Packer, our *C.E.O.* invests fifty million in a product, then upon seeing the presentation about its progress gets so enraged by animated pelican slide transitions that he shutters the entire project completely? Seriously. Who told you that?"

"Ana Forsythe, who works for Greg Belkin, who is friends with Stephanie Wuslow, who is the catering team lead who delivered Chinese Chicken Salad to the meeting, happened to see Packer's Chief of Staff texting someone the story," she said, circling yet another box on the org chart that was positioned right under Packer. It read, "Simone Guerra, Chief-of-Staff."

"I haven't heard anything about any Banana or Boise getting shut down," I said, questioning the Nostra in Elise while questioning my own sanity at the same time.

"I'm tellin' you, dude. It happened. Or it's going to happen. Greg and Ana and Stephanie *especially* are like really reputable sources. Plus," she continued, highlighting a box near the edge of Packer's line of direct reports, "Lu Kei is no longer showing up as even reporting to Packer anymore in the Company address book." She crossed out Lu Kei's box, then took a whiff of the dry erase marker before she put the cap on.

"Smells like blood in the water," she finished.

"Ready for our one on one?" a voice chimed in from the door. We both turned. It was Dustin. Ah, yes. I looked at my watch – my time with Elise was up. She got her things, and passed Dustin on her way out the door.

"Pelicans," she said one last time for dramatic effect, pausing at the doorway, flapping her arms in some kind of bird-like homage.

She exited and Dustin sat opposite me, rocking a *Pac Man* t-shirt and holding a spiral notebook. "You ready to talk social networking and tech bloggers?" he asked, excitedly bouncing in his seat, as the intel about Packer bounced around in my head.

"Yes. *Yes I am*," I said in as excited a voice I could muster, while concurrently looking at my phone's calendar. "Just let me make sure I know where I'm going next," I said. The calendar was *packed*. In fact, after Dustin, the entire rest of my day was filled with more one on one's than fingers on my hands.

"Where are you going next?" he asked.

"*Nowhere*," I said, dejected. "Nowhere at all."

With the Summer fully upon us, Seattle became the paradise that every local tried to keep secret from visitors and outsiders for fear of polluting the so-called population waters with unworthy Californians and Portlandians. Still, despite all the cloak and dagger, residents took to the lakes and the mountains and pathways and trails with an almost superhuman athletic gusto. Families stocked up at REI and ascended tough mountain trails. Bicyclists crossed the cities back and forth, pedaling in perfect formation, clad in local company-sponsored stretchy-pants and tops. Alongside freeways into Seattle, swimmers trained for aquatic challenges in city-sanctioned roped off water lanes. And die-hard University of Washington alumnae (or U-Dub fanatics) cropped up everywhere for tailgating, pre-season games and a beer or two. Even in Canyon Park Estates, real life finally seemed to exist and thrive as evidenced by the frolicking *Nerf* gun-wielding children, boat-towing aquamen and the periodic appearance of the *Cosmopolitan* drink-wielding neighborhood wives. The summer would be short, as was always the case, and so every single Seattle resident took advantage of the glorious outdoors and clean fresh air as God had intended.

Except for us.

Kate sat beside me, crunching through a fresh apple in the back of the City of Bellevue's all-purpose room, which incidentally smelled as if someone had left it out in the rain then defrosted it for twelve minutes in a microwave. I teased a particularly frayed portion of the carpet with my foot, pushing it back slightly to reveal a slab of rotten wood beneath it. It made me think of the time I had come across a half-eaten sourdough bread bowl with remnants of clam chowder in it. The *white* kind. Which had instantaneously made me puke. Which made me feel queasy. Which made me think of Romy Wallace. Who was also *white*. And *also* made me want to puke. Ah, the dastardly circle of sense memories, how they haunted me so.

"Please, don't take this as a threat or some intimidation tactic," Jess' voice echoed throughout the room, "but if you open *Fro-yo Joe's* on Main, I will call every well-respected journalist and celebrity I know from my days in Hollywood and get them to tweet the crap out of this story. Actually, come to think of it," her voice smiled, "it *is* a threat."

I looked up to the front of the room, just as the handful of citizens standing alongside Jess at the podium began *cheering* her on. Across the aisle, a fatigued-looking Businessman shook his head and wiped the sweat from his brow. And at the front of the room, looking official and depressed that they were dealing with this injustice while they could have been outside hunting real live animals and drinking beer out of well-engineered plastic hats, were three City Officials in suits.

Since the *Not So Ethical Ethics Meeting* at The Company, the depressed, over-caffeinated, woe-is-*me* Jess Murphy had taken a turn for the better. Realizing, as she had, that no city had cornered the market on conflict or the daily mundane problems that plagued humans of all shapes and sizes, had spun her up into resolution mode. While the Jess of January shuffled around her life like a shadowy, soulless automaton who spent all of her time obsessing over how badly things had turned out in her head, the Jess of July had turned her focus outward towards others. There were people out there facing problems that Jess vowed she could solve. No matter where, no matter how, it was her newfound goal to emerge into the light, listen for the whispers of discontent and return to her glory days as *The Solver*.

It had started with *The Starbucks Sofa Scuffle*, just days after the *Not So Ethical Ethics Meeting*, in which two ornery old early birds tussled over the ownership of a particularly cushy couch. Jess, pen in hand and scone wrapper in the other, had jumped in the middle of the tirade, sketching out a valid sofa-sharing plan that rotated by the hour.

The Starbucks Sofa Scuffle segued into *The Target Toy Tussle,* which transitioned into *The Pre-School Personnel Project*. Where two people found themselves unable to resolve an issue or where pre-school parents were too busy or self-conflicted to call out the less-than-stellar teachers because they feared being the center of attention – Jess was there. With bells on. And a spring in her step. And a glow on her face. The eerie looking creature that had shared our almost paid-off bed with me had disappeared, replaced with the hot, driven woman I had married. And while her dedication to *many* causes had been eating up some of our down time together as a family, it was better than the alternative.

"Let's just go in for a quick sec," Jess had said, as we walked out of the organic food market earlier that day, stopping to notice a sign that had read 'Bellevue Community Council Meeting Today.' "We should know more about what's going on in our town."

Your stinking overcast town is now *our town*, I marveled at her changed perspective, as we entered the moldy-smelling defrosted room at the back of an old city office. There we had found two factions fighting to thwart the opening of an infamous chain of horribly-reviewed frozen yogurt stores, notorious for hocking yogurt that actually wasn't yogurt *at all*. Apparently, calling it yogurt didn't actually make it yogurt at all.

"Fructose, Dextrose, Maltodextrin," Jess had announced, reading it off her iPhone as she held it high above her head like Mel Gibson brandishing his sword in *Braveheart*, bringing the crowd to a frenzy in what we would later refer to as *The No Fro-yo Show*. It was the Jess I had imagined in all those publicity meetings she told me about after the fact. Full of energy, a commanding presence, and a confidence like no other. After months of searching, Jess had finally found the version of herself that made her happy. That fed her soul. When you saw her, there were no illusions that she was in her element.

"There are no *probiotics* in this Fro-yo," she cried out. "This isn't yogurt *at all*," she shrieked. "Now, either you open *No-Yo Joe's* or you don't open *anything* at all," she demanded, only turning once to share a look with her fans at the back as she reveled in her time in the limelight.

Heck, it wasn't the sun. But seriously – who was complaining?

It was a *feeling*, but not one with any real data or evidence to back it up. It was like all those poor souls sitting in dark cars, unaware that someone with a disfigured face and a horrific backstory that had driven them to kill dozens of innocent victims, was seconds away from vaulting over the backseat and gutting them completely. I tried to explain it to Jess, laying there next to her in the blistering sun at the local park, texting her how I felt. Despite the troubleshooting mode we were in on Memphis, the algorithm was still very hungry for data. Everyone was doing their part.

"You're likening the politics at work to *Friday the 13th*?" she texted. *Ding.*

"It's an allegorical metaphor," the writer part of me texted back. *Bloop.* "I'm saying that I can *feel* something coming." *Bloop.* Jess was more amenable to my crazy work requirements, but there was always a line in the sand. After a few minutes of *dinging and blooping*, she always got fed up and retreated back into the world of verbal communication.

"Don't write a check for a bill that may never come," she verbalized, channeling the latest string of Instagram self-help mantras. "Deal with it when it happens. Until then, what can you do?"

"I can obsess."

"And you are doing a bang-up job of it, Cam."

We paused for a moment as we both scanned the playground for Kate. Every park conversation included a pause every two minutes for the "where is our child" query – it was always a given necessity. I located Kate at the far end of a sea of wood chips, ascending one of those kid-friendly rock-climbing walls, competing with a trio of children all desperate to get to the top like mice fleeing a rapidly filling bathtub.

"She's over there," I pointed out, nudging her. "Still *here*."

"That's two for us, zero for the kidnappers," Jess jeered back, then she went right back into the conversation that had preceded it. We were true parents in that sense – we could start a thought, handle a potential kidnapping crisis, skull fracture or Lego ingestion, then get right back into the meat of it all. "I mean, do you really think Romy was behind the sabotage?"

"Beckham's Razor," I reminded Jess in her own ragmag-focused terminology she would understand. "The simplest answer is always the right answer. Who else would want to see me fail so completely?"

"Oh, I don't know," she thought, "what about all those people now looking for jobs from MediaMesh?" It was a valid point. *Damn*.

"Do you think *all of those people* are out to get me, too?" I worried, rubbing my weekend stubble as I imagined angry townspeople, torches and my glorious house as a medieval castle.

Jess pushed me back on the blanket. "I think you should just enjoy the beautiful weather. And your wonderful, problem-solving wife. How about getting out of your head for five minutes and doing *just that*?" She leaned down and kissed me. I looked up at her smile, sunlight passing through her hair as it blew gently in the cool breeze. For a split second between worrying about Romy and the rest of the people out for my head on a stick, I found some joy in the change I saw before me. Flashes of a similarly-smiling Jess matched the moment in the present, reminding me of all the moments that had felt like this in the past. At a concert at Griffith Observatory on the grass. Waiting for the fireworks to begin on a Malibu beach. On a high grassy bluff overlooking the Pacific Ocean. In my cramped, one bedroom apartment, her sitting atop me on my couch. Holding Kate next to her face, the two of them quietly waking me up on a warm summer morning. There had been hundreds of these moments before. And despite a six-month hiatus, the moment reminded me that despite the ups and downs, there was always the potential for happiness. It was there. *Always*. You just had to believe in it, find it and hold on tight.

"You're happy, *aren't you*?"

"You sound surprised," she said, cocking her head slightly.

"When I was wiping your snot and cradling you in a *Little Mermaid* blanket, I didn't think I'd see this person again, any time soon." She kissed me. It was my payment for the aforementioned moment of intense nurturing.

She turned to spot Kate again (it had been two minutes), realized we were still outsmarting the kidnappers, then turned back to me – tongue slightly protruding from between her lips. It meant she was about to ask a serious question I was going to have to deliver a serious answer unto. "But the question is…are *you* happy?" she asked, eyebrows at full mast waiting for the answer.

"I think I *can* be," I replied.

"OK. So, what's holding you back?"

"It's that *feeling*," I said, harkening back to my hockey-masked serial killer reference. "It's hard to be completely happy when you feel like something's just on the horizon ready to screw it all up for you. It's like the feeling Charlie Brown has every time he's about to kick that football that Lucy is holding. Until he kicks that ball, he doesn't know if he's going to find success." It was true, Schultz-reference aside. If I could kick that football, it would mean that Memphis had made it into the keynote and become a success, solidifying my position and job at The Company. If that football was pulled out from under me, everything I wanted for me and my family would be gone.

"So get Romy in a room and *take away the football.* If you think she's out to get you, call her out. Make her admit it. Make sure she knows you aren't going to go down without a fight," she said, causing the adrenaline to rise up inside of me. "Take control and become the kicker," she said as she gave my shoulders a squeeze.

I am the kicker, I repeated to myself. *I am the one in control*, I thought. *I can do it. I will do it.*

Ah, yes. *The Solver* was officially back.

The cigar was imported. Perhaps it was *illegal*. But all I kept thinking was *this cigar is the most heinous thing I have ever ingested in my entire life*, while I choked myself through every single puff and I tried to look cool. Just so you know, it didn't look cool *at all*.

"You have smoked cigars before?" asked Sudhir, sitting next to me on his porch, looking out at the setting sun, smoking his own cigar with ease and smoky professionalism.

"All the time," I choked violently. "I l-love these things." I sneeze-coughed, sending a phlegm-like protrusion from my throat onto the cement in front of both of us. *Smooth.*

Sudhir rolled his eyes, yanked the cigar from my hands and placed it in an ashtray on his other side, then took another deep inhale of his. He savored the taste, slowly releasing the smoke and his stress all at once. "So. This algorithm."

Oh, the *algorithm*. It had been the thorn in my side over the last week or so, with Rafi and team working around the clock to get us back on track. They had made some progress in changing the algorithm's filter, but hours later it would revert back to a problematic state. Knowing Sudhir was an engineer with *three beepers*, and knowing very little about engineers myself, meant that Sudhir would *obviously* know exactly how to solve the issue. At least, that had been my thinking when I had intruded on his nightly ritual of smoke inhalation. He had gladly welcomed me to join him, listening to the problems I was currently facing.

"Have your engineers identified where the data is being redirected from?" he asked. "Have they thought to go to the API's source? Have they ensured that the metadata feed is not, in fact, what has been compromised instead?"

I stared at the phlegm stain on the concrete. That was more my speed. Sudhir realized I wasn't the guy to be spinning API yarns to.

"I could, if it would be helpful," he began, "have a conversation with your lead engineer and relay my thoughts. It would have to be off the record, obviously, as it is against the corporate policy my employment agreement outlines."

I looked back up, nodding with a smile.

It was gun-metal grey. And spherical. Its ultraviolet-protected windows had been treated in a luminescent film that reflected the sun so perfectly, that they gleamed a color so mind-numbingly bright that the entire structure looked like a white globe magically hovering above a green, grassy knoll. *It looks like the Death Star*, I thought to myself as I approached the menacing Building 111, wishing I had someone like Admiral Ackbar at my side for the lunch meeting I had dropped on Romy Wallace's calendar just three days prior. Being a well-revered military tactician, I had come to realize, was a benefit for anyone who had found themselves working at The Company.

"I used to be a military tactician," a GM had once been rumored to have said.

I had spent three long hours crafting the single line of text that accompanied the calendar request. It had to seem casual, but not meaningless. I spun for hours, sitting next to Jess in bed, trying to write the perfect one liner that would make Romy curious enough to meet me but ambiguous enough to hide my true motivations of intelligence gathering and sabotage surveillance.

"*Romy. Would love to catch up. Let me know if you don't have time,*" the first version had read.

"Don't give her a way out," Jess critiqued, watching over my shoulder as I typed, retyped, deleted, repositioned, reformatted, changed the font, and ensured the spacing communicated the right tone for the message. "You need to want her to be there. Besides, you shouldn't let her make the decision – then you're already giving her the power up front. Don't ask. *Tell.*"

"*Romy. Let's congregate for lunch. It's time we talked,*" the second version had read, after twenty-five minutes of writing, re-writing and consulting a Thesaurus. *Assemble* and *rally* had been close runner-ups thanks to the Thesaurus at hand.

"If I was Romy and I read that, I'd want to know two things. First, what soap opera were we on? Second, why were you breaking up with me," Jess chided. I practically threw my laptop out the window in frustration. Apparently, it took a village to write a one liner e-mail message.

"I'm taking your advice," I shot back. "I'm not asking. I'm *telling.*"

"Enough with the drama. Be a *man.* This makes it sound like you've been obsessing over telling her something for months."

I had.

"Which *she doesn't need to know,*" Jess said. "Keep it simple. Just say, Romy – let's meet for lunch, would be good to catch up. Then *you* pick the place and drop the invite on *her.*"

"Would be good to catch up," I repeated, letting it bounce around in my over-obsessive brain for a moment. "Seems innocent enough. Good natured. But it's my idea, so the power remains in my hands." I liked it. And two hours after fixing the punctuation, we were off to the races.

"*Romy – Let's meet for lunch; would be good to…catch up,*" read the final e-mail. I sent it at 10:32pm on a Tuesday night. At 10:34 on that *same* Tuesday night, Romy had received it and sent back a proposed change to the calendar invite. She would accept the time, but proposed a different location – none other than Building 111.

The Death Star.

"The Death Star," I said out loud. Jess rolled her eyes at me.

"Just get in *that* room with her, Cam. Show her she's underesti-mated you. Show her who's boss."

"You mean *me*, right?"

Jess reached over and accepted the calendar invite *for* me.

There was so much wrong with Building 111, *a.k.a. the Death Star*.

Aside from its obvious design flaws, color choices and imperson-able decorating details, it had an ominous feel that immediately put me on edge. There were kitchens, but no free beverages. Vending machines, but nary a package of *Oreos*. Focus rooms, which across The Compa-ny's campus would often be filled to the brim with sociable employees, were isolated and empty. Even cubicles, which I passed on my way to the second-floor cafeteria, were positioned in such a way as to shield its employees from prying eyes in what I could only imagine was a covert attempt to hide whatever evil was *truly* going on behind the scenes.

Yes. *Evil.*

I checked my e-mail as I walked towards the elevator bays, cy-cling through a slew of congratulatory e-mails from Rafi and team. As promised, Sudhir had dug in with Rafi and team, determining that the actual issue of the now-unspoken porn debacle had been caused by the external data feeds supplying the Movie and TV metadata to Memphis. Whoever had sabotaged the project was smart, technologically savvy and had done so with the help of someone on the inside. Needless to say, the issue had been fixed and Memphis was back on track. *For now.* But what would come of tomorrow? Who knew what was *next*?

I bet Romy does, the obsessive-compulsive voice in my head who liked to imagine workplace politics as ancient medieval battles, said. I shook it off as I exited the elevator, walked down the hallway, and found myself face to face with the double doors to the *Death Star*'s cafeteria. I took a breath and flung open the doors. It was a virtual ghost town. Devoid of cooks, stoves, people and *laughter*. Chairs sat upside down on dusty lunch tables, while signs affixed to the outside of empty refriger-ators read '*Nothing to See Here*.' It was the kind of place a foursome of teenagers out for a rebellious night on the town would find themselves right before their untimely (and tied to some cafeteria-centric death prop) demise.

Behind me, the *schhhllppppt* sound of a carbonated beverage being opened, echoed throughout the room – startling me into a full turn-on-my-heels moment and revealing none other than Romy. She sat across the room, at a far table, taking a cultured (and evil) sip from a can of Diet Soda. She smiled at my fragile state of affairs, then motioned to an empty seat opposite her. In front of it sat a second *unopened* can of soda, perched on the edge of the table.

"Glad you could join me," she said, coldly.

Show her who's boss, I reminded myself. I had invited *her*, after all. "Glad *you* could join *me* since it was *I* who initiated this one-on-one sync," I replied clumsily, moving behind the chair opposite her and pushing the unopened soda can gingerly just to make sure there was nothing sketchy about it. It was clearly *fine*. It was a can…of…soda. I was being overly cautious. I pulled the chair out, sliding down into it, and took the still-cold can of soda into my hands. I flashed her a confident look as I peeled back the tab of the soda and watched in slo-mo as it *exploded all over*.

In my imagination, the Sorceress-Bitch had held up a poisonous cobra, forcing it to spray my face with a pungent death that would clearly spell the death of me.

"Oops," Romy sniped sing-songy, back in the real world.

There weren't any napkins. Remember, this was the cafeteria that time forgot. I shook off my shirt, causing some of the caramel-colored beads of carbonated chemicals to roll onto the floor, then suavely slurped the remaining drink off my forearms and hands. *Show her who's boss*, I reminded myself.

I looked around at the bizarro cafeteria, abandoned and cold. "What's with all this, Wallace?" I said with attitude, believing that by using her last name I was, you know, kind of…potentially…showing her *who…was…boss*.

Wallace wasn't fazed. She took another sip of her soda, then eyed my stained shirt and flashed a barely perceptible grin. "When they make you a GM of a new product," she said, leaning against the back of her chair and shoving her breasts in my face, "you get a building."

I didn't know they were giving away buildings.

"And when you get a building," she continued, "you kick out all the loose-lipped sissies who aren't contributing *shit*. The café staff went first. And I'm currently preparing a list of riffs for any employees who can't get with the plan." She took another glug of her diet soda, tilting back on her chair and careening back towards the table where she slammed the can down and crossed her arms across her chest. "Ok, now. Start talking, Murphy. Why are we here?"

Ah, how I longed for the innocence of the Chicken Cordon Bleu days.

But as *The Solver* had advised me, this was not the time to back down. Romy was up to something with Shane McCullough. I knew *she knew* that I was focused on getting Memphis into the Vegas keynote. We both, clearly viewed the other as our main competition in getting there. And while I didn't have the evidence, I was almost sure she had something to do with Memphis' algorithm debacle. She had to know I was onto her. I had to force her into admitting what she had done, and then wield such intel against her – forcing her to back off completely.

I had to kick the football.

"Look," I began, "I *know*. I know *everything*."

It was a strong start. I was feeling good.

"I know you have very specific goals," I continued, meandering slightly, "and let's just say I know how far you'll go to accomplish them."

Okay, I thought. Aaron Sorkin would have been proud.

But Romy stared at me, unimpressed. Seemingly, waiting for more. Her jury was still out on *my* speech. The coherence of my monologue began to teeter under the strain of second-guessdom.

"I'm not stupid," I continued. "I know your origin story and I know your work ethic. And I know what you're focused on and you know what I'm focused on. There's a lot of mutual focusing going on here and..." I trailed off. It didn't even sound good *in my head*. "And let's just say, like the Raptors in *Jurassic Park*, I know you're the kind of person who will keep testing the fences for weaknesses so you can leverage them for your own success."

Huh? I was losing my footing.

I picked up empty soda can, purely due to the fact that I had no idea where to put my hands, and tilted the opening up to my mouth. But it was empty, *which I'd forgotten*. I looked like an idiot. "We can coexist," I said, dropping the can with dramatic flair as if that had been my plan with the empty can all along, "and then *me* knowing *you* the way I do, and *you* knowing *me* the way *you* do, won't have any bearing on anything whatsoever."

Fuck.

I looked at Romy, waiting for something. *Anything.* It was a weak ending. I needed *more*, so I swung my hand towards the can and it went flying, feebly, onto the floor. Romy eyed the can, eyed the table, eyed me and then *smiled.*

"You had me at '*I'm not stupid*'," she grinned, "because only stupid people need to convince you that they're *not.*" She sat back, smiled, seemingly waiting for *something.* It was right about then that my cell phone vibrated in my pocket, startling me out of the *mano a mano* discussion. Romy reveled in how it shook me, watching as I pulled it out of my pants.

"I'll wait," she said. "It's probably an important text."

I unlocked the cell, pulling up my texts and was met with *an emoticon.* Just like the one I had received after Memphis had been sabotaged. A yellow face, making an awe-stricken *Home Alone* post-shaving expression, hands slapping its cheeks in surprise.

It *was* her.

"It *was* you," I said, accusing.

"Good luck proving it," she smiled back.

I stared at her, eyes wide. *Stunned* at her blatant honesty. At a loss for words. She got up, flipped the chair around so she could sit on it backwards like a coach ready to give you a pep talk, and leaned in even closer. She cleared her throat.

"Here's the deal, Cameron. I am going to do everything in my power to completely discredit and dismantle this Memphis product of yours. No matter how many hours in the day it takes. No matter how many people I have to bribe to do it. No matter who gets caught in the crossfire. When I'm finished with you and your quaint little application, there will be no way in Hell that the Las Vegas airport will even grant a plane, carrying you and your insignificant software gnat or the team who built it, permission to land." She put her hand on mine, then looked directly into my eyes. I gazed at hers, black and cold. "You and I," she continued, "we come from the same effed up place. We've got history. So, I'm doing you a solid here by being completely fucking honest with you."

"Why?" I really wanted to know.

"It's not complicated," she replied. "Or *personal*. It's just business. And for any product, that Vegas slot is *just...good...business*. Mostly, for *me*."

She sat back, crossed her arms and waited for my response.

I didn't ask why. I didn't ask how. I didn't ask *with whom*. I just got up quietly, doubled-back for my empty can of soda, and started to walk out. Inside, I was filled with a combination of worry, horror, envy, frustration, desperation, nausea and a toxic cocktail of vitriolic juices that caused anger to rise up and take center stage. I wanted to punch something. To kick something. All the damn chairs were upside down on tables, making it tough. Nonetheless, I tried – swinging my foot and pulling my groin in the process.

I limped my way out of the *Death Star's* cafeteria as Romy stood up to watch me go.

"Oh, and Shane says hi," she yelled after me as I pushed my way through the double doors and inside the elevator.

Shane says hi, indeed.

"Nothing *personal*," I grunted to myself as I *smashed* in the passenger side window of a very familiar silver Mercedes in the parking garage. "Nothing *personal*," I grumbled, making my way around the front of the luxury automobile, lifting a stray piece of rebar I had found outside, and jamming a hole in the windshield and the steering column -- causing the air bag to *poufff* in a loud deployment, spraying white powder every-where like a carbonated drink.

I threw down the rebar and went running off into the distance. As fast as I could.

August

It's quite possible it was sunny out. After all, August *did* represent the most amazing, most consistent eighty-degree superhuman summer weather Seattle ever saw over the course of a twelve-month period. It was also fairly probable that a majority of The Company's employees were in the midst of their two- or three-week long August vacations, spending time with their families and turning the campus into a virtual ghost town. And I wouldn't deny the fact, although I'd be hard pressed to provide proof in the moment, that Jess' recent obsession with solving the world's problems had finally bled over into the suburban mirage some called Canyon Park Estates. Apparently, aside from the *Seattle Freeze* and the unsociable Dark Times we had experienced, Jess was under the impression that there were issues abound that needed to be resolved. Although I didn't technically know that since I wasn't listening to her real-time tirades, instead obsessed with micromanaging every single aspect of Memphis in order to protect its future from a complete and total aspirational destruction courtesy of the Company's resident *Sorceress-Bitch.*

"How do they let someone paint their front door *hot pink*?" Jess said to Kate and I in the SUV, both accompanying her on a completely productive yet emotionally-draining excursion to either *Target, Costco,*

Trader Joe's or *Rite-Aid*. "Cardinal red, sure. Rose, ok. But hot pink?"

"Totally, babe," I said, not even listening, as I scrolled through e-mails, approving a request for funds from Dustin to hold an on-campus VIP tech blogger roundtable. At The Company, tech bloggers represented the best opportunity for making a great first impression on the Web, and so we would fly them up, shower them with schwag, and hope that all the unofficial payola convinced them to write glowing reviews about a product that was still in its infancy. Often, they would not, as History had dictated, yet they still held an unofficial celebrity-like reputation and power with Engineers and the design staff. So much so that a products' features would often change at the last minute due to blogger/journalists like Wade Bernstein at *The Wall Street Journal* or Peter Gainsburg at *Engadget*. One allergic reaction to a feature or one distaste for a font, and the entire Company could be sent into crisis mode. The hope with Memphis was that this would not be the case. We would show them the early app, talk about our strategies and goals, and ask them to rate the product's market potential.

Jess paused the car at a stop sign, then continued down the hill past playing children and fellow resident Susan Gibbs – known unofficially as the person who had spent the most money, per square inch of skin, on plastic surgery for her face and upper torso. She would often weave in a reference to giving "Gwen Stefani a run for her money" in every conversation, when the opportunity arose. In addition to adoring the hobby of facial reconstruction, Susan, it seemed, also loved dogs and alcohol. Perhaps that was why she adored her precious show poodle Belvedere who had won 'thickest coat' two years running. Perhaps that's also why she openly refused to curb her canine. And next to putting the silverware face *down* in the dishwasher, abandoned dog poop was Jess' biggest pet peeve.

"Excuuuuuse me," she rolled down the window to sing out to the sweat suit wearing, poodle-walking Mrs. Gibbs. "Your dog just dropped a load on that resident's front lawn." Susan Gibbs just smiled and kept walking, so Jess pulled the car up to get alongside the fleeing poop perp. "Miss? You going to clean up after your dog?" she yelled. Susan Gibbs pointed to herself like she had no idea why Jess was talking to *her*, made a hand motion to her ears like she was mute, then waved off Jess as she continued down the street.

"The nerve," Jess *huffed* to me, as we approached the bottom of the street.

"Seriously, babe," I said, still barely aware of what was going on outside of my cell phone, focused mostly on replying to a draft message Jane had sent me at four thirty in the morning. It was the draft message she intended to send to the Business Development lead at *FlixFix*, requesting an audience for a potential joint venture confab. Aside from ensuring such overused phrases like "with all due respect", "that being said" and "are you ready for your close-up Mr. DeVille" were torched and buried in a digital landfill, my only advice was of the *Fight Club* kind. Tell no one about the meeting. Tell no one about the mail. If no one knew, that meant Romy and Shane wouldn't know either. What they didn't know existed, they couldn't kill.

"You're going to *kill* someone!" yelled Jess out the now-lowered driver's side window at a speeding sports car that flew past us going the opposite way into the heart of Canyon Park Estates. The yell snapped me out of my brief texting with Elise, who had run into an old colleague at a bagel shop, who did hot yoga twice-weekly with the Programming Director for the Seattle International Film Festival (or SIFF), who incidentally had already invited the late Roger Ebert's wife Chaz to this year's October event to accept an award in her husband's honor.

"What's going on?" I asked Jess, beleaguered, looking up with eyes so swollen from tiny-screen syndrome. The real world where people did things that involved exercise, eating and connecting emotionally. This was, of course, versus giving an employee direction on how to convince a woman to revive her dead husband's image in hologram form to become the spokesperson for an application that was basically negating everything he had strived to do over the course of his entire career.

"I'll tell you what's going on," she said, putting the window back up. "Speed bumps are what's going on…*this street*, if I have anything to say about it."

Kate, in the backseat, now at the age where every single sign represented an opportunity to pester someone else to read it while never filing it away for future reference, was focused out the window on the opposite side of the car at a standee at the entrance to our neighborhood. "What does that say?" she asked.

We all turned to look out the window. It was almost too good to

be true…for Jess. "HOA Annual Meeting," she read, "in two weeks."
"Well, that can't be good," I said.
"For whom?" Jess replied, wheels turning in her Solver-esque head.

The hallway between the bathroom and the living room of Simon Davis' underground lair was covered by dozens of framed magazine articles, all dated somewhere between 1980 and 1990 – and highlighted in one exclamatory statement after the other, how the men and women pictured were either "visionaries", "geniuses" or "millionaires." Besides the words, the mullets and the Benetton *Cosby Show*-like sweaters, there was one other thing that was consistent throughout. Their demeanor. These people were happy. Looking at the pictures was like watching movies from the 50's – filled with an innocence that knew nothing of evil, jealousy, backstabbing or politics, forcing the spectator to ask themselves if a time like this ever *actually* existed in reality or if it was just the creation of some skilled production designer, ad agency and copywriter triumvirate. But times changed and so did the people involved.

"Tell yer bladder to stop wastin' my time," Simon yelled from in front of his Company-wide wall o' cameras, collating printouts into a stack and taking a seat at a tall metal table where he had already procured two opened Mexican Cokes. "It's time to get schooled by one of the few in this place who *actually* can." I took one last look at a *Newsweek* magazine, dated September 1983, with Simon and three others standing in front of a stack of mass-produced circuit boards and the accompanying headline, "*Circuit…Board of Directors. Leading The Company Into The Future.*"

Simon Davis had changed. Then he changed again. Now, the one-time creative visionary-turned-disgruntled-hermit had turned into a mentor *slash* protector *slash* annoyance – whisking me away from the main campus in his rocket-fueled golf cart whenever he saw fit. Still, having a personal project like me seemed to lift him out of the doldrums of tech-overload, and open a door into a world of *Risk*-like strategy, where the secrets and actions of a few warranted a full-fledged investigation into what their true aspirations actually were. In other words, Simon Davis was enthusiastically playing the game of corporate espionage with Cameron Murphy as his guinea pig.

Simon took a swig of his Coke, then dealt the first photo onto the back-lit table we were leaning on. It was a corporate headshot of Romy Wallace, grinning a grin so fake, it reminded me of every single studio or network Executive Shuffle press release – inundating the internet and industry weeklies with the faces of people like my old friend Derrik. Simon placed one of those useless crystal weights, in the shape of a rook, atop the image and turned my attention to the screens behind him. Romy's image exploded across the left side of the screens, with W.O.P.R. like text filling in her statistics on the right. You had to give Simon credit – if he was going to do something, he was going to do it balls out.

"Romy Wallace, thirty-six," he began. "Born in Southern California, Calabasas specifically. Schooled in the San Fernando Valley, then attended USC for degrees in Business, Entertainment Law and a minor in Bokator."

I blessed him, since *bokator* sounded more like a sneeze than a word.

"USC is only one of twelve universities that award minor degrees in Bokator," he continued, "which is a Cambodian martial art whose name literally translates to 'pounding a lion.'"

And the hits just kept on coming.

"Wallace joined The Company six months ago after leaving her post as an agent at Legendary Artists. Came in as a Senior Biz Dev Director, then promoted to General Manager of Calabasas right around the same time you took on Memphis."

She named her product after where she was born, I choked and wrote it off as something completely self-absorbed which was completely unsurprising. It was common practice at The Company for leaders to give code names to projects that had some personal connection, but this just made me squirm in my seat. What was next? Tattooing the image of her face on the butts of every malnourished employee she had trapped in her own personal *Death Star*?

"As for Calabasas, there ain't much on the Company's secure SharePoint databases about the initiative, but I *was* able to retrieve a simple-minded overly-written brand document that said this…" A page of text was blown up on screen, zooming in on a particular string of text. Simon read, "Calabasas will turn ordinary TVs into extraordinary high-fidelity experiences, and all for the price of a cup of coffee." A vector-drawn schematic of the product appeared on screen – it was the size of a USB drive, and showed a virtual consumer holding it in the palm of their hand.

"What is *on* that drive?" I wondered. "And what costs less than three bucks that can do what that text says?"

What if her product is better than mine? That was the real unknown. It was one thing to avoid getting pounded like a lion. It was another thing to get *just plain beat.* Simon threw a picture of Building 111 on the table, using another dark crystal rook to keep it in place. It was like a mini-Stonehenge up in there.

"That's where all the magic, or lack thereof…is happening," Simon said, tapping the photo.

Over the next thirty minutes, Simon would walk me through a handful of Corporate players who all represented an opportunity for my success or failure. There were the obvious foes like Shane McCullough, who had a history of sabotaging others' work when they had stood in his way. There were questionable folks like Mitch DeForrest, despite being my direct manager, whose motivations were shrouded in mystery and punctuated by extreme sports injuries. There were neutral parties who could help my cause like Rafi in Engineering, the CEO's Chief of Staff Simone, and my entire team of potentially-dedicated employees. And then, there was The Company, often hobbled by its own bloated processes and illogical rules. Above it all, however, Simon had seen thirty years of political machinations, so ignoring his advice was ill-advised.

"Beware the blatant baddies, always question the motivations of the friendlies, and never trust the people who blend into the background. Everyone has the potential to fuck up your shit." I eyed the table of pictures before me, arranged like an FBI's wall of most wanted criminals.

"Is this supposed to make me feel better?" I said, feeling an empty hole in my stomach start to digest the surrounding organs. "Because it doesn't." I lost a liver and part of my kidney while I was waiting for Simon to respond. "We need to hit Romy before she can hit Memphis again. Knock her down. Fuck *her* shit up."

Simon came to a full stop. "No."

"You said it, not me – everyone has the potential to fuck up *my* shit. "Well, why sit around and wait for that to happen? Why not *act* first?" I mean, if there were people out to get me, why play the passive game?

"Don't you get it?" He pushed all the pictures of the baddies to one side, and tossed another picture on the table – which happened to be my horrible New Employee Orientation photo, which had subsequently been used as my employee photo, which would *forever* be the photo that would accompany my ups and downs at The Company for *life*. If I ever made it to my ten, twenty or thirty-year anniversary at The Company, my half-blinking, swollen-looking eye, overdosed on *Nyquil* photo would be the one everyone would celebrate. Simon held up the picture, regarding it himself. "If you do *that,* you're no better than the lot of them. That's not *you.* You're one of the good guys."

I was one of the good guys?

My face, more apt to look tired, frustrated or annoyed as of late must have immediately brightened up. Simon noticed, downplaying a positive opinion that would clearly had ruined his public persona of being a tortured, genius asshole.

"I'm not saying you're going to change the world or anything," he grumbled, "I just meant – who knows. Obviously, no one can predict what's going to happen within a one-percent probability factor. But if there's even a sliver of a chance... But we have to be smart about it. No careless mistakes. Ingenuity *not* idiocy."

"So, then," I said, sliding out the rendered picture of the Calabasas project, "what costs less than three bucks and can revolutionize your flat-screen TV?"

Simon swung around on his chair, hitting a few keys on a keyboard, bringing up a rapidly scrolling screen of numbers and symbols. "Once I break the code to the Calabasas firewall, I'll hopefully have the answer to that," he announced matter-of-fact.

"And once I know more, so will *you.*"

I was in the *shit.* Crouched low to the ground, my aching limbs pulled my fatigued body across the dry gravel and towards my next opportunity for cover – a stack of particularly inviting hay bales that stood a mere *thirty* pelvis thrusts away. My grey and silver camouflage had done the trick so far, keeping me hidden from my enemy and therefore invisible to their sensors, ultimately protecting my pink, squishy, extremely prone-to-pain body from what I imagined would be a surprisingly-painful gun-shot wound. I checked my weapon, ensuring that the safety was off and that I had enough ammunition for a firefight. I did. I was ready.

I got on my knees, slowly rising up to get a view of the field before me. There were acres of gravel and grass, with periodic hay bales placed at strategic positions. Yet there was no one to be seen. I clenched my gun more tightly, bringing the sight up to my eyes and scanning the battlefield before me, sweeping back and forth at the edges of the bales to find my target. "There you are," I whispered to myself, having spotted the edge of a designer sneaker peeking out from a particularly close location. The excitement and potential of victory swelled up inside me as I went into *Full Metal Jacket* mode, springing up and emptying what appeared to be half a can of green paint balls upon the sneaker.

Which was *obviously* protecting a foot. Which was *plainly* attached to the body of one Mitch DeForrest. Whose idea for what a one-on-one meeting was *supposed to be* was radically different from my own.

I let out a guttural *scream* that was more low-budget alien than Navy S.E.A.L. as I descended upon my victim, unloading the rest of the paintballs as I ran in slo-mo towards him, ascending the hay bale, flying up into the air, and landing on the ground like a Marvel superhero next to the foot in question.

But there was no foot. It was just a shoe. I had been *tricked*.

Behind me, the sound of an automatic paintball gun unloading hundreds of the painful orbs, reverberated, pelting me in the neck, face and ear. I turned, barely, noticing Mitch DeForrest as I collapsed onto the ground, clutching every now-painted orifice as I screamed bloody murder.

Mitch DeForrest sat next to me on the bench, outfitted in full camouflage, full idiotic face paint and a hat that made him look like a desert shrub, tossing back a fluorescent green bottle of *Gatorade*. Despite having one arm in a cast and a surgical bandage on his left neck where an arrow had "barely severed his carotid artery" the previous week at a Company-sponsored "Fiscal Year Strategy Planning & Archery Off-Site" – he had still beat me in an impromptu paintball one-on-one. I looked far worse than he, with a swollen neck, cheek and forehead that caused me to resemble one Rocky Dennis from the classic "deformed-kid-changes-lives" movie *MASK*. Somewhere, Cher sang *"If I Could Turn Back Time"* which was, incidentally, not included on the feature-film's soundtrack album.

"You need to move faster," Mitch D. said, wiping his mouth with his sleeve. "Faster delegation, faster decision making, faster progress. I want you executing at *supersonic* speeds. It's been weeks and your team has still not delivered what I asked for." He rapped his gun against my head, causing my forehead to throb, "Get this thing going *mach five*."

"Everyone is moving as quickly as they can," I said, defending the team.

Mitch D. put down his empty plastic bottle, turning his entire comically-encased body towards mine. "Have you threatened to fire them if they don't work more quickly?" he asked, completely serious. "Or given them some *reason* to work harder than they normally would?"

"They understand what's at stake," I said, feeling the Mitch D. vice tightening around my swollen neck. "I've been very clear about the goals for Memphis."

"I see," he said, furrowing his brow and tightening his lips as he gazed up at the sky formulating his thoughts. I bit my lip through the pain of blood pumping into swollen areas of my head as I waited for Mitch D's next meandering speech. In the moment, I half wished for my welts to burst open so I would have to be rushed to a hospital instead of hear what he was about to say. *Death or speech*, I lamented in my head. Death. Or. Speech.

"It was nighttime," he began. *Oh boy*. Anytime Mitch D. started a story with the time of day, you knew it was going to be a long one. No one started a story about stubbing their toe or eating a great meal with the time of day. Only stories that took place during the Earth's full rotation required a time-of-day check-in. And this was one of them.

Mitch D's eyes glossed over like he was going into a trance – continuing: "I was hiking across Central America after ten months in South America, on my way back to the States. I had promised my Amnesty International colleagues that I would cross the border to Mexico in three days, at which point we would all board the Greenpeace boats and travel home along the Eastern seaboard to New York. But on this particular night in question, as I paused in an abnormally-thick area of brush to re-set a makeshift splint on my broken left leg, which is a different story for a different time, I was ambushed by a particularly venomous predator – the *Bothreichis Schlegelii.*"

"Wow," I said, having no idea what a bladdedy-blah schlabladdedy-blah *was.*

"That's the deadly Eyelash Viper of Belize," he clarified, thankfully. "The venom normally passes-through ones' blood quickly, but I had delayed that by swallowing a mixture of flora and fauna, buying me twelve hours in which to ingest the antidote and save my own life. Do you have any idea where that life-saving potion actually was? Can you guess?"

What is…"a hospital?" I answered, knowing deep down for the thirty-seventh time that I would never, no matter what, despite the number of human beings that had been wiped out in a freak asteroid *slash* tsunami disaster, *ever* end up on an edition of 'Corporate Motiva-tional Story' *Jeopardy.*

"*No,*" he replied, annoyed. "Mexico. But Mexico was three days away. I only had twelve hours. I was moving as quickly as I could." He stood up, for added effect, and looked me straight in the eyes. "A broken leg. Poison coursing through my blood. Dysentery. Hallucinations from the peyote I had ingested four hours earlier to stave off the pain of my broken leg. One single day before death would become my bedfellow. If you had been *me,* what would you have done?"

"Hauled ass," I said. "Or died trying."

Mitch D's face lit up – his misguided corporate advice was finally coming around full circle with true allegorical resolution. "*Exactly,*" he said, sitting back down, giving my left knee a manly squeeze for extra dramatic effect. "Everyone can always go faster. Everyone can always be more productive. People with dysentery can still execute on their goals. You just have to motivate them to do so. You have got to be the CEO of your own *damn* business, Murphy. Take ownership. Crack the whip. Up the stakes. Destroy your competitors before they destroy you. Because if *you* go down, everyone who depends on you goes down too. If *you* don't move quickly? If *you* don't succeed? *No antidote.*"

For a split second, coloring in the cells of an Excel worksheet, all day long, seemed like a simple-yet-rewarding day at the office. "How many cells did you color in today?" Jess would ask me, as we sat around the table for our usual (yet early) five-thirty dinner, since coloring the cells of a spreadsheet rarely required overtime hours.

"One-thousand six hundred and twelve," I would say proudly.

"Wooooooooow," Kate would say, completely impressed with her Dad, the *hero*.

"That's seventeen more than yesterday," Jess would point out, giving me a long, passionate kiss then flashing me one of those hidden looks that promised me a night I would never forget. And I would sit back, reveling in the love and respect that my family would shower upon me, and dig back into my cup of spicy Top Ramen soup with the nutritious little carrot squares, since that would be *the only food we could afford to eat*.

Screw that – I wanted the antidote. And I wanted it badly. I didn't want to die two days out from Mexico.

Crack the whip. Up the stakes. Be the CEO of your own damn business, Murphy.

The expressions on most of their faces told a varied, yet emotionally-aligned story of shattered expectations and unvarnished surprise. The expression on my face, despite the swollen areas that had been levied in a previously inspirational *tete-a-tete* with my own manager, was one of stark disappointment. Who were these people I had hired onto my team? Where had all their optimism gone? Who had hobbled their entrepreneurial spirit and squashed their ability to think outside the box? Since when had they required a babysitter skilled in the art of coddling and cuddling? I had spent the last ten minutes of our latest team meeting criticizing our collective inability to move the needle while Rafi and his island of misfits had continued to keep the software roadmap relatively on track by launching our Alpha build to over six-hundred internal testers just three days prior. While Chloe, the sultry-voice of Memphis, had been delivering personally relevant entertainment recommendations to Company employees, the business and marketing team had just been spinning their wheels. I was harsh. Harsher than I had ever been before, mostly due to the fire that Mitch D. had fanned up inside of me. And I knew exactly what each of them were thinking, but were not saying.

Who is this asshole? Why is he being such a dick? Am I really that useless?

The thing was, I was feeling pressure on all sides and was taking active steps to ensure that we were giving ourselves the best chance at success. We were three months from the go/no-go Vegas Keynote decision. It was do or die. But despite the fact that I had no desire to *die*, didn't necessarily mean I could *do everything* for them.

Had this group of individuals been the right people to hire? Had I overlooked others that might have better weathered the storm? Perhaps *The One With The Bermuda Shorts* would have thought to establish a Twitter account for Memphis weeks ago, instead of Dustin, who had sat on the work while a twelve-year-old in Provo, Utah had mysteriously decided that "Memphis", "MemphisRecs" and "MemphisProduct" were the three hip handles he desperately had to own. Was it possible that *Clam-Hands*, faced with the opportunity to discuss a joint-venture with stock darling *FlixFix*, would have actually followed up his introductory e-mail with a call or a request to set the actual meeting in person instead of waiting for the largest global media streaming company on the face of the Earth to do it themselves? I wondered, deep down, if *Soul Patch Sister* might have come up with the idea to book a hotel room *directly next door* to Roger Ebert's wife Chaz while she was up in Seattle for the International Film Festival instead of assuming that a chef's, delivery boy's, concession-stand worker's roommate would find a way in a dark theater to get us somewhere, somehow near the widow in question.

Meanwhile, Bernard was livid. "I don't care what you *think*," he said, shaking with anger, "and I will not sign off on us automatically opting-in consumers for Memphis. It's idiotic, dangerous and legally questionable. And how do you even know that *this* is what consumers want..?" There was an extra pause at the end, where his usual 'you shithead' tag often landed, but despite its absence I knew it was still there, hanging in the ether.

"Because I know," I shot back. "First, the app-store landscape is a fickle, often changing beast. You're up one day, out the next. You get one chance to attach a consumer. The minute someone tries out Memphis, we need it already collecting their data so they can see how spot-on the recommendations can be. Second, there are no legal precedents that preclude us from doing this, as long as we provide a link hidden somewhere in the app for them to turn off the data capture feature." Bernard *scoffed* as I cruised past the word "hidden", obviously at odds with the sneaky machinations I had chosen to engineer in order to grow our user base as quickly as technically possible. Whatever it took to convince the senior leadership at The Company that this wasn't a flash in the pan, but that it had true potential to grow a significant install base.

"Show me some irrefutable data that proves consumers don't care about making *the choice* to share their personal crap," he shot back, slamming his fists on the table and causing his Tupperware container to shoot garbanzo beans out and all over the table. Everyone watched as the orbs of protein spun in all directions; only Jane made any attempt to corral them back into the container from which they came as if returning the garbanzo beans to order would immediately cause the argument at hand to dissipate.

"I don't have to show you *anything*," I said, calmly, while inside I was all wound up. "Because you work for *me* and this my *final* decision." It was truer than it had ever been before. It was my way or the highway. Despite Bernard's strongly opinionated position on the matter, he was out of line. He was also being short-sighted. And if he couldn't get on the train with the rest of us due to his own tunnel vision on the issue in question, perhaps *Vin Doozie* would.

Bernard, having had the luxury of me never taking the "you work for me" position before, seemed taken aback. He didn't say a thing, nor did anyone, for what seemed like an eternity. It was about twenty-two seconds before Bernard picked up his laptop and his half-finished lunch and stormed out the door. I wasn't sure if he was coming back, but if he did he'd have to realize that if you wanted to ship a product you had to sacrifice some of your babies.

I turned back to the team, who were all suddenly at attention. "Action items," I demanded.

"Trip to Provo. I'll get it on the books," Dustin proclaimed.

"I'm going with you," I said. Dustin scrawled something down, nodding along.

"On the phone with *FlixFix* this afternoon," Jane piped up, next. "I won't give up until we have a date and time for the L.A. meeting."

"Good," I said. "I want to see the deck at least three days before we get on that plane."

"Done," she replied, tapping away at her laptop.

"I'm meeting with brand tomorrow," Elise began. "I'll have the full plan around how we market this asap. I'll also book us that room at the W in Seattle. The one directly next door to Chaz. And since I know the concierge's best-friend's psychotherapists' first-"

"I don't need to know the *how*," I interrupted. "Let's just get it done."

I *clapped*. Or maybe it was a *clap-snap*. There may have been a smattering of claps and a cacophony of snaps. God knows I had never had the rhythm or coordination to execute a move like that in the past. Who knows where it came from. But it rallied the troops up from their chairs and they stormed out of that room like I had just announced there had been free donuts in the hallway and a gas leak right there *under the conference room table*. I watched them go and the door shut behind them.

"Who's the asshole?" I asked myself, aloud. "It's the guy who gets shit done."

I leaned back on my chair, arms behind my neck. I was the guy who was getting shit done. Whether or not I had multiple wolves circling, it didn't matter at that particular moment in time. Nothing else mattered but the feeling that tingled all the way down to my feet.

It felt pretty damn *powerful*.

It was orange. With brown accents. And French cuffs that necessitated silver cufflinks. Jess held up the shirt in front of my naked torso squinting to determine if it went with my dark jeans or if there was a different, yet more appropriate outfit I should model to the Canyon Park Estates Homeowner's Association meeting instead.

"I refuse to look like a candy corn," I grumbled, pushing away the hanger.

"Color looks good on you," Jess smiled, cocking her head to get the side-view look of the ensemble.

"Why did I agree to let you dress me for this thing? Remind me."

"Because, you said – and I quote… I *love* and support you."

"Did I *say* that? I don't remember saying that with respect to tonight."

"You don't remember anything these days not having to do with work. Remember?"

"No, I don't remember." I kind of didn't.

"Exactly," she said, replacing one hanger with another – this time a shirt with far less candy-coating. It was blue. With stripes and no cuffs. It would cut down my dress time by at least three minutes per arm since getting a cufflink through a narrow cloth hole was akin to opening any brand-new electronic device hermetically sealed in bulletproof plastic. "Can you just get on board with this one?" she sighed. "I just don't want you to look like you don't care about your own personal hygiene. Especially if I'm trying to get the board to start taking this dog curbing thing seriously."

"I see what you did just there," I said, grabbing the hanger from her.

"I hope so," she said as she pat my butt and walked out of the closet. I watched her walk into the bedroom where she picked up her yellow pads and index card notes for the meeting. She had actually done homework for this thing. You'd think she was going to speak in front of Congress, she was taking it *that* seriously. Didn't she know? This was a *homeowner's* meeting. With people's work and family lives, the last thing anyone wanted to do was show up at an Elementary school cafeteria on a weeknight, discuss pedestrian neighborhood issues that would never truly impact anyone personally and generally realize why the legal system took so long to enact justice.

I put on the blue shirt, hoping the night would be quick and painless. Yet unbeknownst to me at the time, but very obviously *beknownst* to me after the fact, the event that would forever be knownst as '*The Happening*' (and other naming conventions not currently available for disclosure or *Shakespeare-ification*) was mere minutes away.

The Canyon Park Elementary School cafeteria could have won an award for "Best Stereotypical Elementary School Cafeteria" if John Hughes had still been alive and if there had actually been an award to give. Between the sticky juice drenched walkways, the grammatically-incorrect graffiti, and the afterschool special-*esque* wall poster messaging ("*Bullying Stops Here*", "*Strangers Aren't Your Friends*"), I half expected Zendaya or the androgynous mascots from *Yo Gabba Gabba* to jump out from behind the pitifully-sized stage curtains and start singing about multi-cultural friendships and peanut allergies. Oh, and it also reeked.

"Of sloppy joes and ass," Jess texted to me, as Jerry Pascal, our wife beater-wearing, manual lawnmower pushing HOA President stood in front of a *packed house* of residents, recapping last year's agenda items and their present statuses.

"I smell the sloppy joes for sure," I texted back to Jess, while eyeing the entire room of strangers. Sure, there were some familiar folks, including the Kirkmans, Mooreheads, Chens and Shaffers. Sudhir sat a few rows ahead of me, texting away on his device, while Susan Gibbs sat at full attention, just like Belvedere – who sat quietly at her side. "I'll trust you on the ass," I whispered back to her, trying to keep the obscenities from overloading my smartphone, which was still tapped directly into the recommendation servers of Memphis.

"Or a rotting ferret," she whispered back, breaking out the olfactory skills that would someday, probably never, bring in additional income to the Murphy financial trust.

Jerry updated the room on a myriad of less-than-compelling items. There had been a family who had refused to pay their four-hundred dollars in annual HOA dues for three years running. The HOA Leadership Forum, made up of Jerry and his VP and Treasurer, had sent it off to a collection agency who still had been unable to recoup the money. There had also been quite a political dust up last September, when the HOA-contracted leaf blowers had started blowing before nine AM in the morning. A few hard-partying residents who needed their beauty sleep had complained, and so this September they would be starting at nine twenty; a compromise of epic proportions. The landscaper's contract had been renewed. This year, residents who paid their dues on time would receive a twenty-dollar refund. The city snow plows that had previously refused to clear out our hilly streets in isolated times of global warming-caused ice and slush, were still refusing to make our small neighborhood a priority. Oh, and the Girl Scouts had now been completely banned from selling *Samoas*, due to the fact that the cookies were made in plants where peanuts were also handled, thus categorizing them as a threat to Canyon Park Estate's health-focused ecosystem.

"I'll now open the floor for new business," Jerry announced, keeping from locking eyes with any of the residents for fear of someone actually *having* new business. Why he was so worried was beyond me since most of the residents were already checking their watches in the hopes that the sixty minutes scheduled for this useless session could easily get resolved in half that.

Jess eyed the room, nudged me, then motioned to her note cards and yellow legal pads. I gave her as much support as I could via my lethargic, but supportive, shoulder shrug. She smiled, then shot her hand up to the ceiling with such force that I half expected her to take off into the sky. Jerry, realizing this would not be a thirty-minute meeting after all, pointed to Jess and let the air out of his lungs.

"Fellow residents," she said, standing up, "I'm Jessica Murphy, new to Canyon Park since January." There were various head nods and a myriad of mumbles that ranged from apologies for not yet having come by to welcome us to compliments on our landscaping. Like a perfect politician, Jess nodded and smiled to each and every one of them before digging back into her list of concerns.

"Having been new for most of this calendar year," she continued, eyeing her notes, "I have concerns in a variety of areas that I'd like to bring up."

Gary Shaffer, obviously the Parliamentary Procedure Nazi of the group, was more than happy to chime in. "You have to make a motion to introduce new business items," he said. Jess looked at him – she had no clue. "I…make a motion to introduce…*what* as new business?" he tutored her from across the room. She got it. She wasn't stupid. She hit the ground running.

"Residents of Canyon Park Estates. Thank you. If you'd allow me, I'd like to make a motion to install speed bumps in the neighborhood," she said, causing some of the previously dozing residents to look up. Loretta Pascal turned around to look at Jess, about to say something in support-

"One second, hon," she stopped her. "Let me get through my list." Oh, and did she have a list. "I'd also like to make a motion to fine residents who do not curb their pets. I'd like to make a motion to establish a Color Council that approves or denies a resident's exterior paint choice before allowing them to employ a contractor. I'd like to make a motion to establish residential welcoming committees for new residents, create a social club responsible for planning annual entertainment and cultural events for the neighborhood, and increase the HOA dues to support additional upkeep and beautification programs so Canyon Park Estates doesn't start looking like *Crap* Park Estates. Which it's starting to look like." She looked down at me. "It is, isn't it? We were just saying that the other day."

"Uh, yeah?" I half-heartedly agreed, feeling the burning spotlight of judgment directly on my skull.

"My husband, everyone," Jess acknowledged, but there was no applause as I would have hoped. Instead, the room was silent as it had been before anyone had even showed up in the first place. Jerry was having a quiet, internal aneurism at the front of the room, bracing for the eventual self-caused spontaneous combustion that was seconds from occurring. He tried to manage expectations.

"I was unaware you had a *list*," he said, "which seems extremely well-researched and thought out. Perhaps, as these will require significant discussion, we can table them for a few minutes while we address the major new business for this session?"

"Major new business?" Jess asked, confused.

"The nominations and election of the new HOA President, of course," he replied. "Assuming someone chooses to run against me."

Somewhere, a chorus made up of inspiring young adults who had beat the odds of living homeless on the streets and had graduated from high school sang *Hallelujah*. Elsewhere, in a dense forest in China, multiple Panda babies who had been saved decades prior by a British conservationist and reunited with their mother, recognized their savior in an emotionally-breathtaking YouTube reunion. Parents everywhere finally admitted that their criticisms and second-guessing had actually all been the result of their lack of real-world knowledge and jealousy. Salon stylists, working with brand new clients like Jess, miraculously got her hair color right *the first time*. Laser hair removal came in a pill form, *KFC* increased your metabolic rate and luxury department stores everywhere adopted the subscription model that had worked so well for streaming movies for high-end purses and shoes. At least, these were the thoughts of inspiration and ecstasy I imagined were passing through Jess' brain as she slid down next to me and looked me straight in the eyes, internalizing the words that had just come out of Jerry's mouth. *Nominations and election of the new HOA President.*

"What," I whispered to her, as the room began quietly discussing the first major order of business.

"Nominate me," she spoke methodically, ensuring I wouldn't miss any of the words or syllables. "For President."

I sat there for a moment, as the rest of the room buzzed with discussion. She nudged my leg so no one would see, still staring ahead, smile plastered on her face. She was ready for her entre into local passive-aggressive politics. What choice did I have?

I raised my hand. Jerry looked my way. And I said the words.

September

The red and blue flashing lights from the multiple police cars lit up the front of the *Death Star*, giving off the feel of a Bellagio-like fountain extravaganza mixed with the mystery of a *Cirque du Soleil* contortionists' death-defying act. There were campus police cars, local police cars, even backpacked Company employees watching on with curiosity and concern. It was rare that something required so much backup support, but from the look of things – whatever had been going on inside was dangerous enough to require the same level of response that was necessary for the famous incident that had occurred at the legendary Nakatomi Plaza.

Minutes after the sixth cop car had arrived, the double doors to the white sphere opened wide, revealing a crew of Blues, shepherding out four individuals whose arms were cuffed behind their backs, eyes squinted to avoid the spotlights and attention. Three were men, wearing black t-shirts and jeans, all wearing sunglasses and stunned at the welcoming party before them. In front of them, leading the pack, wearing a painfully-ironic smiley-face emoticon t-shirt, was none other than Romy Wallace. Yes. Romy Wallace was being *arrested*.

"Are you seeing *this*?" I vomited, excited from the driver's side of my car, half scooted down in the seat so just my eyes could see over the dashboard but so no one could *see me*. It was unbelievable. It was inconceivable. This was better than the first five minutes of *any* single episode opener of *Law & Order*, where some unknown character actor was found in a precarious yet dangerous situation. Who needed TV when this kind of drama was unfolding in reality, right before my vindictive eyes?

Dustin, crouched in the passenger seat and half committed to a powdered jelly doughnut, coughed in excitement – sending a fine mist of sugar cascading onto the floor. "Eff yes I am seeing this," he said, still chewing. "Totally balls, boss. Totally *balls*."

As the officers jammed Romy and her lackeys into the back of the patrol cars, I started the engine to my car. I slid up slightly, watching the cars exit the building's driveway and onto the main campus streets. Dustin pointed after them, and I put the car into gear, following them down the street and onto the main thoroughfare feeling more 'suave governmental spook' than 'tortured getaway driver.' No matter which persona was piloting the car, there really was only one thought going through my head.

Oh, yes. Romy was going to jail and I was going to watch it happen.

Five days earlier, I had miraculously found myself in a position I would never have predicted or expected – sitting wedged in between Dustin and old man Bernard on an airplane, descending into one Eppley Airfield, serving the gloriously humid city of Omaha, Nebraska. Omaha, as it had turned out, was the hometown of one infamous twelve-year old named Garry Hitchcock. Garry lived over on Hamilton Street in the Midtown area, loved his Legos and split his time between school and *Animal Crossing,* where he had built up a fairly lucrative digital turnip trade business. In addition, Garry also seemed to get off on registering Twitter accounts using the confidential product names of Fortune 500 technology companies like ours. After turning down multiple offers of free game consoles and trips to visit our exciting data storage facilities, cold hard cash seemed like the only solution to a problem we couldn't afford to ignore. And since the Memphis code name would be the official product name, the Twitter screen name (which *someone* had forgotten to register in our early days) had to match. I had brought Dustin since it was clearly his fault, a check for one-hundred and fifty grand, and the only legal support I had – who had incidentally returned to the Murphy fold after a short yet agreeable exchange.

"You're a real *shithead*," Bernard had used as an opening line the day after our most recent argument, surprising me in front of the magic *Starbucks* robot, where I often relaxed to the gurgling sounds of mad scientist coffee creations when I needed to get away. I had put aside my four latest concoctions of coffee; turning to meet the geezer's gaze, no longer scared of his bark nor his bite.

"Yes, but I'm the *shithead* who you report to," I had said, matter-of-fact, having started to feel comfortable in my managerial shoes. "I'm also the *shithead* who can fire your ass for insubordination and turn off that health benefits spigot you so clearly love to drink from." He looked at me, stunned, as if I knew something I wasn't supposed to have known.

Thank you, Nostra*dame*us.

The three of us sat at an uncomfortable wooden table, opposite an oblivious gum-chewing Garry Hitchcock and his Wilford Brimley-*esque* grandfather, Sam. This was *not* the scene we'd seen in movies before where the College recruiter came to the house of a small-town athlete to convince his grandparents (his parents had died in a tragic boating or ski-lift accident) that he should sign the contract for a better life. No, this was more depressing than that. *This* was the scene where the old guy with anger issues, the computer nerd and the failed Hollywood screenwriter tried to convince a wise old man that the check he was holding in his hands was literally, totally and completely all that The Company could offer.

"The Company made billions of dollars in profit last year," Sam Hitchcock said, tapping an article he had highlighted, which sat in front of us. "You're tellin' me that one hundred fifty grand is all they can afford?" He slid the article towards me, ensuring I had seen the selected passages.

"Sir," I began, respectfully, "This is all I am authorized to pay your grandson. It is, in my opinion, very generous in light of the fact that we are not pursuing further investigation to determine just *how* your grandson came upon details of what is currently a confidential project."

Sam Hitchcock eyed the three of us, squinted through it, then turned to look at Garry. "Five hundred thousand," he threw out. Dustin choked on *absolutely nothing*.

"It isn't going to happen," I said. "It's one hundred fifty-grand. That's the offer." Sam Hitchcock was not pleased. He had experienced financial bait-and-switches in his past. There had been the bank loan interest rate on his farm. That *Columbia House* Ponzi scheme. Now, from the look in his eyes, he was all in a twist due to the obviously unfair situation before him – where someone was going to *hand him a hundred and fifty thousand dollars* for no reason whatsoever. *Thank you, lazy America* – I cursed in my head.

"Then Garry ain't signing crap," Sam replied, sitting back arms crossed.

I looked to Dustin. Then I nodded to Bernard, who sat up from his reclining position and pulled a stack of papers out from a folder on his lap. They were filled with lines and lines of intimidating legal wordage, covered everywhere by pencil scrawls that looked like they were written by someone competing for the "Smallest Words in a Legal Document" Guinness Book of World Record. They did the trick. I got nervous just barely glancing at them.

"Mr. Hitchcock. I'm Bernard Denman. As one of the legal representatives for The Company," he began, "it is my duty to make you aware of three things." The old man talking to the old man seemingly held more weight over the geek and the writer. Sam leaned in. "This document before you is a legal filing that The Company will revise and deliver to the courts in the event we cannot reach an agreement. This document will charge one Garry Hitchcock with corporate espionage, as well as charge him with intent to distribute intellectual property to the public without permission. This document, Mr. Hitchcock, if filed, will have the potential to ruin your grandson's future. I have grandchildren, Mr. Hitchcock. Knowing how I care for them; I can't imagine you'd want to allow that to happen to Garry here. Especially with an opportunity to ensure a successful, financially stress-free environment as the alternative."

Go, Bernard, you motherfucker!

Even Garry had taken notice, swallowing his gum and leaning in with his grandfather. The two of them tilted their head to get a look at the legal document, as we picked up our bags and Bernard started to reach for the check.

"*Waitwaitwait*," came the words out of Sam's mouth, while at the same time he slammed his oaky hand on the check to keep it from disappearing.

Fifteen minutes later, while Bernard, Dustin and Sam were shaking hands and admiring a totally unremarkable wall of stuffed fox heads, I sat in front of Gerry's tricked-out desktop computer changing the passwords on the three Twitter accounts that The Company had just recently purchased. In case you missed it, for the completely insane price of *one hundred-fifty thousand dollars*.

For a conglomerate as large as The Company, which was *not* skilled in the art of moving quickly in any aspect of its business, there was a *Fuck-Up Fund* which was strictly reserved for buying off the general public when they had squatted on a soon-to-be-released product name, or been maimed, injured or burned by a product or service. And the *Fuck-Up Fund* was huge. I could have gone as high as four-hundred and twenty-five grand, so I was proud at our collective bargaining ability. *Go team!*

"So, how'd you know about Memphis?" I asked Garry, casually, while changing the final password for the Twitter screen names.

"Just luck I guess," snapped Garry, lying oblivious on his rat's nest of a bed comforter.

I got up, gathering my laptop bag, and moved towards his doorway. On the way there, something curious diverted my attention. A framed picture, hanging just over Garry's light switch, including Garry himself and an eerily-familiar looking Zombie popping out of a FedEx shipping box. But it wasn't just any Zombie. It was a Zombie with a familiar face. It was more than just a Zombie with a familiar face. It was a *slap in mine*. "Who's this?" I asked, leading the witness.

"Just a guy dressed up as a zombie," he replied, sitting up on the edge of his bed now with mild curiosity. I knew it, and he knew it. There was a significant reason to be curious as I hovered, feigning fascination with the picture. The picture that also, incidentally, included an autograph. A *readable* autograph.

"Signed by RJ Zimmer, I see," I said, tapping away at it clear as day.

"Oh, you know him?" he was now standing up, next to me, trying to get the conversation to move out into the den.

"Anyone who is a *YouTube* fan knows about *Undead Snark* starring RJ Zimmer," I said. Especially Romy Wallace. Who had represented the 'corpse of comedy' during what no one but Romy called her *Age of Snark*. "Plus," I said, smiling as I walked out of the bedroom and back into the den, "we kind of go around in the same circles."

Garry just stood, mouth agape, watching me with fear as I walked towards his grandfather – who was loosely holding the check. I'm sure he was worried I was going to snatch the check and any chance at a real life out of the old man's hands, but I didn't. Inside, I had imagined how the whole situation most likely played out. Romy called RJ. RJ called Garry. Garry typed Twitter in his browser's address bar. The rest was History.

Somewhere *in my imagination,* as I made my way to the rental car outside, the *Sorceress-Bitch* turned her back to my sword-wielding warrior, having no idea what wicked things were coming next.

The East Seattle Police Station had wonderful, understated eco-friendly lighting, vending machines with gluten-free protein bars and soups, and a wonderful one-way window that allowed the ultimate in voyeurism as perps went through the motions of getting photos taken and fingerprints logged. I watched, completely engrossed, as Romy argued on the house phone in the background, then made her way to the fingerprint station mere feet from the window where Dustin and I gazed wide-eyed.

"Are you sure she can't see us?" I asked, cautiously touching the glass without fully committing, much like I'd do when an evil insect appeared on the driver's side window but you couldn't tell which side it was actually on.

"One way glass. Sweet, right? They make it in Korea using a special next-generation smelting process," Dustin bragged. "See?" he said, *knocking* loudly on the window.

Romy turned quickly to the window, staring directly at me, despite actually not being able to see anything but her own face. To which she smiled at. Then, she checked her teeth, thrust out her chest and puckered her lips. Yes, even while getting her fingerprints taken, she had time to revel in her own brand.

A Police Officer sidled up, eyeing the two of us and our fascination with what was going on behind the glass. "We don't get many of *those* coming through here that often," he said, grinning.

"What'd she do?" I asked, wanting to hear it in his own words.

"Breaking and entering into a secure Company building," he said. "Key cards looked real, but none of their names were even registered in the system. I'll tell ya, we'd be pretty bored and never hit our quotas around here if it weren't for all the anonymous tips coming in." He gave Dustin and me a healthy pat on the back, continuing on down the hall.

"*Anonymous* tip," I said to Dustin.

"Yeah," he nodded, smiling, holding out his fist in a welcoming fist-bump kind of way. "Anonymous."

We bumped fists. Of course, we did. We deserved it.

Three days earlier, Memphis was getting its own coming out party, in the dark wooden depths of The Company's "Great Room" – a living room simulated in the basement of Studio D, tricked out with all the latest technology and casual enough to feel like home. There were embarrassingly-large HD flat panels, couches and chairs, drinks and snacks. I sat off to the side, checking my mail, as a relative Who's Who of "famous" technology bloggers and journalists watched on as Rafi demonstrated the Memphis application working in Beta mode, projecting entertainment recommendation results on the largest screen of the bunch.

The technology VIPs included well-known, established journalists like Wade Bernstein from *The Wall Street Journal*, Peter Gainsburg at *Engadget* and Cade Johnston from *Wired*. There were the lesser-known flash in the pan bloggers like Felicia Thompson (*Gadget-to-Go*), Kain Belford (*InputOne*) and Tegan Hess (*BlogherGeek*). And then there were the folks no one had ever heard of, but had written something incoherent *once*, that had garnered them a slot on a previous year's list that someone in PR never got around to scrubbing. People like, *Guy with the Unicorn Man-Bag*, *Asian Girl in Pigtails* and the Patrick Stewart of wheelchair-bound grumpy geeks everywhere – Eric Grimwood. All of them wore fluorescent green Company badges, hats and bandanas that glorified the Company's logo, and all guarded their cans of carbonated caffeine-infused drinks on the table in front of them.

The questions came in waves, with each individual getting the opportunity to ask five, as Rafi coordinated the clockwise rotation. Could we share with them the equation behind the algorithm? *No, it was confidential tech.* What made it stand out versus other recommendation engines? *It was personal, not crowd based.* When was it coming out, what was its name, and would we partner with media companies? *Soon, no comment, and maybe.* Then Rafi got to Eric Grimwood, who had come extra-prepared with a list of questions printed out on a wrinkled, ratty piece of paper. "How is the Company handling the leaks of confidential product information?" he asked, pulling me out of an e-mail thread that had been going on for days about whether or not the "M" in Memphis should be capitalized. Rafi and I shared a look of mutual concern.

"The same way we always do," Rafi responded, on point, "swiftly and with consequences." Eric Grimwood seemed satisfied, taking a swig of his fifth can of soda as Rafi made it around the horn again. What devices would it ship on? *To be determined.* Would the Company be putting significant Marketing spend behind its launch? *Only if it was chosen as a pillar of this Holiday's campaign.* Why build something that others have already built? *Because if you see an opportunity or opening for improvement, why not give consumers something better?*

It was back to Grimwood, who looked past the mustard to read his second question. "So, when you say 'swiftly and with consequences' does that mean writing checks for hundreds of thousands of dollars?" Rafi's eyes bugged out as I *sprung* up to my feet. The rest of the VIPs were already writing and typing as fast as they possibly could.

"How about you elaborate on that," I asked, causing the VIPs to turn around and wonder why the guy in the corner had suddenly chosen to speak up. It was highly uncharacteristic for the person who *wasn't* the moderator to say *anything.* It was also highly uncharacteristic for *me* to say *nothing.*

Grimwood manipulated a small joystick and *whirred* the wheelchair around to face me. "I'll withdraw the question," he jeered, smoothing out his piece of paper on his damp, soda-stained belly of gluttony and then *whirring* his mechanical nuisance back around.

Inside my head, the alarm bells were going off like crazy. *Where was he getting this stuff,* I wondered. *Who was feeding him this information?* Rafi made like there was nothing wrong, going through another cycle of questions. I was sure they were good, thoughtful questions with vague, ambiguous answers, but they all came out as *waah waaah waaaaah*. Because I wasn't listening. Because all of my senses were trained on Grimwood. The bald-headed bastard in the wheelchair. When it came back to him, he referred once again to his sheet of paper, directing the question in my general direction.

"Bring it," I said. He raised his eyebrows at me, accepting the challenge.

"Is it true that you've made what will most likely be a very *unpopular* decision, to automatically opt-" I leapt at him, covering the distance between us in less than a second, ensuring he wasn't able to complete his question about our completely secret and *totally confidential* decision to automatically opt-in consumers to our personal data collection without their knowledge. But I didn't just leap. I *tackled*. With enough force to cause *Guy with the Unicorn Man-Bag* to drop his bag and knock Grimwood out of his chair and onto the floor.

"Give…me…that…list…" I demanded, as I tried to rip it from his sweaty, calculating hands. He fought back wildly, guarding his eyes and screaming bloody murder. Rafi pulled me off him, pushing me back as the rest of the room helped forklift Grimwood back into his chair. Rafi grabbed me, shuttling me quickly out of the Great Room and into the hallway.

"What are you *doing*?" he demanded, pulling me off to the side.

"*Sabotage*," I said, accusing Grimwood of the act, body heaving and out of breath.

"Him or *you*?" he questioned, frustrated.

"I had to stop him," I said, "before it became a story the press could *actually* tell." Rafi looked back into the Great Room, where the other Company VIPs were discussing my inappropriate pile driver. "I need to know what was on that paper," I demanded. "Get it for me."

Rafi, or *The Sleight of Hand Master* as I would call him within seconds, revealed the paper and offered it to me in a gesture of solidarity, respect, and because he hoped it would make me disappear quickly. He had to calm down the VIPs and salvage the session. "Take it and go," he said. "And when I say go, *jefe*, I mean go *quickly*."

Twenty-four hours later I found myself crouched atop a milk crate, sitting in the back of an old-school ice cream truck, wearing a hoodie and backwards hat as I had been directed, and listening to Dustin translate the *seemingly English phrases* coming from the mouth of his hacker friend, NoDoze.

"DNS tracked, domain confirmed one-eleven," NoDoze said to Dustin. "GAL is online, ready for the go." I longed for sub-titles. Could I get some?

"The e-mail came from *her*," Dustin said, saving me from the endless loop of incoherence in my brain. "He can wipe her name from the global address list and revoke all her security privileges from her badge. Then it's in our court."

"Do it," I said, without thinking about the consequences, perception or what the Company policy was on asking one employee to help erase another employee from existence then alerting the authorities. If only Bernard had been here, maybe then I would have paused. But I didn't. Harsh actions were necessary for harsh times. *"Do it now."*

NoDoze went to work, playing the keyboard like a digital virtuoso of data. He reached under his makeshift, ice cream truck hacker's desk and handed me a red portable phone that didn't resemble anything I'd seen that also came with a two-year commitment.

"What am I supposed to do with this?"

"It's untraceable. *Anonymous*," said NoDoze. "Go ahead and make your call."

I got to the dial tone and pressed 9, 1, 1.

It was fascinating how a person's goals changed in the heat of the moment. It was ironic, in a *rain on your wedding day* kind of way, how an initial aspiration of basic corporate success had evolved into a complicated and vindictive framing of a co-worker. If someone had asked me why, after hearing that Romy Wallace's bail had been paid and that she would be set free within the half-hour, I had made the choice to sit and wait on the couch in the front lobby of the Police Station – I wouldn't have had a great answer. It was insane, wasn't it?

Actually, no.

If Romy could so transparently announce her plans to destroy me, right to my face, did I not owe her the same? Why shouldn't I stand up to her and tell her exactly what I had done? Why not? It was time for me to actually prove to her that she wasn't fucking around with someone who couldn't give it back in the same way she was serving it up. She was dealing with Cameron Murphy. That's right. The list of brave, careless, edge-of-your-seat actions I had taken throughout my life could fill up a hundred empty journals. In lowercase. Without any spaces or punctuation.

KickedThatDudeInTheBalls

TriedtoSimulateWaterboardingOnMyOwnSelf

...

So, maybe not a hundred. But I could fill up at least *three* journals. Three journals was a lot of pages. If I died today and someone at my wake got up and said, "*all the brave things he did couldn't even fill up four journals*," I would have been okay with that.

"Murphy."

There standing above me was Romy, backed up by a trio of black t-shirted, gaunt-looking skeleton coders who had obviously not been fed in weeks.

"Why are you here?" she said, as I stood up to face her, slightly weak in the knees.

Because it was me, I thought to myself, doing my best job at practicing blatant transparency. *Because it was time you felt what it was like to get burned yourself.* Because I saw an opening and took it. Because, because, because.

"I'm here waiting for a friend," I said.

"Didn't know you rolled like that," she replied, surprised.

"Well, I do. *Roll*, that is." *Oh, yes.*

"What's their name?" she asked, prompting me to think *extremely fast.*

"NoDoze."

"NoDoze?"

"Yeah, exactly. Who names themselves after an over-the-counter drug?" I said chortling, while feeling the cowardice completely eat me up inside. *Tell her! Be a man! What's the worst she could do?*

Romy leaned in more closely. "This was *you* tonight, wasn't it?" I looked at her as she leaned in mere inches from me – our noses barely touching. "Man up, Murphy." She eyed her coders behind her, who all seemed to be enjoying the scene before them.

In my imagination, the *Sorceress-Bitch* no longer had her back turned to me. She faced me head-on, with her goblin warriors at her side, getting closer and closer as I was backed up against a stone wall. I was blocked on all sides as she raised her staff above her head and it began to glow a painfully-bright, menacing fluorescent green. She came closer... And closer... I looked for a way out but there was none. I had to fight.

"It *was* me," I said, jaw clenched in defiance. "All me." The adrenaline shot through my body so quickly and so wholly that I felt more powerful than I had ever felt before. The rush was intense. I felt all-knowing. My senses were completely alert. My reflexes..?

Almost like she was possessed, Romy's face was taken over by an angry determination. Out of nowhere, and without warning, she swung her fist at my face. My reflexes were *good*. It was like I saw it coming a mile away, like everything was in slow motion. I thrust out my left arm, sweeping her punch away from my body like I had been well-trained by a small immigrant man with a penchant for polishing antique 50's automobiles. I grinned so wide, everyone could now answer the question, "Has Cameron Murphy ever had his wisdom teeth removed?"

Then Romy kneed me in the nuts. And it *connected*.

Oh, how the Groin Kicking Incident has come around full circle, I thought to myself as I collapsed to the floor with my full body pain replacing the full body rush I had felt just seconds before. It came in waves, accompanied by a blurred vision that obfuscated most of what surrounded me and a ringing in my ears didn't help much either. I *groaned* from the ground as a familiar face leaned down to get a better look.

"Now who's the bloody clown?" the voice attached to the face of Shane McCullough said. I squinted, trying to get a better look. I tried to speak, but it just came out as a painful-sounding *eccggggthhhh*. Everyone laughed in unison, muttering a slew of gang-rallying phrases, and walked out the doors. I faded in and out as I grasped my pulsating crotch.

I really need to stop this blacking out thing, I started to think to myself as the pain intensified and crept into my lower abdomen. But not before attempting to give myself a virtual pat on the back. I was a *badass.* A *motherfucker to avoid.* A guy passed out on the germ-infested faux-linoleum floor of a police station.

Life wasn't going to get any better than this.

The fliers had been printed in four colors and with a glossy sheen that made them look more like brochures than posters. The design had been farmed out to an L.A. based graphics house that had been responsible for multiple Emmy campaigns and "For Your Consideration" ads in *Variety.* The words, although originally crafted by Jess, had been "sweetened" by a pair of copywriters in Hollywood who were best known for the phrase "*this Summer you can't escape the heat*" from those TV commercials for that hidden camera crime drama *Kitchen Investigators* – of which Jess' former studio had produced. Kate, comfortably perched in her chariot (a.k.a. *Radio Flyer* red wagon), held tightly onto the stack of the fliers as I pulled her along the sidewalk during one of the first of many promised "community outreach tours" that had been a part of Jess' political platform.

The HOA election for President had been a bloodbath. For Jerry, at least. Despite garnering two votes from *himself* and his wife, the rest of the residents had put all their faith in Jess. Some had been sold by her laundry list of neighborhood improvements. Others had found her subtle joke about Jerry's wife-beater tank top to be just the right amount of "dirty politics" to get the job done. For most, though, it had all been due to her speech. An inspiring, fifteen-minute opus documenting her fall from grace into a dark pit of depression that she was only able to climb out of by disregarding her own egotistical shortcomings and instead solving for the needs of *others.*

"Canyon Park Estateeeeeeees," she cried, pounding on the desk at the front of the cafeteria, startling the residents every time her fists met formica. "This is about *you.* This isn't about *meeeeeee.*" There were tears streaming down her face. The residents were caught up, sniffling along in unison. At one point, someone rushed to the front to lift Jess back up from the table, where her head had slumped through the last minute of her rousing climax. Meryl Streep would have been proud.

And *jealous.*

"Were you really crying?" I asked her, on the way out of the Elementary school, as she cleaned the smeared eye shadow from her glowing, triumphant cheeks.

"Yes, I was."

"Because of the dark pit of depression?" I wondered.

"No. Because I was afraid I was going to lose. Jerry's whole *free bagels on Sundays* thing had the potential to upset the apple cart."

Jess had moved quickly, wasting little time getting her new administration up to speed and delivering on her promised actions. She had established a new Color Council, solely responsible for approving any external painting or landscaping *before* a resident could pull the trigger. She had contacted the city, providing justification and gaining approval for the neighborhood speed bumps. She had set up a myriad of events that would encourage neighborhood residents to leave the safety of their four walls behind and emerge into the sunlight (and at times, the overcast skies) to bond with their fellow Canyon Parkers. The old neighborhood tag line of *'Canyon Park Estates – Turn Left From 106th Court SE!'* had been given a makeover as well. Now, *'Canyon Park Estates – Community Unbound!'* emblazoned the top of the fliers in a gloriously italicized font, highlighting all the amazing new neighborhood opportunities that would be "*heating up the hillside*" and "*turning faux-ships into friendships.*" You could take the job out of the publicist, but you could *never* take the publicist out of the *person.*

I grabbed a pair of fliers from Kate as we approached the infamous *hot pink*-painted front door of The Hemmingers that had been the bane of Jess' existence for months now. So much so that it had started to (at times) unknowingly impact her everyday slang. If you had done Jess wrong, you could potentially have been classified as a *total hemminger.* If you were in the act of doing something that would eventually be viewed as idiotic, you were *hemmingering away.* You could fool Jess once, and it would be her fault. But if you fooled her twice, it was because she had the qualities of a *hemmingerist* – someone who observed the world without logic or common sense.

In the last couple of weeks, Canyon Park Estates had already begun to feel different. *Lighter.* Like more of a community. Perhaps it was because Jess was always on the lookout for an opportunity to say hello to a new resident or talk to one of the "founders" who had been in Canyon Park Estates since it had been built. She fed off the personal interaction and it made complete sense why this was the right opportunity for her. It put her in the spotlight, gave her an excuse to build relationships, and gave her *carte blanche* to take her personal idiosyncratic issues and create processes and rules that were legitimized by the HOA's bylaws.

Jess was dressed to the nines, having rehung all her L.A. power suits in the "regular usage" section of our walk in closet. As we walked up to the front door, I glanced at her ensemble. Suit, stiletto heels, hair blown out like it had been done professionally. She snapped for the fliers and I handed them to her, while at the same time she looked down her nose at my weekend wear. Jess had *also* become quite concerned with the image of what she was now comically calling "the first family" – and her husband was seemingly not getting with the program.

"I need you to be my *Doug Emhoff*," she said, serious, as she knocked on the *Angelyne*-colored door. "Don't you want to be my *Doug Emhoff*?"

"What does that even *mean*?" I said. "That would make you *who*? Kamala Harris?"

But she didn't have time to answer, as Cliff Hemminger answered the door, wearing basically the same pair of shorts and generic t-shirt I had chosen for the day. I felt a slight victory inside as Jess handed him a flier and shook his hand.

"Cliff… Jessica Murphy, your new Canyon Park HOA President," she smiled, putting on the charm.

"Hey hi," he said, tussling his own bed-head and eyeing the brochure. "Heard we had a new President from Tammy." Cliff looked my way, extending his hand. I shook it, genially.

"This is Dou- …Cameron," Jess informed him, like I was some out-of-town friend who had decided last minute to pull her four year old daughter around in a plastic wheelbarrow just for the hell of it.

"Her husband," I clarified.

"I'm just making the rounds this morning," Jess continued, "as a part of the Association's community outreach efforts." Cliff nodded, looking like he had no idea what either word meant as it related to the neighborhood. Still, he feigned interest as Jess pointed to the flier. "I just wanted to make sure you were aware of next month's Canyon Park barbecue, right down under the event list for October there… We're also taking sign-ups now for the Canyon Park book club, which will have its first discussion on *Cloud Atlas* in November. You like to read books, Cliff?"

"Not for fun," he said. "Mostly in the bathroom."

"Well, let Tammy know that there's limited spots in case she's interested. And in case you change your mind, Cameron will be there."

I would?

It was news to me. I didn't have enough time to get through my e-mails. Books? They were impasses to success.

"Okay, thanks. Good to meet you," Cliff replied, starting to retreat back behind his *hot pink* colored door. Jess put her heel in the doorjamb, preventing it from closing. I took a step back, having a pretty good idea of where this one was going.

"Oh, and one more thing," she said, confounding Cliff. "The Color Council met yesterday and we're going to need you to repaint your door black, beige, brown or mauve. You've got thirty days."

"Repaint our front door?" Cliff questioned, now more alert than ever. "We're not repainting our front door."

"According to section three, paragraph twenty-two of the Canyon Park Estates Homeowner's Association CC&R's you are. If you don't, you'll be fined twenty-five dollars a week until it's changed." Cliff, who had probably been in the middle of navigating the hot and cold areas of the Pepperoni *Hot Pocket* he had been eating in front of the TV, was now legitimately upset.

"Says who?" Cliff shot back, annoyed.

"Says *me*. The President. Look, don't be a total *hemminger*." *Aaaaand, there we go.* The subconscious always found a way through.

Cliff eyed Jess, confused, then slammed the door in our faces. Jess shrugged completely unfazed, then refocused on a neighborhood couple walking by on the sidewalk. It caused Jess to stop in her tracks, then pull me close into a deep, messy kiss that completely surprised me. It went on far too long, or at least until the couple disappeared up the street, at which point she pulled back from the passionate embrace.

"What was *that* for?" I asked, surprised. *Pleasantly* surprised.

"We're *in love*. They should see that. Perception is *everything*, babe."

"But we *are* in love. We don't need to pretend."

"Yeah yeah," Jess waved me off, "Kiss me again!" She attacked me, swallowing my lips, as an SUV passed by and *honked* its horn. Jess smiled and waved. The show was over.

"I am still *not* coming to book club," I said.

"Let's talk about it later," Jess said, turning and walking towards the sidewalk.

I stood there, still holding the handle to the wagon, and looked to Kate. She shrugged, basically telling me in no uncertain terms that she wasn't going to get in the middle of *The Solver* and *The King of Memphis*.

I was going to book club. I fucking *knew it*.

Hal, the endangered African parrot, sat perched on the edge of a glass wall, guarding a piece of technology that resembled a pair of glasses without the lenses. Instead, the edges of the frames were wrapped in copper wire and connected to a gleaming metal box of circuits on the table that looked strangely familiar. I reached out to the box, to get a better look.

"Don't touch. *Sqwaaaaaaak*," said Hal, causing me to pull back my hand like I'd just touched fire.

"Who made you the bird in charge?" I wondered aloud, regarding the parrot with a sense of wonder and total annoyance.

"I did," came the familiar gruff voice of Simon Davis, who had asked me to meet him in his Building 12 lab at this exact time, and came bearing gifts in the shape of a Commons' salad bar container. He tossed one into my lap as he sidled up on a wheeled-chair and dug into his lunch. Both culinary creations had been arranged meticulously in the color-coordinated mathematical fashion I had first taken notice of but had never actually called out. Now was as good a time as any.

"What's the deal with the color-coded salad?" I asked. "Because it's *weird*."

Simon jabbed his fork into a tomato, taking a bite and regarding the other red-hued items on the plate. There were red peppers, seguing into dark red beets, transitioning into purple eggplant and coming in contact with a strip of black olives. "It's not *weird*," he said, "it's math. It's order. Whether or not you realize it – everything every *single* person does in this world, is guided by order. You execute tasks in an order that makes sense to you. You eat a bag of candy with a structure that makes sense – perhaps you eat all the colors you dislike first, or eat them in handfuls of even-numbered groups. That's what makes us human. Except most humans are clueless that they're doing any of what I just mentioned."

"So, this is your way of making sense of salad?"

"This is my way of telling the Universe to *screw off*," he grumbled. "I'm not going to be a slave to my subconscious need to find order in a salad. Instead, I'm going to force my own will on that salad and eat it in *exactly* the way I decide to. I'm going to retain total and complete control over my destiny."

"Makes sense," *to an insane person*, I thought, as I took a bite out of the yellow section of my salad and turned my attention to the technology I had been asked by the parrot to avoid. "What's this?" I asked.

Simon took a deep breath through his nose while still chewing voraciously with his mouth. He rolled his eyes, finished chewing, then put the salad container and his fork down on the desk at his side. "It's nothing," he said.

Upon further examination, the circuit board was totally familiar to me now. It had powered the helmet that had almost fried my brain into oblivion. Now it was attached to a new "wearable torture device" that was smaller and more fashionable. What was Simon Davis up to?

"It's not nothing," I said. "It's definitely *something*."

"It is beyond you, so stop asking."

"Well, despite it being beyond me, it also is the technology that was responsible for *electrocuting* me. So, you kind of owe me an explanation."

There was a long beat of Simon sizing me up, annoyed and frustrated all at once. Finally, he let out a *sigh* of defeat and grabbed the glasses from their holster in the workstation. He held them out to me. "Put them on, you *bastard*." I cautiously took them, eyeing what looked like conductive electric wiring all around the frames. "They won't electrocute you."

I put them on carefully, resting the bridge of the frames on my nose. They fit perfectly fine, like a normal pair of glasses – except there were no lenses. Simon spun the gleaming metal circuit box towards him, opening up the top of it to reveal a set of switches and lights. He continued to grumble through the exercise, obviously annoyed that I had strong-armed him into demonstrating whatever it was that he had been working on.

"*This time*," he began, "you will *only* feel a small tingling in your face. Then, just look straight ahead and tell me what you see. Simon clicked a switch, which was accompanied by a *humming*, then a pins-and-needles feeling in my cheeks and lips.

"It's tingling," I said, nervously.

"Eyes forward." Simon turned up a dial and flipped three more tumblers. Then it happened.

First, a flash of light filled my vision, which blinded me for a split second. Once it had dissipated and everything came back into focus, what I saw was absolutely stunning. There were digital heads-up displays everywhere I looked. But they didn't exist in the real world, they were hanging in mid-air, in front of my very own eyes. Some played videos, others scanned through data – the information was less important than the fact that I was *seeing* these things without any of them actually being there. If I looked to the left, they were there. If I looked to the right, they were still there. When I closed my eyes, they hung virtually in the black space of my eyelids.

"This is *amazing*," I said, reaching my hands out into mid-air to try and touch them. "How are you doing this?"

"Yes. Now it's *amazingly* going to go away and you'll pretend you never saw it."

"But *wait*," I said, frantic. "What *was* that?"

"If you must know, I projected visual representations of data that you could see without a screen, projector or display of any kind. Electrical impulses translated the desired visuals directly onto your retina. Your eyes became the screen. At least, that's how it *could* work."

"*Could?* It did." It was fantastic. While people were struggling over making augmented reality glasses a thing, Simon was pumping data right onto the surface of my *eyes*. It would revolutionize the way people "saw" their data. It would usher in a whole new world where hardware and physical technology could be rendered useless. This was bigger than the start button. *Way* bigger.

"It *won't*," he said, as he closed the box and put the glasses away.

"This is why I didn't want to show it to you. It's never going to see the light of day."

"But why? That's insane."

"Because."

"*Because* is *not* a reason," I shot back.

"But it's *my* reason," Simon returned, getting up and walking away from where we'd been sitting. I followed him over to the far side of the lab where he began tinkering with his motorcycle.

"What you just showed me could change the world," I demanded. How could Simon create something so innovative and groundbreaking and hide it in a dark metal box? "If you don't show this to someone, you'll be doing the world a disservice!"

He straightened up, livid, like a bear rising up on its hind legs. "I served for twenty *damn* years," he said, his face finally growing the shade of red I had always imagined would have been a great compliment to his beard. "I served and I served and I served. And where did I end up? It doesn't matter how great your product is or how much you think it will change the world. In the end, someone else will just take it all away from you. It is *not* worth your time *or* the heartbreak." The bear got down off its hind legs, kneeling back down to examine a crank shaft on his bike.

"All your *damn* advice," I said, doing my best rendition of a bear on its hind legs. "You can't preach one thing and not practice it yourself. You've been hammering me for months. Be yourself. Be passionate. Help others. Make a difference. Be one of the good ones. *Change* things. And guess what? I took all your advice and it *did* make a difference. I *am* changing things. I'm going to deliver on a product that will change the status quo. So, if I can, why can't you?"

Simon looked at me, disappointed. "You aren't changing things, Cameron. It's just an illusion and a thinly-veiled one at that."

"But I am changing things. I *have*." I did.

"Whatever modicum of change you've made," Simon looked up, "is because of the tools I gave you."

What a bastard, I thought. So, big deal. He gave me the tools to change things. Isn't that why I had sought Simon Davis out in the first place? To benefit from his experience. To get advice and inspiration. You could teach a man to fish, but you couldn't always guarantee that he was going to like being out on the water. It would, ultimately, always come down to that one person's drive and determination. I was holding the fishing pole. Sitting in a boat. In the middle of a lake. Trying to snag a big one. *Then it hit me.*

"I'm salad," I said.

"You're not salad," Simon shot back.

"Yes. I am. I am Simon Davis' big leafy bowl of salad. Croutons, peppers, lettuce, tomatoes, onions, garbanzo beans, the whole nine. Shaped and controlled by *you*. You forced your own destiny on me." Shane said nothing. He waited for the question that I think we both knew was coming. "All so that I could enact revenge on the one person that beat you. Has all of this, all these months, been about Shane Mc-Cullough?"

I asked, not really wanting to know the truth. It had been haunting me for months, but I had found a way to keep it from coming back into my head. Had every leaked bit of information and every piece of advice all been provided to me so that I could bring down Simon's ultimate nemesis?

"Some of it," he said, emotionless. "*Most* of it. But not *all* of it."

"So, you're just *mostly* a lying bastard?" I shot back, completely enraged. Everything was crumbling around my psyche. My confidence was taking a beating. I was in the midst of a battle with the *Sorceress-Bitch* and Simon's nasty nemesis, with my family and future on the line, and every action I had taken up until this point had been, in one way or another, influenced by a man who had ulterior motives. The twenty-fifth hire at The Company had used me. *Mostly.* And it was not a good feeling in the least. I felt like total and complete *shit*.

"I meant what I said about you being one of the good ones," Simon said, backpedaling. "And Memphis could be a stand-out. I still believe both of those things."

"But you used me. You're a *user*. When was the last time you actually did something for someone else?" Simon opened his mouth, but I wasn't going to let him answer. "What is…*never*," I spat back in his face, making sure to knock his bullshit color-coded salad onto the floor as I stormed for the door. I could hear him stand up, behind me, but he still couldn't find the words. I opened the door to the lab and stopped, turning around for one last punctuating thought.

"You know what I just realized? All those pictures of you, in those articles, on your walls? The Simon Davis who worked as a team with his colleagues to bring technological wonders to the world? Keep hoping and dreaming all you want, my friend, but *that* Simon Davis is dead. May he rest in Peace." I swung the door closed, causing the glass window to break into a billion pieces as I walked down the hall without ever looking back.

October

The clouds that the airplane descended through weren't clouds at all. They didn't even look like clouds. They were Hollywood clouds, primarily made up of a noxious cocktail of factory smoke, diesel fuel and premiere party dry ice – slathering a haze so grey across the horizon that all it made me think of was a painful eyesore of an Excel spreadsheet. I held up the *Alaska Airlines* in-flight magazine, its cover highlighting the glorious majesty of Mt. Rainer's snow-capped peaks, and compared it to the city below. The dichotomy wasn't just a joke, but it was stunningly unfair. I had never seen the difference more clearly than I had at that very moment.

I had abandoned this concrete jungle a quitter. I had let the system stagnate my creativity and deplete my determination. It was clear to me now that I had let Hollywood turn me into Simon Davis. But there was a distinct difference between the two of us. While Simon languished in his own anger, seeking out his passive-aggressive revenge when it suited him, I had leveraged the end of one disappointing chapter into the beginning of another more advantageous one. Eyeing the Los Angeles skyline from the window, I felt no disdain or hatred for what lay below. Leaving had helped me to evolve. Like a modern-day *Lee Majors,* I had the technology to rebuild a better Cameron Murphy. I was stronger. I was nimbler. And if successful, barring some technicalities regarding the vesting of Company stock awards, I would be rich. The *One-and-a-Half Percent of the Six Million Dollar Man*, they would call me…*somewhere*, where people reveled in the act of meshing 80's TV metaphors with present day financial success metrics.

The plane passed through a particularly-rough patch of turbulence, bouncing the cabin back and forth on the air stream as LAX started to come into focus. It didn't bother me in the least, like it had used to – I was free of the paranoia of an untimely death. Perhaps it was because I knew that there was so much to do over such a small window of time, that the Universe wasn't going to just gift me an easy way out of it. Jane, on the other hand, must have felt differently – she grabbed my arm in fear, trying to smile through the terror. I looked down at her wrists, both which were modeling the latest in motion-sickness armbands, and gave her a knowing glance. "Talk to me about the *FlixFix* agenda," I said, trying to get her mind off all those movies where fellow airplane passengers ate each other after being sucked out the back of the fuselage.

Besides having a product that worked, a partnership like *FlixFix* and a spokesperson like *Holographic Ebert* would lend us the cache we'd need to get past Ben Packer's gate keeper of the ETS Keynote, Simone Guerra. As in previous years, only two products would make it through the November evaluation process, giving those teams the opportunity to execute a full-dress rehearsal presentation the night before the Keynote in the Company's Vegas auditorium. From there, it was *Thunderdome* all over again. Only one up-and-coming product would get the coveted *"And Before You Go…"* slot, where Packer would close the show by singing the praises of a next-generation product that was considered to be an up-and-coming opportunity for The Company. Simone *knew* Packer. Packer loved to announce big partnerships and celebrity support. Therefore, the key to getting Simone on board was to deliver just *that*. Which we would strive to do, without the help of a flying elephant or a check drenched in gold, the following AM.

"Tomorrow at t-t-en th-irty," Jane stammered. "Trip Hawkins, their CEO, will be in attendance, along with his trusted advis-s-*oh no we're going to die aren't we*?" she shrieked as the plane pitched and leveled out as we crossed over the 405 freeway and headed for the runway.

"Agenda items?" I looked her directly in the eyes, while grabbing her other hand. I was the Mother Teresa of air terrors. "Give me the rundown."

She swallowed, gave me the glance back. "Opportunity overview. Real time demo. Joint partnership pitch. Leave behind d-d-documentation." The plane landed with a *thud* just as she had rattled through the list, engines reversing at an extremely high decibel. "Eat better, more exercise," she repeatedly stuttered, bouncing along with the shaking cabin.

As the plane slowed down, taking a turn towards the gates, she released her death grip on my arm and turned to explain. "I promised myself, *if we survived*, that I'd eat better. And exercise more." Like most in-air turbulence-inspired resolutions, *this one too shall pass.*

"You're going to do fine tomorrow. And do you know why?"

"Why?"

"Because you *have to*," I said. "We need this. And I know you understand that." She looked at me, puffing up her chest and taking a deep breath. Her mood completely changed like a boxer walking from the dressing room and out into a stadium filled with screaming fans.

"You're *goooood*," she said, patting my hand. "How'd you get so good?"

It was a question for the ages. That was for sure.

FlixFix had been a Silicon Valley startup with Hollywood-sized aspirations when its relatively young CEO, Trip Hawkins, brought its business model to the world. Hawkins, who had spent his college years managing a Bay Area boutique video store called *The Reel Stuff,* had dreamed of bringing video to more than just two-hundred customers a day. It was only through years of coding, content deals and customer growth that his dreams had come true. With over one hundred and fifty million subscribers watching streaming video on *his* platform, Hawkins had blown his modest goals out of the water. As a result, both he and his company were the media darlings of the digital entertainment world. But they were missing something significant that had the potential to transform and explode their engaged user base into the stratosphere.

That something was *Memphis.* And this time, *it was personal.*

While *FlixFix* had a recommendation engine, it was just like every other engine on the planet. It told you what to watch based on what you just *finished*. It showed you what you might like based on what your friends *enjoyed*. It couldn't hold a candle to what we'd put in motion. Partnering with Memphis would mean our algorithm and data mart would power *FlixFix*'s recommendation engine across the entire world. We would be everywhere and anywhere *FlixFix* could stream bits. We would be heroes of The Company. We would be immortalized in bronze sculptures that would be placed in the center of the Commons, just behind the Indian food restaurant and to the left of the salad bar. *Which I didn't want to think about.*

Jane and I had arrived early, nursing our complimentary bottles of water in the lobby of their third floor Beverly Hills offices. It was an open and inviting space, walls covered with movie posters and conference rooms with movie quotes emblazoned across the walls. Did you want to meet in the *"Say Hello To My Little Friend"* room, which had A/V connections for all your small video devices? Or would you rather get down to business in the *"If Andrew Gets Up, We'll All Get Up, It'll Be Anarchy"* annex, where the luxury chairs included lumbar support and massage arms that would keep you in your seat for the length of the meeting, *and then some*. The young Hollywood elite made their way in and out of the office, smiling genially as they walked by, but gliding past with the all-knowing air that they were a part of something big that everyone else wanted to glom onto. For a split second, before the doors to the Executive *"What Am I, A Clown?"* Conference Room, opened – I felt a tinge of jealousy. Here I was, in my old hometown, feeling like an outsider. I was a visitor in a city more familiar to me than my current place of residence. Yet I didn't work in Hollywood anymore. I worked for The Company. It was a sobering moment that was shattered momentarily by what I would later refer to as the "cackling laughter of despair."

Had I been blindfolded, I would *still* have recognized that laughter. Had I been born with the ability to hear and lost that hearing in a horrible underwater diving *slash* stingray accident that had caused my eardrums to rupture – I would still have recognized the laughter solely based on the way Romy's mouth moved when she cackled. Had I come to the *FlixFix* headquarters with my trusty shot put, I probably would have hurled it at her and Shane McCullough, who shook Trip Hawkins' hand mere inches from us as they finished what was *apparently* a strategic meeting that had ironically been scheduled *right before ours.*

"Fantastic, Trip," gushed Shane, in his cultured *Bridgerton* accent.

"We would truly value the opportunity to align both initiatives into one superior offering." Romy, taking second fiddle position, repeated the word "fantastic" about three more times, ensuring she looked back at me and smiled at least *twice*.

"Who is *that*?" Jane leaned over, whispering.

In my imagination, the *Sorceress-Bitch* and the Black Knight kneeled at the feet of the King of *FlixFix*, falling all over him like their lives depended on it. I was helpless, trapped in a cage that was suspended from the ceiling, with a muzzle around my mouth.

I waved off Jane, unable to enunciate even a simple phrase, as Trip turned around and walked back towards the Executive Conference Room. Shane and Romy hovered for just about a second, then stared directly at Jane and I in our chairs.

"Cameron," Shane acknowledged, then walked out the front door.

"Enjoy that water," Romy said, raising her eyebrows, then pivoting out.

I slumped down in my chair, not doing Jane's psyche any favors with my sudden lack of enthusiastic support. "Great," I lamented, my head spinning into oblivion. "Just great."

Jane was freaking out. "What's *great*? Or, what's *not* great? Is that a sarcastic great? What just happened there?" Jane popped a third Xanax, or maybe it was a fourth. With her, you could never keep track. She kicked back a swig of water as an Assistant approached us at the front. "They're ready for you now," she said. "Follow me."

The two of us stood up, collected our things, and shared a look of hope mixed with uncertainty. "We just do our best," I said. "That's all we can do."

Jane nodded, satisfied, as we followed the Assistant and entered into the Conference Room, where Trip and his team were already seated, waiting for the show. I couldn't help but notice the quote from *Goodfellas* mocking me from above. "*What am I, a clown?*" it read.

I shook Trip's hand, smiling genially, and wondering what the deal was with all the clowns. *The bane of my existence*, I thought, as we got down to business.

The plane ride had been uneventful and smooth. Jane had remained calm, cool and relatively kept to herself the entire return trip. The walk from the gate to the baggage claim area had been free of distractions or complications. The trip up the escalator, across the bridge, to the long-term parking lot and into fourth floor garage had also been seamless. My credit card had been accepted in the long-term parking lot's automated pay kiosk within thirty seconds, and the arm keeping me inside the lot opened up to the sky as if to say *'you are free now, dear weary traveler, may your trip up North bring you into the arms of those who care.'*

It was the *Flix-Fix* meeting, on the other hand, that didn't go so well.

It had all started with the clowns. And my idiotic inability to stop *thinking*. The *Goodfellas* quote made me think about clowns. And clowns made me think about Shane. And Shane made me think about Romy. And Romy made me think about her alliance with Shane. And the alliance made me think about the *Death Star*. And the *Death Star* made me, momentarily wonder why the exhaust shaft had been built in such an idiotic place as to allow for the Rebel forces to shoot a laser beam in it and destroy it so completely. And the Rebel forces made me think of myself and my team – a virtual rebel force defending Memphis from an armada of evil, Wallace-style. And in imagining ourselves as defenders of Memphis, it also begged the question as to why we couldn't, sometimes, shake things up and go on the offense. And if we were going to go on the offense, we would have to be proactive. And if we were going to be proactive, we shouldn't pitch Memphis to Trip Hawkins until *after* he told us what his meeting with Shane and Romy had been about. And if Trip Hawkins declined to reveal the information I was seeking, I would throw him in an oil drum and send him to where the fishes slept.

Yes, it was all Martin Scorsese's fault.

"We're very intrigued to hear more about this *Memphis* product," Trip Hawkins had said to us, as I stared wide-eyed at the clown quote above his head. Jane looked to me, then smiled to Trip, then looked back to me – I was mute, staring blankly, like I'd been entranced.

"Thank you," said Jane.

"We're ready to hear about it, whenever you are," Trip prompted us, looking directly to me, as I continued to stare up at the quote. I was somewhere in the "being proactive" part of my internal monologue that had been spurred on by the pasty-faced, red-nosed, mini car-stuffing bastards.

"But first, I need you to answer a few questions," I demanded, snapping out of my trance as I turned away from the quote and looked directly at the King.

"Go ahead. Use the thirty minutes however you like."

It was at that point, and I was somewhat hazy on the entire turn-by-turn rollout of what I would later call my *FlixFixation*, that I leaned across the table and pointed at Trip Hawkins with a look of total and complete *bastar-tude*.

"What was that last meeting about?" I demanded to know. I had to know. He had to tell me. I may have even *slammed* my first across the top of the uncomfortable wooden table a few times.

"We hold our meetings behind closed doors for a reason," he smugly shot back. "Now do you have a proposal to share with us or not? We're very busy and don't have time for games."

I walked around the table, glaring at Trip. "Games!?" I was insulted. "Don't play games with me. I demand to know what you talked about. Was it *Calabasas*?"

"How do you know where I live?" Trip asked, now slightly uncomfortable.

"I…I…" I stammered. That was the problem with naming products after real, geographic locations.

Trip Hawkins stood up. As did his leadership team. They began to walk out of the conference room in a single file line. "Wait!" I yelled after him. "This didn't quite go how I had expected. Give us another chance. Please."

Trip stopped at the doorway. "*No do-overs*," he said, pointing to the wall behind me where *that exact quote* was stenciled on the wall. He then pointed us towards the exit.

I must have sat in my car, in the driveway, for at least forty-five minutes replaying the incident again and again in my head. I cycled through my phone's text messages, which had also captured the incident in hindsight, through my messages to Jess.

"*I ducked up the nesting*," my 1:12pm text read, auto-correcting my true explicit, curse-laden text. Over and over and over again.

"*You did what?*" she had responded at 1:14pm.

"*I scrawled IP,*" I tried again at 1:19pm.

"*You know I don't get that computer speak,*" Jess texted back at 1:22pm. "*But how did the meeting go?*"

"*I'm such a tucking idiom,*" I re-tried at 1:25pm. Then I gave up. I had fucked up the meeting, screwed it up, and was a total fucking idiot. Jane was livid, although she wouldn't admit to it, because after all my speeches about 'getting it done' – I was the one who had caused it to fall apart. I would have spent another twenty minutes obsessing over my inability to control my deepest, most caveman-like instincts, but I had another dire situation to deal with. I looked up at the house, warm lights glowing from a slew of windows in the living room. I knew Jess and Kate were up there, dealing with it right at that moment. Although I would be fatigued, frustrated and take a hit to my ego, I couldn't leave my family alone up there with *them*.

They were *evil*. They were *heartless*. They were *my parents*.

She was five-five and decked out in wool-vests and dangly earrings, single-handedly supporting the fiscal year-over-year growth of *Chico's*. She knew something about *everything*, sent daily e-mails about how people who ingested [insert processed food item here] got terrible cases of [insert debilitating illness as diagnosed by WebMD here], and treated her children like they still had the emotional maturity (and knowledge) of a twelve-year-old. He was five-eight, wore the same sweaty baseball jersey and matching cap as often as he could, and always had an unrelated, barely poetic, but often confusing inspirational quote at the ready. Quotes, *incidentally* that had nothing to do with baseball. At least the outfit would have made sense if he had cited Abner Doubleday every once in a blue moon.

The two of them sat on the couch together, fawning over an excited Kate, who enthusiastically walked them through a picture book about Princesses who turned into pixies.

"And what are those things over here?" Mom asked, pointing to something on the page and making a sick-face to my Dad. "They're so… *interesting looking*."

"Pixies," said Kate. "When the moon comes out they sprout magical wings."

"And *fangs*," snarled my mother. "This is so obviously a subversively demonic book," she opined to Dad.

"One man's demon is another man's yeoman," he quoted, except for the fact that it was not a real quote that could be attributed to anyone whatsoever. Still, he was proud, straightening his lopsided cap and turning back to the apple of his eye.

Kate looked at both of them, giggling due to not understanding what in the hell they were talking about. Over at the edge of the living room, Jess and I watched on – she perched her chin on my shoulder, her arms around me.

"Have they asked anything about you?" I asked.

"I'm just the mother. Of course not."

"Do you have any credit card debt?" my mother asked, downing her third glass of wine across from me at the kitchen table. The first of three bottles had been corked roughly two minutes and twelve seconds after Kate's bedroom light had gone off and the door had been shut.

"No debt, Mom."

"What about savings?" asked Dad. "You should always have at least a hundred thousand dollars in your account, *just in case*," he would always say, because you never knew when you wanted to start up your own meth lab in the basement.

"We're *fine*," I said, shaking my head.

"You just shook your head," my mother noticed, due in part to a class she had once taken at an Arizona Community College that was called *Decoding Modern Day Mannerisms*, and which resulted in a pulled neck muscle that had been caused by her constant dozing off.

"Because we are fine." My parents looked to Jess, then all three of them looked back to me. It appeared as if Jess had lied. Perhaps they hadn't spoken *a word* to Jess about *her* before I had arrived. I was another story, altogether. In fact, they had probably spoken *many* long, complicated, Cameron-centric phrases to one another as I had been winging my way back home from the now-infamous *FlixFixation*.

"What's going on at work?" said Dad, nodding to Jessedict Arnold. Jess just shrugged that typical, adorable, annoying, two-faced, back-stabbing shrug she so clearly had practiced over the years for use in this *very specific moment*. I was livid. It was one thing to have your parents ask uninformed questions you were not in the mood to answer. It was another thing to have your parents ask *informed* questions provided to them by your *wife* that you were not in the mood to answer. My kingdom was being overthrown before my very eyes. Somewhere in my imagination, I visualized a catapult hurling a fiery boulder at my front door.

"What's going on at work, you ask?" I said, winding up for the pitch and giving them exactly the show that they had paid for. "Aside from being promoted, of which none of you took the time to congratulate me for, and above and beyond the fact that I am under a significant amount of pressure to deliver on a product that will wow our CEO enough to talk about it in December at our Las Vegas keynote, and compounded by the fact that I ruined one of our few opportunities for a significant partnership that would have garnered us the support of said referenced CEO, and further exacerbated by the fact that there are many people out to destroy my product and my future if I do *not* succeed... Not a whole hell of a lot. If you *must* know." I looked to Jess, punctuating the word "must" so she knew I was pissed at her. She gave me one of those 'really are you going to hold a grudge' kind of look. Yes. *I was.*

"I am still not a fan of this CEO," my mother said, completely misconstruing my entire tirade. I looked at her, fatigued. "Here he is, going off to Vegas to enjoy himself, and he still hasn't stopped by your office to congratulate you on your promotion."

"Well, neither did *you*," I said, tersely.

"I am *not* on The Company's payroll," she raised her voice, getting noticeably frustrated.

"Mom. You have obviously missed the point."

"I don't think she has," defended my father, which he always did, even if her logic made you wish for a torturous year of nothing but *Soduku*. "What happens in Vegas, stays in Vegas. If you're not staying in Vegas, you ain't gonna be what's happening."

Good God. "I am trying to *get* to Vegas. With the product. That's what I am saying. That is why work is so crazy right now." There was a long pause. My mother looked at me. Then looked at my father. The two of them looked to Jess, who averted her eyes to look down at the floor.

"Don't take this the wrong way," my mother ventured out of the quiet and into the storm of my own personal discontent, "but Vegas is no place to go in December. The weather is horrible."

And yet it was much more pleasant than the current atmosphere in my beloved kitchen.

It was pitch black in our bedroom. I had strategically positioned myself on the far side of our still-not-paid-off *TempurPedic* bed so there would be no risk of *my* foot touching *hers*. The fleeting toe touch would have meant that I had forgiven her, which I had not. It had been at least fifteen minutes since the light had gone off and there had been zero communication whatsoever. Total radio silence. At least until the sixteen-minute mark.

"I'm sorry," Jess whispered from her side of the abyss. "It just kind of slipped out. I just thought, maybe, they'd have advice you'd listen to." I turned my head on the pillow, facing the opposite way, being as much of an immature jerk as I could be. I was good at that, too.

She deserves it, I thought. There were certain things you didn't bring the geriatrics in on because their pre-iPad birthed brains just wouldn't get it. Besides not knowing the difference between *Dermot Mulroney* and *Dylan McDermott*, they also misconstrued every other single story and misunderstood every modern-day detail we had ever relayed to them.

"What was I supposed to do?" Jess asked, whispering. "You've just been *so* obsessed with Memphis, lately. I thought maybe they could snap you out of it. Being so single-minded can't be healthy."

Out in the hallway, I could hear the door to the guest room open up. That was followed by someone shuffling into the bathroom and closing the door behind themselves. Which was followed by the sound of a toilet seat being lifted, then *clanging* against the back of the toilet itself. I clung to my vow of silence, but saving Jess and myself from the impending horror and annual psychological counseling seemed like the healthier alternative.

"Uh oh," Jess said, noticeably concerned, as the *sound of liquid,* squirting in staccato rhythm, began reverberating against a ceramic bowl. My father was taking his trademark eleven-thirty pit stop.

"Get your head down *now!*" I whisper-yelled. I double-fisted a pair of pillows as I jumped from the edge of the bed and landed next to Jess. Quickly and proficiently, I guarded her ears with both of them while digging my face as deeply into the covers as I possibly could. The *staccato sound of liquid* quickly evolved into other sounds no human child should ever hear their parents' body exude, but I had successfully delivered under pressure. There would be no psychological counseling today *or* tomorrow.

Somewhere in the padded walls of pillows and covers, Jess kissed me. "Just accept my apology, you idiot. In case we don't make it out of here alive."

"Fine," I said, reluctantly. "But something must be done about my parents."

"Already all over it," Jess shot back. "Nordstrom is sending a few things over for Saturday."

"Nordstrom?" I asked, now completely confused.

"For the barbecue. You can't expect the HOA President to show up with a bunch of homeless people for her coming out party."

I would have said something, except there wasn't enough oxygen to do so.

Quentin Tarantino put his hand on my leg. All I could do was stare at it, as the world slowed down around me, and imagine all the words that had been typed with those fingers. Words that had turned into stories. Stories that had turned into screenplays. Screenplays that had turned into Oscar gold. He shifted his hand slightly as he used the other to reach for a beer, taking a swig as his baritone laugh lit up the hotel room like a carnival game. I smiled back, more affected than I had ever been during my years in Hollywood, taking a swig of my beer at exactly the same time. *I am just like him*, I thought, as he continued to wildly recount some story from some set of some movie and give me that trademark Tarantino chin-nod as he likened *that* story to what was happening *right now*. *Just please keep your hand on my knee*, I begged inside, knowing that the story would give me mileage for years to come.

The door to the top floor penthouse suite of the W Hotel *burst* open, revealing Director Ryan Coogler of *Black Panther* fame. He was sweating, out of breath, balancing two huge silver buckets of ice from his shoulders like a Dutch kid coming down off the mountain with pails of milk. "We're good, all's good!" he yelled, scanning the room for someone or something. "Where's she at!?"

Quentin took his hand off my leg and pointed towards the floor to ceiling windows that looked out across the city of Seattle, the Space Needle standing tall in the background. Just as he had extended his finger and pointed it with purpose towards the balcony doors, they opened, blowing the curtains apart in slow motion, compounding the surreal mood even further. As they parted, they revealed two figures, walking slowly side by side.

One was Elise. Holding her left hand, wrapped in multiple bloody bath towels, looking woozy and drunk. Holding her up and helping her walk into the center of the room was none other than Chaz Ebert. The African-American woman was strong and nurturing, carrying most of Elise's weight over to the couch opposite Quentin and I. The minute Ryan put the buckets on the table in front of them, Chaz was quick to take Elise's still-wrapped hand, and shove it quickly into the pile of ice.

"Murphy…I knew this was going to happen," Elise mumbled, slightly slurring her words as two award-winning Directors, a holographic movie reviewer's widow and the *supposed* King of Memphis watched on in fascination and concern.

Had she known this was going to happen, I thought to myself – she probably wouldn't have ever picked up that knife.

Three hours earlier, Elise was standing outside the cab, waiting for me to follow her out. "Alright, clown town," she said, poking her head inside the back seat. "It's show time."

I reluctantly got out and shut the door to the cab, which was quick to leave us alone in what seemed like an abandoned alley right out of a scene from *The Warriors*. Elise made some kind of bird whistle, despite the fact that I was standing right next to her, then scuttled along the brick wall like an amateur cat burglar and towards a closed metal door. I followed close behind, making sure to match her position – back against the brick wall, flanking the metal door, as she let out the same bird whistle again. She looked both ways, giving the door a quick repetitive knock three times, then doing it once more for effect.

From behind the door, a metal lock disengaged – rusty gears that had not been turned for what seemed like years grinded open. Then the door itself clicked out from its doorjamb, opening just enough to shine a dim light out into the alley. Elise motioned to step back as the door pushed open, revealing a nervous looking Mexican dude in a kitchen uniform of some kind. He poked his head out, looking both ways, then ensured he hadn't been followed on the inside.

"*Hola, Hector. Gracias,*" Elise spoke in a perfectly-pronounced Spanish accent. "*Este es el clown town del que te hablé.*"

"*Andale!*" Hector whispered, motioning for us to get inside quickly.

Elise nodded, then turned to me. "In case anyone stops us? We were here delivering the vegan cupcake samplers to Dusty, the pâtissier."

Things moved quickly from there. Hector took us to the far end of the kitchen, behind the salad station and through a two-sided walk-in freezer so none of the chefs could spot us, and directed us to the freight elevator. Once inside, we rode it up to the twentieth floor, banked a right, raced down to the end of the hallway, then used a keycard that Elise had already been given days prior by her former roommates' chiropractor's administrative assistant's locksmith boyfriend to unlock the stairwell to the penthouse floor. We climbed the stairs quickly, *bursting* out into the main hallway of the top floor, and right into Quentin Tarantino.

He was having a smoke in the hallway. Drinking a beer. And picking shit out of his cowboy boot with a huge *Crocodile Dundee*-sized knife. He turned, spotting the two of us at the stairwell door, and gave us an extra close, suspicious look. Elise and I shared a look of concern, worry, wonder and amazement. I, personally, shared a look of nausea.

"Elise Jenner!?" Quentin yelled out, squashing his cigarette out on the wall and spilling his beer all over the ornate carpeted floor. He ran up to us, still brandishing the now-scarier looking knife. I turned to get the *hell out of there*, but Elise reached down and grabbed my arm as Quentin came to a full stop mere inches from her face. "Elise Jenner. *Pupchuck*? Is that you?"

She smiled, sheepishly, shrugging her shoulders and giving me a look of embarrassment. "Yes, it's me – Pupchuck."

Quentin handed me the knife and gave her a huge, super-sized hug.

The Seattle International Film Festival (or, SIFF) had been around since the late seventies, highlighting independent cinema year-round. This year, they were hosting a special retrospective of movies that Roger Ebert had given nothing but glowing reviews to, and they included such films as *Pulp Fiction, Reservoir Dogs* and one of the last films he had seen before his death, *Fruitvale Station*. The festival had invited none other than Chaz Ebert to the special event so she could accept the award post-humously for her beloved, well-regarded husband.

With the pressure mounting from Mitch D. to find a way to bring *Holographic Ebert* into The Company's fold, we had identified this particular night as our one window of opportunity to get close to Chaz. Elise had promised to find a way. I had been skeptical. But we had both never expected that Elise's old Production Assistant life in Hollywood, where she had worked forty-five days on Quentin's flick *Four Rooms*, would have ended up being the catalyst to get us in the same room.

"Beals brought this show dog she named Chuck to the set every single *fucking* day," Quentin growled, downing a beer along with myself, Elise, Ryan and Chaz. "Whenever we broke for lunch, she'd ask a Pro-duction Assistant to hold her damn dog."

"I was that Production Assistant," Elise laughed, taking a swig. "Every single day. Per Jennifer that damn mutt's feet weren't allowed to touch the ground. Something about not staining those *beautiful* white paws. She was going for some most lustrous fur award or something."

I just sat there, watching the Hollywood tennis match go back and forth. I pinched my own leg without anyone seeing, just to be sure it wasn't a dream. I was sitting in a Hotel room with Quentin Tarantino, Ryan Coogler, Chaz Ebert and Elise. Who I had fully decided at this *very* moment, was the real McCoy. Not only could she get us into a re-stricted area of the W Hotel through back channels and secret alliances, but she had enough celebrity contacts to get us into Chaz Ebert's pent-house hotel suite.

"So why the nickname *Pupchuck?*" Chaz asked, sipping a glass of red.

"You tell her," Quentin prompted Elise.

"Ooh, I just *hated* that dog. After five days of not being able to eat lunch because I had to keep that dog's feet from touching the floor..."

"She chucked Chuck into the garbage pail," Quentin ruined the story, laughing so hard he sprayed beer all over the coffee table. Everyone laughed, even Chaz. "*Pupchuck,*" he chortled.

"That's messed up," laughed Ryan Coogler.

"Way," I chimed in, having zero impact at all.

Everyone let the laughter wash over themselves, lying back on their respective couch cushions. Chaz put down her wine, then looked over to me. "So, are you folks going to the retrospective tonight?"

"We don't have tickets," I said, "but we are huge fans of your husband and his work."

"Oh, thank you," she said, genuinely. "So, then you're just staying in the hotel?"

"Not exactly."

Quentin turned to Elise. "Pupchuck. Fill us in."

Elise turned to me, seemingly looking for my approval to broach the subject. How could I do anything but give her the 'go' sign. We were here because of her. I would let her make the case.

"A hologram? Of my husband?" Chaz asked, trying to hide a smile. "You *do* know that during his last years he took all of his television and radio appearances and had them digitized and stored? His words, in his voice, preserved for later when technology could better leverage them."

"Technology can leverage them *now,*" I said, picking up after Elise had given Chaz the full overview of Memphis, to which she had seemed intrigued by. "We consider him to be the undisputed legend in the movie review space. What better way to honor his memory than by bringing back his *digital* self to be the spokesperson for The Company's product?"

"This thing takes all my *personal* e-mails and records them?" asked Coogler. "That's kind of George Orwellian and *shit.*"

"Maybe you shouldn't be e-mailing what you're e-mailing," laughed Quentin.

"Roger was fascinated by technology," interrupted Chaz. "He wanted his voice to live on through many yet-to-be-invented mediums." Elise and I shared a look, not wanting to get too excited. But the writing seemed to be on the wall. "I think he would get a kick out of this. So, assuming The Company grants me the opportunity to both review and approve the final output, I would say *yes.*"

It was clearly time for drinks.

We picked up our glasses and *clinked* them across the table with Chaz. Quentin got up, dancing Elise around the room while Ryan, Chaz and I grabbed some more drinks off the glass tabletop. Someone put on some music, blasting it throughout the room. It was wild. It was crazy. It was completely *unreal*. Quentin paused for a moment, grabbing his huge knife off the side table and brandishing it for Elise. "Remember the movie *Alien*?"

"Who doesn't?" Elise shot back.

"Remember that trick with the hand, the knife and the table?"

Elise rushed to Quentin, half-drunk and half-excited. "Give me that *schmeelie*," she said as she grabbed the knife out of Quentin's hand and went to town.

All I could look at was the uncomfortable wooden table her hand was touching, knowing deep down how these things always turned out.

Mitch DeForrest had spent the weekend out on Lake Washington, taking advantage of what was rumored to be the last sunny weekend before the ominous clouds of inclement weather covered Seattle in a sheet of depression. It had been his final opportunity to test what he had dubbed "watershielding" which was an invention of his own creation – and which was a combination of waterskiing, wakeboarding, pole vaulting and adrenaline-fueled idiocy. The logistics took far too long to explain, but the most recent outcome which involved flying three hundred feet in the air and slamming against a static, wooden barge at least explained his current posture-challenged situation.

I sat across from him in his office, trying not to stare, but you were instructed to do so *at a particular angle* or else he couldn't even see you. That was because he was encased in a full body cast, with his head fully encased in plaster except for a stray patch of hair, an abnormally small hole for one of his eyes, his nose and a slit for his mouth. His left arm was positioned up into the air at a ninety-degree angle while his left leg was supported upright in the wheelchair that had been specially engineered for his ludicrous set of injuries. His left hand, which wasn't his "writing" hand, had three fingers available for pinching and grasping. Yet despite his current ailments and handicapped classification, it didn't stop him from reading me the riot act.

"Completely *fucking* unacceptable," he shouted, which was

slightly slurred because of the stringy plaster that was tweaking the corner of his mouth. "If someone's screwing with you, they're screwing with me. I vouched for you. I went balls to the wall to get you ownership over this program. You've let this Romy screw with *my*, I mean *our* chances at getting Memphis to Vegas and put everything at risk."

"Well, I did get her arrested," I said, trying to find the silver lining.

"And she made bail," shot back Mitch D., "which gave her the opportunity to hop a plane to Los Angeles and *fuck you again!*"

"Let's not forget we got *Holographic Ebert*," I suggested, trying to calm him down. "As we speak, his words are being edited into his holographic testimonial for the '*This Time It's Personal*' introduction spot."

Mitch D.'s good eye rolled into the back of his head. Then…he went crazy. He screamed, shaking the body cast back and forth like he was a mental patient trying to get out of his straightjacket. His left leg's erector set-like mechanism snapped off from the wheelchair and his leg went crashing through the glass tabletop in-between us. It caused him to stop shaking and focus his good eye back on me.

"There's two types of people in this world," he said, still breathing somewhat labored. "There are the people who get *hit* and then *hit back harder*. Then there are the people who get *hit* and sit around obsessing over a virtual representation of a movie critic. Can you guess which one of those people ends up disappointing their whole family because they have to sell their house and move into the back of their SUV?"

There was no use battling the beast. I'd fucked up. So, I had tried to battle the *Sorceress-Bitch* myself without looping Mitch D. in on the vortex of drama. It was a double-edged sword. Had I told him what was going on, he would have concluded I was completely useless as a leader at The Company. Had I told him *nothing*, he would have concluded I was completely useless as a leader at The Company.

"You are completely useless as a leader at The Company," he concluded, without any of my own personal evaluations to help him in the endeavor.

I looked away from his one good eye, staring down at the ground with my *two*. What could I do? We still had *Holographic Ebert*. We still had a product and a tagline and a chance at convincing Simone that it was worth taking to the dress rehearsal *Thunderdome* in Vegas. It's not like I'd been asleep at the wheel. I had *tried*.

"You need to try *harder*," he barked, wheeling his body and trailing gimpy left leg towards my side of the couch. "You need to *destroy* her."

"How?"

"You destroy her product before she ever has a chance to show it."

"But *how*?" I said.

"Do you know where the product is being developed and coded?"

I did. "I do. Building one-eleven."

Mitch D. swung his wheelchair around, making his way back towards the window that overlooked the campus and the soccer field. The sun, which had been shining when I had entered the double-wide office, was now obscured behind a sheet of dark clouds as they swept across the sky and towards the horizon. He turned, swinging himself back around.

"I once spent twenty nights straight in a Middle Eastern underground sewage tunnel imbedded with a Navy SEAL team, which is all I'm legally permitted to tell you," he bragged through the cast. "Get your team together and meet me tomorrow night at eight o'clock in the fourth-floor Executive conference room. I'll tell you how to destroy her product. I'll show you what it looks like to *hit back hard*."

Somewhere in the distance, I could have sworn I heard the echoing sound of thunder. I turned to look, but there was nothing there.

It was a Saturday at six-thirty in the evening when Hollywood had come to Canyon Park Estates.

At least, the Hollywood "after party" had come to our simple, quiet neighborhood in the form of the *1ˢᵗ Annual Barbecue for Peace*, sponsored by the Canyon Park Home Owner's Association Leadership Board in conjunction with *Whole Foods*, *REI*, and the hit reality TV shows *Extreme Barbecue Masters* (airing Wednesdays at 7 and 8pm) and *Super Extreme Barbecue Masters: Arctic Edition* (airing Wednesdays at 9 and 10pm). Contrary to popular belief, the soon-to-be released *Extreme Barbecue Mistresses* (airing only on *YouTube*) had no connection to anything whatsoever. All the sponsorship funds Jess had secured from the brands, after she'd covered the costs, would be donated to The American

Red Cross. Had someone told me that *Entertainment Tonight* would be showing up to cover the event, I might have believed them.

There were food stations set up everywhere, with servers carrying trays filled with BBQ goodies like ribs and seared tuna and Philly Cheesestake sliders. Holding court over two sliced-open oil drums that had been converted into *Extreme* BBQ pits was none other than Sam Gantino, last year's outspoken *Champion o' Charcoal* who had walked away with the $250,000 prize on *Extreme Barbecue Masters*. The American Red Cross had even brought one of their Blood Drive vans to the neighborhood, and was filling up their blood bags with Prime USDA Bellevue hemoglobin.

I sat next to my father, dressed in a tight-fitting pair of khakis, button down shirt and a sweater tied around his shoulders, who was completely distraught at what he'd been forced to wear. Sudhir, who sat on the other side of me, watched the circus that had unfolded before our eyes, staring dumbfounded at the size of the production.

"Well, she may not be my first choice in preparing a meal," he said, turning to myself and my Dad, "but she can plan my mukhagni any day."

"Still that bad?" I asked him, referring to his continued despair over his job at the start-up.

Sudhir said nothing, but simply referred to his waist as he lifted up his shirt. What once revealed three pagers now revealed *four* pagers, one cell phone and a long-range two-way radio. He was a kept man, that was for sure.

Each time any resident walked by the three of us, they made a point of stopping to ensure I was aware of "just how great" Jess was. She ranged from a "breath of fresh air" and a "catalyst for change" to "a modern-day Jonas Salk." We watched Jess as she worked the cul-de-sac, brightening up every pocket she stepped into with an energy that was infectious. She even had found a way to mend her relationship with Jerry after the election had turned it sour, and had appointed him the "HOA At Large Correspondent" who would be responsible for, basically, *tattling on people* who were acting out against the HOA guidelines. He was perfect for it. He was already a *fink* in my book.

That "outlet" Jess had been looking for back in May when I had found her depressed, dirty and downtrodden? That purpose that had been sorely missing from her day to day? She had *found it*. It was *here*. It was none other than *Canyon Park Estates*.

"C'mon c'mon c'mon, gentlemen," she chanted as she fluttered around the three of us, grabbing my hand and my father's. "The photographer is only here for an hour. We've got to take advantage and document this neighborhood's first step into its exciting new phase."

The two of us got up, reluctantly, leaving Sudhir to himself as we approached an already-in-progress staged photo moment that would put Jess, Kate and me opposite my parents – standing in front of the BBQ where The Great Gantino was holding up a rack of lamb. Jess rallied us all, bringing us together so we'd fit in the frame.

"Now everyone laugh – this is a hilarious moment," the Photographer excitedly projected.

We laughed. Over and over again. It was silly and ridiculous and everybody who was watching thought it was the funniest thing they had ever seen, which made me personally judge each and every one of them. *No, I would not pretend I was about to eat the entire rack*, I readied as a response just in case the Photographer asked.

"Having fun?" I leaned into Jess, whispering to her.

"What do *you* think?" she whispered back, flashing a smile and waving to a few folks off in the distance. "This is my bag, *baby*."

I nudged her gaze in the direction of my father, who was seemingly frustrated as he attempted to find the adjustment straps that often came in the waistband of a tuxedo. "When do you think you'll give him a reprieve from the outfit?"

She looked at her watch. "Eight-thirty. No sooner. That means *you*, too."

I looked at my watch. It was seven o'clock. I had to be at the Studios building by eight for our impending experience with Mitch D.. "But I have my thing. Remember?"

"I know you *think* you have to go, but what would happen if you just blew off that idiot Manager of yours?"

"Well," I ran through the options in my head, "you would have to segue into being the HOA President of our Dodge Durango." The look on Jess' face was priceless.

"You should go," she said, patting me on the back. "Go do…that *thing* with the *stuff* with *whats-their-names* for the Company."

"I love how you *listen*," I said, kissing her.

"I'm sorry, *what*?" she joked, giving my butt a slap.

I turned and walked towards my car, taking a moment to stop and look back. Not being in the center of it all gave me some added perspective at just how significant the moment was for Jess and the neighborhood. Until now, no one had made a concerted effort to bring the *people* of the neighborhood together. But Jess had. And she'd done it in four weeks flat. As I got into my car and shut the door, I could still see Jess at the far end of the cul-de-sac making an immediate impression on every group she approached. It gave me faith that come January, there would no longer be a *Seattle Freeze* to speak of – at least when it came to Canyon Park Estates.

That's because we had found an ice breaker…and her name was *Jess*.

"The taking of Calabasas, one-one-one," announced Mitch D. from the front of the Executive Conference Room, periodically taking a sip of water from a straw being held by his admin Esther, who stood loyally by his side. There was no white Persian cat on his lap, purring as Mitch D's three good fingers scratched its neck, and that was a shame – I had always hoped for a run-in with a real-life Bond villain. Mitch D. would have made a stellar one, especially in his current condition. Unfortunately, it seemed as if tonight would not be that night. But Bond-attribution or not, Mitch D. was still wielding a great deal of power and intimidation over all of us, as he always did, demanding our attendance for a Saturday evening meeting that I *knew* wasn't proper protocol at The Company. *Other* tech companies, yes. But *ours*?

The lot of us included Elise (sporting a single-finger bandage and splint), Dustin, Jane, Bernard, Rafi and myself – we all stared down at a printout that had been handed to us as we walked through the door.

THE TAKING OF CALABASAS 1-1-1
ACTION ITEM #1: INFILTRATE FACILITY
ACTION ITEM #2: DUPLICATE CALABASAS DATA
ACTION ITEM #3: TAKE ORIGINALS, LEAVE CODE
ACTION ITEM #4: SIT BACK AND ALLOW CALABASAS
TO FAIL

<u>O.A.R.P.</u>
OWNER: Mitch DeForrest
APPROVER: Mitch DeForrest
REVIEWER: Mitch DeForrest
PARTICIPANTS: Cameron Murphy & Team

"Memphis is at a turning point," Mitch D. began. "All of you have done a wicked job in birthing this sticky fetus of ours. But as we all know, bringing the baby into the world is the easiest part of the process. It's *protecting* that baby from a vindictive and violent death that is every parents' ultimate challenge."

We listened, although the metaphors weren't landing exactly as I think Mitch D. had hoped. Still, he continued. "Do you want to keep your baby *alive*?" he shouted from inside the body cast. We all agreed, somewhat wholeheartedly in unison, that *yes, we did.*

"Your action items are clearly defined in the handouts Esther gave you, which you should be sure to burn and scatter in multiple lo-cations once you have memorized your responsibilities. It's simple and elegant, people. A smash and grab, duplicate and switch, copy and re-position, retreat and exit plan. Esther, bring up the overhead."

Esther stepped away from Mitch D. and turned on the overhead projector. There was an animated schematic on screen of Building 111, represented by a large octagon-like shape made out of green vector-like rectangles. As Mitch spoke, Esther stepped through the animated as-sault plan with a wireless clicker.

"After-hours infiltration, access provided via Blue Badge autho-rization." The front to the octagon building opened up, zooming in on a handful of little dots as they entered the facility. "Once inside, you will proceed to the third floor, where a security-code guarded data center is located in the belly of the beast. Esther will provide the code. You will be responsible for entering the room, locating the hard drives that contain *Calabasas'* code, and jacking into the data port." The animation segued into a third floor 3D view that approached a closed door. The security code "XLJ32" flashed on screen and the door opened up.

"Once jacked in, it's a simple file switch. You download the data files and code onto a portable drive, then upload files back with the same names. Except these files are dummy files with no data at all. When they've finally realized this and attempt to launch the executable files, it will be too late for them to recover." The presentation showed a list of computer files, the copying and replacing happening in real time, and then pulled back to illustrate the entire facility blowing up with a flash of light.

We stared dumbfounded. Perhaps it was because of the elaborate presentation. Or perhaps it was Mitch D.'s enthusiastic support of a plan that involved breaking and entering into a campus facility with the expressed goal of altering the intellectual property of a competing project. I was less concerned with that – the motivations made perfect sense. I had been an annoyance for Romy but hadn't truly carted out the big guns. *Yet*. But if she ultimately had no product, she had *no chance*. That was inspired. Yes, that made sense. But… It was the *specifics* of Mitch D's plan that were bothering me. That felt *off*… But why?

Because Mitch D's plan mirrored the exact plot of the movie *Oceans 12*.

Which sucked.

When Mitch D., suggested we *infiltrate* building one-eleven to steal the Calabasas data, all I could hear was George Clooney suggesting his rag tag team of con men *infiltrate* a facility to steal a *Faberge* egg. When the man in the golden cast explained how we would *duplicate* the data so no one would know it had been stolen, all I could see were the horrible flashbacks of watching Brad Pitt create a holographic version of the egg, so no one would know it was gone. When the man who wrestled rabid Iguanas suggested leaving a mere "shell" of the original files behind, the *Oceans 12* egg-conceit also hung out there in the ether, like an identical twin of the *heist*-kind.

The result Mitch D. was shooting for made sense. The way in which he suggested we execute felt like a badly-executed rewrite. Despite Mitch D.'s cultured, dangerous and extreme life experiences, he had phoned this baby in. I decided somewhere in between the moment he finished spouting his "genius" plan and the moment where I told him we were on board, that I would completely rewrite his heist like I had done to other writer's work while in Hollywood. I wasn't going to let Mitch D. cause us to "Soderbergh-it-up" – that was for sure.

"We're in," I said, with the caveats monopolizing my thoughts.

Mitch D., nodded from within his body cast. "Good man," I think he said, muffled.

My team, on the other hand, seemed reticent and unsure. Standing there, watching as two senior managers from The Company planned a covert heist under the guise of an officially sanctioned initiative. I suspected they wondered just what kind of person their Manager was. Had they asked me, I would have told them.

"I'm one of the good guys," I would have said confidently, trying to convince them of a fact that I was, in the moment, no longer sure of.

November

*T*he darkness had returned. The skies, once sunny and sea blue, were now shrouded in a thick blanket of greyness, signaling the beginning of a six-month period of inclement weather that would embody the central theme of every casual conversation and drive-by salutation that occurred in retail establishments, indoor fitness facilities and the hallways of everyone's corporate workplace.

I pulled back from the bathroom window, where I had also been evaluating the weather in light of the evening's pending events, and turned towards the mirror to take one last look at what I had been so diligently focused on. I, too, presented my own version of the darkness – but it had nothing to do with the weather. It was, instead, all about what I was wearing – a black pair of jeans, black turtleneck t-shirt and a black knit cap that was pulled over both my ears. I touched up the black shoe polish that I had liberally applied across my face and neck, taking particular care to ensure there were no spots I had left untouched. If Brian DePalma had been looking for a cat burglar foil for his next movie, I would *not* have been his choice.

I stared at myself, having trouble even recognizing who the guy in the mirror was with all the caked-on gunk. I wasn't Cameron Murphy.

No. I was someone far more dangerous. Someone who others feared for their raw manly strength and intimidating stature. I was Jason Statham. Or I was Dwayne Johnson. Or I was-

"-inappropriately dressed?" Jess said, sauntering into the bathroom and sidling up next to me. She reached up and swiped a finger against my darkened face, holding up a black finger. "There's no world where painting your face black and dressing up like a criminal lands you in the positive column," she quipped. "Not even for a Sunday night team *whatsthisagain*?"

I hadn't filled in Jess. Not truly. But she didn't need to know. Besides, if she knew the truth, who was to say that she wouldn't involve my parents *again*. Or try to change my mind. Or sign me up for an episode of *Intervention*. To folks on the outside, perhaps what we were about to do was questionable. Or crazy. But those were opinions by folks who had no concept of the seriousness of the situation laid out before us. There were stakes. *Big* stakes. Unless you were deep in the shit, you had no right to give your opinion, criticism or feedback. And we were deep in the *shit*.

"It's another one of Mitch D's management training off-sites," I said, turning back to cover my left earlobe as she stood behind me, toes tapping while she gave me the twice-over.

"Uh huh," Jess eyed my outfit. "And *this* helps train you as a Manager, how?"

"Managers don't often truly *see* their employees for who they are," I spun, as fast as my creativity would take me. "If you can find your employees in the dark of night when they are covered up like I am, then you will never look past them in the workplace ever again. Because people *matter*, Jess. No matter what their level, they all contribute to the larger picture." Inside, a giddy excitement tingled throughout my extremities. I was *good* on my feet.

"So, basically you're playing hide and seek?"

"Kind of," I said.

"It's nice to see I am living with *two* children," Jess said as she slapped a copy of *Cloud Atlas* on the bathroom counter in front of me. "Good thing the bigger of the two kids can *read*. Don't forget about Book Club. Starts at eight, but you can get there as late as nine."

Ugh. Book club. The thought passed through my eyes, mouth

and nose – and Jess saw it plain as day as my nostrils flared one of those "Ugh Book Club" nasal hole blows.

"You promised," she said. "You know how important this is to me. And to our image as the First Family."

"I'll be there," I said, reluctantly.

"Don't just say it. Do it."

Jess came up close, turning me towards her. "If you don't show, then Dylan Packmore will be the *only* man to attend Book Club. If Dylan Packmore is the only man to attend Book Club, Dylan Packmore will never come *back* to Book Club. If Book Club becomes a female only event, it will quickly turn into an estrogen-fueled disaster. Book Club *cannot* turn into an estrogen-fueled disaster, because that will mean we will have to discuss *Little Fires Everywhere*. Which I promised, in my electoral platform, was something that Canyon Park Estates would *never* ever do." She had obviously put a lot of thought into the significance of Book Club on her political performance.

"First rule of Book Club, Cameron?" she said, pausing for dramatic effect. "No matter what, you don't miss Book Club."

"Is there a second rule?" I asked, joking.

"No. Because if you can't follow the first one, you ain't sleeping in *this* house," she said, then walked out of the room as I turned back to the vision of myself staring back from the mirror – it wasn't smiling at all. But it did notice the book Jess had lobbed onto the bathroom counter.

I picked up *Cloud Atlas*, opening up to the first page – it was written in the form of a diary. *"Beyond the Indian hamlet, upon a forlorn strand,"* it began, continuing on about rotting kelp and sea coca-nuts and one Dr. Henry Goose, surgeon to the London nobility. I rolled my eyes. *A surgeon to the London nobility*, I scoffed in my head. *With the last name Goose.*

"Henry Goose has nothing on *Fancy Pants*," I imagined my mother saying, just before she lectured an entire room on the horrors of how geese were inhumanely corralled and cooked for unsuspecting foodies.

As for the book, I hadn't even read the damn thing. And I wasn't going to. I'd show up, under duress, and manage to say just enough to be considered a mediocre participant. I'd seen the parts of the movie I hadn't fallen asleep through, and that would have to do. Because I had more important things to focus on than the reputation of the First Family. I had bigger fish to fry.

The *Death Star* was waiting. And we would be there soon enough.

The Magnificent Seven, which no one would call us *ever*, stood side by side where the grass ended and the concrete began – extending to the front double doors of the *Death Star* and surrounding the massive structure like a figurative moat of sorts. As instructed, *almost* everyone had dressed appropriately for the occasion in all black, albeit each with a slight shade of personal flair. There was Rafi, hair concealed under a black bandana and sporting a pair of Bono-like dark shades. There was Dustin, head covered by a ski-mask and chest framed by two strips of black fabric – each which contained a minimum of five silver throwing stars. Elise came rocking a black hoodie, dark jeans and a pair of black driving gloves despite there being no driving portion of the night's events. Jane, seemingly unclear on the concept of 'breathable heist-wear' came in a pair of slinky leopard leggings, perched atop a pair of high heels that not even Serena or Venus Williams could have handled. And speaking of tennis, Bernard wore a black headband, a backwards hat, and a look of discontent. And then there was NoDoze. If there was anyone who looked like a real, bona fide criminal, it was him. Which was a compliment.

The dude was *gangsta*.

The *Death Star* was ominously quiet, but there was a perfectly good reason. At The Company, whenever one or more employees moved in or out of a building, it was mandated that no one move it themselves or *witness* the movers doing it either. The movers, who had been employed by The Company for decades, had kept their trade secrets shrouded in mystery and wanted to keep it that way. Just how it took them an entire day to move two desks, three monitors and an empty filing cabinet was anyone's guess – but they were paid handsomely for it and no questions were asked. *Ever.* No matter the reason, the information had come in handy, giving us the perfect window of time to strike, when none of Romy's minions would be present *or* accounted for.

I stepped forward, facing the team and pulled my walkie-talkie from my waistband – nodding to each of them to do the same. As they turned theirs on, I opened my palm and looked at it closely – everyone's previously agreed-upon covert call-signs were scrawled in ink. It had taken many painful hours to land on the names, no thanks to the Internet – which had turned what had once been a simple, ten-second choice into a significant life-altering decision that no one ever seemed fully satisfied with.

"All agents confirm readiness factor," I spoke into the microphone of the walkie-talkie. My team responded, one by one, as the evening fog began to roll in.

"TRS-180 standing by," said Rafi, referring to the first personal computer he had ever owned, on which he learned the Basic programming language.

"Night Owl standing by," said Dustin, referring to his favorite character from the classic comic book *Watchmen*.

"Pupchuck standing by," said Elise. Because, well, *you know.*

"June standing by," said Jane, who had toiled for hours over finding a satisfactory call-sign and had eventually done nothing but change one vowel to reach her goal.

"NoDoze standing by," said NoDoze, which wasn't his name anyway so he got a pass.

Everyone stared at Bernard, who stood arms crossed defiantly. I made a "go ahead" motion with my hand, pointing to my own walkie and my watch to ensure he understood that timing was everything and that he was slowing us down.

"This is *bullshit*," said Bernard. I glared at him, angrily, and he scoffed back. "Standing by," he replied, reluctantly.

I circled my hand in the air and turned towards the *Death Star*, making a motion for everyone to follow me as I crouched low to the ground and made my way to the double-doored glass entryway. I made it there quickly, and so did the rest of the team, but with one exception. It was Jane. She lay halfway between the grass and our final position, clutching her ankles in pain with one hand as she stretched out the other to the group. She mouthed *help me*, like she had just stepped on a land mine or been shot by a sniper.

"Go get her," I whispered to Dustin.

"On it!" he whispered back, making a point to remove a Chinese throwing star from his sash and clench it in between his teeth. He scuttled back towards Jane's position as we all watched on. Dustin reached her quickly, wrapped his arm around her waist, and attempted to pull her to the safety of our group – but she kept stopping him. She wouldn't go. She whispered to Dustin, who picked up his walkie-talkie and spoke into it.

"*Night Owl to Memphis Leader One*," came the voice through my walkie.

"Go, Night Owl," I whispered back, already fatigued with all the names.

"*We've got a problem*," came the voice again. "*She can't wear them while she's crawling or they'll get scuffed.*"

"Put her on," I whispered back, then watched as Dustin handed Jane the walkie-talkie. She looked at me, speaking into the device.

"*June to Memphis Leader One*," came the voice through my walkie.

"Drop the shoes, grab onto Dustin and get over here now," I whispered back. I looked at my watch – we didn't have time for this crap.

"*These are expensive shoes*," said Jane through my walkie. "*They're Louboutins. If you knew what I went through to get these you wouldn't be asking me to do this.*"

"Drop the shoes," I repeated, sternly.

"*I am not leaving my red bottoms behind*," argued Jane.

I put down the walkie-talkie and took a sanity breath. Then looked at the team surrounding me. Nobody was touching this one, and I didn't blame them. This was on me. I was Memphis Leader One. Memphis Leader One was the *owner* of *The Taking of Calabasas 1-1-1* for better or for worse. That and a dollar got me...*a dollar*.

"Throw them to us," I said into the walkie, only fully realizing the error of my suggestion as the eight-inch heels came hurtling towards the group. The first one came flinging past us so rapidly we couldn't even catch it – its heel slammed into the front door, planting a spider-web crack across the glass panel. *That was close*, I thought, as the second one came even faster – whistling through mid-air, red bottoms whipping end-over-end, its heel finally finding a home in none other than Bernard's left eye.

He screamed. So did I. But it was mostly because of the sprinklers. Which had suddenly turned on, pelting the group with a wave of freezing cold wetness. Bernard collapsed, clasping his eye in pain as the rest of us dove for cover in a nearby set of foliage.

Foliage + rose bushes + thorns = pain.

"Good thing you've got health benefits," whispered Elise to Bernard, as an aside.

"So, Julia Roberts poses as a *pregnant Julia Roberts*?" asked Jane, addressing the entire group as they stared slack-jawed and confused at the end credits to *Oceans 12*. "I don't get it. Is Brad Pitt playing Brad Pitt?"

I had summoned the team to my office, just three days prior, forcing them to watch the entire one-hundred and twenty-five minutes of the film in order to make a very simple point. That Mitch DeForrest's plan to end Calabasas was the *exact plot* of *Oceans 12*. And that the *exact plot* of *Oceans 12* was *not* a blueprint to follow. Ergo, did we want to put ourselves at risk utilizing a ludicrously-confusing plan that resulted in more questions than answers? Simple *always* trumped complicated.

"So, they're replacing the egg with the holographic egg but then the egg was already stolen by the French dude years earlier so they're really replacing a fake egg with a virtual egg?" Dustin couldn't wrap his head around the plot either.

"That Clooney kid ain't no Sinatra," grumbled Bernard.

I flipped off the TV, turning on the lights and moved to stand in front of the group. They were all deer in the headlights – having just had two hours of their life stolen by a meandering, brain-twisting plot of epic proportions.

"Here's my point. Plain and simple. While we look to our leaders at The Company to make smart decisions that will allow us to excel in the highly-competitive world of technology," I explained, "it doesn't mean we shouldn't question those decisions if we feel they are misguided or stupid. If someone at The Company suggested we get into the business of building cars, using the same business models that DeLorean used, they would get laughed out of the Studios. If someone wanted to commit massive resources to reboot an already-successful operating system much like the way in which *Coca Cola* rebranded its popular soda as *New Coke* – that someone would most likely be sent packing as well.

Innovators learn from past failures in order to drive future successes. Let's do the same and give ourselves a fighting chance."

"So, what do you suggest?" asked Rafi.

"If the goal is to stop Calabasas once and for all… We stop Calabasas once and for all. No copying and replacing. No fake file names with empty containers. We break in, hit them hard, and destroy every last bit of data in their secure servers. We annihilate them." The words echoed throughout the small office, bouncing off the walls and back into the ears of everyone on my team.

I imagined myself standing atop a castle's wall eyeing the armies of the *Sorceress-Bitch* and her Black Knight. My leaders stood around me as I moved the stone pieces around the board, indicating just how we would go about destroying our enemies. They nodded, taking note of what part of the plan would be theirs to deliver on. *We annihilate them*, I could see myself mouthing.

Back in the real world, Elise raised her hand. "I'm on board, but only if we get to make up our own call-signs," she suggested.

"Yeah!" replied Dustin, "Top secret aliases." The energy in the room grew exponentially as the group got excited…*about making up fake names*. Whatever it took.

"Of course," I replied, happy to oblige such a simple, insignificant request. Besides, how long would it take to pick *those*?

Rafi and I stood cautious in front of the infamous third floor data center, eyeing the security keypad as we referred to the code Esther had previously provided. Inside, the Calabasas code base was protected and encrypted on multiple drives and backup servers. All I would have to do is take the black market electronic-pulse devices given to me by No-Doze, stick them in the server's exposed data ports, and turn them on. Within thirty seconds they would rip the hardware to shreds, destroying the data and leaving nothing but a smoking mess behind. *E-mail, schme-mail*, I thought to myself.

"We're in," whispered Rafi, as he completed tapping in the code and the locks disengaged. He pushed open the door and we stepped through into the glimmering, humming den of the beast – lights flickering in a rhythm only the servers knew the reason for.

"We've gained access to the data center," I spoke into the walkie, alerting the team throughout the facility of our current progress as we closed the door behind us. Everyone checked in from their respective posts. Elise and NoDoze had the first-floor control center secure, where they had unlocked the elevator bays for Rafi and I to take upstairs. Dustin and Bernard guarded the outside perimeter, there in the event any local campus police came into the picture. And Jane, with her swollen feet up on the table, reclined behind the lobby's front desk, monitoring the campus security radio band in the event anyone was dispatched to our location. Everything was going according to plan.

I flipped on the switch for the electronic pulse device, eyeing the exposed data port on the first server with fascination. "Look at this," I pointed out to Rafi. "Someone goes to all this trouble to build this elaborate, secure piece of technology, only to make it so easy to destroy. Who does that?"

"Engineers," Rafi replied. "Simplicity and logic always win in the battle of product development."

"Well, here's to simplicity and logic," I said as I slid the device into the exposed data port, placing my finger on the activation button. "Let's do this."

But I didn't get to hit the switch.

Without warning, the entire third floor lit up with what appeared to be daylight. Startled, Rafi and I hit the ground, sliding under a desk as what was now identified as a vehicle's headlight pulsed back and forth across the face of the *Death Star,* then completely disappeared.

"*Oh my god,*" came Jane's voice through my walkie. "*You are not going to believe w-*" The walkie-talkie signal to Jane went dead, replaced with an ominously-sounding static.

I pulled the walkie off my belt, speaking into it. "What is it? Who's down there?" I whisper-shouted, scuttling over to the edge of the room to try and get a glimpse of whatever it was through the tinted windows. There were no vehicles anywhere, but there was something else slightly more disturbing.

It was the remaining *five members* of my team. Running. Quickly.

They sprinted away from the *Death Star* and into the distance, each focused on their own individual survival. Bernard, with only one good eye, shuffled at a meandering angle that made him look drunk while Jane struggled with her heels as she ran across the road and to-wards another building. I repeated myself through the walkie-talkie again. "Report in. Someone!"

But there was nothing but static. I shared a look of worry with Rafi. "Where are you going!?" I yelled into the walkie. I looked at Rafi. "What the *hell* are we supposed to do, now??"

"You *abort*," came a voice from the doorway of the third-floor data center. Rafi and I turned to look – there was nothing but the hulk-ing silhouette of a very familiar-looking individual. I stood up and ap-proached the figure, taking a portable flashlight and shining it in their face.

It was Simon Davis. Looking more ominous than ever in a full-body leather jacket and pants – holding a motorcycle helmet at his side. "I'm here to stop you idiots," he said, "before you do something you will never be able to take back."

"Bullshit," I said, still angry at what he had revealed the last time we'd talked. "Why are you *really* here?" Why was he still in my business? Why couldn't he just leave me alone? Of course, behind me, Rafi was having a completely different reaction to the appearance of the twen-ty-fifth hire at The Company. Almost as if he was in a trance, Rafi sleep-walked towards Simon and reached out to feel the leather of his sleeve.

"Is this really *you*?" he asked, dumbfounded, looking up at the guy who invented the Start button.

From outside, more headlights appeared, accompanied by the growling of a dozen or so car engines. I ran to the window, looking out – this time spotting a fleet of campus police vehicles. I turned around – Simon had removed the electronic pulse device from the data server. He shoved it at me. "I'm here to *help*," he grumbled. "Now let's go before I can't."

I watched Simon, fuming, as he bolted through the door and out into the third-floor hallway. Rafi and I stared at each other for a split second. "That can't be him," he stated, still dumbfounded. "He's supposed to be in Guam working on some top-secret project for The Company."

"Well…he's not in Guam," I said, dejected. "*Unfortunately.*"

I sprinted out the door after my least favorite Company employ-ee, who was already lumbering down the third-floor stairwell. I reached for the handle, realizing that Rafi was nowhere to be seen. I quickly bolted back to the third-floor data center doorway, where Rafi was still standing. Entranced.

"That was Simon Davis," he said, enamored.

"And that's the *police* downstairs," I yelled. "Come *on!*"

I took the steps three at a time, feeling the pressure pound back up into my knees with each leap. I could see Simon a floor below me and hear Rafi a floor above. The sweat was pouring down my face, black paint stinging my eyes as it hitched a ride down my forehead and over my face.

I hit the first floor hard, spotting Simon as he sprinted towards the back door – pushing his way through the exit and onto the back of his motorcycle. I followed close behind, pushing my way out into the brisk night air – as I exited, I could hear multiple people yelling from the other side of the building, with police car lights bathing the trees in red and blue. I swung around and checked for Rafi as the door started to close – he was running full force towards me and I motioned for him get the lead out.

The door closed as Rafi reached it, and was accompanied by the sound of an internal *security lock* engaging into place. Rafi tried to open the door, but it wouldn't budge. I pulled at it hard, but to no avail.

I looked at Rafi, through the glass of the back door – he put his hands up to the glass, and shrugged. "Go!" he yelled to me, as I heard Simon's motorcycle *growl* to life.

"Rafi... I-"

"Cameron!" rang Simon's voice from behind. I turned, then looked back at Rafi one last time before I booked towards Simon's rig and jumped on the back. He revved the engine and took off into the darkness. I looked back at the *Death Star,* eyeing Rafi as the campus police pulled him away from the door. As he was getting arrested, I could have sworn I saw him smile.

But then, that would have been *crazy.*

"What in the *hell* were you thinking?" lectured Simon Davis, as he paced back and forth beneath the night sky, pointing at me every so often with those big hulking digits.

I sat, perched up against a tree, in the center of Campus, face smeared, hair damp, clothes soaked and ripped. I let Simon continue to rail on me as I retreated into my head. All I could think about was how this was going to impact Memphis. Would Rafi implicate us? Would HR get involved? Would Simone get wind of this and disqualify us from the Vegas opportunity? What would Mitch D. say when he heard how I had revised his plan? Maybe he wouldn't have to know. Was this the end for Cameron Murphy?

Simon repeated his question again. "Why would you do that? Why would you put your own employment at risk?" Why, why, why. Boo hoo. The marvelous innovator I had been so fascinated by in the beginning had now evolved into a nag with a penchant for salad reconstruction. He didn't even intimidate me any longer. In fact, he just plain *annoyed* me.

"Why do you *care*?" I stood up, challenging him. "You never cared before, truly, so what's suddenly changed? Was I about to do something that would have benefitted your longtime nemesis Shane McCullough? Please. Tell me how my destruction of Calabasas would have impacted your own self-important life in some disastrous way?"

Simon put his digits down and took a deep *breath*. He backed up against a tree opposite mine and slid down to the ground, opening his jacket and taking it off. "Listen to the big man," he shot back, shaking his head. "Had you actually gone through with that idiotic stunt tonight you would have destroyed any future you had at The Company, not to mention any future opportunity you'd hope to get after the fact. I showed up tonight to *help*. It had nothing to do with me. It had everything to do with *you*."

The words *sounded* nice. But they were too little, too late.

"Well, I'm hoping it won't be much of a surprise to you after all we've been through," I shot back, looking at my watch for the first time since we had entered the *Death Star*, "but I don't *believe* you." I stood up, realizing that I could sit here and try to mend an already fractured relationship or get to Book Club on time and preserve another. "I'm late for an appointment," I said, turning and starting to walk away.

Simon stood up. "Well, if you believed me when I told you that you were one of the good guys," he began, calling after me, "then I hope you'll believe me when I tell you that I was *clearly* wrong."

It didn't hurt, because I didn't *care*.

"Screw you," I said over my shoulder as I kept walking, heading towards the parking lot where I'd left my car. Simon Davis didn't know me. He hadn't taken the time to understand what motivated me or what made me who I was. And I didn't need his *damn* help either. I was doing perfectly fine without him.

"Where did Cameron Murphy go!?" Simon yelled after me in the darkness. "Where's *that* guy?" he continued. "What happened to *him*?" I just kept on walking, then threw up my middle finger over my shoulder while I ascended a hill and hiked towards the concrete structure in the distance.

Although I'd given my fair share of donations to the homeless population of Los Angeles and New York, and despite feeling as though I understood their plight through their simple yet emotionally-manipulative cardboard messages – I never had quite understood what it felt like to be *looked at like you were homeless* until I had found myself at the Canyon Park Estates' first official Book Club gathering.

The fifteen most well-read residents of Canyon Park Estates (yes, including Dylan Packmore) sat in a circle of metal fold-out chairs, generously provided by the hosts for the evening – Rosalind and Joesph Shaffer. They stared at me, marveling at just how horrific I appeared. Between the damp hair, black-stained face, ripped clothing and saggy black wool hat, I was either doing an extremely credible job at dressing up like *The Cure*'s Robert Smith or doing an extremely horrible job at *just plain living life*. They *had to know* just where I had been and what I had been doing. Jess, on the other hand, knew *exactly* what I had been through, if by "exactly" she believed that to be a misguided evening of Corporate hide-and-go-seek. I could see it on her face – it didn't much matter where I had been or what I had done, she was livid that I had shown up looking like someone who even The Bidens would have turned away from a homeless food bank on Christmas Eve.

Loretta Pascal, the wife of the Canyon Park Estates' very own HOA *At Large Correspondent*, looked down at the list of discussion questions she'd been managing for most of the evening, and repeated the same one she had asked me three and a half minutes ago, to which she'd gotten no more than a blank look of confusion. "Cameron, is this a cautionary tale…a prognosis…a diagnosis?" she asked. "In Mitchell's tales, what do humans seem bent on doing to one another…and why? With little left at the end, what, if anything, remains?"

The questions hovered out there in front of me, echoing throughout the room. *Cautionary tale… Humans…bent on doing to one another… What, if anything…remains?* My head was spinning, in part due to a night of confusing, frustrating and borderline *maddening* events. The questions that had come out of Loretta's mouth seemed less appropriate for *Cloud Atlas* and more tailored to the box I was stuck in; walls closing in from all sides. From where I sat, looking back at the events of the last eleven months, my experiences *were* a cautionary tale about biting off more than one could chew. And generally, being an *imposter*.

Somewhere amidst the silence, Loretta asked me if I was okay. Elsewhere, Jess made excuses for my strange behavior, which were obviously the result of working extremely long hours at The Company. Next to me, Dylan Packmore handed me a cold glass of water and gave me a clearly-heterosexual knee squeeze of support, securing a place in my life from that day forward as my only BCBFF (*Book Club Best Friend Forever*). Loretta's words circled back around and hit me again. *She's not asking me about the book*, I justified in my head. *She's asking me about what's been going on with me.* I had things to say. And a pulpit from which to say them. So, I did.

"Yes. A cautionary tale," the words came out of my mouth, startling most of the circle back into focus. "This *is* a cautionary tale," I clarified, emerging from within my psyche and finding myself totally lucid in front of the entire Book Club coefficient.

"Tell us more," spoke Loretta, seemingly engaged. Jess, on the other hand, looked *horrified*.

"Humans," I continued, "seem hell bent on doing *anything* to one another that puts them in the power position. It's not about *why*. No one knows *why*. No one cares about the *why*. They set out to dominate others for the pure sport of it all."

"Just like what happened to Somni~451," said Susan Gibbs. "So demoralizing."

"So true, *so true*," I said, having no idea what or *whom* the woman was even talking about. Did it have something to do with Tom Hanks? Honestly, it *did not* matter since I wasn't talking about the book or the movie. *My* thoughts were in lock step with my anger, which was slowly rising up inside of me. I took the glass of water and downed it, then wiped my mouth with my damp sleeve as I stood up in the center of the meeting, rallying the group's attention with a "people…*people!*"

It was possible Jess was trying to get my attention, but I hadn't looked at her in minutes, rather spinning to make eye contact with the others as I continued to spout my thoughts. They were coming fast, with my synapses firing on all cylinders, driven by pure emotion.

"Prognosis?" I asked. "*Prognosis!?*" "People, there's no prognosis. You get a prognosis when there's a chance at curing what's wrong with you. This is a *diagnosis*. Society's diagnosis. And let me tell you something, people – society is *sick*. Society is *dying*. Society doesn't *deserve* a prognosis. Not when there are people out there who are hell bent on destroying each other. Not when the people who pretend to be your friends are secretly coordinating your undoing while complimenting you at the same time. Not when *people* are more interested in ruining others' lives than bettering their own!"

I spun around the room like a whirling dervish, the faces of Romy and Shane and Simon hovering in my head while I spat and shouted at each and every one of the fifteen Book Club participants. Most of them hung on my every word, engaged with my passionate sermon and jotting down notes in the margins of their books as I ranted away. Jess gave me a look that I wasn't sure I had ever seen come off her face. Had I been logical, I might have stopped in that very moment. But there was no *logic* anywhere to be found.

"What remains at the end, if anything?" I asked, picking up my copy of *Cloud Atlas* and swinging it around the room with every enunciated word. "When your courage…and confidence…and dignity have been ripped from your weakened hands!?" The book got loose from my grip, flying across the room and smashing into the fireplace mantle. Multiple glass swans, whose home had once been the mantle in question, came *crashing* down onto the ceramic tiles. Everyone *gasped*. Especially Loretta. *Perhaps those were collectible glass swans*, I thought to myself for a split second.

"*Nothing* remains," I said, motioning to the broken swan pieces and letting a deep breath out of my body like a possessed soul had just been exorcised. Loretta rushed to the fireplace mantle only to turn and glare at me with a look of disdain. *Oh, now she wasn't feeling it,* I thought as I felt the first signs of true fatigue wash over me since the night had begun. Between the night at the *Death Star* and my run in with Simon and now *this?* I had nothing left.

I turned towards the foyer, walked out of the Book Club circle past Jess, and went right for the door. No one tried to stop me. And no one called my name. Someone in the background whispered to someone else, "He was talking about *the movie,* right?"

I walked out of the house, closed the door behind me, and headed home.

"You knew how important tonight was to me," Jess texted. *Bzzt.*

"You ruined the entire evening," she texted minutes later. *Bzzt.*

"You're an asshole, Cameron," she sent my way, finishing off the *Texting Trilogy. Bzzt.*

I mindlessly swiped my finger across my smartphone's screen, jostling the most recent three messages over and over again, as I sat unmoving on the living room sofa. For the first time in months my mind was empty. *Blank.* I just laid my head back, staring up at the light in the lamp on the side table, counting every time that there was an electrical pulse which caused the bulb to flicker. I was up to three-hundred and seven when Jess finally came through the front door.

"Jess," I said, sitting up. But Jess didn't stop, instead ignoring me as she walked through the foyer and into the kitchen without saying a word. Drawers were opened, kitchen cabinets were closed. I heard dishes clink and clang. What was she doing? *She will poison you, so don't eat anything she gives you over the course of the next forty-eight hours,* the *Investigation Discovery*-watching part of my psyche suggested as Jess walked past me again and towards the stairwell.

"Jess!" I said, again. "Can you please just-" But that didn't stop her either, as she tromped up the stairs to the second floor. Closets opened, cabinets closed. Papers shuffled, pens and pencils clanged within a glass jar. *She's drafting divorce papers,* the part of me that had seen the late night *Be Your Own Lawyer* infomercial, thought. But as Jess came downstairs again and approached me in the living room, I realized my suspicions were way off base. She wasn't going to poison me. Or divorce me. She was just going to force me to do something I vowed never to do.

"Go ahead. *Put it on*," she said unemotionally, shoving the now-dusty Happy Lamp into my lap.

"Jess, please." I put the Happy Lamp on the side table, attempting to get it as far away from my cranial area as humanly possible. She picked it up and put it right back in my lap.

"You obviously *need* this, Cameron. If tonight's little show was any indication."

"Jess, I don't need the damn Happy Lamp. I'm fine."

"You're fine?" she said, matter-of-fact. "Is that so?"

"YES. That *is* so."

Jess grabbed the Happy Lamp with one hand, and my hand with the other, dragging me out of the chair and towards the foyer. There, she shoved me in front of the mirror. It was probably the first time I had seen my reflection since earlier that day. So, I was a mess. Big deal. Anyone else who had been through what I'd been through wouldn't have looked nearly as rough. *You look rugged*, I thought to myself – I was pleased with the evaluation.

"What's your happy quotient?" Jess prodded me.

"What's *your* happy quotient?" I asked, redirecting.

"Before tonight? Ninety-five percent," she said.

"That's impossible, no one can have a ninety-five percent happy quotient," I shot back.

"Says who?"

"Says…the… National Organization of…Happy, or whatever they're called, assuming there's an organization who establishes this *ludicrous* and illogical quotient of delightment," I shot back, annoyed.

There was a long pause as Jess looked at me in the mirror's reflection, examining every nook and cranny of my face in the hopes that she would see something different. "Where were you *really* tonight?" she asked. "And don't tell me it was some ludicrous corporate game of hide and seek."

"You don't want to know," I reluctantly blurted out.

"Since when do I *not* want to know anything that has to do with you?" she said, making me feel guilty.

"I'm trying to protect you," I said, lying.

"Protect me *from what*?" she let out a breath. I was actually trying to protect *me* from *her*. She wasn't going to let me out of this one.

I shook my head. I had to tell her. God knows I had told her *everything else* up until this point. "We broke into Building one-eleven tonight with the goal of destroying Romy's product and data files."

Her face turned red, and that was in the low light of the foyer. "And *whose* ridiculous idea was *that!?*"

"Well, it was Mitch D.'s. And I agree – it was *ridiculous*. It was the same *exact* plot as *Oceans 12*. You know, with the egg and the-"

"Yeah, yeah," she had heard it a thousand times, "the holographic replacement and the pregnant Julia Roberts. I'm your wife, remember?"

"So, I *revised* his plan. And I made it better. Or *worse*. I'm not quite sure what went wrong. I mean, besides Rafi getting arrested."

"Cameron!" she shouted, then self-quieted herself for Kate's sake. "What were you thinking?"

It was a great question. I didn't have an answer. I said nothing, just stared slack-jawed at my wife, who shook her head.

"You're not yourself, Cam," she said. "You haven't been for a while now."

The hypocritical train was running on time, it seemed. "I seem to remember a similar situation with *you*," I defended, making reference to her many months of depression-fueled lethargy.

"And I snapped out of it. With *your* help."

"But I don't *need* your help. And I don't need Simon's help. And I don't need my parents help. I just wish everyone would stop trying to *help* me. I'm doing just fine without anyone's damn help."

Jess took a step back, placing the Happy Lamp on the shelf beneath the mirror, then did her best Vanna White impression as she revealed my dirty, damp, disheveled version of myself in the mirror. "Then have at it," she said, appearing hurt. "But I'm not going to stand around and watch it happen."

"What does *that* mean?" I asked, as a twinge of nervousness shot through me. "What, you're going to leave me? Abandon your husband and take his child where she'll be without a father figure? It's *tough* out there for a single mother, Jess. I've seen it. And there will be no one to help you with bath night. Bath night is *all* you. I wouldn't wish bath night on the worst of human beings."

"It means… I'm *just* going upstairs, you *Hemminger*," she said, rolling her eyes and disappearing to the second floor. I watched her from below as she entered the bedroom and closed the door.

I stared at myself in the mirror. What was *my* happy quotient? I tried a smile on for size, but it just looked creepy and fake.

Two bags of *Doritos*, three *Diet Cokes* and one delivery pizza later found me sitting in my office, Happy Lamp around my neck, tapping away at the soundboard interface we had created for our very own *Holographic Ebert* program – allowing us to record video of the Memphis spokesperson using any and all digitized audio he had captured from his days on TV and radio.

"*Memphis…is…a…blockbuster,*" the glowing-blue avatar of movie reviewers said, stringing together audio clips from completely different television appearances to get the message across. It wasn't perfect, but it would do just fine. "*Forget about…those impersonal…movie recommendations. This time it's personal. I give it two thumbs up!*"

"You don't really believe that," I said to Holographic Ebert, suddenly second-guessing myself about everything that we had done on the project to date, especially in light of Jess' extremely vocal opinion about how I was screwing up left and right.

"*It's a blockbuster!*" Holographic Ebert repeated as I mindlessly clicked on various sound buttons.

"Even after tonight?" I asked, now partially convinced I was talking to Holographic Ebert after all the drama, salt, caffeine and carbohydrates had taken a hold of my biological systems.

"*Everything works…out in the end,*" Holographic Ebert replied.

"Well, it sure doesn't feel that way," I shot back. "I mean, look at me. I'm a total wreck. Even my wife can't bear to look me in the eyes. Have I changed *that much*?"

"*Let me tell you something,*" Holographic Ebert said back, giving me a digital wink. "*Sometimes…you've gotta take…a step back.*"

"A step back? But why?" I asked Holographic Ebert.

"*Because…this time it's personal,*" he said.

I sat there, taking it all in, still buzzing from the diverse variety of chemicals and trans fats that were swimming around in my blood. But *Holographic Ebert's* meandering yet allegorical statements turned my attention towards something I hadn't thought about in months. My *own* personal recommendations. Since the beta program had begun, Memphis had continued to capture my texts and e-mails in a massive database that had gone unchecked and unvalidated for months. If there were any unbiased way to take a step back and look at who I had really become, it would be through Memphis. And Chloe. My how I had missed her.

I wasted no time. I pulled out my phone, connected it to my laptop and clicked the quick launch button to activate the recommendation engine. It powered up quickly, opening my own personal textual reference box on the left of the screen as the lovely voice of my long-lost British concierge returned from beyond.

"Memphis ready," said Chloe.

I clicked "execute" and sat back to see just what Chloe would have to say. Suggesting that I had been unprepared for the results would have been an understatement.

The phrases came fast and hit hard. As they scrolled up the screen, I caught glimpses of some of them. *Self-absorbed* and *absent* and *asshole* were just a few of the words that flew by. *Careless* and *single-minded* and *hypocrite* were others. Where was *dedicated* and *driven* and *resourceful*, I wondered. Where was *hard-working* and *generous* and *dedicated to his family*? Apparently, those phrases were all in my self-absorbed, single-minded, hypocritical head. Jess' words took on even more meaning as the remaining recommendations populated. *Had I changed?* Was Simon right? Was Jess on the money? I turned the Happy Lamp up to its highest setting as Chloe rattled through her list.

"You might like *Scarface*," Chloe said. "And *Nixon*," she continued. She was on a role, serving up other movies she thought I'd love, all which were the product of my words, actions and electronic communications. Did these recommendations truly represent me? There was *One Flew Over The Cuckoo's Nest* and *The Godfather* and *Amadeus* and *The Shining* – movies all about major characters so obsessed with one thing that everything and every*one* in their lives were ignored or abandoned or *killed*. There were books focused on building better marriages and how-to's on time management. And there was even a song. One *particular* song that hit me harder than any other recommendation. Harry Chapin's *Cat's in the Cradle*. You remember – the one where the absent father one day discovers that his son has grown up to be *just…like…him?* Right through the heart. It stung.

There was no denying the fact that the technology under Memphis' hood was amazing. But it was also *way too personal.* And *depressing.* It made me angry – who the hell was Chloe and what gave her the right to evaluate who *I* was? My first instinct was to smash my computer with something heavy, silencing that annoying, egotistical British voice once and for all.

There was that anger again. I took a breath and pushed the laptop away from me. I eyed the recommendation engine from afar as it continued to say libelous things about my life, criticizing everything about *me.* It made me wonder, would any consumer *ever* want this kind of honesty delivered conveniently to their smart device of choice when all they wanted to do was *watch a movie?* For the first time, a wide gaping hole appeared in my entire bulletproof pitch for Memphis. The realization was staggering. I tried to turn the Happy Lamp to an even higher setting, but it was as high as it would go.

Happy quotient? Fifty-one percent.

I pulled the laptop back to me, eyeing the visual representation of who I had become. Was this the person Jess had been referring to? Is this what I looked like to people outside my own head? Had I truly grown so laser focused on one single goal that everything else had fallen to the wayside? Had I become Ahab and was the success of Memphis my Moby Dick?

"*Not impressed…stay far away from this one,*" came the words of Holographic Ebert, who was still running in the background on my laptop and obviously tag-teaming with Chloe.

I went over to my desk, opened the top drawer, and pulled out my *now* obsolete iPhone that I had carried with me during my loops at The Company. I connected the power cord to the phone, then turned it on, and opened up the Notes application. Exactly what I was looking for was still on it – the entry from that infamous date in December. The pep talk I had typed to myself glowed from the screen – the words were simple and impactful.

You're smart.
You've got great values.
She loves you.

Those were *my* words. I had typed them. They had come from *me*. But much like that old recording of ones' voice which *sounded* like you but didn't *really* sound like you – the words seemed foreign to me. I was sure that I had believed them almost a year ago, but did I believe them now? Were they even still true? Had I evolved? Or just *changed* for the worse?

The realization did *not* make me happy at all.

Rafi Johansson was not happy *either*. Although, if you wanted to get technical about it, it was Rafi's half-Swedish part that was having a bit of the *moody Mondays*. This, of course, was due to the fact that Rafi's half-Indian part had never made any attempts to remind his half-Swedish part (which also happened to be the part that retained citizenship in Sweden and *not* the United States) that his work Visa, if not renewed, would be invalid as of…*six months ago*.

The Company's campus police and local authorities, after holding Rafi for questioning the previous night, had not found any evidence significant enough to hold him. There had been no signs of breaking or entering, no intellectual property ruined or stolen, and the rumors of limping geriatric cat burglars could not be substantiated. I was relieved that my careless actions had not put anyone at risk. In light of the previous evening's epiphanies, there was some silver lining to it all. At least, with respect to Rafi, I *thought* there was.

"But…" Rafi explained, "when they ran my I.D., they noticed that I was working with an expired VISA. Which is a pretty big deal. So, they're deporting me back to Sweden in two days."

I stared at him through the two-way glass, stunned. "Isn't there anything The Company can do?" I asked. "Is there anything I can do?"

"Just get us to the finish line," he said, placing his hand up on the glass. I put my hand up, matching where his was planted and decided it wasn't the time or place to explain just how the previous evening's realizations had changed my opinion on just *what* that finish line was.

"What are we going to do without you?" I asked.

"Well, you're going to find someone to take my place and lead the engineering side. Someone who can get this product shipped at the end of the day. Someone *damn good*."

"Yes, but what will we do *after that*?"

"If there's one thing I've learned about you, my friend," Rafi said into the phone, leaning in, "it's that you know what to do. You always have. Just trust your instincts." I nodded, appreciating his support, knowing that my instincts would be put to the test in just a few hours. With Mitch DeForrest.

"I'm sorry it had to end this way," I said, apologetic. Truly, I was sorry. But Rafi wasn't going to let anyone rain on the parade. He had a huge smile on his face.

"Eh, I haven't seen my parents in *three years*," he said. "It was time for me to get back anyway. And besides – I got to meet Simon Davis. *The* Simon Davis. I would get deported a hundred more times if it meant getting to touch his arm again. You know, that arm invented the Start button?"

I had never seen *The Phantom of the Opera*, nor had I ever had a desire to see *The Phantom of the Opera*, and sitting across from Mitch DeForrest (who had carved out part of his cranial cast so his eye, nose and portions of his mouth could breathe) only confirmed that *not* seeing *The Phantom of the Opera* had been a wise decision. Perhaps it was his eerie half-face that looked back at me or the anticipation of how he was about to react to the phrase I had uttered just thirty seconds earlier. Either way, I felt nauseous.

"I'm confused," Mitch D. said, half of a furrowed brow now visible through the cracked-open head cast. "Can you say that again so I'm crystal clear?" I took another breath, like I had practiced multiple times in my car on the way to the office that morning, in transit from the Seattle Police Department.

I tried again. "We need…to close down…Memphis," I said, my voice shaking and stuttering much like *Holographic Ebert*. "We were all *too* close to it. None of us ever stopped to ask the question – will the public *ever* embrace this blatant invasion of privacy? We're taking everyone's data without their expressed authorization to do so. And even if they did, who truly wants all their personal data being used to make entertainment recommendations? People want to escape from their lives – that's why they go to the movies. Or read books. Or listen to music. They don't want to be reminded of their shortcomings every time they sit down to do any of those things."

Mitch D. nodded, swinging his motorized wheelchair around and moving towards the glass windows. Outside, it was gloomy and overcast, with rain showers shifting back and forth with the wind. I could hear Mitch D. take what sounded like a breath of relaxation, then swing his chair around one-hundred eighty degrees to face me again.

"Is this because you screwed the pooch with Calabasas 1-1-1?" he asked.

"I'm *glad* we didn't go through with it," I said. I *was*. Simon, despite me not wanting to admit it, had been right. It was an act motivated out of fear, not strength. "Wouldn't you rather quit while we're ahead and not embarrass ourselves in Vegas in front of Ben Packer?"

"Did I ever tell you the Eyelash Viper of Belize story?" he asked.

"Yes. Harrowing story." So harrowing, *once* was enough.

"Well, then you know I pushed myself to superhuman lengths to get that antidote, which saved my life and allowed me passage on a Greenpeace boat to New York. Did I ever tell you about the pirates who boarded that Greenpeace boat and threatened the lives of everyone aboard?"

"Pirates?" I asked. "Like *Somali* pirates?"

"No. Just pirates," he replied.

"What kind of pirates?" I was confused now. Were there other *kinds* of pirates? Did he mean one of those Carnival Cruise pirate-themed vacations?

"*Just* pirates. Forget about what kind of pirates. Christ, Murphy."

"Okay. Generic pirates of some kind, just not the *Somali* kind."

"The point is *this*," he continued, rage starting to build up inside of him. "The outcome looked bleak. But faced with the choice of quitting or playing it out with potentially disastrous results…I did the opposite of quitting. Because no matter the risks, however disastrous or painful, I'd rather *die* trying before being called a quitter."

"This isn't about dying. Or quitting. This is about having *values*," I said, standing my ground. "If we had values and cared about the consumer, we'd never even *try* to push this on the public."

"Someone suddenly grew a conscience," Mitch D. said, addressing that same invisible Corporate lackey he always enjoyed conversing with. "Maybe it's time you grew some balls, Murphy. I mean, come on. Man up. This isn't some environmentally-conscious summer camp where we sit around listening to flowers cry and vegans explaining why fish is okay to eat but chicken isn't. This is Corporate America. Conscience and values don't exist here."

I was about to disagree, but Mitch D. had an answer for that, too.

"You don't like it? *Quit*. But you're not taking Memphis down with you."

"So, then – what would happen to Memphis?"

"Live and die by the OARP," Mitch D. spat back. "You don't *own* Memphis. I do. You're just an Approver. And let's be brutally honest for a moment. The only letter that matters in the OARP is the O. You can *arp arp arp* all day long, but it won't change the fact that you…own… nothing. We're taking this baby to Vegas. Packer's gonna see what this product can do and give us that final keynote slot. We'll take our shot and hope for the best."

"And if *the best* doesn't materialize?"

"Here's the best part, Murphy. If it succeeds, *it's because of me*. And if it fails? It's all Cameron Murphy's fault. Go ahead. *Quit* now and that will be your legacy at The Company."

"And who would believe that?"

"The same people who saw what you did to MediaMesh. So far, you're just the guy who has fucked shit up. Your careless, risky behavior has already torpedoed one product – what's one more?" Half of his mouth flashed a calculating, creepy grin.

I was between a rock and a hard place and Mitch D. knew it. I could quit and take myself out of the equation completely, giving up all connection to Memphis whatsoever and abandoning my team in the process. Or I could stay, however emasculating it might feel, and try to find another way to shut it down. But Mitch D. had already thought about *that* angle as well.

"And don't even think of trying to sabotage it yourself," he threatened, "because I *will* know if it was you. Then you won't just experience failure. You'll experience what it feels like to have The Company's legal counsel slap a multi-million dollar lawsuit on your ass. Which, incidentally, they *love* to do."

I looked at his one good eye, all wiggly and meandering as he tried to gauge my emotional state. I shook my head, realizing that I would have to live to fight another day.

"So," he said, turning his menacing tone into something far more pleasant. "We on the same page?"

"Yes," I said, smiling the kind of smile that either meant happiness or acid reflux. ~~"We are totally on the same page."~~

Sudhir placed his *six beepers, two cell phones, one long range walkie talkie* and *an employee key card* on the table in front of his wife Teha and I. We all stared at them for what seemed like an eternity. To me, they represented the shackles of the startup company he had been hustling for during the last eighteen months. To them, it represented something altogether different.

"The devil," Teha said, eyeing the black devices with disdain.

"Freedom," Sudhir chimed in, as he picked up a pair of hammers from his side, handing one to Teha and wielding one himself. They both raised them up in unison, pausing at the height of their arcs. "This position you have offered me," Sudhir confirmed, "is a long-term position with benefits – I am just confirming?"

"Once you're in, you're *in*," I said, reminding Sudhir and Teha that firing someone at The Company once they'd been hired was like getting honey roasted peanuts on a Transatlantic flight – basically *impossible*. "In light of the current engineering lead position that has suddenly become available," I reminded him, referring to Rafi, "once you have completed your New Employee Orientation, you will be good to go."

Sudhir nodded to Teha. They kissed. And then, like a pair of star-crossed lovers with the same *exact* thought passing through their minds, they smashed the *shit* out of the pagers and cell phones. I guarded my face from the plastic shrapnel as the pieces flew in all directions. The cell phones *whimpered* their failing electronic beeps as the once-glowing digital readouts began letting go of their long, electricity-fueled lives.

Sudhir and Teha put down the hammers, then pulled each other close. They kissed again, smiling so wide that for the first time since we had moved in, that I knew it had been the right decision. Despite what was to come for Memphis, the opportunity for Sudhir would transcend one silly little product and stretch across a potentially-lucrative career for a guy who was one of the most genuine people I had met in all my time in Seattle.

Sudhir was *smart*. He had *values*. And Teha *loved him*. If you couldn't put your faith in a guy like that, you couldn't put your faith in *anything.*

Thunderdome

Over the years, and throughout the halls of The Company, the story had become legendary. It had all started in 1989 with Simone Guerra's earlier than expected birth, which had taken place without warning in a stalled gondola ride from Montjuic as it traversed the Barcelona harbor. Her parents, Hector and Dominique, along with the other surprised passengers were said to have marveled at the voluminous locks of jet-black hair that had grown in the womb – garnering Simone the childhood nickname of *Belleza Negro* or 'black beauty.'

When Simone Guerra, whose last name was synonymous with the word "*war*", turned five, she organized the adolescent Kindergarten population against the instructors, crafting a crudely-scrawled *Crayon Manifesto* to demand that the afternoon *siestas* (or, nap time) be extended to ninety minutes. *She had been successful.* When she was twelve and in *Escuela Secondaria*, Simone took on the role as campaign manager for her best friend Alexandra Toutin, exchanging *polvorones* and peanut butter for embarrassing intelligence about their thumb-sucking competition. Alexandra, having no competitors left in the race after Simone had gotten through with them, *had been successful.* And in 2013, when Simone met White House Chief of Staff Denis McDonough and realized just how perfect she was for a position such as *his* – she set her single-minded, unwavering goals towards securing that very specific role. *She had been successful at that, too.* With one slight, *yet significant,* technicality.

The job was at The Company, and not The White House.

Still, at The Company, the Chief of Staff was more than just a glorified assistant despite what other jealous employees might have had you think. Simone was the *gatekeeper* when it came to CEO Ben Packer. Simone worked closely with all of Packer's direct reports, putting out fires behind the scenes and ensuring that nothing got to Packer unless it truly deserved his final sign-off. Simone was always aligned with Packer's positions, often chairing meetings with his directs while he was out sick, welcoming fellow Tech luminaries to campus, or on a boat, west of Lisbon, spending his own personal fortune hunting for ancient treasure like Nic Cage.

Simone knew Packer better than his own wife. She knew his daily bathroom schedule, where to locate that spot on his back that was always itching and how to pronounce the words *caramel* and *mayonnaise* so it didn't drive him certifiably insane. She often calmed him down when he got irritated, pulled him aside when he was about to say something that HR wouldn't be pleased with, and regularly fought with him like they shared a bed. It wasn't just *ironic* that for a woman with a last name synonymous with *war*, she was fighting one every single day *with* and *on behalf of* the Corporate Almighty.

The Thunderdome, or *SimoneDome* as she had dubbed it, was an annual battle unto itself. Dozens would participate, bringing their polished presentations to the Studio B screening room, in the hopes that they would be one of two to make it to Vegas. Once there, Packer would have the front row seat to view the entire Keynote from beginning to end, and based on how the two projects showed on stage, would select one for the coveted final surprise announcement slot.

"Some clown town told me that the story about Simone in the gondola was only half true," whispered Elise, who was sitting next to me on the left side of the auditorium and making reference to Simone and her lackeys in the center of the room. "Apparently she has an *identical* twin. And whenever you're talking to Simone and you see her wince, which she does every so often, it's her feeling the pain of her long-lost sister."

Yes, the pain was *real*.

Simone presided over her own personal three-ring circus like a hyper-surreal version of Tina Turner in post-apocalyptic drag, replete with the flowing mane of black hair tumbling down her back. She sat atop a specially-erected judging table in the auditorium, flanked on both sides by the *Chieftains*, or other Chiefs-of-Staff who supported Ben Packer's direct reports. It was a *caste system*, that was for sure, with Simone's passive-aggressive *suggestions* and opinions often considered to be gospel by anyone who cared about looking good in the eyes of Ben Packer. Because anyone who wanted Packer's ear or support had to pay their respects to Simone, falling at her feet in the hopes that she would feel compelled to throw them a crumb of attention.

Yes, the unexpected birth on the Montjuic gondola was great as a Simone Guerra origin story. But the true sign of her superpowers were evidenced here, in person, as she granted Romy Wallace an audience in-between the various presentations of the day. I watched her as she gave Simone a welcoming hug, giving me a wink from within the embrace. Romy wasn't stupid, that was for sure, and she was more than happy to kiss some ass and fall at some feet if she knew it would make a difference.

Whether or not it *would* make a difference, had remained to be seen, as Calabasas was scheduled for the last slot of the day. *Bringin' up the rear.*

Holographic Ebert and the Memphis presentation, which sounded like a hybrid Jazz fusion & rock band that was burning up the Alternative charts, was extremely well-received. I put on my best poker face, especially with Mitch D. watching from the back of the auditorium, and delivered the pitch in much the way we'd been practicing for weeks. It *sounded* great. It made sense. People connected with it. Even Simone, typically distracted by her e-mail, cell phone or trademark *edamame beet salad*, had found the idea and presentation especially satisfying.

"This *pleases* me!" she had cried from the center of the auditorium like a Queen reacting to her Jester, pointing to *Holographic Ebert* with glee.

"*Then…we agree*," Holographic Ebert shot back to Simone,

while behind the curtain I watched as Dustin's fingers moved quickly across the soundboard, trying to keep the illusion of a soulful *Holographic Ebert* alive and well.

"You are a wonderful creature!" she shot back to Holographic Ebert, noticeably engaged.

"*She's wonderful...and talented...two thumbs up!*" Holographic Ebert said as he extended his hand and motioned into the audience. Which Simone, obviously, assumed was *all about her.*

I stood on the stage, feeling like a sell-out. It didn't help that Mitch D., in the back of the room, was enjoying the show just as much as everyone else. *Why are you doing this*, one part of me asked myself as I felt the corners of my mouth crack under the pressure of a noticeably-fake smile. *Because you will lose everything if you don't*, the other part of me shot back as I pretended to pat *Holographic Ebert* on the back. *But there's got to be a way out*, another part of me suggested, as I wrapped up the presentation, wondering what type of medication someone with multiple-personality disorder actually took. *Chlorpromazine*, the other part of me replied, having spent copious time on the Internet searching for the answer to just *that*.

Besides being conflicted, I was stunned. Mostly at the rest of the products that had made their way to Thunderdome were the tragic result of three elements that never went well together in a billion-dollar tech Company that had endless funds for R&D. They were *caffeine, ego* and *M&M's. To wit-*

There was the beach ball that had integrated circuits to track just how many calories you had burned by *throwing a beach ball.*

"Al Gore says the excess water from the Polar Ice Caps will drown our nation's beaches and resorts in less than eight months," Simone directed from her throne. "No beaches, no product. And nobody puts Al Gore in the corner."

There was the next generation USB storage device that came in an *edible* form factor. Its purpose, of course, was to allow for the owner of said "confidential" information to ingest the device (and the data) thus keeping it from falling into the wrong hands.

"How many calories per megabyte of data?" Simone had asked, confounding the product owners with the one question they had *not* thought of. "Because if I have to choose between my mid-afternoon snack and protecting some PowerPoint slides...it's a toss-up."

There were plug-ins for existing programs. Fabrics that one could wear that also did double duty as a computer screen. There were 3D printers that turned two-dimensional drawings into physical objects. Simone was ferocious at times, stumping creators with business questions that demonstrated her MBA-savvy past. Other times, the pure spectacle of a presentation wowed her into delivering giddy responses that sounded like a teenager singing the praises of Taylor Swift. If you could get Simone into that sweet spot, you might very well be the smartest person in the room.

And if there was one thing you could say about Romy Wallace – it was that she wasn't *stupid*.

The setup for Calabasas rivaled the Broadway production of *Starlight Express*. There were risers and props everywhere, all surrounding a behemoth ninety-one inch HDTV up on a pedestal. There were concert-sized speakers placed throughout the auditorium, with a full concert-worthy lighting package hanging from the ceiling. Romy had done her homework, that was for sure.

She had also come dressed to the nines, looking as if she had raided Jess' professional wing of our walk-in closet mere hours before the event in question. She grabbed the microphone and landed on stage as the monitor in the front came to life. "Me TV" it read, with the tag line "*Take Your Life to Eleven.*" I gripped the armrests of my auditorium seat, feeling like I was riding down that last leg of the log flume, seconds from plunging headfirst into a pool of chaos.

Then the adult-contemporary heavy metal music that Corporations used to convince consumers they were "edgy" and "hip" starting playing.

"Technology moves fast," she began, clicking a button that flashed through hundreds of new-fangled TVs in a blinding display of seizure-inducing imagery. "Sometimes you have to stop for a minute and take a look around." The images gave way to a vector image of a USB device with the *Me TV* logo on it. It turned from vector to reality, as Romy held up her own prototype device to the crowd. They *cheered* although still having had no idea as to what this product actually did. It was typical at The Company, where enthusiasm always came first, before logic.

"How often do we, as consumers, drop thousands of dollars on the latest TVs, only to realize they're obsolete a year or two later? How many times do we wish that we could upgrade to the latest technology without having to spend the money to do so?" Around the room, everyone nodded – the pitch made sense. "How much would any of you pay for a device that, once plugged into the USB or HDMI port of your now-obsolete television, upgraded your experience to the latest in high-fidelity home theater surround sound?"

"Ten dollars!" yelled Dustin, next to me, along with the rest of the Borg, shouting their own retail price suggestions. I glared at him and he shrugged, sheepishly.

On-screen, the USB device faded into the background as a $4.99 price point came into focus. "For the price of one of those designer coffee drinks," Romy cheered, "you can get your very own Me TV device." The crowd went wild. I looked at them confused. Had I been the only one who hadn't drank the ecstasy-laced *Kool Aid* before coming inside? Had I missed something? "But don't let me tell you what Me TV does for such a competitive low price. Let's hand it over to one of the world's most famous creators of high-fidelity entertainment…director *Michael Bay*!!"

Another huge screen rose alongside the flat-screen TV and turned on to reveal none other than Michael *fucking* Bay. On location for his latest movie. This one was based on that classic puzzle game that *everyone* loved. *Variety* had briefly described the plot as "a rollicking action-adventure movie about a puzzle game that takes over the minds and souls of New York City, then traps its inhabitants inside." There would be huge stakes, big heroes, and a set piece that involved the hero and villain battling over who got to be the *blue game piece*. It would also be produced by Legendary Artists, where Romy had previously been employed.

Michael *fucking* Bay, I repeated in my head again for the added humiliating effect.

The room *obviously* agreed. It was a total and complete zoo. There were spotlights, loud music, people out of their seats. Simone stood tall, rocking her fists in the air as her jet-black mane swung in all directions.

"How are you doing, Seatttttttle?!" shouted Michael Bay, stringing together words and phrases so seamlessly that it made me feel for

Holographic Ebert. "Let Romy and I show you how Me TV brings your television of the past into the glory of the future!"

One of the *Transformers* movies blasted onto the main screen as Romy turned up the volume until the green bar had reached its maximum. Explosions, music and sound effects shot out of the speakers, bombarding the audience. "Sounds great, right!?" yelled Bay, mugging for the group to such an extent that I wondered if Romy had lied to him and told him today's Thunderdome would be broadcast *live* to the entire world. Everyone cheered again, for no reason whatsoever, except for the fact that…yes, it was Michael *fucking* Bay.

"So, now watch what happens when Romy plugs in the Me TV dongle on this flat screen," Michael said, waiting for her to do so. "We just wait for it to connect to the TV's system…."

On screen, the volume bar which had been maxed out at 10/10 suddenly extended slightly to reveal that the volume max had now been increased to 11. "Now watch this!" Romy yelled as she grabbed a remote, pressed the volume button, and maxed out the volume to *eleven*. "11/10" it read, demonstrating that the Me TV had hacked the device in question and added one more bar of volume.

Really?

Michael Bay got up from his chair, from wherever he was broadcasting, and did some kind of karate kick that knocked over the faux-Miami backdrop he was being filmed in front of. Simone stood up from her protected box of royalty to proclaim that it was "a game changer!"

Seriously?

I looked over to Dustin, then over to Elise. They were right there with everyone else. Going insane over a five-dollar device that made someone's TV *slightly* louder. All I could think about was the *pretty* Dolphin and the bouncing ball, and wondered if The Company had reacted this *same* way when Shane *fucking* McCullough had peddled *those* wares.

Probably, I thought.

Definitely.

Oh, yes.

Although it was only *in my imagination*, I felt the faux-log plunge into the faux-pool and completely turn my stomach inside out.

December

Shane McCullough, a.k.a. the Dark Knight, swung his long sword with all his might; pushing himself up off the floor and using the stone column behind him to brace his body for another anticipated attack. In his other hand, he held up an ornate shield, covered in rubies and emeralds and showcasing an elaborate family crest in the center. His hair fell limp towards his eyes, the sweat overpowering the hold that his styling gel had once delivered, as he jabbed the sword once again towards the face of the twenty-fifth hire at The Company – Simon Davis.

Simon dodged and weaved to avoid the sword's blade as it swung close to his head and neck – he was completely unarmed and was doing his best to avoid allowing his longtime nemesis to nail a jab. I stared at the two of them, from fifty-feet away, alongside a dozen or more other onlookers who watched in wonder, eyes agape. *This is all in my imagination, isn't it*, I asked myself, knowing all too well how my oft-distracted mind would take me to the lands of warriors and knights and *Sorceress-Bitches*. But it wasn't my imagination at all. It was real. And it was *really happening*.

In a gift shop called *The Dragon's Lair*.

Down the walkway from a *Baja Fresh* and *The Steakhouse at Camelot.*

In Las Vegas' own Excalibur Hotel & Casino.

Simon dodged another sword-thrust, this time kicking Shane in the stomach and sending him flying back into a case filled with identical plastic swords and shields. Had Shane felt the need, he could have also stocked up on magical wands, Sorcerer's robes, plastic-molded chain mail and a variety of King Arthur-themed costumes and props if he was feeling disadvantaged by Simon's sheer brute strength.

"Had enough, old friend?" taunted Simon, hovering tall above the downed knight in question.

"Clearly not," Shane shot back, tossing aside his plastic shield and picking up a plastic Mace to accompany his plastic sword. He *screamed* one of those "I'm more scared than you might think" screams, throwing everything he had at Simon as he stormed full force. Simon stepped nimbly aside, sticking his tree-trunk of a leg out, and tripping Shane head first into a glass display of elaborate collectible statues of Fairies, which collapsed onto the ground with a *crash*. It was ironic, in an *old man wins the lottery and dies the next day* kind of way.

Simon turned to look at me – I stood, blown away, in front of a faux-castle façade that also served as the entrance to the Castle Walk Food Court. He just shrugged, eyebrows at full mast. It didn't much matter to him that Shane was stumbling up again from behind; he made one last attempt to take down his decades-old nemesis. Simon, of course, heard him coming and threw out a fist. It connected with Shane's head, knocking him back and into a huge fiberglass Dragon statue, which was incidentally wearing a black Excalibur T-shirt. The Dragon stood firm as Shane collapsed and blacked out.

"Well, *that* was an unexpected yet pleasant surprise," Simon said as his deep guttural laugh echoed through the establishment. "Do you think he's had enough, *now*?"

I suspected he did. He *looked* like he did. The punch wasn't an obituary in *The New York Times*, but it was nice to see that someone had finally given the singing-and-dancing, magic-trick enabled Shane McCullough a taste of his own medicine.

One day earlier, I sat in Jess' Dodge Durango, in the loading (or was it *unloading*) part of the *Alaska Airlines* terminal. I was two hours out from a direct flight to Las Vegas from SEATAC, where the Entertainment Technology Show would kick off with The Company's Opening Keynote speech the following morning. Jess squeezed my leg to get my attention, and pulled out one of her trademark attention-driving face grabs.

"You're all set?" she asked, addressing at least three *different* concepts with just three simple words. "Good to go?"

"Good to go, like Jodie Fo," I said, making a reference to the movie *Contact* that no one except for Jess would ever get. "And I've got my suit, so there's that."

"Your funeral, buddy," she shot back, giving my face a healthy little slap.

I turned around to look at Kate, who was stuck in smile mode – flashing a toothy grin as I detached my seat belt and leaned in to give her a nuzzle and a kiss. "I love you, sweetie. I'll be home soon."

"Love you, Daddy," she shot back. "Are you bringing me back a present?"

I shared a look with Jess, then turned back to Kate. "That's the plan," I said, as I pulled my carry-on from the backseat and dragged it with me into the front where I opened the door. "See you in two days," I said to Jess, slinging the bag around my shoulder, stepping back onto the curb and closing the door. Jess immediately opened the passenger side power window.

"Don't forget to text me," Jess yelled out. "I want details."

"How about I call you?" I asked, fatigued from months of texting for Memphis' own benefit. "On the *telephone!*"

"Ah, the telephone," she smiled. "I love it when you get all *Little House on the Prairie* on me."

"Keep the candle on," I said. "I'll be back soon."

I watched as Jess and Kate drove away, then walked into the double doors for the airline terminal as I prepared mentally for what was to come. The Thunderdome results had ended up in my favor. *And Romy's.* Now both product teams were winging their way to Las Vegas where Ben Packer would choose one of us for the final moment of the Keynote speech. Had the entire exercise been recorded for live television, an announcer somewhere might have claimed that the entire rigmarole would end up being "*the most stunning, life-changing, emotionally-charged,*

awe-inspiring keynote ceremony ever."
    And if things went the way I was hoping, those words wouldn't end up being too far from the truth.

The ETS, or the *Electronics Technology Show* was an annual technology and consumer electronics conference that brought global technology companies from around the world to Las Vegas each and every December. The goal, of course, was to provide a forum for electronics manufacturers to preview their upcoming products, give software giants like The Company an opportunity to communicate their long-term strategies and product roadmaps to *said* electronics manufacturers, and to allow business folk with a love of "cinema" to *also* attend the *Adult Film Awards* – and do so on the company dime. *Not that there was anything wrong with that.* There wasn't. It was research. A tax write-off. *Ask a CPA – they'd tell you.*

    Since The Company's software and hardware divisions drove billions of dollars in revenue to the manufacturers and since both groups were so dependent on the other in a symbiotic relationship that had continued to be lucrative as far back as anyone could remember – the show was always opened up by a Keynote speech that was given by the Chief Executive Officer of The Company. This year would be Ben Packer's second go-around, having just joined The Company the previous September. The tradition of doing it at the Excalibur Hotel & Casino, however, had been a tradition ten years in the making – regardless of its aged-look, The Company kept coming back for more.

    I stared out the window of the taxi as it approached the garish façade that *was* Excalibur. Primary-colored castle spires shot up into the Vegas sky, arranged into a bustling city that was more like an adult-themed Medieval Metropolis than the *Disneyland* that some visiting children might have mistaken it for. And despite being built before the most recent high-end casinos had staked their claim on the strip, Excalibur continued to draw hotel and casino guests in through their gates and across their moats because *people loved dragons.* And castles. And swords. And watching real-life jousts, almost nightly. It didn't matter that the plastic stone-brick frontages at every entryway and arch sounded as hollow as the chocolate croissants in the buffet. The dungeons and the dragons were big business. Just ask George R.R. Martin.

I was wearing a suit. *Just so you know it actually happened.*

I strutted through the center of the Casino, through wafting clouds of cigar smoke and cheeseburger grease, alongside the screams of tortured gamblers with their lives on the line. I felt pretty damn good about where I was and how I looked. Periodically, a stray spotlight cascaded across my face, giving me that classic 1988 Dustin Hoffman *Rain Man* escalator look that had taken the world by storm. As I passed the three-dollar blackjack tables, Elise came up out of nowhere, sidling up alongside me. She, too, was dressed like a hundred-thousand bucks – holding a clipboard and ready to get down to business as the strut continued without nary a pause.

We shared a dramatic look, then turned to face forward as we continued to make our way down the center of the Casino pathway, stepping in unison to *Sexy Boy* by AIR – our unofficial theme song, that I had told no one about.

"How we looking?" I asked, checking my watch – it was just after one PM.

"Seven hours until we give the run through. Here's the schmeelie." She handed over a piece of paper, which I grabbed, continuing to walk at a rhythmic pace. "Those include all of Packer's idiosyncrasies. The stuff we know he can't stand. The things that drive him crazy. Good for us to keep all of those things in mind as we approach the zero hour."

"Thanks," I smiled, handing back the paper.

"What for?"

"For saying *zero hour.*"

"No problem, *Chief.*"

"There you go again," I said, flattered by her remembering my list of preferred phrases.

She grinned and wiped the smile from her face as Dustin and Bernard joined the walking tour from opposite sides. Dustin didn't look a hundred-thousand bucks, but maybe eighty-five. He was still wearing his trademark Linux penguin shirt under a sport jacket with jeans. Bernard *was* Bernard, who didn't give a shit what you told him to wear, especially now that he had developed an almost unhealthy attachment to his damn *Newsies* hat.

"Gentlemen," I nodded, as we kept on walking the walk. Trust me, it was *a long corridor.* "Where are we at?"

"Hotel rooms are set," Dustin replied.

"Good. And are we covered legally? With respect to the presentation?"

"We're fine," Bernard grumbled as Dustin responded with a not-so-sure mouth sigh. "We *are* fine, you *shithead*," he threw back at Dustin.

"Just make sure we are before tonight. Cool?"

They nodded as we continued to the theme song, passing by eagle-eyed Pit Bosses, Tommy Bahama fashion-inspired tourists, and a distraught Jane. She sat on the edge of the walkway, mascara ruined and smeared.

We stopped. The theme song music stopped, too.

"Jane," I said.

She looked up, removing her hands from her face. Said nothing.

"What happened?" I asked, concerned.

"I *hit* on an eighteen."

"Never hit on an eighteen," growled Bernard. "What are you, an idiot!?"

"I know that *now*!" she yelled.

"Did you lose a lot?" asked Elise.

Jane covered her face. "My rent. For the next three months." Then she started crying. I looked around at our kick-ass, well-dressed team as we comforted the weak link of the bunch.

"Get in line. *Do it*," I said. Nervous, she did just that. "And pull yourself together. We will worry about you being homeless *later*."

"You always know what to say," she sniffled, straightening herself and her cocktail dress up as we turned and gazed upon the entrance to the Main Gala Auditorium.

The five of us, dressed to the nines, looked up at the cobblestone entryway, with The Company's logo emblazoned on the glowing marquee.

"Well," I said, taking a deep *breath*. "Let's see what we've got to work with." I stepped past the entryway first, with the rest of the team following on my heels as we headed into the belly of the beast.

The Excalibur's Main Gala Auditorium, or *King Arthur's Round Table* was the largest circular auditorium West of the Mississippi, which was an obviously-overboard attempt to find the silver lining by the in-room hotel network TV channel. It had no corners, no stretch of wall or floor that *wasn't* covered liberally with red velvet or faux-stone façade and no eagles – despite the fact that anyone walking in had the inexplicable feeling of dread that at any moment one could be attacked from above. The throngs of Company-employed event planners had been having their way with this room for weeks, bringing in massive rigs and elaborate displays that daisy-chained hundreds of flat screen HDTVs into a mosaic-like experience that allowed for incredible visuals and sound.

At the center of the auditorium sat mission control for tomorrow night's Keynote – with a mammoth sound board, dozens of connected laptops and the Director at the helm. "Go make sure that our interface for *Holographic Ebert* and our sound cues are compatible with the system," I directed Dustin. "And make sure the teleprompter has the most up to date version of the talk track," I relayed to Jane. The two of them took off for the center as Elise nudged me and pointed to the far end of the room.

"Drama at three o'clock," she whispered, pointing out Romy Wallace. She was directing multiple peons around the auditorium while arguing with disembodied voices that were coming through her headset/microphone. "I think it's time you talked to her, don't you?" asked Elise, motioning to her watch.

I eyed her, imagining her body morph into a life size version of the *Brady Bunch* Hawaiian Tiki of bad luck. No matter how confident I felt or how much I thought I knew, the appearance of Romy Wallace always caused me to second-guess, falter and fail. Because, much like the Tiki, she had *bad mojo*. All that being said, I *did* need to talk to her. And it had to happen *now*. It was important that I made an effort to extend the olive branch of friendship before tonight's run-through began.

"Go," she said, pushing me in Romy's direction and snapping me out of my internal debate, which had included a five-step plan to rid the Middle East of Al Qaeda.

When I had reached Romy at the far end of the room, she was in the midst of an argument with someone in the ether, berating someone over her microphone and giving me a "wait just a second" motion with her index finger. I stood there, impatiently, toes tapping.

"I *understand* it is a busy week, trust me I do," she said, "but if you do not get Wolfgang Puck over to this hotel to deliver Mr. Bay his trademark chicken-pesto panini before eight o'clock in the evening, *thenyouaregoingtohaveaveryangrydirectoronyourhands*." She was in overdrive, biting her lip as she listened to the poor soul on the other end of the microphone. "Yes. *Correct.* YES. No. *Good-bye.*"

I smiled at her. Michael *fucking* Bay. "Panini problems?" I joked.

"More like talent issues," she groaned. "Dude, who do these people *think* they are? When Michael *Bay-bee* was making commercials, he had to go get his own damn paninis. Now he needs Wolfgang Puck to hand deliver them to him?" She *sighed*, then refocused. "Not your problem. You've got bigger ones to deal with, like figuring out how to overshadow *Me TV.*"

She was relentless. And blind to what I had seen with my own two eyes. *Me TV* was, for all intents and purposes, something that made your TV abnormally louder. She was living in her own Universe where she was the center of it, drinking from her own vat of *Kool-Aid*. I ignored it, segueing to the real reason I was there. I pulled a piece of folded paper out of my jacket and handed it to her.

"What's this?" she asked.

"Kind of…a peace offering," I said. "Look, NEO was a long time ago, but we agreed to look out for each other. I don't know if you remember, but we *actually* discussed forming an alliance. Now, things didn't necessarily end up that way, but I thought that *just maybe…*"

Romy opened the slip of paper. It had a room number on it – *2801*. It was the Corporate Suite we had set aside for the team. She eyed it and made a face, like something smelled off. "Aren't you married?" she asked.

"Good GOD no," I stammered, meaning something completely different. "I mean, I'm not *asking* you what you *thought* I was asking you. I wasn't. Jesus. I mean… It's our suite on the twenty-eighth floor. Our *Company* suite. I figured, one drink, what the hell. For old times' sake."

Her rigid defensive stance relaxed. "You want to have a drink *with me?*" The competitiveness and spite in her face disappeared and was replaced by one of genuine surprise. "Dude, you are totally effing with me, right? You've got RJ Zimmer somewhere around here ready to jump out of a FedEx box, don't you?"

"No." I wasn't and I *didn't*. It was time to move past all of this. "What I was going for here was… You know, like the night before The Olympics, don't all the major competitors have a friendly drink before the big final competition? Kind of like that. Just *one* drink. I thought it would be nice."

She looked at me cockeyed. "You are…*unique*," she said, folding the paper back up and putting it in her pocket. "But like you say – what the hell."

"Great. So how about six o'clock?"

She paused. For a moment. "Uh, *no!*" she yelled, looking directly into my eyes. *WTF?* Just as I was about to ask why, she picked right back up, "Michael Bay is *allergic* to tree nuts," she shouted as she pulled the microphone closer to her mouth. "If he even rubs up against a tree nut, we are going to have an *Armageddon*-like situation on our hands."

Romy saw I was still standing there. *Six o'clock*, she nodded, confirming that she would indeed attend. I was surprised, but not totally, since any event that had to do with bolstering Romy's ego, was an event Romy rarely (almost *never*) allowed herself to miss.

I nodded and walked back to Elise, giving her the thumbs up, then checked my watch. Six o'clock wouldn't be here soon enough.

We'd spared no expense. The suite at the top of the 28th floor of the Excalibur Hotel came complete with a stunning panoramic view of the Strip, an indoor hot tub, fully-stocked bar, living room, dining room, bedroom and yes, even a small room specifically set aside for *massage*. The team had left minutes earlier, having spent the last three hours closing off on the details for tonight's final run through. I pushed a pair of white boards, which we had been using to walk through the presentation's top talking points, to the far wall and put my laptop bag and portable USB drive (which contained all the final files and assets) for what we were now calling *The Ben Packer Show* on a table off to the side. Room service had delivered a chilled bottle of Dom, as well, which I placed on the top of the bar as the doorbell to the room *chimed*.

I opened the door. It was Romy, looking *human*. She had abandoned the tight-fitting guy gear for an elegant cocktail dress that accentuated more than just her major curves. Her face glowed with a substance I believed to be foreign to her, which some referred to as *makeup*.

She attempted a smile, but it was more like the kind of look a physician gave you right before they asked you to bend over and *cough*.

"Okay. So, I'm here," she said, almost like she had landed the short straw in a game of Corporate Russian Roulette, where the loser had to have a drink with their most annoying, *unthreatening* nemesis. "And in case you are wondering," she clarified, "this dress is for tonight."

"Come on in," I opened the door wide, guiding her into the massive suite, which she immediately started evaluating against her own Vegas accommodations.

"We're tried to get the suite next door," she said, feeling the couch fabric and eyeing the crown molding where the ceiling met the wall. "It was already taken. So, we got twenty-eight hundred *instead* for the same price. It has an elevator, three floors and a mini *jai alai* court." Somewhere, one twenty-sixth of the population of Florida and the editor who cut together the opening title sequence of *Miami Vice* were overjoyed at the reference.

I smiled, clenching my teeth through it all as I reached for the bottle of champagne and held it up. "So, how about that *one* drink?"

"Sure," she said and wandered over to the windows, looking out across The Strip as I moved around the back of the bar and pulled out two glasses. I got to work on the champagne, using both thumbs to urge the cork out as Romy disappeared into her e-mails. With added force, the cork *exploded* free, slamming into the chandelier and shaking Romy to the core. She spun around, hands on her heart, then let out a *sigh* when she realized it was just the cork.

I had seen *the look*. It wasn't trademark Romy Wallace, ballbuster extraordinaire. For a fraction of a second there had been a lack of confidence. A nervousness. Panic. *There is something human inside that woman*, I thought to myself, as I began to pour the Dom into the champagne flutes. Maybe she was not the *Sorceress-Bitch* through and through.

But Romy snapped quickly back into her usual mode, sat down on one of the leather stools and reached out to grab a hold of the glass. I held up my glass to Romy's and *clinked* it. "Best of luck," I said, taking a sip. "I just wanted you to know that there are no hard feelings. May the best product win the spot."

She eyed me, then took a deep look into her champagne flute. It was one of those questioning *did you ground up sleeping pills in my drink* looks, which she shook off quickly. Still, the whole situation had her on high alert. There was something she couldn't figure out.

"I don't get you, Murphy," she said, after swishing the Dom around on her tongue. "After all that's gone down... I mean, who does all *this?*" she continued, referring to the glasses and the bubbly and the general friendly attitude I was putting out there.

"I do?"

"Yes. *You* do," she said, taking another sip. "I mean, how do you not hate *me* like I hate *you?* You and me, we come from the same place. People from the Industry are trained to hate each other."

"Do you *hate* me? I mean, truly hate me?" I wanted to know.

"You're my direct competitor," she said, matter-of-fact. "If I don't truly hate you, I can never hope to win."

"Well, that's kind of sad," I said. And it was. But it wasn't the Industry's fault. It was just who Romy was. So intent on success that she became a person with values that even *she* knew was inexcusable. I thought about Mitch DeForrest in that same breath, reminded of his own guiding principles. *Win or die* were his only two choices in any situation. It wasn't much different from Romy.

It wasn't the person that I wanted to be. *Not anymore.*

And despite coming to terms that one night with Chloe and *Holographic Ebert* by my side – this *one* drink made it all the much clearer.

"It *is* sad," Romy admitted, nodding along with me.

"Well, at least we agree on *something*," I said, tossing back my last sip and missing my mouth altogether. Instead, it poured down my chin and all over my shirt.

"Aw, man," I whined, throwing a stack of bar napkins over my shirt to sop up the mess while I preserved my suit jacket on the chair to my left. "Let me just quick change this," I said to Romy.

"You and *drinks*," she laughed, as I ran into the back bedroom where I pulled another shirt from my hanging bag and did a quick change. I was gone three minutes tops, but the minute I returned Romy's tone had completely changed – she had downed her drink and was getting her stuff together.

"Michael Bay wants his food servers to pretend they're robots," she said, holding up her cell phone as if to reference it had come through e-mail. "Gotta go, but thanks for the drink. I wish I could say it was *nice,* but it was more…"

"*Weird*," we both said in unison.

"Yeah. Best of luck, Murphy," she said, reaching for the door and opening it. "Although, unlike you, I don't really mean it."

I smiled as she walked out the door. Despite there being some element of humanity beneath that rough exterior, it was nice to know the *Sorceress-Bitch* part of her still made up about ninety-five percent of Romy Wallace's total organic mass.

No drink, no matter what, was going to change that.

Ben Packer was never a golden child. He didn't start up his own paper delivery business at seven, erect his own backyard food bank for the homeless at twelve, or patent a device to create clean water for third-world countries when he was sixteen. He wasn't valedictorian of his high school, editor of his school paper or Student Body *anything*. He wasn't even smart in the traditional sense of the word, with a huge vocabulary or a brain that could crunch numbers more quickly than a Texas Instruments' scientific calculator. But where others focused on good grades and sales numbers, Ben Packer focused on *trends*. Like a crazy little concept called the *Internet* and a crazy business idea called *buying domain names*.

Packer got rich selling twenty-dollar domain names for millions of dollars to major corporations that had missed the boat, but that alone would have never prepared him to be the CEO of a billion-dollar company. No, neither did the multiple companies he bought, ran and sold for a profit over the next twenty-or-so years. Neither did his ability to manage companies with thousands of employees across multiple countries, impacted by complicated International economics and laws. No, the reason Ben Packer was offered the job as CEO of The Company was due to one, very specific and somewhat ludicrous personality trait.

Ben Packer was *eccentric*.

While Ben Packer never started up his own paper delivery service at seven, he started up his own global treasure-hunting organization called *Globe for Gold* at twenty-seven. And while he never erected his own backyard food bank for the homeless, he often handed *thousand-dollar bills* to the highway adjacent pan handlers on his way to work. And even though he never patented a device that created clean water for third world countries, he was once lambasted for telling a reporter that *"third world countries are only third world countries because they are unmotivated to become anything but that."*

And as long as eccentric came hand-in-hand with charisma, ego and bottom-line profit, Ben Packer wasn't going anywhere. No matter how often he was "out of the office" retrieving gold bullion from sunken pirate ships, making uneducated snipes at competitor's products or yelling at his underlings for pronouncing the word caramel as *car-mel*, he was a protected commodity.

Yes, even in Vegas.

"How tall am I *now*?" Ben Packer yelled down at his Admin from the center of the stage, who was frantically trying to adjust the platform he was standing atop – which was hidden by the pulpit from where he would give his Keynote speech.

"Five-seven," someone from the rafters announced.

"*Unacceptable,*" he shot back. "We are just over twenty-four hours from this event, people. If you can't execute something simple like making me two inches taller than I am in real-life, then your time at this Company will be short-lived." Ah, Ben Packer's *Something Simple* list. It had grown to be legendary in a comical, sad, depressing sort of way. Especially if you were caught in the crosshairs and had no supernatural forces to help you deliver on some of his requests, like:

Make People Like Me More Than They Do

Make My Face Look More Symmetrical on Camera

Make the Public Embrace My New Saying, "Can You Smell What I'm Cookin'?"

Despite having no clear ideas for causing the CEO of The Company to grow two additional inches in twenty-four hours, the MacGyvers of the moment rushed the stage – carrying new shoes, saws, hammers, and hair gel. I had no idea how'd they'd solve this problem, but there were more pressing issues at hand. Like the fact that we were fifteen minutes out from the final run through for Memphis.

This was it. There was no turning back. The team and I sat in the center of the auditorium seats, waiting for our turn to approach the stage and give Packer the opportunity to see what had gotten us this far. I'd been very specific to the team at what our goals were for the evening, and they were all on board. Unlike the disaster that occurred at the

Death Star, the entire team was fully aligned on *The Vegas Coefficient*.

"Ex-boss in the back of the house," interrupted Elise, motioning with her head to the back of the auditorium where Shane McCullough had found a seat as far away from the action as possible, arms crossed and legs up on an empty chair in front of him. Even the way he sat made me want to punch him in the face. Or watch someone else punch him in the face. Oh, if only someone, sometime would make that happen…my life would have been complete.

"You might want to see *this*," interrupted Dustin, directing our attention to the other side of the auditorium, in the back. Our heads pivoted like we were at Wimbledon, moving off Shane and onto none other than Simon Davis. My former mentor. Shane's nemesis. In that one moment I felt more Daniel Larusso to their Mr. Miyagi/*Cobra Kai* Sensai than I had ever felt before.

"What is he doing *here*?" asked Jane, concerned.

"I have no idea," I said, getting up from my chair on my way to confront him but running into my favorite person *instead*. In his motorized wheelchair. Blocking the aisle.

"Hello, Cameron," I think he said, although I couldn't be sure due to that head cast still causing him to sound like a guy who was eating marbles. "Have a minute?"

I didn't.

But it was Mitch DeForrest.

So, you know.

"I've got to go get ready," I pleaded with Mitch D., as he kept me blocked in a corner while he continued to pepper me with questions about every single moment of the presentation. How long would it be? Who was controlling *Holographic Ebert*? Was the talk track the same version that he had seen over mail the previous Friday? These were all fine questions to ask, but not *ten minutes before I was about to go on*.

Mitch D., moved his wheelchair closer to me, intentionally pushing his front left wheel on top of my shoe and squinting to get a better look at my eyes. "Tell me we're good."

"We're *good*," I said, casually looking past Mitch D. to see if I could see Shane *or* Simon. But in the time I had been talking to the Phantom of the Opera, they had gone MIA. Yet something else more curious tugged at my attention. It was Romy – slinking her way to the stage at the edge of the auditorium.

"*We*," he repeated. "You're finally talking like a team player. It means you understand that Memphis' success or failure impacts us all."

I did. Truly. "I do," I said, still watching Romy with an eagle eye. She reached the stage, disappearing behind the curtain.

"Bring it in," Mitch D. said, using his three free fingers to make a 'come hither' motion.

"Bring *what* in *where*?" I asked, terrified at what his answer might be.

"A hufffggghh," he slurred as his tongue got caught on the edge of the Phantom of the Opera hole in his head cast. "A *hugttthhh*," he tried again, unsuccessfully. Then, fortunately for him but unfortunately for me, his tongue got un-stuck. "*A hug*," he enunciated.

Good God. I held my breath, kneeled so I could get my arms around the cast, and gave him a half-hug, cast-pat thingie. "Now if you'll excuse me," I said, pulling back as fast as I could, "I have something to go take care of."

That *something* was Romy.

Mitch D., tried to spin around to see where I was going, but I was already halfway down the aisle, booking towards the stairs at the edge of the stage.

I heard it as I exited the stage, having ensured that Romy hadn't done anything untoward or unplanned. What I heard seemed innocent enough. The words, with respect to the night's schedule, made perfect logical sense. It was a simple announcement, over the P.A. system, that I never would have second-guessed. After all, we were next on the docket – perhaps there were some audio/visual questions the Director of the Keynote needed to ask.

"*Cameron Murphy to the projection booth, please.*"

Perhaps, not. Perhaps, instead of the Director requiring my attention, who incidentally wasn't using the projection booth *at all* for the Keynote presentation, it was someone who wanted me out of the picture. Someone who had wished me ill will. Someone who had given all British citizens in the History of British citizens, a bad name.

Meet Shane McCullough. *Sacker of people.*

Shane McCullough shoved me up against the massive metal IMAX projector in the Round Table Auditorium's projection booth as he locked the door behind him. He eyed me, out of breath, obviously overtaken by months of anger that had finally had nowhere to go but *out*.

"Are you crazy?" I shouted at him, as I reached back to feel my shoulder – it had been punctured by one of the sharp spokes of the IMAX projector. When I brought my fingers forward, they were slightly bloody. Not death-inducing, mind you, but significant enough for me to use it in my Oscar-worthy performance.

"Are you trying to *kill me*?" I shouted at him, holding out my hand with the blood showing. "I'm *bleeeeeeeding*. Good God, I am totally bleeding."

Shane said nothing. Instead, he went up to the windows that looked out into the auditorium. He banged on them. Even *yelled*. But no one could hear him. That was because the Round Table Auditorium's projection booth was built with some of the newest soundproof technology West of the Mississippi. No one could hear *or see* what was going on inside…West of the Mississippi. But if you were me, having gleaned all of that not-so-pertinent information from the in-room hotel TV network, would you have told him?

"The blooooood, do you see it?" I chose to say instead, jamming some dirt from the floor into my eyes to elicit tears, then looking up at him with a puppy dog face.

"Shut up, you stupid fool," Shane shot back, pacing back and forth in the room. "They can't hear you, so scream your bleeding head off as much as you want."

I pushed myself up against the base of the IMAX projector as Shane fiddled with the controls in the room, eventually able to turn on the speakers in the projection booth. It was a direct feed to the audio boards down in the auditorium, and the microphones from the stage picked up the voices nice and clear. It's just that what they were saying wasn't so *nice*.

"*Cameron Murphy to the backstage area*," one of the voices over the PA reverberated in the projection booth. "*Two minutes to start*."

I looked up at Shane, still breathing heavy, eyes darting between the locked door, my place on the floor, and his view through the two front windows. "They need me down there," I said.

"That was my expectation," Shane said calmly. "A lot of people *need* things, but it doesn't necessarily mean they will ever get them. Someone else will have to do it."

"But I'm the one who knows it best," I said.

"That was our hope," he smiled, evilly. "Then you will witness your beloved product as it crashes and burns first hand," he spat at me. "Perhaps now you will understand exactly what it was you put *me* through the day you destroyed MediaMesh."

"Much like what you put Simon Davis through," I shot back, trying to get his goat. But he didn't show any emotion – just went back to the door, put the key ring into his pocket, and locked me in from the outside. I could hear the dead bolt engage from the outside with a *clack*.

This was *not* how everything was supposed to have gone down, that was for sure. I pulled myself up to the windows and looked down into the auditorium. On stage, my team stood in a circle, arguing over how to handle the current situation. Elise and Dustin were pointing to Jane. Jane didn't like *anyone* pointing to her, especially when it accompanied them handing her the printed-out talk track for the run-through. She tried to get out of it, but there was no other logical choice.

"*Memphis run-through in one minute*," the speakers announced to the auditorium and me, in the projection booth. This train was on the move and there was no one, not even me, who could stop it from happening.

Memphis never had a chance. And it wasn't Jane D'Allegro's fault. It was ultimately Adam Sandler's.

Something had gone horribly wrong between the moment we had locked the presentation and the moment it had gone up in front of Ben Packer. The usually-tasteful intro music that accompanied the beautiful Memphis logo and tagline surprisingly ended up being the song *Baby's Got Back* as Jane strutted onto the stage. Nervous, and following the teleprompters word for word, Jane's talk track was a disaster – previously proofed language had been egregiously changed. Her statements contradicted themselves and made use of certain words that should have never made it into a public forum.

"Today's average recommendation engines are dry and impersonal," she had explained. "But with Memphis, our goal is to make consumers *moist* with emotion."

The transitions between the PowerPoint slides, which had previously alternated between a fade and a push, had turned into garish animations of swans, doves, rocket ships and baby reptiles that hopped across the screen like a retro game of *Frogger*. Even *Holographic Ebert*, once a complimentary and positive force of good, took a turn into the land of the negative.

"*Memphis...is a horrible...thing,*" he had said, making an ick face.

"*Audiences will...not be fans,*" he had revealed, while talking about its potential for success.

"*Short...people...need not apply,*" he said to Ben Packer, looking straight at him, causing him to almost jump out of his seat and attack the faux-movie reviewer had Simone not pulled him back down.

And the *screaming colicky* baby at the front of the auditorium, didn't help matters much either.

I stared through the window, listening and watching as the fifty-car pile-up happened right before my eyes. I imagined the rescue vehicles trying desperately to get to the site of the accident, but there was an even bigger complication that was standing in their way.

That supersized disaster was none other than Adam Sandler's cherubic face.

It had all gone down during the real-time demonstration of Memphis' recommendation engine. Chloe walked the audience through a sample user, who had previously been attached to Dustin's name and face, but which had somehow been reassigned to Ben Packer. What appeared to be an amusing way to include the CEO's persona in the demo turned disastrous as the movie recommendations popped up one by one, with titles that ranged from *Happy Gilmore* and *Big Daddy* to *Billy Madison* and *The Waterboy*. In fact, every single item from movies to TV to books and songs, all were related to Adam Sandler.

Who Ben Packer hated with the heat of a thousand suns.

"Just make sure there's no Sandler in those movie recommendations," Simone had said to the team after we'd presented at the Thunderdome. "Put in Will Ferrell. Ben loves Will Ferrell. The more Will Ferrell you can put in there, the happier he will be."

"But this is based on an algorithm," I explained, eyeing Sudhir who agreed. "We don't manually place movies in those slots."

"You should manually place movies in those slots," she shot back, "that *don't include* Adam Sandler."

"But why?" I asked, with the entire room (including Romy) listening to the debate.

"There is no *why*," Simone said, growing fatigued with my line of questioning. "There is just a *what*."

"What's the *what*?"

"The *what* is Ben Packer, attacking whomever is responsible for Adam Sandler's appearance in a Company-sanctioned PowerPoint presentation, like a piranha attacking a juicy, white-meat triathlete swimming up the wrong river. Don't swim up the wrong river. Avoid going anywhere near that horrible river. Swim up Ferrell Falls and avoid the Sandler Strait."

So, it wasn't much of a surprise when Ben Packer stormed the stage, kicked over the monitor that was so gleefully showcasing the entire career of one Adam Sandler, and grabbed the microphone off Jane's lapel so he could shout his own words to the entire auditorium.

"This is over," his voice came loudly through the projection booth's speakers. "This product, this presentation…I do not want to hear a mention of it ever again. Calabasas team, prepare for the Keynote – you're in."

The stage lights went dark. The microphone *screeched* feedback through the projection booth's speakers. And just outside the door, there was *shouting*. I got up and approached the door in an attempt to see what was going on. Without warning it *blasted* open, knocking me back down to my feet. When I looked up, I saw Shane taking off down the hall and Simon Davis standing there in the doorway.

"What are you *doing* down here?" I shouted. "You were supposed to stay upstairs, out of sight! I had everything under control."

"Disorder is *good*, remember?" he grumbled, impatiently eyeing the hallway that Shane had escaped down. "Besides, this was *our* plan, not just *your* plan. And now that Packer has killed Memphis, I can focus on securing my other goal. Who incidentally, has a pretty good head start."

Simon took off down the hall as I pulled myself up off the ground, stumbling to the doorway where I crooked my head out to get a better look. He was in hot pursuit with Shane rounding the corner at the end of the corridor. I did what any self-respecting conspirator would do.

I ran after the two of them, sprinting as fast as I could.

And why not? *Simon was right*, I thought, as I hit the end of the corridor and booked around and into the first floor Food Court. It wasn't just *my* plan. It had become *our* plan when I had tracked him down in the Commons, apologized for the person I had become, and asked him to help us kill Memphis once and for all.

That had been *two weeks earlier.*

Simon Davis was eating a salad. But it wasn't a normal everyday Simon Davis salad. This salad could have passed for the kind that a five-year old toddler had constructed simply by grabbing errant handfuls of iceberg, veggies and crunchy toppings and throwing them onto a plain white canvas plate like he was the Pollack of lettuce and legumes. In other words, something had changed in Simon. Something *significant*.

On the heels of the Thunderdome decision and feeling as though I had been backed up against a wall, I had sought out Simon in his many areas of *hermittude*. I visited Building 12 to no avail. I crawled into the depths of his underground lair, garnering no more than a sprained ankle and a scratched face. The Commons had been my last bastion of hope. When I spotted him off in the corner, hovering over his latest uncharacteristic concoction, it was both relieving and confounding.

I approached him at the table, hovering at the edge, debating if this was really the card I wanted to play. But I didn't have anyone left on my side.

"Come to tell me I'm an asshole?" he said, mouth full, without looking up.

"No," I replied. "I came to talk to you about Thunderdome. The results are in."

Simon barely looked up, then chased his mouthful of food with a swish of his free, Company-sponsored, carbonated beverage. "Like I care," he said in an emotionless, monotone voice. "Now if you don't mind, I'm eating lunch."

I looked down again at the mess on his plate. It looked like an episode of *Hoarders*. "Yeah, what is that *exactly*?" I asked, trying to keep him talking so he would lower his defenses. "Did *order* and *control* go out the window or something?"

He took another swig, then looked me in the eyes for the first time since I'd approached him. He took another bite, never diverting his gaze, then chewed and swallowed again. "Yeah, well… Maybe sometimes disorder can be good."

"When it snaps you back to reality, *definitely*." Which is what had happened to me. It had taken the chaos of Mitch D. and the assault on the *Death Star* and the Book Club and my arguments with Simon to bring me to my lowest point. It was only then, when all that disorder had turned my life upside down, that I was able to see things clearly and plot a new course. At least, that's why I was here, reaching back out to Simon. I had a new course, but I needed his help.

"You sayin' that you've *snapped* back?" he asked, curious.

"I didn't get what you were trying to *do*," I said, fidgeting with my Blue Badge at my side. "I just saw what you were trying to keep *me* from doing. I was wrong. What I *said* was wrong. Everything I'd been doing was wrong. You were trying to help. And I didn't see that for what it was."

Simon's eyes widened, then narrowed with suspicion. "You just got booted from Thunderdome, didn't you? Kicked in the ass, now you've suddenly had a complete catharsis because of it. Is that the deal? You've got nothing now, so you're crawling back on your hands and knees with apologies spilling out from all sides?"

"Actually, we're going to Vegas," I said. Simone had chosen Memphis and Calabasas for the Keynote run-through. One of us would land the coveted spot. The other would be branded a failure, see their product funding dry up almost immediately, and watch as all previous senior-level support was reattributed somewhere else. I wanted to be the failure. But I had to do it without Mitch D. ever holding me responsible.

I pulled out an airline ticket and slapped it down on the table in front of him. "You offered your help once, and I turned it down. I'm here because I changed my mind."

"Why? What am I supposed to help you do? Win it all? Go for the Gold? Impress the CEO? Not my game, Cameron." He slid back the ticket, uninterested.

"I don't want you to help me do any of that," I said.

"Then what. What do you want me to do?"

"All that disorder? It made me realize that this product should never see the light of day. I want you to help me finish off Memphis once and for all." I slid the ticket back towards Simon's side of the table. "I want you to help me *kill* it." Simon looked up, confused. Then surprised. Then excited.

Then he picked up the ticket and shoved it into his pants.

The chase was on.

Shane McCullough booked as fast as he could through the Excalibur Hotel's Castle Park Food Court. Tourists swarmed back and forth, carting bags and children from one side of the walk to the other. Shane, realizing he was now being pursued by the twenty-fifth hire at The Company and his shoulder-punctured sidekick, determined his options were limited. Despite the ego and the strong words, when it came down to it, Shane McCullough was a coward.

He weaved in and out of the dense group of tourists, slamming into a family and throwing their bags back towards Simon. He flipped over tables and shoved them into the walkway. The closer Simon and I were on his heels, the more he tried to disrupt our pathway to success.

Shane McCullough crashed through fifteen of *Popcornopolis'* nineteen offered flavor tins, barely escaping the grasp of Simon Davis as I weaved through the minefield of pre-packaged food, wheezing the whole time. Simon leaped after his nemesis who was making his way around the Food Court fountain and past the stairwells that led to the downstairs Buffet.

I struggled to keep up. I was "in shape" in an elliptical, low carbs, circuit training kind of way. But, no, when it came to chasing down ones' nemesis, through crowded hotels and food courts, all the while dodging tourists, *not* breaking a sweat and tossing off hilarious one-liners to my partner the whole way through – not so much.

"I'm too old for this shit," I yelled to Simon, *trying*.

Six hours earlier, the entire team sat around the living room of Suite 2801, directing their attention to Elise at the front of the room. She referred to a pair of white boards, each with lists of items scrawled across them, all under the header *Things Ben Packer Can't Stand*.

Elise used a laser pointer, excitedly walking the team through each of them like she was briefing an entire room of CIA operatives. "Alright, clown towns. Thanks to my own personal network of admins, Directors at The Company and my boyfriend, we have pulled together this list of *really annoying* things that make Ben Packer want to eat his own face off. That being the case, we'll be incorporating each and every one of them into the *fake* Memphis presentation docs, assets and files. These items include…"

Elise went on to describe each and every one. There were the infamous animated PowerPoint transitions. There was Packer's aversion to being referred to as *short*. There was rap music. Reptiles. The word *moist*. And anything starring Adam Sandler. There were other items, not completely confirmed, which ranged from Packer's fear of alien abduction, aversion to the movie *Titanic* due to his public feud with fellow Treasure hunter and nemesis/film Director James Cameron and screaming children of *all kinds*.

We had more than enough to drive Ben Packer mad.

Three hours earlier, that "one drink" with Romy Wallace was coming to an end.

"Yeah. Best of luck, Murphy," Romy had said, reaching for the door to Suite 1801 and opening it wide. "Although, unlike you, I don't really mean it."

I smiled as she walked out the door, standing there for what seemed like a minute before I slowly turned to look at the table where I had previously left my laptop bag and portable USB drive. The drive, incidentally, that we had loaded with alternate Memphis files and assets that no one would have ever wanted Ben Packer to see. The drive, not so ironically, that was no longer there. It was *gone*. And so was Romy.

Connect the dots.

The door to the adjoining suite burst open, revealing Simon Davis with a Cheshire cat kind of grin on his hairy mug. "We got 'er," he said, opening the door extra wide.

I walked past Simon and into the other room, completely outfitted in a tech setup that rivaled the control room of N.O.R.A.D., *circa War Games*. There were surveillance cameras, GPS tracking maps, laptop computers and a myriad of infra-red eyes-in-the-sky that gave me a giddy feeling that I'm sure the entire lot of the NSA felt every single morning they woke up in bed.

"Check it out," Dustin chimed in, spinning around in his chair, and hitting a key on the control panel – a recorded video stream began playing on the screen. It showed Romy, the snake that she was, snatch the USB drive mere seconds after I had left the room to change my shirt.

Like a sleight of hand artist, Simon waved his hand in front of my face and produced a mini-computer disc. "We've got her taking the files," he said. "Now we've just got to hope she'll use them to screw you."

"She *hates* me," I said. "You heard her. That alone should be enough."

Simon Davis had caught Shane McCullough.

Had it not been for the crowd of onlookers, I might have sped right past the kitschy gift shop o' fairies, appropriately dubbed *Dragon's Lair*. But the crowd was so engaged and so vocal, as they watched the red-bearded Simon Davis hurl the thin, cowardly Shane McCullough into a wall of 3D *Magic Eye* framed dragon posters, that there was no way I could have missed it.

"I think this is part of the jousting show," a churro-eating Father explained to his churro-eating Kid despite there being no jousting equipment or announcer anywhere in the general vicinity.

The store emptied out quickly as Shane stumbled to his feet. Simon stood unwavering as his nemesis approached him, attempting to hide the fact that his left leg was already in bad shape. It was David vs. Goliath. There was no way Shane was emerging unscathed from this one.

"It's been a long time," Shane said to Simon, straightening up.

"What did he *say*?" asked an elderly woman with a camera next to me, snapping a multitude of shots of *the talent*.

"He said it's been a long–" I started to say, then realized the ludicrousness of it all, turning back to the real action.

"Indeed, it has," Simon replied, eyes red with fire. "Looks like you've created yet *another* mess. A mess that, once again, I'm going to have to clean up."

One hour earlier, I had fled from Mitch D. and his creepy embraces of servitude, racing to stage right where Romy had ascended the stairs and disappeared behind the curtains. It was the exact area where the brain of *Holographic Ebert* and the hard drive containing our entire presentation was locked and stored.

As I passed by the front row of seats, on my way to back stage, I caught a glimpse of Bernard sitting with a Baby Bjorn attached to his chest. He held a bottle just out of reach of the little kid, seemingly trying to elicit a not-so-positive response. I passed by, did a quick nod, then passed through the curtains to the backstage area. Where *she* was.

Romy hovered over our security-enabled digital lock box, keying in a code that she had obviously obtained off our confidential USB files. Once it unlocked, she connected the stolen USB drive to the master hard drive for the presentations, then copied all the sabotaged files we had handed to her on a silver platter over *the good ones.* She activated the *Holographic Ebert* sound board, editing the phrases and words in the sound bank. She even changed the teleprompter text, adding her own unique edits to the ones' I had memorized.

I stood there, hiding in the shadows, watching Romy do exactly what we had predicted she would do and *more.* And I didn't try to distract her. Or reason with her. Or stop her.

She was going to kill Memphis for us. Just like we had planned.

Shane McCullough was engaged in a certain activity I liked to call *The Nemesis Tries To Redirect Blame.* He was doing a fairly good job, at that.

"Please. Spare me with all your holier than thou, savior of The Company's future crap," Shane shot back, wincing at a pain in his side. "It's been *thirty years,* Simon. Wake up. Nobody cares about The Company like you do anymore. It's not some precious little club that you founded in your cousin's garage. It's a corporation. Corporations die every single day and no one sheds a tear." Shane motioned to his head, faux-knocking on it and making a *tick tock* sound with his mouth. "Might want to check the noggin," he said. "Being locked down in that bunker may have really screwed you up."

"I am in that bunker because of what you did."

"Come now. Be a *man.* Stand up for yourself. Maybe if you did that back then, instead of shrugging your shoulders and disappearing…

Maybe if you fought for what you believed in... Maybe then things would have turned out differently. But you didn't. Survival of the fittest, I always say. And I'm the guy who's still standing..."

Simon looked to Shane, then back to himself. They were *both* standing.

"It's an allegorical statement," clarified Shane.

Simon didn't like allegory. Especially when it was focused on his actual, real-life, downfall. Simon faked like he was going to hit Shane, which put him off balance and caused him to collapse back into a display of sword-in-the-stone coffee mugs and onto the floor.

"Allegory or not," Simon shot back, "I'm the one who's standing *now*."

On the ground, Shane eyed two bins filled with faux plastic weapons. "I'll believe it," Shane started to say as he picked up a plastic long sword and an ornate replica shield, "when I see it." He pushed himself up off the floor and used the stone column behind him to brace his body for another anticipated faux attack.

His hair fell limp towards his eyes, the sweat overpowering the hold that his styling gel had once delivered, as he jabbed the sword once again towards the face of the twenty-fifth hire at The Company.

The crowd had grown, and they were on the edge of their seats. What would happen to the back-stabbing Brit? Would the lumbering red-bearded giant emerge triumphant? Would Shane McCullough get a well-deserved punch in the face?

Only time would tell.

The Company was a Goliath of sorts, with hundreds of thousands of employees worldwide, an annual profit in the hundreds of billions, and rumored to be on the cusp of changing the industry again with groundbreaking technological advances, pushes into the new media space and a digital entertainment strategy that would revolutionize and disrupt the current tech landscape as we knew it.

That is, if the *consumers* believed in the products.

The Company's ETS Keynote had gone off without a hitch. Ben Packer had chaired the event with charisma, confidence and a slew of great fiscal results that got the consumers *and* the stock holders all worked up in a frenzy. The updates to our new products had been well-received and the new hardware we'd be shipping in just a few short weeks would take the gaming and personal computing space to the next level. And Ben Packer even *looked* two inches taller. Needless to say, he was overjoyed and enthusiastic when the "*And Before You Go...*" portion of the Keynote kicked into high gear and he brought Romy Wallace up on stage.

I was on my laptop, monitoring the minute-by-minute Keynote live-blogs as the *Me TV* logo lit up the room. I was reading my Twitter feed when Michael *fucking* Bay burst onto the stage with a pair of Vegas showgirls dressed up like *Transformer* robots. I was reading *Engadget* when Romy announced the price-point and Michael Bay took the volume of the TV monitor up to eleven.

The *consumers*. And the *bloggers*. And the *technology press*. And even Eric Grimwood, the Patrick Stewart of wheelchair-bound grumpy geeks everywhere. All of them, in real time on the beloved Internet, proclaimed what I had known to be the case when I had first experienced the wonder that was *Me TV*.

Me TV blew. Big, gnarly, *raisin-filled* chunks.

Had it been that hard to see? Had it been so hard to predict? Had anyone inside The Company really thought that a five-dollar USB peripheral, that increased consumers' TV volume by one metric unit, would really, honestly, take the world by storm?

Yes. *All of them.*

I sat there in the dark of the auditorium, watching Romy smile her way through the performance of a lifetime, having no clue that every word she uttered was being recorded, replayed, typed back and lampooned across every technology site that mattered. And even the ones that didn't. Her hatred had kept her from seeing the forest from the trees, and now the trees were falling on *her*.

Had it not been for Chloe, Memphis and all the people in my life who cared enough to tell me what an asshole I had become, some pretty big oaks would have also pulverized me into oblivion.

I pulled out my cell phone, almost by instinct, and activated my text messaging program. I typed in the start of Romy's name, which populated in the TO: field. Then I found the same exact *Home Alone* emoticon face that she had sent me on that very first day when the sabotage had begun. I placed it in the message, regarding it as I felt my own hatred surface for a split second, then seep completely out of my body.

Must…find…hate, the Hulk part of me grumbled.

I tried. As best as I could. I relived all the evil things she had said and done to me, but it just kept dissipating. I even mock-stabbed myself in the left leg with my *Bic* pen. But it wasn't happening. I wasn't Romy. I couldn't play the game. I couldn't *hate* in order to win the game. I hit cancel on the text message and put away my phone.

On stage, Romy was smiling like she'd just won the lottery.

Mitch DeForrest was demanding satisfaction.

We stood around the motorized menace, on the stage of the auditorium, after everyone had gone on to the overblown parties and self-congratulatory events. Mitch D. had summoned myself, Romy Wallace and Shane McCullough. Simon was there, too. But no one, except maybe Ben Packer, ever summoned him.

"I demand satisfaction," Mitch yelled again, echoing only slightly due to the fact that having a huge plaster-covered body in a wheelchair often dulled the surround sound effect.

"I think you mean to say something else," Simon chimed in, having no fear of Mitch D. or Shane McCullough, whose face was half-swollen shut. "You demand satisfaction when there's a pistol duel."

The three fingers protruding from Mitch D's right-handed cast, along with his one good eye just about had an aneurism as he tried to calm himself down in front of the guy who invented the Start Button. "Someone is going to take the blame for the Memphis debacle," he stated, "and no one is leaving here until that blame has landed on someone's head."

"If I may," Shane spoke up, "but I'm unsure as to why you've asked myself and Romy here tonight. The Memphis debacle, as you so appropriately put it, was the result of a bad presentation. How are we to blame for something that was so squarely in Mr. Murphy's court?"

Mitch D. flipped the wheelchair motor, spinning himself in my direction.

"That's where you're wrong," I said, producing the disc that I had been previously handed by Simon and the team. "The Memphis presentation was perfectly fine. Until Romy came into our suite, stole our USB drive of files and assets, and replaced them right before the dress rehearsal. This disc has surveillance video footage that proves exactly that."

Romy stared at me. Pissed. Flummoxed. "You *bastard.*"

"Well, I am stunned," lisped Shane. "This is deeply disturbing." Romy spun to Shane, completely livid at how he had gone so quickly from *zero* to *betrayal* in 1.8 seconds. McCullough factor, *Schma-cullough factor.*

"Not as disturbing as *this,*" chimed in Simon, who produced a digital tape recorder out of his pocket. "This is the call that Romy placed to Shane just *after* she stole the Memphis team's USB drive."

He pressed play. Romy's voice came on first. Then Shane's. Romy marveled at how easy it had been to steal our files, and how idiotic we had been to leave old, imperfect draft assets lying around. Shane congratulated Romy on a job well done, then reminded her that he would do his part to keep me from ever making it to the stage. Faces drooped. Eyes widened. All we needed was the cast of *C.S.I.* to show up with a blue light to make the scene complete. That notwithstanding, the last-minute evidence reveal was a pretty satisfying moment.

Mitch D.'s one good eye glared at Romy and Shane. "You know how some people say how hard it is to fire someone at The Company?" he asked from within the cast.

Romy and Shane nodded, despite not wanting to.

"Yeah," Mitch D. said. "*Not so much.*"

I was hammered. On the balcony of the Octane Lounge. Watching my team down tequila shots as they celebrated the fact that their beloved product was *dead.* They'd been at The Company long enough to know that when one product was shuttered, another one took its place. And since there was the equivalent of two hundred unique companies within The Company's mega-corporate structure, if you weren't getting riffed (or fired) you always had time to find your next gig.

They weren't getting riffed. That was someone else altogether.

I shook my head, grinning, as I spotted Elise holding court with a slew of Vegas tourists, telling stories about some celebrity or secret bit of gossip that no one knew about the place we were in. Jane and Dustin leaned in to each other at the edge of the bar, apparently having developed some form of attraction right under my own nose. And Bernard and Sudhir played a nasty yet competitive game of shuffleboard.

I eyed my cell phone's lock screen, proclaiming that there had been "439 new e-mails" since the last time I had checked. I unlocked the phone to look, then scrolled through my inbox, only to have my tired eyes recognize a fluorescent stream of *red* – the "bangs" were out in force tonight.

"No rest for the weary, I see," came a voice behind me. I turned, it was Simon. He pulled up a chair and placed a beer stein the size of a carton of milk in front of him as he sat down.

"Oh, no. You misunderstand, good sir," I said, showing him as I clicked a box that selected each and every one of my four-hundred plus *extremely important* e-mails. "There will be rest. Indefinitely." I clicked the delete button, sending a nuclear command to my phone and removing every single e-mail from existence.

As soon as they were gone, forty-eight new ones appeared. Simon laughed, having to spit some of the beer in his mouth out onto the floor. I deleted *those*, and then watched as they were replaced by a hundred more. Now, *I laughed.*

"Screw it," I said, taking the phone and throwing it with all the drunk-energy I had off the balcony and down thirty stories to its own concrete death. "I'm taking a page out of *your* book," I joked, referring to Simon's proclivity to do the same.

"Very bold," he said. "Impressive."

We were silent. For what seemed like an eternity but was probably just a few seconds. Still, I sat back, using those seconds to reflect upon the journey that had landed me at a table with Simon Davis, in Las Vegas, hours after destroying the one thing that had meant so much to me. Where had these last twelve months gone? Who had I become? I had left Los Angeles intent on starting a new life, with a new *me* at the center of it all. *Me being me.* The one man off-off-*off* Broadway show that would have had critics praising the actor in the title role (read: *me*) and his stellar, uncompromising, confident performance:

"Cameron Murphy is a revelation in his unwavering dedication to sacrificing nothing that he truly believes in." – New York Post

"Me Being Me takes the forces of evil that exist in modern society's corporate conference rooms and hallways and demonstrates how one man can remain unchanged and steadfast in the face of greed, money and

success." – The Village Voice

"In a daring, uncharacteristic and exhilarating choice, Me Being Me presents a character so confident in who he is that the core of his person never changes once for the worst. It is a daring first in the theater and in the world." – The New York Times

But none of that had happened. The Industry wasn't so different from The Company. The grass wasn't any greener. The politics and back-stabbing and bullshit were the same anywhere you went. Had I tried to convince a room of Company employees that an intergalactic dictator *did* lose his powers when he passed through the Earth's atmosphere, I would have been met with a long list of action items to determine the at-mospheric pressure, previous power-losses of intergalactic superheroes as real data to drive the analysis, and three more conference calls to de-cide on just which of the participants could review and approve the new direction of said intergalactic dictator.

Derrik with a K was looking pretty damn good right about now.

"So, what's next?" Simon asked, putting his quart of beer back on the metal-grid table.

"Well, I suppose I should get a new phone," I replied. "After that, I guess I'll kind of take it as it comes. What about you?"

He cocked his head. Thinking. "What about *me*?"

"Yeah. You know. *You*. The guy who lives in an underground bunker. The twenty-fifth hire at The Company. The legend who invented the Start Button."

"I never invented the Start Button. Who told you that?"

"Elise did."

"Well, that's a whole load of bull-crap," he said, laughing. "No one *invented* the start button. It's the *start button* for god's sake." He shook his head, and so did I – eyeing Nostra*dame*us back in the bar.

"You *are* Simon Davis, though. She was right about that?"

Simon Davis *rolled his eyes.*

I let out a breath, preparing myself for another swig of liquid courage. I tilted back, pouring it down my throat. I slammed the table, turning to Simon. "So, then? What's next for Simon Davis?"

"Well, for one," he said, "I'm going to stop working on my damn motorcycle only to leave it in my lab. If I'm going to take the time to work on it, it might as well get the opportunity to see the world."

"Amen," I said. "Although you could probably say the same thing about the *other* things you've been working on in that lab." After seeing what the rest of The Company was developing on their own, it was obvious to me that Simon's work did not deserve to remain under wraps and underground.

"One step at a time," he said. "After that, I guess I'll kind of take it as it comes. Someone I once knew... One of the good guys... He said that."

I reached out to shake his hand, and missed it completely only because I was stinking drunk. But it didn't much matter. To him or me. We both knew what I was going for.

"We did it, you *bastard*," I said.

"Oh, so now I'm a bastard?" he ribbed back, amused.

"The minute I found out you didn't invent the Start Button," I grinned, "everything changed."

Jess stared over my shoulder in the mirror as she helped secure the bowtie on the tuxedo, which was a double-breasted custom job we had been out of our minds to purchase, but which had been a part of a spending spree we would forever refer to as *The All Is Lost So Spend It While The Credit Card Companies Will Still Let You* incident of December. While we were at it, we had also purchased a brand-new refrigerator and a bread-making machine that had a timer so you could wake up smelling that cinnamon raisin scent in your brain.

Oh, and there had been the dress. *That* dress. The one she was wearing as she stood behind me that made her look like a Princess on her way to the ball. The kind that "Princess Di would have worn if she was the President of the HOA." We had spared no expense. Which made no logical sense. Since there was no corporation or Company who was paying our bills.

"Now *this* is what I was talking about," Jess said, moving around the front of me and swiping her hands across the lapel to remove any remaining dust. "You look like a million bucks, dude." She leaned in, giving me a passionate kiss without any of the neighborhood residents watching on, then moved to the window overlooking Canyon Park Estates.

It was *snowing*. And why not? It was December.

Again.

But it didn't faze either of us because we had made it around the horn and back to the Dark Times version 2.0. We were fearless. We had been through it all and emerged unscathed on the other side. And while the weather outside seemed harsh and unforgiving, the climate inside was far from it.

"You remember the talking points?" Jess asked, as I gave myself one last look in the mirror.

"Yes."

"Their names. You memorized the list of attendees? Can't have you calling such influential people by someone else's name. You've got to connect with them. Make them trust you. Make them want to take that journey with you."

"Now you're just talking crazy."

Jess rolled her eyes, ignoring my statement, continuing with her interrogation. "And what do you tell someone who asks you what you do for a living?"

It was the mother of all questions. I had moved from Hollywood to come to Seattle for an opportunity at greatness, then squandered said opportunity for greatness because of some minor, insignificant thing they called "values." In the wake of Las Vegas and the death of Memphis, despite having no pressure to move on or distance myself from The Company whatsoever, I had made the decision that the experience had run its course. I had walked right into Mitch D.'s office seven days later and told him flat out that I was leaving for good.

"Nice to have *fuck you money*," was all he said before he waved me out of his office due to a meeting with a newly promoted Senior Director who was heading up the *Chico* project. Which was also known as *Humboldt.* And *Cantaloupe 3.18.* I knew I hadn't mistaken the words because by that point he no longer had that cranial cast around his skull. His hair had mysteriously rubbed off, but at least he was speaking with true eloquence once again.

"I tell them that I'm exploring exciting new opportunities in a multitude of fields," I told Jess, cinching my belt and smoothing out my tuxedo pants. "A work in progress."

It was a lie, but how different was it from all the daily lies we told ourselves in the quiet solitude of our own thoughts? We were all works-in-progress, at every single stage of our lives, rarely aware of that fact until yet another milestone reared its ugly head. The truth was, the two of us had no idea what was to come. The future was unwritten. We had no Nostradamus or Elise Jenner telling us what would come next. As long as *Skynet* wasn't on that roadmap, we could figure out everything else in due time.

Jess moved to the bedroom doors, resting her hand on the doorknob and looking back to me in the bathroom. "Are you ready, Doug?" she said, practicing her "public" smile.

I pulled out my phone. My *iPhone*. And scrolled to the notebook application where I pulled up those same words that I had written to myself almost exactly a year ago to the day.

You're smart. Check, I thought.

You've got great values. Work-in-progress, I reminded myself.

She loves you.

I looked to Jess, who reached her hand out to me, as I put the phone back in the inside pocket of the double-breasted coffin I had agreed to seal myself inside. She *does* love me, I thought. There was no question about that. Despite the hell we'd both been through, there was one single constant throughout it all. And it hadn't changed, or wavered, or faltered.

That love? *It was mutual.*

I grabbed her hand as she opened the door, following her onto the landing at the top of the stairs in our house. There was the warm glow of candles, the sound of clinking glasses and laughter, and the flickering ornamental lights on the twelve-foot high Christmas tree in the foyer. The house was packed to the hilt with what seemed like every single resident of Canyon Park Estates. In fact, they were *all* there. *All* participating. *All in.*

It was December. Outside it was dark, snowy and depressing. Yet inside, it was the complete opposite. A crowd of onlookers noticed Jess and me walking slowly down the circular staircase, arm in arm, making our way into the center of the social storm. "They're coming," someone shouted and the rest of the residents crowded into the foyer to get a glimpse.

"Wave, like we practiced," Jess whispered to me as she lifted her hand and started turning it like the Queen of England. I rolled my eyes, doing exactly the same, and feeling silly for it. Sudhir, standing next to Teha, mocked me outwardly with his own ridiculous wave.

In my imagination, I stood at the center of a throne room, me in my gallant (yet uncomfortable) suit of armor, and my Queen standing beside me. There was a crowd of our royal subjects there to greet our arrival, which had partially been the result of the battle we had won against the hordes. I glanced off to the side, where my fellow warriors held our two captives – the *Sorceress-Bitch* and her *Black Knight*, now on their knees looking up at the throne for mercy.

It was a ridiculously imagined moment, which I immediately shook out of my head.

"Camelot," Jess whispered, all breathy and giddy.

"Ah, Camelot," I whispered back, more mocking than anything else.

"I *know*," she said, out of the corner of her mouth, misinterpreting my faux-joy. "Isn't it great?"

"Yes," I said. "It's the most wonderful thing *ever*." It was obvious that she loved me. I, however, wearing a tux, waving like the Queen, and smiling a smile so fake that it made the corners of my mouth hurt?

I loved her *more*.

Epilogue

Kwincy with a K was Harvard educated, hazed for eighteen months under one of Hollywood's most prolific and alcoholic producers (remember *Danger with a Cherry On Top 1, 2, 3D and 4-Play?*), and completely convicted in his opinion that Calen, the Warrior Prince from the Iron Stronghold of Tehan, didn't have to defeat the blood-thirsty horde in the end.

"We're entering a new renaissance of the Hero's Journey," he said, while his furiously scribbling, underpaid (but overly enthusiastic) Assistant took copious notes as my Manager and I listened. "A hero doesn't have to win in the end. A hero doesn't even have to defeat the nemesis. We could kill off your hero and let a tangential character pick up where he left off."

"The circle of life," my Manager chimed in, having now fulfilled his quota of repurposing references from successful animated movies as creative developmental asides.

"What do you think?" Kwincy with K asked, as the room turned towards me, the writer of the idea that had spawned a treatment that had resulted in a script that the studio had purchased three months into our return to Los Angeles. Now here I sat, six months since we'd left the Pacific Northwest for the consistent, boring, smoggy eighty-degree weather of the San Fernando Valley, wondering less about how many ways I could refine the spelling of Kwincy's name (although Kwincee was a potential front-runner) and more about how the new version of Cameron Murphy would handle the question.

The question, along with many others, seemed astute and logical. They didn't strike me as thinly veiled attempts to change my ideas just for the sake of making change. They didn't piss me off and put me on the defensive like they used to.

Had Hollywood changed?

The town had not. Neither had the jobs. The people, despite having differently-spelled eccentric names, were still going through the same motions. In fact, the same thing was happening back in Seattle, where I had left a vacancy that the next Cameron Murphy would secure, in the hopes that *he* would have a chance at becoming the next *King of* [insert product name here]. Hollywood was to Seattle, which was to New York, which was to Chicago. Corporations, small businesses, fast-food restaurants and libraries.

The world rarely changed. It was the people who did.

So when Kwaynsay suggested that the hero didn't have to win in the end, the new and improved version of Cameron Murphy, who had been through the gauntlet and not won himself, found the suggestion legitimate. And reasonable. And if being legitimate and reasonable was the quickest path to bringing something to fruition, then wasn't that path the right one to take?

"It's a fair point," I said to Kwincy. "Perhaps the loss is also, when one looks more closely, a triumphant win? Loss and failure often breed more success than the latter."

Kwincy smiled, nodding. "This is why we want to be in the Cameron Murphy business," he said. "I think this could be a trilogy. What do *you* think?"

"To infinity and beyond," chimed in my Manager, apparently still fulfilling the quota.

"I think it's exciting," I shot back. "Let's make it work."

"Get this man all the free water he wants," Kwincy said, getting up and rifling for something in his desk as his Assistant sprang to action. "We're going to be here awhile."

When I ran into Romy Wallace at the *Whole Foods Market*, she had to introduce herself at least three times before I believed it was actually her, having convinced myself in the aftermath that she had been a figment of my chemical-imbalanced imagination.

"*From* The Company," she said.

"In Seattle?"

"We used to work together when I was at Legendary?"

"The agency?" I asked, squinting to try and find something familiar in the tanned face that was blathering at me.

"Romy *Wallace*," she said, punching me in the left arm. The pain triggered a sense memory that sort of, kind of, brought back some memories of my interactions with her.

She rang up her items, then met me outside the market, arms carrying the kind of health food I had never seen her ingest. She was single handedly supporting *Lululemon* with the hoodie, the yoga pants and the ergonomic flip flops. She looked good. Well-rested. Disconnected in a homeless kind of way.

"Those bastards at The Company had no sense of loyalty," she ranted. "Sucked the life out of me. Challenging me to launch a product that would change the landscape of the industry all at once while punishing me for destroying any blockers that stood in my way? I delivered for them and theyblameditallonmeandhungmeouttodry."

Ah, Romy Wallace. The joy *of nothing whatsoever* washed over me.

"So, what have you been doing?" I asked.

"Been off the grid," she said. "Picked up, sold my shit, put the rest in storage and hitchhiked down to Mexico. Just got back last week. I had made it through the letter "M" in my digital music collection and it was starting to wear a little thin. I had to get back."

"Back, *for what*?"

"Who knows. I don't know, Murphy. Some gig where I can leverage my skills and experience to break into a brand-new disruptive opportunity.

So, cockfighting? I asked, only in my head.

"You know, I never got a chance to ask you," she continued,

prodding. "How the hell did you do it?"

"Do what?"

"Lose. But still end up on top."

"The only way to win the game," I said, leaning in, "was to not play the game at all."

Romy cocked her head, letting it process through her complicated and twisted internal thought circuits. Her mouth hung crooked, like she was chewing an invisible piece of gum, then it closed as her thoughts came full circle.

"No, it wasn't that," she said, unconvinced. "I picked the wrong horse in the race. That was why. Stupid-ass Shane McCullough. He flipped like a catfish on dry land the minute Mitchy D looked at him cockeyed through that retarded costume. I should have known that from the beginning and chosen someone else."

Time off the grid hadn't changed Romy, and I suspected nothing ever would. You could see the wheels turning again in her head as she plotted her way back into the next industry she would seek to infiltrate and destroy. It was a circle, that was for sure, just maybe not one that you could consider a *life*.

"I don't know what to tell you," I said, grabbing my bag of groceries, "except that I've got to get going."

"Yeah, whatever Murphy," she said, also getting up. "Good to see you. Maybe I'll see you around sometime? Maybe our paths will cross again?"

"Yeah, maybe" I stood up, hoping *not*.

"Alright," she said, and then punched me in the arm so hard that it caused my entire bag of groceries to break open, littering the concrete below. She just smiled as I raced to pick it up.

And she didn't even offer to help.

The Canyon Park Estates' *Farewell to Jessica Murphy* party had been elaborate, fancy and tugged at the heart strings. There had been photo montages set to some of the most emotionally-contrived ballads, with *Every Rose Has Its Thorn* playing three times as much as *Faithfully*. There were prize packages, gift bags, and an emotional speech by the guest of honor, who was more conflicted over the items on her list she had not followed through on (*i.e. seceding from the city and buying her own snow plow*) than the ones she had hit out of the park. The residents were truly going to miss her, which was further illustrated by the tears and hugs that kept the party going until dawn.

But it was nothing compared to the speech Jessica Murphy had given to her Los Angeles-based constituents, who had contributed roughly $79,150 to her campaign for a seat on the board of the Los Angeles Unified School District, of which she had won.

"What organization has more problems that need solving than the LA Unified School District?" Jess had posed to me, three weeks into being back in our old digs.

"The United States Government?" I'd suggested, not kidding at all.

I stood, once again, in a suit and tie – back stage at the local Community center, with Jess and Kate at my side. Out beyond the curtains there were crowds, churning and cheering as an interim speaker spoke up at the podium.

"*Thanks to all your support,*" the voice echoed throughout the hall, "*we now have our new District 3 delegate for the LAUSD,*" he said. More cheering. Kate, between Jess and I, clapped for her Mommy, enthusiastically.

"Had you told me when we got married, I'd be marrying into politics, I'm not sure what I would have said," I joked, whispering to Jess as she checked her lips in a compact.

"People change, *First Husband*. People change."

"That's an understatement," I smiled back.

"Well, it's like they say," she continued, smacking her lips and getting ready to go on stage. "Life is like a box of diamonds. You never know what kind of carats you're going to get."

"You mean chocolates."

"No. I mean diamonds."

"Of course, you do." Of course, she did. What woman wouldn't want a box of diamonds including a wide array of different karated goodness?

"Hey buddy, this is me," she nudged, as the curtains started to open. "Think you can handle it?"

"Of course, I can," I said, accompanying her out on stage, pulling Kate along for the ride.

I had done it *once*, I could do it again.

After leaving The Company, I never heard from Simon Davis again. So, you can imagine my surprise when, almost six months later, he surprisingly came back into my life.

But it wasn't in person, or on the phone or even via e-mail. It was in the car, over the radio, as a part of an NPR report on a brand-new slate of innovative products that The Company would be bringing to the public in just ten months' time.

One of those products had been created by Simon Davis.

The codename meant nothing to me, but the concept – of delivering data and imagery to individual consumers without the need of a screen, monitor or glasses technology *was*. NPR called it "revolutionary." The Company claimed it would "deliver the ability to interact with real-time data to anyone, anywhere, no matter their ethnic background or financial status." Simon Davis just kept referring to it as "foo".

The interview byte with Simon was short and to the point, but ended with a question about where he had been for the last decade and why he had chosen, at this point in time, to resurface with a new product. His answer was more telling than any conversation that had ever taken place over a plate of color-coordinated salad.

"I was lost," he said. "And it took a stranger to find me. Once he did, I could see clearer than ever before."

Acknowledgements

You always have to use the first paragraph of your Acknowledgements page to thank the people you live with or else you'll get in trouble. Then you have to thank the people who you lived with before the people you live with now or else you'll get in even more trouble. Then you have to thank the people who periodically have stayed with you in your home for more than three days because those are probably extended family who would be mad if you forgot them. So. I'd like to thank my wife for always encouraging my creativity and passionately supporting it, my children for blindly supporting it despite never wanting to read anything I've written and my dog. He doesn't care what I've written, nor does he probably even know what writing is. Then, you know, my parents, my sister, my in-laws, my brother and sister in laws and that one guy who crashed on my couch for a week back in '97.

Since this is a book "inspired by" my experiences working in one of the world's biggest tech giants, I'd like to posthumously thank them for the experience. It was amazing and fun and tortorous and insane and fun again and amazing at times and despite never going to graduate school for an MBA it was basically like going to school and getting my MBA. I had great bosses and co-workers while I was there and it was a period of time in my life that really allowed me to mature and grow in a corporate gig. So thank you for all that. Clearly, if you've read this far you know that underneath all the humor and lunacy of the book, there's clearly a lot to love about the experience that I will never forget.

Now for the inspriational paragraph. The one where I say how writing is not a solitary job, truly. Because despite sitting in a room, in your head, for hours upon hours creating fake worlds and fictitious characters, there always comes the part of the process when you call up those friends who take time out of their own busy life to read your stuff, give you notes, and make you better for it in the end. I've got a great circle of friends who have been there for me whether it's this book, a previous one, a screenplay or even a greeting card (yes, there was that phase). Those folks include my good friends Fabian Marquez, Jeff Schectman, Owen Renfroe, Grant Nieporte, Andy Berman, Matt Walsh, Brad Morris and many more. Thank you, gents, for your tireless ability to read my stuff, give me thoughts, and still be my friend.

Was that last paragraph inspirational? I hope so.

Then, there are those who took time out of their own busy writing lives to read this book and provide advance priase. The Quest for Blurbs as I often refer to it. I'd like to thank them as well, and they include: Kevin Roose, Keith Wisniewski, Wayne Gladstone, Dustin Kidd and Sarah Walker.

Finally, I'd like to thank the memory of Roger Ebert. If you read the entire book instead of skipping to the Acknowledgements first, you know that the spectre of the most awesome movie critic in the history of the world, figures prominently in the novel. If you came to read this section first, then SORRY FOR THE SPOILERS. All to say, Roger Ebert has always been an inspiring figure to me every since I was a kid. His love of entertainment, his dogged personality and his total and complete brutal honesty sets him apart from the rest of them. That's why I made him a hologram in this book. I hope his wife Chaz is cool with that, and if she's not I just want to take the opportunity to say...satire. This book is satire. Satire is legal under some section and some paragraph of some legal document somewhere.

Thank you.

About the Author

Paul Davidson is an entertainment executive in Hollywood who also manages to find time to be a producer, screenwriter and four-time published author. Along the way he ran the digital entertainment division at a major tech company in Seattle whose name may or may not rhyme with Sycrosoft.

He lampooned corporate America in his first book *Consumer Joe: Harassing Corporate America, One Letter at a Time* and imagined what the world would have been like if historical figures had been able to blog in *The Lost Blogs: From Jesus to Jim Morrison.*

Most recently, he released his debut fiction novel *The Small Stuff* which Publisher's Weekly called a "quirky debut rom-com" that was "sure to stick in readers' minds."

His writing has been featured in *Wired*, the *Los Angeles Times* and *Mental Floss* and he also hosts the film commentary podcast *The Side Track.*

Paul lives in Los Angeles with his wife, two daughters and an emotionally-needy dog.

Printed in the USA
CPSIA information can be obtained
at www.ICGtesting.com
JSHW082015220823
47026JS00004B/30

9 798891 450431